Eve
Ann

ANGEL OF DEATH

"A very powerful novel, dealing intrinsically with life and death and the ugly side of murder. A very impressive, powerful story that grabs you, sucks you in, throws you around and dumps you out, dazed but richer for the ride." *Science Fiction & Fantasy Books*

"*Angel of Death* had me turning the pages with a sense of terrified fascination. This is the first of King's books that I've encountered, and his strong prose and stark characterizations have me firmly hooked and looking for more of his work." *Examiner.com*

"It's quirky, it's different and its definitely a novel to make you think… Not something to rush and will remain in the reader's subconscious long after the final page." *Falcata Times*

"I am at a loss of words. *Angel of Death* is the book you hold, no clutch, until your eyes smart, you can't really focus on the words and you are not sure whether you are making any progress, because it's way past your bedtime, but it's too good to put the book down. A must-read." *Temple Library Reviews*

"An utterly *masterful* novel – one of those novels that truly only comes along very, very rarely. And it's still echoing through my head – I replay scenes, hear the dialogue, see the imagery, feel the emotions… I haven't read anything quite like this before; it stunned me completely, and I truly hope that this book finds its way into the hands of many, many people." *Fantasy & SciFi*

J ROBERT KING

Angel of Death

ANGRY
ROBOT

ANGRY ROBOT
A member of the Osprey Group

Lace Market House,
54-56 High Pavement,
Nottingham
NG1 1HW, UK

www.angryrobotbooks.com
Fear the reaper

Originally published in the UK by Angry Robot 2009
First American paperback printing 2010

ISBN 978-0-85766-019-0

Printed in the United States of America

9 8 7 6 5 4 3 2 1

ANGEL *of* DEATH

BOOK I
SON *of* GOD

ONE

Old man, old man – I see you with your lake-rights cottage and your knotty pine paneling, dark as walnut with cigar smoke. Even now, the blue haze tangles in your hair. You've burned your dining table all to hell – the table your wife bought to refinish four years back, though a heart attack finished her first.

I'd helped with that one, too.

I see you, old man. You were a widower even before she died. Of your own design, you marched backward in measured retreat. You never had to battle the army in front of you, nor run out of ground behind you. Until now, the day you will die.

Or rather, the night.

(The old should die at night, and in the fall or winter. The young should die in the morning and springtime. It is an aesthetic concern that had been ignored until the districts were parceled out to individual angels. The middle-aged adult can die any time in the day or year, according to whom or what is left behind. They are

9

mourned as themselves, not as archetypes, as are the young or old.)

Old man, you die tonight in your home, cigar in hand, or better, in mouth. Your recliner would be an easy place to go and... ah, I have the perfect idea.

You see me now, don't you? I can tell by that glassy-eyed stare that sees past all the world and sees nothing at all.

I am that nothing, old man. I am the Bastard Being, extension without substance. I am not the garden shears that snip a rose from the vine, but rather the un-explainable and persistent shadow that overcasts bush and bloom until both are dead. I am an angel descended of the archangels Michael and Samael and Azrael, the bringers of death.

You do not want to go with me. I should not have let you see me so soon. You leap up from the ash-pitted tabletop. Your hamstrings fling back the chair and it barks to the battered hardwood between us as you flee. But I am an angel. Chairs do not bother these sharp Caucasian shins, the linen pants I wear. They are appearances only. I bound through the chair.

You've left your cigar beside the ashtray on the table. I grapple you. Your hair is greasy on my arm. You bite my shoulder, no more than a cornered badger. I need to calm you down, so I drag you downstairs to the basement. You claw at the pictures on the wall. Some fall. Glass breaks. Those will leave people wondering.

Ah, the furnace room. The exhaust usually goes through this white pipe. Not with a nest of mice in it.

Now it comes out here and here, but mostly here. You're gasping anyway now, so with your face rammed up into that galvanized triangle, it's not long before you are limp in my hands.

The gas will go through the rest of the place by the time I'm gone.

Strange how much heavier you feel as dead weight. Your pants mop the stairs of glass shards as we ascend. I pick up the broken pictures, a nice touch in mind.

You look comfortable in the recliner, especially with the leg-rest up and the pictures on your lap like you are reminiscing. Ah, here's your cigar. With a couple of long draws from me, it flares hot. Your chair catches easily, with all the towels draped over arms and back, and I stand to watch your bruised chest slowly breathing.

You won't awaken. No, not with the carbon monoxide in the air. Your pants peel back like curling parchment, and your leg hair is flashing with orange and sending up white smoke.

I breathe that smoke, sweeter than any cigar.

I must leave. In this form, the carbon monoxide will make me dizzy. Soon the chair will catch the drapes, and the drapes the walls, and there will be neighbors calling the volunteers.

I shift, no longer a thirty year-old white male with a disarming smile and a predilection for murder, becoming nothing at all, the Bastard Being. I move through the back door without opening it and disappear among the bare boughs of autumn.

Time means nothing to me. Time means nothing to any creature in the heavenly choir. But when one must work among humans, to whom time means everything, one must enter time and exit it. There are many such special dispensations for those of us who choose to descend the ladder of being.

Do not be mistaken. There is a true ladder of being – a Jacob's Ladder, as humans might call it, and angels ascend and descend it all the time. There is an unbroken path from God down to the simplest virus, and humans are somewhere halfway up that infinite climb. Angels are a little more than humans.

Just as dog breeders work in the cycles of canine heat and dirty their hands with dog blood and sperm and shit, so I work in the cycles of humans and foul myself with human frailties.

See, here? I am down in a cafe just off the Dan Ryan, sitting in a vinyl booth and staring at a compartmentalized plate. The cafe is small, with a sixteen foot ceiling covered in dusty tin filigree and insulated pipes from the apartments upstairs. Smoke struggles to cling to the dark heights but is channeled downward from teetering fans that trail threads of soot.

They sit here and eat their congealed grease and smoke their cigarettes, at once adding puffiness to cheeks and taking it from lips. Their faces look like pantyhose puppets with puckered thread marks instead of lips. They sit here and talk of trucks and fish and wallow in German insistence upon old, stout ways. But I am not here to kill any of them.

I am here to kill the jogger who, in fascistic spandex, will be along any moment. He is a forty-four year-old vice president with eyes that recede into his head behind burling brows. He's shaved every day since his thirteenth birthday but even now has the blue-black aggression of denied animality sheening within his jaw. He is a modern positivist, believing that all of life is explainable by him, that anyone who wishes to be successful must merely become him, and that there are no such things as accidents or mysteries.

Here is a moment of accidental mystery for him.

I appear in his path as he reaches Ohio Street and slows to jog in place until the light changes. I have timed the moment perfectly. The eleven-forty CTA is five minutes behind and gunning for the yellow. The runner has a fly darting at his ear. I have a foot in the way and a helping hand-slap on the man's back. He launches from the curb into the accidental and mysterious cliché of the bus's path.

When there's a red spray and a shriek of tires and the sound of screams, everyone notices the victim; no one the angel. As a final touch, I have one of the fat German smokers burst from the corner cafe and – disregarding the blood and its threat of AIDS and the fact that the man's chest is a mere bag of bones – clamp his collagen-depleted lips to the dead mouth and inflate the corpse with lungful after lungful of nicotine and bacon grease.

It is what I do. I am assigned to the Chicago sprawl, reaching south through Lake County, Indiana, and north past Kenosha and Racine to Milwaukee. It is a natural unit. Heavy industry, mob operations, bedroom communities, ethnic tensions, lake-effect snow, mosquito wetlands, crime, drugs, dirt, and a sort of brutal grandiosity that belies a deep and corporate inferiority complex.

I cannot kill in Berwyn without mourners driving out from Hammond and Whiting. I cannot orchestrate a gang slaying in Racine without the Skokie Sears ending up with fenced diamonds. I cannot release a steel roll on the Edens without it bouncing atop a family of four from Wauwatosa and decapitating the sophomore quarterback of the Hobart Brickies.

Consistency of service is why I have the land I have. With hundreds of murders a year in Milwaukee alone, it is no wonder so many senseless deaths once occurred.

Not that what humans call senseless is what angels call senseless. The death of a child on a bike can be a very meaningful and worthwhile event. It makes for good, heart-wrenching drama. On the other hand, the death of a child in bed through the simple cessation of breath – that holds very little in the way of meaning. Only if the mother is a suffocating presence or the father is an oxygen salesman who is never home – only then would such a death have its poetic effect.

That is what I do, assure that the deaths in the megalopolis of Chicago-Milwaukee have a poetry to them, that the death fits the life. Mr Jacob Sonnenbean, the widower with the cigars and the flaming recliner, died alone in the safety and caustic comfort of his cottage, asphyxiated by his own cheery furnace and burned by his own sources of comfort: cigar and throne. It would not have served for him to fall off a pier and drown or be killed by a shooter in a convenience store. To die of his own vices and devices – that was a beautiful death.

There it is. Beauty. Aesthetics. Keats was right about beauty and truth, and it is my job to assure true deaths. The deaths are many – eight murders a day, on average, ten suicides, seventeen accidental deaths, and ninety-three by natural causes.

I do most of my work with the accidents.

Murders, suicides, and deaths by disease or age have natural resonations. Murderers are usually loved ones, friends, or neighbors – people with a history of involvement with their victims. In these cases, the killer does the job of making sure the death fits the life. He selects the time, place, and means of the demise. Suicides do the same. So, too, bodies have a certain knack for paying back their owners with fitting ends – the dancer has a heart attack after years of bulimia; the businessman yellows and dies beside his basement wet bar; the whore lies in a back room of some dive, her flesh dismantling itself as though every sperm that ever entered her is slicing outward. Of course, I monitor all these incidents, and if a death occurs in a particularly disappointing way, I often will go back in time to manipulate events for a more pleasing outcome.

Accidents and random violence, however, are chaotic, and their results are often pointless. I have, on occasion, saved a person from one meaningless death on a given day only to subject him to a better end that evening. The old phrase "going down for the third time" has its origin in this phenomenon, that a doomed person may be saved once or twice before finally being slain.

Accidents are my main work, yes, but there is one type of murderer whose work runs entirely counter to mine: the serial killer. Their victims tend to be unknown to them. Their murders are orchestrated to satisfy their own fantasies, not to provide a fitting end to a victim's life. It was because of the likes of Heirens, Gacy, and Dahmer that I was assigned this area. I cannot stop such humans from killing, not until it is their own time to die. Nor can I do much about victim selection, since these men act according to random opportunity or elaborate fantasy. On a night that such a man is prowling for a kill, I struggle to keep up, saving those I can and attempting to tweak the deaths of those I cannot.

My jurisdiction does not go back to the time of Gacy, but does to that of Dahmer. They were similar murderers, in many ways, luring their victims to their homes and tricking them into vulnerable positions. Gacy used a pair of real handcuffs, saying he had a magic trick to show his guest. Dahmer used drugged beer. A mere queasiness was enough to save some of the victims. I caused one young man to throw up on the carpet, and while Jeffrey cleaned up the poisonous mess, his prey slipped out the door.

But I could not save all of them. Some were marked for death, and even if they escaped, I killed them later that night. Nor could I kill Dahmer, for his time had not come. When at last it did come, it was out of my jurisdiction, in the Columbia Correctional Institute, a maximum-security penitentiary. The job was sloppy – bludgeoning and stabbing with a broken broomstick. I had had a much more fitting end in mind.

Even now, there are three serial killers in my domain. One, Clive Darrow of Griffith, Indiana, hasn't killed in over a decade. A white man, he had been an assassin-style killer, getting drunk and driving his 1976 Ford Grenada past toll booths, open garages, car washes, and other such places and slaying his white victims with a shotgun. The police suspected a race crime by a black man, but the FBI profiled a white man of a little less than Clive's age – 54. The police arrested their black man at the same time that Clive struck and killed a pedestrian and was imprisoned for reckless homicide. He happened not to have the shotgun in the car because he had just lent it to a friend for duck hunting. The killings stopped, the police were satisfied, and Clive sat in a cell for five years of an eight-year sentence. A model prisoner, he found Jesus.

Since his release, Clive has spent his time working as a janitor for Harvey's Department Store and volunteering his time at Hoosier Boys Town. His witness to the young men there includes frank discussions of his serial killings and the difference Christ has made. The listeners give Jesus little credence, and the talk of shootings even less. The police have been called fifty-seven times to investigate Clive's allegations of serial killings, but have found no evidence, and have ceased responding.

The other two serial killers are still somewhat active. Jerome "Jerry" White is twenty-nine years old and has been killing since he was seventeen. He lives winters at his mother's house in Evanston but spends his summers at a rundown cottage at the flood-prone Methodist Campgrounds in Des Plaines. Like Darrow, Jerry is a born-again Christian, though his conversion yielded the opposite effect.

Always an unbalanced zealot, Jerry's conversion to evangelical fundamentalism at age fourteen gave him a whole new ground for obsession. While most boys his age were handling themselves and, if lucky, a breast or two, Jerry was turning all his attentions toward a leather-bound Bible. He considered his sexual desires to be a form of demonic possession, and eventually convinced himself that even humor was ungodly and evil. On several occasions, he stood with knife in hand and began slicing off his erect penis, only to quit after inflicting tiny cuts.

If he had gone off to college, as his parents had insisted, he likely would have outgrown his delusions. Instead, after high school, he moved to an upstairs apartment in Gary, Indiana, and began trying to rescue prostitutes. He was beaten bloody more than once by angry pimps who wanted twenty dollars for the half hour he'd spent preaching to the women. In time, he came to believe that all the abuses he suffered at the hands of black pimps and drug dealers had been, in turn, forced upon them by whites of all stripes.

Jerry got himself a junkyard car, painted it black, and used masking tape to write warnings all across it. He rarely had enough money to buy gas, but when he did, he drove the car until it ran dry. Then he would leave it and walk home. He stole the car back a number of times from various impound yards, in the last encounter running down the security guard.

This accidental killing convinced Jerry of his mission, to drive his car by day and slay whites by night until they heeded his warnings. Since that time, he has killed twelve. After his fifth kill, the very pimps and drug dealers who had once beaten him up began hiring him to do hits in white areas. Jerry considered the money a sign from God that what he was doing was right. The police have not yet linked all of his crimes.

Now, Jerry's mental aberrations are so extreme as to prevent him from driving or committing untraceable crimes. His deterioration is severe enough that he may be captured in the act of one of his next murders. He probably doesn't have the wit or the time to kill again, though. He will be dead before Friday this week. I'm planning for him to break into Wesley Tabernacle on the campgrounds, lie down on the altar, douse himself with gasoline, and die as a burnt offering to God.

The last of my three killers is on the prowl even now. I will step down one rung and see if I might direct his hand a bit.

* * *

Young man, I see you. I see how you move among them, like one of them. Your battered old London Fog coat comes almost to your knees and sticks too far out as if you are some kind of flasher – the coat of a Goodwill shopper and a murdering madman. Keith McFarland. I know you will kill even tonight. I know you are prowling.

You look lost in your trench coat. Your shoulders are too narrow for the smudged gray polyester that drapes you. Even your thin neck – it should be red but is white and stubbled with the new growth of an inattentive razor – holds an Adam's apple two sizes too large. A greenish Granny Smith, swallowed whole.

You have not bought gas. You duck your oil-sheened black hair away from the cashier and move toward the compact orange bags of peanuts. There you stop. You seem to be looking at snacks. In fact, you glance at the T-shirted man who stands at the counter.

The man has his hand out. He waits for the small flask of Mr Boston spiced rum he will be sneaking tonight on the walk with his collie mutt. He stinks already of a cheap cigar that smolders on the painted board of the gas station stoop.

The cashier knows this man. Not his name. Only his addiction. The man knows it too. He has already doled out the three dollars and ninety-four cents it will take to buy two hundred milliliters of oblivion. Sometimes he pays in nickels and pennies fished from the tie tack drawer and the couch cushions.

The rum is set in his hand. For a minute it glints, liquid gold. Then it is gone in a fold of loose canvas pants.

"Have a good one," the cashier says, sliding closed the ringing register drawer.

The rum man nods and pushes his way out the door. Around him rises a breath of petroleum on asphalt in late autumn. In the momentary gap of the door, the collie is visible, eyes wide with anticipation beside the leash that holds her to the two-by-four stoop. The door closes. Through mud-spattered glass, you see the secret drunk loose his shaggy dog. They make their way out into the lifeless light of the gas station dolmen.

From within your trench coat, you watch.

They move toward the road. Cars whir past in the rushing, gravel-cracking haste of a November night in Wisconsin.

"You need some help?" asks the cashier. He is young. A baseball cap brim curves between his shoulder blades. A sleek, thin ponytail rides his spine.

Your black hair shifts listlessly above your sallow face. "N-N-No."

The trench coat moves; not you, just your coat. Then you, too, are gone into the anonymous glare. You are just another wedge of light in the dirty-paned door.

You pause on the stoop and look toward the angry, shushing cars. A newspaper tumbles over wet blacktop, crumpled but still airborne, not yet soaked and plastered to the road. You follow, white trash after white trash.

Avatar. You do not know that term, but I do. You are the avatar of all backward inbred hicks – a disaffected loner from a silent race that has never been invited into the modern age. Sullen. Fitful. Gaunt. Enraged. As murderous as the night.

You stutter-step along the gravel margin of the road, in the very footsteps of the man with the secret rum. Human eyes cannot detect it, but I can: the rum man's feet leave faint prints of warmth on the autumn stones, and your feet fall in those very prints. As you pass, the stones turn cold again with night and death.

The rum man turns down that dark road and takes the first bitter swallow of the gall he hides from all but himself and his dog. You stalk and follow. He will be your kill tonight.

These eyes of mine see more than footprints. I see who this man is, and that it is indeed time for him to die. He is a newspaper editor for the local rag, a man using distilled spirits to fill up the gap between what he is and what he had intended to be. A writer. A novelist. A family man. That's what he had hoped for, but instead he lives alone, hacking apart the words of other hacks and making them into the bland garble of modern journalism.

He takes another drink.

Thirty-eight is young to die, but not young enough for this one. A depressive, an alcoholic, a loner, family off in Wichita, and friends... what friends, aside from that collie mutt?

Oh, you have chosen your victim wisely, a moody man who'll be fired for not showing up before he is truly missed, who will be replaced by one of the clamoring young reporters who attack a job posting like piranha on bloody meat. The FBI would call this a low-risk victim, a drunken man walking alone at night on an untraveled country road.

Except for the dog. I might have had to step out of time to do some orchestration, but you hesitate; you fear the dog. And well you should. A gap-toothed cracker such as yourself had first owned her and kicked her daily until she ran off. She might seem friendly enough, but once there's a shout and a scream and blood, she'll remember your kind and go for your throat.

Ah, though, that's the key. The man has only this dog in all the world. The leash he holds does not so much keep the dog next to him as keep him next to the dog. Ambush them and kill the dog. Let him see you kill the dog. Use your gun on the dog, not the man, and then let him worry over the thing's body. Or, better yet, it's deer hunting season, and this fellow's a budding author – he has an imagination. He'll put the pieces together.

I whisper the idea in your ear. You are too disorganized to do anything but listen. There's a deer path that heads off from the road here through that little stand of trees and out onto the access road. If you walk quietly along it…

You stalk from the road, pulling your coat around you as if it were a rain poncho and you a little girl. Maybe that's what he thinks when, on the red rim of road, he looks back and spits, then takes another drink. He thinks he is hiding from you, and not the other way around. You pick your way across the vacant field then among the autumn-hard rows of broken cornstalks. Already, he is down the other side of the hill.

Oh, what fun, to hunt this way! The pines are black and murmurous in the settling dark. You see the road beyond, where he will be shuffling into view in moments. You crouch down among tenacious roots of pine and pull out your pistol. It gives you a hard-on every time you touch it. Yes, here will be a good place. They will pass within ten feet. The shot will echo, and the editor will not know the difference between a pistol and a deer rifle. He'll think you're just a bad hunter.

He comes, leather-soled shoes on a chip-and-oil shoulder. He looks around. His face is slack already from drink, though his eyes squint against the night. The bottle in his hand glints purple inside its wrinkled skin of paper. He drains it one last time and throws it into the trees, just near you.

You fire. It's all right. You were afraid, but it's all right.

Half the dog's head is gone. It whines a moment and turns as if to scratch its remaining ear, then goes down upon the chips and quivers sickly.

He doesn't look toward you but sinks down atop the dog. Already he is wailing. He holds the thing stupidly. The thrown bottle was all the better, as if it had triggered the bullet. An accidental but elegant nuance.

He looks up. Blood is on his face, with tear tracks through it. He is furious. Some of the blood is his own, from a lip he has sawed open between teeth. He is murderous.

"Fuck you, God damn it! Fuck, fuck, fuck!" he cries.

Yes, crouch lower, but grin still. That erection feels like a jabbing stick among the pine roots. Enjoy the moment, killer. Your day will come, too.

"Fuck you! Fuck you! God damned fucking asshole hunter! Fuck you!"

His shouts are like the moans of a lover. Don't come yet, killer. Keep it in until he is dead, too.

Ah, he has stopped his shouting. He lifts the still body off the road and sets it gently on the shoulder. He kisses the mutt's tangled fur and whispers something. Now he rises.

He's coming to find you. He expects you to be in the glade beyond, a man who feels bad for having accidentally killed a leashed dog. A man with a rifle that the editor can grab and swing against a tree to break it. That's what he expects to do. That's what he would write about.

He rises, scarred leather soles on the smooth humus of pine. More curses grumble from him, these meant not for you but for himself, stoking his engine. He wants to be good and angry. Hunker down, now. He grabs the brittle bole of a nearby tree. He steps beyond it and keeps going.

You rise. Dead needles fall from you as if you are some monster of humus. He doesn't even hear you, raging to himself. You follow him a couple paces.

"T-T-T-Turn around, quiet n-n-n-now, or you'll be d-d-dead as your d-dog," you say.

Your door-hinge voice is enough to spin him. His bravado is gone. He is white in the dead evening. You point the gun at his head. He holds his hands up, as if in a movie.

"Kneel!" You manage to say it without your stutter. He complies. Very good. You move up to him, getting the gun to his forehead. Your other hand fiddles with your fly, almost too slow. You'd wanted to be inside him, but this is almost as good.

He pulls away. You shoot.

His head is like a fountain as he falls back. You let him fall and strip off your coat. That's why you had worn it. It will cover the blood on your clothes after you are finished.

The killing has not happened as I had hoped, as I had planned. You were supposed to ask him to write his own obituary before he died, so that the editor could become a published author only by writing his final words. I am distressed by your impulsiveness.

Still, you do the rest. You drag both bodies away from the road and into a cornfield. Then you take the man's wallet, and cut off his head and hands. This is hard and messy work, but you've done it before. You used to do it because you heard it kept the body from being identified. Of course, in such a small town, it'll take only days instead of weeks to do a head count and figure out who's missing, but the amputations are now part of your fantasies. You'll carry the head and hands home inside plastic and burlap.

These arrangements also happen to serve my ends. The man's head and hands were what he worked with as an editor, and his work was always separated from his heart, which makes this death somehow fitting. Also, he lived a life of quiet desperation and inner anguish, so a death of overt anguish and loud desperation is also ironically satisfying.

I could have done better and may even return to the event to make certain you get the obituary written, but there have been serial killer victims who have done much worse than this one.

I will be glad the day I get to kill you, Keith McFarland.

TWO

Burlington, Wisconsin had not had a murder in five years when the headless, handless body was discovered. Despite spitting sleet, the nighttime cornfield was crowded. Detective McHenry, Investigator Leland, Sergeant Banks, Medical Examiner Schmitt, the volunteer fire department, half the staff of the *Gazette*, a few dozen farmers, and a handful of police scanner jockeys stood in the carnival glare of the three dispatched squads.

The body had first been found by Daryl Jamison's dogs, which had gnawed on it awhile before returning to their owner. Jamison, spooked by the sight of dogs with bloody muzzles, had gotten his brother Carl to go with him. Shotguns in hand, they had walked the fields. They'd followed the dogs' tracks and found the body soon enough. Daryl claimed he had checked for the man's wallet and, not finding it or any identification, gone straight away to call the police. The crime scene, though, looked as though Daryl and Carl had held a barn dance around the body, boot prints crushing every bit of soil for a twenty-foot radius. The old farmer had paced around the body, trying in vain to obliterate the tracks of his two unlicensed dogs. It hadn't mattered. The dogs got loose while he was on the phone and were down chewing on the body when Detective McHenry arrived. To prevent further damage to the crime scene, the detective ordered nearly a quarter mile of road and farm field cordoned off.

Investigator Donna Leland volunteered to set up the roadblock and string the police line. She had seen enough of the ghastly scene. Just now, she wielded her ten pound sledge to drive the last rebar rod into the partly frozen field, and then let the muddy mallet rest in a black furrow.

As she tied the police line, someone in the crowd shone a flashlight toward her. She raised a hand before her eyes and blinked. *Who's shining that light?* The old maxim was true: murderers often returned to the scenes of their crimes, wanting to relive the excitement of the moment. Some even injected themselves into their own investigations, monitoring the facts and providing false information to lead police astray. What if this is the murderer?

Leland gripped the sledge haft tightly in one hand and gestured with the other. At last, the light darted downward, becoming a short column of gray.

She finished tying the yellow plastic ribbon to the last crowbar and hoisted the ten pound sledge to her shoulder. It comforted her to carry that sledge. Whatever demon had done this would think twice about coming after her, what with the sledge and her .45.

At five-foot three, Leland was too short to step over the waist-high tape, so she crouched beneath it, making sure to keep the knees of her blues out of the mud. She straightened and tucked her braid into the collar of her jacket. Cops were supposed to be short shorn, like Dobermans, with nothing to grab in a fight. Cops were also supposed to be men, at least in rural Wisconsin, though men had one extremity that begged grabbing during a fight.

With a nervous sigh, Leland trudged across the avaricious cornfield, toward the crime scene. It was a man's world, and this was a man's crime.

The brutality alone made it such: a dog with half its head blown off and a dog walker with grisly stumps where hands and head should be. Even in the dark, before the scene was set up, the vertebrae and severed muscles stood clear. Now, though –

Lights glared down on the body – flashlights moving fitfully in the hands of cops and cop buffs, a couple of spotlights glaring from patrol cars on the road, a kind of miner's helmet on Francis Schmitt, the county coroner, and even the flashes of the cop photographer. The place looked almost like an operating room instead of a lonely stretch of cornfield.

Leland approached, gut turning even as her eyes grew wider, taking in every detail.

The victim had been big, probably two-hundred-twenty pounds. He wore a pair of canvas pants, a T-shirt, and no jacket, though the last day that had been warm enough for such clothes was November 29, five days ago. A leash was found attached to the collar of the dead dog, and bits of tar were stuck to the dog's pads. Despite the boot prints of the Jamison brothers, the ditch and trees between the road and the body showed no signs that the man had been dragged, nor did his heels or clothes contain any ground-in mud. It was quite clear that this was no mere dumpsite, but also the scene of the murder.

"Mother of God."

She was close enough now to see the dog-gnawed leg of the man, and the neck and wrist stumps. Francis was leaning beside the body and checking beneath the shirt hem. Despite what must have been massive blood loss from the severed limbs, there had been enough left in the body to create a brown line of lividity on the man's back.

Another flash went off. Leland turned away, seeing spots. Someone yelled. There was a scuffle. Her hand fell immediately to her gun before she made out what was happening.

Sergeant Banks was wrestling someone – the Burlington *Gazette* photographer-reporter, Blake Gaines. All she could see was the patrolman's steel-wool hair and his muscular bulk straining against a scarecrow-thin man.

"Can't you read? 'Police Line, Do Not Cross!'" Banks growled through gold-capped teeth.

Blake, a gaunt and shaggy young artiste, did not answer, snapping off a couple more shots as he was propelled back toward the road.

The investigator reached the pair, slipped one of her own arms into Blake's and helped to speed him on his way.

"We're going to confiscate that film," Banks warned as two more flashes went off.

"You can't," Blake yodeled. "Freedom of the press!"

"We can and will," Investigator Leland said, "unless you cooperate."

"I'm going! I'm going," the bewhiskered man said, trying to break free.

Leland leaned toward him and whispered, "Not that. I want you to take pictures of the crowd. Get everybody you can – faces – but don't be obvious about it."

"What do I want with–" he began loudly, but she broke in.

"Get me the crowd, and we'll let you print what you've got. Otherwise, I'm taking your camera now."

"All right, all right," he said as they muscled him to the police line and bundled him over. He regained his balance just beyond the tape but rebelliously lingered against it as he checked his camera rig for damage.

Leland turned to Sergeant Banks, poised there like a wolverine ready to strike. She touched his shoulder, meaning to appease, but got a startled jump from him. "Banks," she said with quiet urgency, "you'd better get back to the scene. They'll be wanting you on hand."

The muscle nodded, not even recognizing the flattery. He trotted back to the scene.

Leland turned to the photographer. "Listen, Blake, we've got to work together on this."

"What are you talking about?" the man asked, coddling his camera as though it were an injured baby. "You're not going to dictate what the *Gazette* prints–"

"It's a lot easier than that," responded Leland in a hushed voice. "You need good footage to sell papers. We need good footage to catch this guy. Work with us, and I'll keep you close, on the inside. Fight us, and all your shots will be through fence holes."

He seemed ready to make a rebuke but blinked it away in uncertainty.

"You get us a shot of the killer, and we'll tell you. That's called an exclusive. And a byline."

Blake nodded, tight-lipped.

"And it's not just that. I'll have to talk to McHenry, but if he agrees, we can do some proactive strategies with the paper to flush this guy out. I'm sure the *Gazette* wouldn't mind being credited with helping to catch this guy."

Again, he nodded. A small smile crept onto his face.

"Good," she said. "Now get at it."

He loped away among the crowd.

Men knew so little about working with each other. Or, perhaps, they thought it beneath them to play to bruised egos. Better to bruise them some more until it comes to broken noses and black eyes.

No wonder there are no female serial killers, Leland thought.

That was not actually true, but the number of women who committed such crimes was almost statistically insignificant.

Of course, this was a serial crime. The last murder in the Burlington area, five years back, was a similar decapitation and amputation in Bohner's Lake.

After closing down the crime scene, Investigator Leland returned home, showered, dressed in PJs, and leaned back in her favorite chair. It was a worn and low-slung piece of furniture, what she had considered a couch when she was a kid. Her mother had reupholstered it in bristly curtain fabric and set it in front of the upstairs TV. Then, it had room enough for Kerry and herself, a calico cat, and a Tupperware bowl of popcorn. Now, it was not quite even a love seat, and, crowded in a drafty bay window, was only just big enough for Donna and her books.

She pulled one of the books from the stack, a true crime expose about criminal profiling. Though modern mythology had made FBI profilers into supermen – divining the state of a killer's underwear and his taste in movies from the position of a shell casing – the science of profiling was still largely unknown in small-town police work. What Donna knew of it was second-hand, pieced together from books by former members of the Quantico Behavioral Science Unit.

By dismembering victims and burying hands and heads separately, organized offenders can make identification difficult. A victim's identity is a critical piece of evidence for narrowing the field of suspects, determining motive and opportunity, and rallying community assistance in tracking down the killer. The removal of these parts takes time and effort and produces large quantities of blood. It is a technique used almost exclusively by psychopathic personalities.

Donna paused. The dark bay window behind her breathed coldly and she drew up the tattered afghan she kept on the chair arm. Out of old habit, she crossed herself. How could a person think of heads and hands merely as forms of identification? She glanced up at the crucifix hanging above her twenty-four inch TV and reflexively imagined Christ dismembered. She crossed herself again.

By contrast, psychotic personalities engage in dismemberment not to eliminate clues, but for symbolic reasons and to fulfill personal fantasies. Their mutilations tend to center more on genitalia, viscera, hearts, and eyes.

Sickened, Donna closed the book. Sociopaths did what they did by design. Psychotics did what they did by instinct. One group were humans who thought they were gods. The other were humans who thought they were animals. Both were monsters.

Donna stopped that thought. Her hand strayed to a picture on an unvarnished end table. He was a boy. Only a boy. Her twin, Kerry, at fourteen – bright-eyed, hopeful, and human. In her mind, he would never be older than fourteen.

By their fifteenth birthday, Kerry had lost all his friends, dropped out of school, and never came out of his room in the basement. Father John, principal of St Mary's, joked about getting an exorcist. By their sixteenth birthday, Kerry was so sedated that he never spoke or even smiled. By their seventeenth birthday, he was institutionalized in Elgin. He didn't reach his eighteenth, hanged by a noose he had made from his own torn-up shirt.

Kerry had not been a monster. A bipolar schizophrenic, they said, with homicidal fantasies. A manic-depressive with multiple personality disorder. A cyclops. A Grendel. A steppenwolf...

No, Kerry was not a monster. He was a sick boy.

Sighing sadly, Donna set the picture atop her pile of books and leaned back on the seat. *Road to Utopia* was on tonight. Kerry had loved the *Road* pictures. Donna got up, turned on the set, and moved the rabbit ears to pick up WGN. Then she went to the kitchen.

"I've got a bag of popcorn around here somewhere."

Assuming after the third ring that the doorbell didn't work, Investigator Leland knocked. She stood in the lee of a storm door held together by duct tape. The cool gray winds of a December 7th morning breezed past her.

It had been standard police work. Lots of dead-end leads. Lots of waiting for someone to file a missing persons report. Lots of phone conversations assuring cottagers and farmers that everything that could be done was being done. After two days of office work, Leland had at last been asked by Detective McHenry to help him knock on doors and canvas the Bohner's Lake area to find out the identity of the body.

She looked down at the crime scene photo in her hand. In it, Sergeant Banks squatted gravely beside a dark pine tree and propped up a stiff collie mutt. At the zenith of a washed-out foreground, the dog looked spectral. Its frozen legs were poised in a flat line on tip-toe. The effect made the collie appear to be dashing pell-mell through the picture, past Banks's stern, down-turned face. The dog's eye glowed with the flash, as if Banks held a light to the blown-open back of its skull.

"I feel like a Goddamned trophy hunter," Leland murmured to herself.

The door eased back, shuddering a little. Warm wet air came from within, along with the mill-wheel tumble of a stove-sized humidifier. A thin old woman stood there in a faded cotton housedress. A Kleenex jutted out, ready between two buttons. "Yes?"

"Sorry to bother you this morning, ma'am. I'm Investigator Leland of the Burlington Police Department–"

"If you're here about the cardboard, I didn't know it could be recycled until just last week, and I've got it ready for the bin this time, if you want to come see–"

Leland laughed in quiet dismissal. "Actually, ma'am, I'm looking for the owner of this dog." She held up the photo.

The old woman peered, unblinking, at the picture. "You probably think I should have reading glasses or bifocals to see something like this, but I've had the new cataract surgery, which lets me read a book and look out at the sunset without any glasses at all, or see this picture of the dog and see Mr Koenig walk that dog just about every evening at eight thirty before the gas station stops selling those little flasks of devil water that I've signed petition after petition against, always the first or second name…"

"Mr Koenig?" asked Leland, writing. "And he lives where?"

"Three houses down, on the right, toward town, the one that still has the Christmas lights from three years ago up on the eaves even though he hasn't plugged them in for two Christmases and he's not turned them on yet this season if they work at all anymore. I haven't seen him in a while, but he keeps those irregular hours, a newspaper man for the *Gazette*, and coming and going at all times and working on that old junker of his in the middle of the night sometimes, trying to keep a twenty-year-old car going with these two-day-old computer car parts they have nowadays, and him without the first bit of mechanical skill but too cheap to buy something better…"

"Thank you, ma'am," Leland said, tucking the photo into her breast pocket. "You've been a great help."

With no trace of humor on her face – the shape and hue of a garlic clove – she said, "Too bad about that dog of his. Sometimes it would break loose and dig in my petunias. Not that I would have wanted it dead – hit by a car, right? Forty-five's too fast for a residential block."

"Thank you, ma'am," Leland said, backing out of the door space and letting the storm door sway inward.

The old woman caught it and held it ajar as Leland backed away. "And if you're going to get so up in arms about cardboard in the garbage, what about these folks that pile it in with their leaves to burn and we have to be breathing that all day long?"

Leland marched away. Her black boots splashed through the dead oak leaves, brown and gold like muddy water. Behind her, the woman's voice continued to labor shrilly, a too-small pump struggling in anonymous obsession to empty a too-deep pit.

The oaks were tall and stout here, their crags deep with gray shadows. The sky above was an acrylic blue, and a wintry wind tumbled brown leaves over the rim of the Bohner's Lake bowl and down toward the water.

Mr Koenig's house was on that rim, perched like a ship breaching the head of a standing wave and about to plunge down the trough beyond. The land dropped away behind it, baring a line where clapboards gave way to gray cement block. The white Masonite boards on the main floor were curved with inexpert installation and years of seepage, but they clung to the frame with all the tenacity of a gunwale on a ship.

She knocked. In good intention, someone had painted the white door red, and then left it to peel behind a rusting screen. No answer. Again she knocked, and again, nothing.

It was a Tuesday. He could well be at work, but a rust-riddled gray '89 Olds sat on the cement slab beside the chimney. He couldn't have walked to the *Gazette* from here, but could have carpooled. It wasn't enough to warrant a search.

Unholstering her walkie-talkie, she switched it on. "This is Investigator Leland. I'm in the fourteen-hundred block of County P. I think I might've found our victim. Anybody near a phone? Over?"

The crackle and hiss of static answered at first, and then Banks's butch voice: "What do you need, Leland?"

"I need somebody to call the *Gazette*, see if a Mr Koenig – a newsman – see if he's there."

"I'll get back once I know something."

"Thanks, Bill. Out."

Leland stowed the walkie-talkie and knocked again. Still, no response. She stepped from the front stoop and strolled slowly around the cottage. It had the decent dirtiness of most middle-class bachelor places, eaves stubbled with dirt, shingles beginning to curl, storms and screens in random assortment, flower beds gone to volunteers and weeds, grass left overlong after the mowing season, sticks lying on the walk. Ah, a dog tether, and no dog on it – and no dog barking inside. Perhaps he and his dog were at the vet, or on vacation.

She glanced back at the old woman's house. The storm door was closed, though the woman still haunted its frame. This man was the same as she. Perhaps this whole block was the same, shipwrecked souls clinging to whatever sargasso they could gain and hold.

Leland descended a set of concrete steps beside the house. She came to a wide window of the walkout basement, a sixties design in aluminum and single pane glass, actually releasing more heat than it held in. In fact, the window where she stood poured dry furnace air out through its open side casement –

He had worn no jacket the night he was killed.

On the desk within was a framed photo of a shaggy collie mutt and a similarly hairy man embracing her. His bearded face smiled, and the dog, too, smiled.

Leland blinked, and the photo changed – half the dog's head was gone and its remaining eye was gray with death, the man's neck was vacant and his embracing arms ended in a pair of stubs.

"Leland, come in, over," crackled the walkie-talkie.

She lifted it. "He's not been in since the 29th, has he?"

"They've already given his job away."

THREE

Death comes in threes; everything comes in threes. It is the mathematics of God's universe.

When Keith McFarland killed the editor in Burlington, I knew two more would die there, two people somehow connected to the rum man. This occurs naturally enough – a heart attack, a suicide, or some other resonation of an individual death. I typically do not have to do any of the arranging but merely approve the results.

I wasn't surprised, then, when some days later I needed to oversee the death of Detective McHenry of the Burlington Police Department.

The man was a stereotypical career policeman: heavyset with a steely bristle of gray hair, blue eyes with yellow edges, a piercing stare that was half command and half reproach, a neck permanently scarred by worn razors and tight collars, a barrel body that could wrestle a mule to the ground, and narrow legs better suited for driving than running. If he were older – say, sixty-three – he would die when the last bit of grease that he had poured down his throat solidified across the web of his coronary arteries and made his heart explode.

But he was fifty-five, and it wasn't to be a heart attack today. Only an accident. The detective deserved an elaborate death, with its measure of ceremony and civic pride.

Detective John McHenry had been a cop in Racine County for forty-five years and in Burlington for the last twelve. He'd been known as Officer Friendly by two generations of kids before landing the detective job in Burlington; had pushed for D.A.R.E. programs and started anti-graffiti campaigns; had rescued one adult, seven children, four dogs, a cat, and a hamster from various house and apartment fires; had organized the Tornado Task Force for the Union Grove Fire Department after the twister of '83; and done countless other works for good.

He'd paid for it all with a bullet still in his left lung, a pack-a-day habit for his right lung, a hardened liver from nightly drinking, a few bar-fight scars on knuckles and face, two back-to-back failed marriages, and an addiction to twelve-hour days. He was a stereotypical cop and deserved a death better than what would be scripted for the average cop show.

Here's what I came up with.

You still look like a cop, John. The faded blue Dockers don't change what you are or who you are. You tug at your belt as you walk across the hardware store parking lot. You hold the plastic ball cock as if it were a black-jack, and the hardware receipt crouches in your shirt pocket. Nobody uses shirt pockets anymore, John.

Smile and nod, yes, greet your townsfolk, but what about the bright belligerence in your eyes? Always scoping. Level and unapologetic suspicion. Only sun-glasses could mask that, but those are still in your squad.

In moments, it won't matter.

Then you see her. After all these years, she still has her hooks in you. "Ah, Susan – how are you and Ed-ward?" you ask the once-lithe creature on the sidewalk in front of the store. Her pageboy hair shifts as she turns toward you. A distant train bellows mournfully.

"Ed, please," she says. "Can't you call him Ed, after twenty-five years? And he's fine."

Even you notice the twitch in the corner of your eye, and you wish for those sunglasses. The windshield of a nearby car glares mirror-like, showing fragments of tat-tered sky. "Good to hear."

The train's marching feet clang on the track.

You stare at each other, nodding. A rebel thought re-minds you that you were once inside her. You blush and look away.

Something's going on in the elementary school park-ing lot across the street. The child's fingers still show above the hard gray line of the Chevy's roof when the rumple-faced man slams the door. Her scream is loud even through the glass. He tries the latch. It is locked.

He drags keys from his pants and shouts angrily at her, "Shut up! Shut up!"

The ball cock trembles as you run across the parking lot and into traffic.

He has the passenger door open and the screaming girl tries to fight out past him but he throws her back into the front seat. The man's plaid flannel shirt sticks to him, sweaty, and flaps a warning from his belt line. He rounds the hood and half-runs to the driver's side door.

At best an abusive dad. At worst, a kidnapper.

"Hold it!" you shout. The cars around seem to hear, bunching back like wildebeests before a predator. The man, too, hears, swinging wide his door and lurching in beside the girl.

"Hold it! Police! What's going on here?"

You catch the door he's trying to slam and almost get your own fingers caught. You yank it open and grab thread-worn plaid that tears beneath your grip. He tips half out of his seat.

"Get up!"

The engine roars. As you reach to snatch the keys, you see something. Had you lived longer, you would have sworn it was a knife under her throat, but how can a man start a car and hold a knife under his own daughter's throat? A reflection in the glass, your friends would have said. A hallucination, a prejudice of a white cop against a Latino father, the prosecution would have said. You'll be dead before you even recognize his race or his daughter's.

It is I who hold that phantom knife. I sit in the back seat of the car and hold the blade to her throat so that you will see it – so that what happens happens.

The car lurches. You grab the man's shirt. Your own weight pinches your arm in the door, but you won't let go. Tires squeal. Lights flash red. A claxon sounds. You fight to keep your feet, but the blacktop potholes steal your toes. The ball cock only now clatters to the ground. You cling to the man.

The car drags you fifty-eight feet before, at forty-five miles an hour, the undercarriage strikes the tracks and jolts you loose. You tumble, arms flapping like rubber from a stripped tire. You come to rest on the southbound line that hooks up with the Illinois Central.

Susan screams. The horn is louder and nearer, and the brakes, too. You hear nothing, though, and see only sky before your body is struck by the cattle catcher, rolled over twice, and then cleaved by the wheel. It rolls through you like a pizza cutter.

Cops die well. Cops and gang members. Soldiers, doctors, mobsters. They understand death. They face it at least minimally every day, and some are neck-deep in it. They have given death a lot of thought, and know it for what it is, a ubiquitous necessity. It is no less mysterious to these folks than it is to everyone else, but it *is* more a reality to them. They dwell at the edge of a black and endless ocean that others have only heard about.

Michael, row the boat ashore, alleluia…

Slaves face death, too. They know that the river of death is black and chilly and endlessly wide, and that the ferryman must row them safely across. And what of the Jews at Buchenwald and Dachau? Did they not pray to the angel of death for release? Mobsters know their saints and go to their confessions. Midwives go softly. Hookers, addicts, fugitives, and freaks – all those marginalized by the world and therefore pushed to the ragged edge of death, they know.

Only the soft white belly of America dies badly. They know more about Canada than they do about death, and that's not saying much. They thrash and scream or go dumb in amazement. Most do not even realize they are dying until it is all done. In the face of all religion and science, they believe that if they want to live they will not die. They go about life in ruby slippers that will always fetch them home, wishing upon stars and cars and pensions to keep them alive.

But they will die. Every last one of them. That black sea is insatiable, and it rises. One day, it will lap at the doorstep of anyone, will fill the basement and rise until it swallows the man crouched in the attic and the woman waving from the rooftop.

Everyone dies. Pray to me, and die well.

It's interesting how one glimpse can change a town. The white majority had called for and gotten the arrest of Manuel DeGarcia on charges of reckless homicide and child abuse.

He, in fact, could not have been telling his daughter to "Shut up!" since he neither spoke nor understood English. Nor could he have known McHenry was a policeman. Rattled from having accidentally slammed his daughter's fingers in the door, he panicked when a fat man ran up, shouting, tore his shirt off, and tried to take his car keys. Manuel drove off, trying to escape, but the assailant wouldn't let go.

That was the Latino's story, once an interpreter could be found, and it was the truth. The truth didn't matter. The police and community wanted someone to pay for the death of the detective, and a non-English-speaking, foreign, apparent child abuser was without defense.

The death had been very satisfying for me. It was public, involved an ex-wife and a school-aged child, allowed Detective McHenry to play the hero one last time, included a harsh repayment for selfless action, used the trains that daily criss-cross Burlington, occupied the staff of the *Gazette* for months, and divided the community that McHenry's jurisdiction had done so much to unite.

I had overseen the deaths of one hundred twenty-two others in the Chicago-Milwaukee megalopolis before Keith McFarland went hunting again. This was the third death connected to Burlington – the editor, the cop, and now the priest. This time, I had little to do but observe and prevent things from going awry. Though Keith had no real plan – too psychotic for that – he was heading in a direction almost sure to satisfy us both.

It was Christmas Eve. The ground was white with hoarfrost, all that the Midwest would have of a white Christmas, and a priest from Burlington happened to serve at St Francis in Woodstock, Illinois.

Keith steps down from the bus and looks around. The town glows beneath a woolen sky. The steeple of the Nazarene church scrapes the belly of the clouds. Behind his gray polyester trench coat, glass doors close. The bus hisses and moves on.

Keith ascends from the road to the curb. On the concrete, the frost has etched tiny stars. His Converse high-top All-Stars look very red against the wintry ground. He imagines standing there through the next frost and the first snow and wonders how his shoes would look then.

Alone and lonely, that's how. If I stand here all those days, I'd be alone and lonely for Father.

That last one wasn't too good. He was not much of a father except to his dog. There were plenty of fathers there who got scared, maybe, which helped. But still, one bad father was bad enough. He would have to be replaced by one very, very good, good father.

The chimes of St Francis on the hill at the end of the street say it is two o'clock: time for confession. Mass is at six.

Keith doesn't put his hands in his pockets as he shuffles up the cracked sidewalk. Maybe if he holds them really still they will turn to ice and he can break them off at the wrists and put Father's hands on in place of his own.

He walks. The round-leafed weeds that worked so hard to push through the sidewalk cracks are now bunched and dry, shaded gray by frost. He can probably kick them out and they will be the shape of manhood, long and with a ridge underneath. They are pushing to get down into the ground – the sky is always trying to burrow into the hard, cold earth.

Someone nods to him as he passes. Keith gestures in a way that looks like he is taking a DVD down from the rack. He wonders which DVD it is. Probably a naked one. He thinks of *The Manhood of Eddy's Father*. That was a good one. For a while he walks with the scenes playing in skin-colored neon across his mind.

All the store windows have bright fantasies: lights, snowflakes, pictures, statues, TVs, smiling men, pointed toes, metal rods up into the back of the boy's new pants, deer with targets on their sides, guns with those hard long ridges beneath them, men in white furs that cover their long chastities, a man who crouches and turns a screwdriver in a wall box, a little train that puffs real gray smoke and always swerves away from the dark, round tunnel through the cotton mountain, silvery sausages made out of the dirty parts, amber bottles wearing little red collars around their necks, elves working hard and fast beneath Santa – what a wonderful world.

He stands on the corner and waits for the light to change. It goes to yellow, and a black sedan roars up and dashes through the red. Someone shouts out of the window, "Fuck you!"

That is what the rum man had said. What a wonderful world.

Keith crosses the street and takes the sidewalk toward St Francis. The church is massive. It is built of yellow brick. The cornerstone says *A.D. 1953*, but it looks older than America. He wonders if there is a cat in the cornerstone. They do that to give a building good luck. It is bad luck for a cat. It is not a good cat they use. It is an alley cat that isn't fixed and has one eye and half a paw on one foot.

Maybe the luck isn't in the cat. Maybe it's just in the fun of killing it.

The windows are tall and colorful and shaped like manhood. The steeple has a wiry cross on top like an unbent coat hanger. It is a bigger church than the Nazarenes have, and higher. It needs lightning rods so that when God blasts out of the sky, He doesn't burn it all up. It is bigger than the Nazarene church but it is still really small under God and it belongs to God and He can do whatever He wants to it.

There are three big red doors on the front, for Father, Son, and Holy Spirit. Keith McFarland wants to go through the big Father door, but it is locked, and the Holy Spirit door is, too. The Son door is just right, and he goes in.

It is dark and damp and still cool inside. There is a smooth floor of stone like in a cave, and coats hang on one wall. He hangs his with the others.

The big part of the cave is up ahead. It opens up so the colored windows are standing tall and shining on both sides. There are two men sitting in fur coats in the dark pews, their heads down like they're tired. The Father is in that cabinet with the curtain, behind a little square with a screen like he is about to do a puppet show.

Keith McFarland walks there.

"Hey, get in line," says a man with big yellow hair – no, a woman. She is one of the tired people in the pews. The other one, who also has breasts, looks up, too.

Keith looks from the one man to the other and makes a dotted line in his head. He walks to the end of his dotted line and sits in the pew there. No sooner has he sat than a man comes out of a red curtain and walks slowly toward the hanging coats.

"Hey, g-get in line," Keith shouts to him.

He keeps walking. He is tired, too. He must have been working very hard before he got here.

The man with the big yellow hair is gone, but Keith sees her high heels under the curtain. He listens hard in the buzzing quiet and hears everything. This man talks like a little boy: "That hurts, Father. No, not there. That hurts. That hurts. Don't."

There is one more man. She goes. Then it is Keith McFarland's turn. He feels his pistol and his hunting knife.

He goes past the curtain into the cupboard and stands in there, waiting for something to happen. His gun is ready in his pocket.

"Kneel, my son," says the voice through the screen. "Begin when you are ready."

Keith McFarland kneels on the little velvet cushion on the little wooden ridge. He still has his hand on his pistol.

"What troubles you, my son?" the voice says.

"N-nothing, m-my F-f-father."

"Have you any sins to confess?"

"I-is killing a s-sin, my F-f-father?"

"Killing what? An animal? A person?"

"A p-person."

"Oh, yes, my son, that is a very serious sin – unless it was during a war. Did you kill this person during a war?"

"Yes."

"Ah, but it troubles you, still. Are you Catholic, my son?"

"Are you C-Catholic, my F-father?"

"Yes."

"I am C-Catholic, too, my F-father."

"Have you confessed about this killing before?"

"Y-yes."

"Ah, but it still bothers you. Have you spoken to Our Lady of Mercies about it?"

"I d-don't kn-know."

"Are you C-Catholic, my son?"

"I don't kn-know, my F-father."

"What is troubling you? Speak freely. You have no need to fear."

"I don't l-like the w-way you touch m-me."

There comes a pause. "What do you mean, my son?"

"Th-this way."

"My son, this is a holy place. You must not do such things."

"It is when you touch me here, and put your hands in here, my Father."

There comes another pause. The Father is speaking, but Keith hears another father, a father long dead and gone. "Oh, so you don't like that? You don't want me doing this? Or how about this? Well, that's too bad, Keith. When you're the father, you can make the rules."

"I am very angry about this."

"Go ahead and be angry. Go ahead and go in the back yard, spitting and kicking the cat. The neighbors know what you are, what you've been doing. They could care less. The cops know, too. They just say, 'Well, he's a re-tard. At least he's found something he's good at.'"

"I'm good at shooting you with this."

"You keep your hands off my guns. How did you get into the rack? Give me that. You want to shoot the thing? Shoot it down your own throat. You ought to be used to that by now, you little fuck."

The bullet blasts out. It's loud in the little box, and it echoes in the rest of the cave. There is a hole in the screen and something heavy leaning on the other side. Keith McFarland comes out of the cupboard and sees there is not a line, or anyone in the church at all. He opens the door where his father is and goes in with him.

The gun is hot in his pocket but the knife is very, very cold.

* * *

Father Mike could not have asked for a more fitting
end. He was a young priest, very caring and sensitive.
Such attributes lay a cleric open to charges of homosexuality and misconduct with younger parishioners,
but Father Mike had not let suspicions prevent him
from his work with the youth of Woodstock and nearby
Rockford.

When his superior, Father Clayton, had advised
against his volunteer work at the Boys Club of Rockford
and in the intramural basketball league of Woodstock,
Father Mike had shrugged it off and said, "I cannot and
will not abandon these kids to the streets just because
gossip mongers want something to talk about. My ministry and message come first. If they want to ruin me,
let them take up the matter with God."

Some had, and others with the parish council, but
Father Mike was innocent of any offense, and the con-
flicting stories' lack of evidence only served to prove the
fact.

Then, two years after the last such rumblings, a
youth he had never known not only accused him of a
crime he was innocent of, but also executed him for it.
Father Mike had been willing to be martyred for his
ministry and now, in the way of a true martyr, he had
died for his beliefs without anyone but his killer knowing why.

I am convinced that if he had seen Keith coming and
known who and what he was, Father Mike would still
have patiently counseled him, been similarly misheard,
and would have died in much the same way.

It was a rare and beautiful thing to have a serial murder in which victim and killer were so attuned that I had only to sit back and let the music of the spheres well up around me.

FOUR

The radio in her squad car went off during the eulogy. Phil's voice carried from the open window of the vehicle, across the frost-laced grass of the cemetery, and out to where Donna Leland stood beside the grave.

Leland at first tried to ignore the sound, her eyes averted to the frozen broadleaf weeds that had been sliced neatly in half when the grave was dug. She looked at the chocolate earth, silent and respectful beneath the silvery casket, and wished Phil would have the sense to shut up. The whole department was up in arms about Detective McHenry's death and the recent murder, but there were enough others on duty to see to anything that might come up.

Whatever had happened to the chance to mourn? McHenry was a good man. Though she had spent most of her time patrolling, whenever he'd needed a hand, they were partners. He'd taught her all she knew about police work. Now she would be stepping into his position, alone. Her mentor – her friend – was gone, and she had been promoted: Detective Donna Leland now was Burlington's first line of defense.

Phil's voice continued, shrill.

"Mother of God," she murmured.

Leland's white-gloved role in this affair could not be interrupted. She clutched the folded flag to her dress blues.

Louder, more strident, Phil's radio crackle rose, carrying above the bowed heads.

"… another death investigation … a priest in Woodstock. Same MO, same signature … the Illinois cops want you to see the scene …"

The new detective uncomfortably cleared her throat. Her jaw flexed. Another murder. A priest. Now no one could deny this was a serial crime. Her attempts to tie the first case to the decapitation and manual amputation five years back had brought criticism from many of her colleagues, most notably the man whose remains were evenly distributed through the closed casket before her.

The critics came back to one question – what had the killer been doing since the last murder in Bohner's Lake? There were numerous possibilities. He might have been doing prison time for some lesser offense. Or, perhaps he had been institutionalized for mental illness, or gone to live with a relative elsewhere, entered a relationship that stabilized him for a time, faithfully took his medication, got a job, joined the army…

Now, she wondered if he'd merely been spreading his kills through various jurisdictions, in various states.

"... coroner is finishing crime scene work ... still looking for the severed remains..."

"– would have wanted his able successor, Detective Leland, to tend to her duties," the priest intoned above the noise of the radio. He gave her a significant look. "It is the sort of man he was, that his duty to the department and service to the people came before all else."

Leland returned the priest's nod, pivoted, and headed for the squad car. The flag that had draped the coffin was still clutched tightly to her jacket. She circled to the driver's side, climbed in behind the wheel, snatched up the mike, and said, "This is Unit Four. Where's the crime scene, Phil?"

"St Francis in Woodstock, across the border. He killed a priest in the church."

"Here is where he killed him," said Bob Cabel, McHenry County coroner. The old man had a lean physique, attentive eyes, and a mantle of silver hair that he wore in a ponytail. Despite the cold, he wore a thin, short-sleeved button-down shirt and coarse-woven nylon trousers, cinched by a wide belt.

Leland looked from the old character to the blood-stained confessional. The puddle on the floor was the same deep maroon as the curtain.

"It was still warm when I got here," said Cabel with some agitation. "Wasn't an hour old then."

The detective scanned the floor around the puddle. Tennis shoes had left red footprints down the side aisle, leading toward the chancel and altar. The rest of the sanctuary was filled with flashbulbs and cups of coffee and men in long coats.

"Anybody follow the footprints?" Leland asked. "Outside, I mean."

He waved away the thought. "They go to an alley behind the bookstore and disappear on the gravel. He must have taken to the road, or maybe he just hiked out. They're bringing dogs out from Evanston."

She nodded. "Sorry. You were saying...?"

The feverish light returned to his blinking eyes. "Yes... he cut off the head and hands – I imagine he shot him first, since there's a hole in the screen – and judging by the blood, took them up to the front of the sanctuary."

"Blood on the altar?" she guessed.

"No," the coroner said, silvery brows lowering over his eyes. "That's the thing. Look at the prints. They don't go straight. Some are darker, with puddles in front of them, like he stopped and stood, holding the head and hands." They both took a moment to look along the line of footprints. The worn shoe soles wandered slowly away from the confessional, as much space between steps side to side as front to back. "He never got to the altar with the body parts. That would seem a symbolic act too tempting to turn down."

"He was masturbating," said Leland flatly. "That's why his feet were so far apart. His ritualistic fantasy is not about God. It's somehow about hands and heads."

Cabel's brows continued downward as he glowered at the footprints. "There was semen in the confessional, but we didn't find any elsewhere."

"Find the head, and you'll find the semen," Leland said. The words, once said, made her nearly retch, and she half-expected Cabel to do the same.

He only nodded.

"Afterward," prodded Leland, wanting to move on, "where did he go?"

Cabel shrugged. "He went to the basement, poured out a bunch of garbage from one of the Sunday school rooms, washed his hands, climbed the stairs, went to the coat rack, and left through an alarmed door. It's covered with bloody fingerprints."

"Well, that's something," Leland said. "As to the rest of it, let's see. He dumped out the garbage so he could put the body parts in the bag. He's not organized. An organized killer would have remembered his own bag. Besides, he's left too much evidence. Dismemberment like this is usually done to keep the victim's identity secret, but here – everybody knows who this is. The head and hands are for fantasy use, that's all."

"How many killings is this for him?" the coroner asked. "Guessing?"

Leland shook her head. "I couldn't say, yet. Three, at least, though he's been out there a long time – five years or more. He travels a good distance before hunting, but once he arrives, he will kill. I suspect that's why the murders haven't been linked – one in Burlington,

Wisconsin, the next in Gary, Indiana, the next in Pontiac, Illinois, then Woodstock, and so forth."

"He's a canny devil," said a new voice: Detective Elwood of the Woodstock police department. The black-haired and neatly clothed man had met Detective Leland at the door and put her in Cabel's charge until he finished interviewing the other parish priests. "He's got to be brilliant to think of separating his crimes by jurisdiction so as not to get caught."

"I don't think he's trying not to get caught," Leland said. "He's left plenty of evidence at each of the scenes and taken high risk victims in public places. I don't think he has the presence of mind to be canny."

"Well," Elwood said, blushing just slightly along his clean-shaven jaw, "even a dog knows not to shit where it lives. I guess he's no more canny than a dog."

Leland blinked, amused. It had been a long time since a man had felt uncomfortable in her presence, desiring to please. She rather liked the feeling. "I think you're right. We're dealing with a stray who instinctively trots off into the sticks to do his business. I'd guess he doesn't even drive himself."

Elwood's amazement was plain on his face. "Someone else drives him? And doesn't ask why he's all bloody?"

"He wasn't bloody – he put on a coat before he left. I'm guessing the sleeves and body of the coat were long enough to cover bloody hands and clothes. He walked out of here carrying a black plastic bag, got on a bus or train, and rode home."

"Leave the driving to us," said Elwood grimly.

"Even when the dogs get here, I bet they'll lead to a bus or train station," Elwood said. "Damn it. This train stop's a main feed into Chicago. He could have gone anywhere."

"What about the ticket office?" asked Leland. "Wouldn't he have to buy a ticket?"

"You buy them on board," said Elwood. "Hundreds of people every day buy them on board, unless they have a weekly or monthly pass."

Leland took a deep breath. She glanced around at the church, wondering how long it had been since she'd stepped into one.

"Keep your boys busy. Get samples of everything he came in contact with. Check both sets of fingerprints against Father Mike's personal possessions, and eliminate the priests' prints. I'm going to take what we know and punch it into the Criminal Information Bureau and NCIC. I'll bet we're seeing just the tip of this iceberg."

At last, Detective Leland was back behind her desk, hiding behind a redoubt of paperwork. John McHenry had liked being the man in the field and had often saddled Leland with the desk duties. She'd resented it then, but tonight – tonight, the benign stacks of forms were welcomed. None of them bled. None of them committed heinous acts. They lived in a flat and quiet world and feared nothing.

If I'm going to feel so lonely, this is the place to feel it.

The phone rang. Leland jumped. She grabbed the receiver and said, "Leland."

"Detective? This is Elwood, from the Woodstock PD."

"Hi, Detective. What's up?"

"Just got the prints back from the doorknob. Something strange. Thought you'd want to know."

"What is it?"

"The prints are the priest's."

"What?"

"They match prints we pulled off stuff in his room – private stuff. Even the communion cup."

Leland sat, breathing quietly. "He used the priest's hands to open the door?"

"Just thought you'd want to know."

"Thanks, Detective." Leland hung up the phone and stared into space for a while. "Got to keep going, or I'll never get home tonight." Leland pulled her keyboard toward her and tapped into the Wisconsin Crime Information Bureau. She entered the vital characteristics of the crime scenes: decapitation and manual amputation, high risk male victims, gun use, necrophilia, male Converse basketball shoe prints at size ten, crimes crossing jurisdictions, use of public transportation. She punched in the data and pressed Enter.

As the computer grunted quietly within its casing, Leland doubtfully scanned the list she'd made. This offender was disorganized, psychotic. That was also comforting. To know this person was sick made his actions somewhat less horrifying. She understood mental illness, knew it was a thing of brain chemistry, not a matter of demons and monsters. This guy needed a doctor, not an exorcist.

But if he's psychotic, why's he so tough to track down? In most cases psychotics were easier to find than psychopaths, more likely to do something obvious or stupid. But not here. Whenever the killer required a particularly subtle act – like riding the train or bus to and from the crime scenes, committing murders in different county and state jurisdictions, taking off his coat before killing and then putting it on again, cutting off hands and head to prevent victim identification and ballistics match-ups, carrying the dismembered parts in a bag beneath his coat – he was suddenly capable of doing it. Jeffrey Dahmer exhibited similar presence of mind when it was needed, and thus avoided detection. It was as though the guardian angels of these killers were especially adept at protecting them.

A slow scroll of matching cases began to slide up the screen, listing first the murder of editor Jules Koenig, and then the homicide of butcher Lynn Blautsmeyer in Bohner's Lake, five years back. Leland watched intently, scanning the case information for new clues. Koenig's case was too fresh in her mind to provide new insights, but Blautsmeyer's...

Leland's eyelids drooped with fatigue as she recalled that scene.

The sign read "Blautsmeyer's Homemade Sausage" and pictured a wiener dog snapping at the last frankfurter in a chain of them. It had always seemed to Leland that the dog was part of the string of sausage. That image was enough to drive some customers away, and Lynn Herman Blautsmeyer's missing index finger brought even more jokes – speculations of accidental cannibalism in Bohner's Lake.

Lynn was missing more than a finger, now.

The young investigator drew a handkerchief from her pocket and opened the blood-stained glass door. Within, yellowed tiles and walls were stained with blood. Even to eyes unfamiliar with homicide scenes, the stains formed a portrait of the murder.

"Mother of God." Leland positioned the cloth over her face.

In front of one old-style deli display, blood pooled in the shape and color of a liver. That's where the killing occurred – a quick slash to the neck while victim and killer stood face to face. The two concavities on the upper edge of the puddle were from the toes of Lynn's shoes. He'd stood just there. The blood had been a gushing spray. The killer had held the man up for some moments before pushing him over. Lynn fell back and cracked his skull where the larger pool was. The killer knelt beside him, knee prints in the blood, and used the cleaver he'd snatched from the butcher to hack off the man's head and hands.

This was messy work. The killer had left fingerprints all over the body and clothes as he performed his inexpert butchery. He had done a ragged job of it, as if he had not known how difficult it would be. This might have been his first kill.

Once done, the killer went behind the counter and experimented with the shrink wrapper. Tangles of red-spotted plastic wrap showed various trials with the machine. Once he had learned what he was doing, he apparently wrapped the hands and head and stowed them in an Igloo cooler that Mrs Blautsmeyer had reported missing. A very clear handprint hung like a sunburst on the tile wall above where the cooler had been.

As for the body, a wide red path wound like the yellow brick road back behind the counter to the meat locker. There, the butcher at last was hooked and hung among his stock. By the time Blautsmeyer's wife discovered the scene, the blood beneath her husband had thickened to a syrupy brown.

The killer had dipped his left index finger – the prints were positively confirmed from three other locations – in the blood and written on the parchment-pale chest of the corpse, "*Samael 5:2:356.*"

Leland blinked away the scene. The only Wisconsin crimes that matched the priest's murder were the two she had already been involved with.

Strange that I've worked both cases. I was only an assistant investigator five years ago. It's like the killer has me targeted.

She shook away that idea. The long hours and gruesome scenes, the memories of poor Kerry and his homemade noose, the death of her partner – all of it was tumbling around in her head. Chronic loneliness had deepened to bona fide isolation. Perhaps she would go to Lakeland Animal Shelter to see if they had any calico kittens, but it would only be cruel to leave a kitten alone for so many hours a day. Besides, in the midst of all this welling inhumanity, she needed human contact.

How late is Fred's Burgers open? She checked her watch. Not tonight. Tonight, she'd hit the NCIC and get to bed.

Sighing, Leland switched to the National Crime Information Center computer network and began typing in information. While she did so, she thought back to that most puzzling clue: *Samael 5:2:356*. Debate about the other clues had quickly been replaced by speculation about that one bit of writing in blood. What was it? A Bible verse? A date? A license plate? A verse of poetry?

The Bible verse seemed most promising. Though there was not a book of Samael, there were a pair of books of Samuel. The first book of Samuel, chapter 5, had no verse 356, but one young patrolman, formerly a seminarian, calculated on a long night shift that, starting with Samuel 5:2, the first 356 words read thus:

¶ When the Philistines stole the ark of God, they hid it in the temple of their god Dagon, and set it by the idol of Dagon. Early next morning, the men of the house of Ashdod rose to find that Dagon had fallen upon his face on the ground before the ark of the Lord. And they righted Dagon and set him in his place again. Next morning, Dagon had fallen on his face on the ground before the ark of the Lord;

and the head of Dagon and both hands were cut off upon the threshold; only the stumps were left on the idol.

Therefore unto this day, neither the priests of Dagon nor his worshipers tread on the threshold of the temple of Dagon in Ashdod. The hand of the Lord was heavy on Ashdod, and he annihilated them and plagued them with genital boils.

When the men of Ashdod saw these terrible things, they said, "Let us take the ark of the God of Israel away from us: for his hand is hard upon us and upon our god Dagon."

The men of Ashdod called together the Philistine lords and said to them, "Where shall we hide the ark of the God of Israel?" And the lords answered, "Carry the ark of the God of Israel to Gath. And they carried the ark of the God of Israel to that place.

But when it arrived, the hand of the Lord struck the city of Gath with a terrible annihilation: and he struck the men of the city, both poor and rich, with boils in their private parts.

The people of Gath sent the ark of God to Ekron. But when the ark of God arrived in Ekron, the Ekronites cried out, "They have brought the ark of the God of Israel to slay us!"

So all the Philistine lords met again and said, "Send the ark of the God of Israel away, back to its own place so that it will not kill us or our people: for there was a terrible annihilation all through the city; God's hand was very heavy on them.

The fact that the false god Dagon's hands and head were missing was taken as an ominous sign. So, too, was the mention of tumors in the groin, which some interpreted as a reference to sexual perversion. A columnist of the Burlington *Gazette* irresponsibly speculated that the killer considered himself to be the ark of God, righteous and powerful but captive to the Philistines – corrupt society at large. As long as he felt trapped in this hostile world, the reporter said, the man would kill again and again, and be the Death that brought panic to the city. God's hand was heavy upon him.

The young patrolman who had discovered these things had collaborated with the columnist and was suspended for it. He took the suspension as a sign, quit his field training, and went back to seminary.

Leland's remembrances were interrupted by a beep, and by a listing of violent crimes in the three-state area of Wisconsin, Illinois, and Indiana. Bleary-eyed, Leland scrolled through the accounts. Some involved decapitation, others amputation, and still others necrophilia, gun use...

She began to read the individual entries but glanced up at the list tally – the screen showed only five of four hundred eighty-two entries. She requested a cross-index of amputation and decapitation, and sat back as the computer began its contented grunting.

The piggish sound reminded Leland of another speculation about *Samael 5:2:356*. One officer, speaking facetiously, said that since the corpse had been hung up among the pork carcasses, 5:2:356 must be a reference to the act, scene, and verse in Hamlet: "Now cracks a

noble heart. Good night, sweet prince; and flights of angels sing thee to thy rest!" A fitting enough verse,
except that the butcher had been no prince, and the
killer no singing angel.

Dead ends everywhere.

The cross-check came in, narrowing the field to two
hundred thirty-one cases. Though the name "Samael"
had not been found on either the priest or the newspaperman, Leland's recollections had piqued her curiosity.
On a whim, she typed in a check for the name Samael.
She leaned back and took a sip of coffee.

Officer Greenberg had said Samael was the name for
the Jewish Angel of Death.

"Mother of God."

The screen blinked, producing a list of eighty-eight
murders in the tri-state area, each of which included
decapitations, manual amputation, and, somehow, the
name Samael.

Angel of Death.

FIVE

At last, Keith McFarland is slated to die. The death will come in a month, so I have plenty of time for orchestration. I want his end to be bloody, slow, and somewhat perverse. Already, I have many ideas, most shaped by the fact that the detective assigned to his case, a Detective Leland, is scheduled to die the same day. I might as well let them kill each other.

Before that sweet moment, though, I have a very difficult case before me. A newlywed couple.

Many cultures believe that angels of death seek to steal virgins on their wedding day. Actually, we do. A rose is best snipped before it opens. Also, deaths become tricky around any rite of passage. A death date scheduled for a virgin adolescent will be inappropriate for a sexually active adult. Once a rite of passage is completed, the person is new, and a whole new death date must be arranged.

There are various traditions meant to prevent virgin abductions. One is the white wedding runner, which can supposedly stop an angel of death from reaching up through the floor to snatch a bride on her way to the altar. Oddly, virgin grooms are not similarly guarded. Another is the Jewish tradition of breaking the wine glass, a symbol of the broken hymen. It is thought that this symbolic consummation will fool angels into giving up. If such preventions are unsuccessful, grooms must ready an arsenal of tricks and wards for battling angels throughout the wedding night. They will appear in various hostile guises – drunk drivers, fires, jealous boyfriends, muggers, poisonous snakes, and so forth – until consummation is achieved. Some noble grooms lay down their lives to protect their brides, all the while unaware that it is their own virgin soul the angel has come to collect.

Today, though, I must collect them both.

The couple is driving through Chicago, en route from Waukesha, Wisconsin, to Kissimmee, Florida. It is the morning after their all-night wedding party, and they plan to drive to Louisville for their first day and on to Kissimmee afterward.

They will not reach Indiana.

It will be a car accident. That much is simple on the Dan Ryan Freeway. Husband and wife both, at intervals, break into tears at how beautiful their wedding has been. That fact will make the moment's inattention even easier to arrange. The difficulty is organizing a suitable end for such promising young lovers.

He drives. The roads are dry and cold this January. The shoulders hold filthy snow. The sky is white like paper.

His brown hair is combed back long, like a prophet's, and his beard is coarse and reddish. His blond mustache disappears against lightly freckled skin. From a distance, he looks Amish, or Lincolnesque. He does not disapprove of either impression.

He talks. He talks and talks, in a fluid, self-impressed bliss of hopes. The breath pulsing in and out of him fans the eager flames in his eyes. He pauses now for a comment from his bride, but when she does not immediately volunteer, he turns up the CD player and points at intervals toward it, as though a guitar solo could be seen as well as heard.

Sighing at the sublimities of feedback, he clutches the wheel in large, strong hands. Since puberty, those hands had moved with the rhythm of mantis claws. It makes sense. He has spent much of his adolescence in trees.

A bit of egg and Canadian bacon is perched on a groin fold of his thin canvas pants. Ratty deck shoes leap from gas to brake to gas again in the graceless dance of young nerve on the Dan Ryan. Despite an athletic build and a freckled tan from life guarding, he is no true athlete. His disabling fear of competition extends even to card games and attempts to drive through Chicago.

His bride sits beside him, glowing in their first morning together. Her oval face and bright hazel eyes are intense. She listens, mostly because she loves him, but also because she has nothing to say about the bizarre flurry of fancies he spins out. This particular eruption will be spent as quickly as all the rest. She waits, patient and powerful. A force of nature, the bride is both fragile and indomitable.

Her shoulders shiver beneath her coat. Long-nailed fingers flick the heat control to the foot well symbol. Those actions are enough to draw the man's attention. He looks suddenly concerned – no, worried – and reaches out one of his mantis hands to fumble inexpertly with the temperature controls. She stretches and yawns. His attention drifts from levers and knobs to her figure. The drifting asteroid has been snagged by the grand silence of a spinning world, and he curves inward, willingly and eternally captured by her.

Oh, how deeply they will be mourned – twin roses plucked just as they begin to open. If this were the sixties, there would be a folk song.

Now is the moment. They both must die, and I know how it will happen.

He glimpses me. I stand in the salty freeway lane before him – the slow lane, in which they are overtaking a semi that rumbles along in the center lane. He can see me for but a moment. If I were real, my pierced feet would even now be striking the undercarriage as my shins break upon the bumper and my loincloth is sucked from my shattering pelvis into the front grill. Bleeding hands would strike the fiberglass fenders as my pierced side slides in its own blood and water to send my thorn-crowned head through the windshield to slay him. But I am not real. He swerves, too late, loses control on a sheet of black ice, spins once completely and strikes a cement piling of an overpass.

The impact has the sound of a plastic toy being crunched.

Then it is done. That quickly, the car is stopped. The man sits, dazed, scraped, bruised, but otherwise untouched.

The oblivious semi roars onward. In the empty windshield space, the next vehicles slow. Emergency lights begin flashing like mournful fireflies. January bites cold against the man's hot red belly. The rumble of traffic slows, like the sudden reverent hush that comes to a crowd when something has gone terribly wrong.

He has often thought that a fatal accident should stop traffic: human death should never occur conveniently or unobtrusively. A man after my own heart.

"That was… close," he says hoarsely, realizing only then that he has screamed his throat raw. He turns to his bride and sees only the sheared away edge of the car and the cracked piling that now brushes his right arm. He blinks, uncomprehending at first, and looks into the back seat, as if she will be sitting there.

Gone. Folded away in metal and plastic.

He turns forward again and watches the cars and their firefly lights. One of his mantis hands lifts to the horn and honks it twice, a bleating sound. He begins to pick glass out of his body, tossing the bloody fragments out onto what is left of the hood.

They aren't enough to kill him, he knows. Nor is the shoulder dislocation, already swelling beneath a strained strap. Nor is the bleeding band of his forehead where it crunched against the steering wheel.

But he will die tonight. He is not strong enough to survive this.

The planet has been destroyed, and the asteroid flies free again, pelting toward a sun that waits, fiery and voracious, ten or twelve hours ahead.

(I would not have done it the other way. The bride would not have committed suicide. Even had she tried, her own elemental flesh could not slay itself. She was life.)

He, on the other hand, is treated, counseled, and given a room at the University of Chicago Hospital. Despite his sore shoulder, the tree climber makes his way down from a third story window to the ground, walks along the South Side, is mugged and beaten when it turns out he has no money, continues to the Skyway, and leaps, tattered and bleeding, from a viaduct to land before a semi.

As I say, he was a man after my own heart.

Not so long ago, there was a madman who talked to God. (Any mortal who hears the true voice of God goes mad, just as any mortal who sees God is slain by the sight.) This man truly spoke to God and was truly mad.

Divine madness allowed him to rise to power over his small, oppressed nation, brought to its knees by a series of hardships caused by the old regime. The madman wanted more land, better land. But the land he wanted was full of people already – lesser people, slave races. They needed to die. God agreed.

God told him to kill every man, woman, and child of the lesser races. Genocide, purification of the land for the divine, master race.

And the madman succeeded. In a ferocious rush, the tiny country took on the world. City after city fell. The madman's soldiers rounded up the lesser races, and according to God's will, slew them and buried them in vast mass graves, or burned their bodies away to ash and bones.

Do not be surprised by this. God has not only the right but the obligation to decide when everyone will die. Whether God decides that ten thousand should be slain all in one day, or over the course of fifty years, God decides when they will die. Assuredly, he slays them, and sometimes in their multitude, like a man mowing grass or spraying for termites.

Yes, I assure the quality of individual deaths, and the tool of my work is sometimes a madman like Keith Mc-Farland. It is not merely my right to slay via such mortals as he, but my solemn obligation to do so.

Just as I have been assigned by God to oversee the deaths of individuals in their thousands – sleeping, driving, working, eating – so the mad dictator was assigned by God to slay men and women and children in their hundreds of thousands. Either God could not stop these mass executions, or he would not stop them. A God who could not stop them is not God. A God who would not stop them has ordained them.

Either there is no God, or the mad genocidal dictator was God's servant.

"So Joshua took all that land, the hills, and all the south country, and all the land of Goshen, and the valley, and the plain, and the mountain of Israel, and the valley of the same; even from the mount Halak, that goeth up to Seir, even unto Baal-gad in the valley of Lebanon under mount Hermon: and all their kings he took, and smote them, and slew them. Joshua made war a long time with all those kings. There was not a city that made peace with the children of Israel, save the Hivites, the inhabitants of Gibeon: all other they took in battle. For it was of the LORD to harden their hearts, that they should come against Israel in battle, that he might destroy them utterly, and that they might have no favor, but that he might destroy them, as the LORD commanded Moses."

Not a sparrow falls from heaven without your Father knowing it. God knows of every death, and approves of every death. Men who play God are murderers and mad dictators, but men who truly hear God can do the same things and be holy prophets. Ask the extremists. They still understand the idea of holy war.

When Keith McFarland kills, he is a monster. When I kill, I am an angel of the Lord.

Joshua could not have slain his tens of thousands, Napoleon his hundreds of thousands, Hitler his millions, and Stalin his tens of millions if God had not willed it so. Mad and murderous they may be, but these folk are servants of God.

And people get so upset over Manson, who never killed a soul, or Keith McFarland, who hasn't even gotten into triple digits. The difference is that they do not really hear the voice of God.

One last fling for Keith? Why not? He has time to kill, and I have people.

They call him Mister Strange. He is tall, stoop-shouldered, and heavy, with kinky blond hair standing from his head and a gap-toothed, idiot grin beneath his wire-rim glasses. He is a garbage man in Griffith, Indiana. The loping ape has few friends, one sister, and no car. A graduate of Griffith Junior High, he landed his first and only job after the death of his father. He has hauled the garbage of Griffith for twenty-four years now and is known mostly as a harmless idiot.

When he was twenty-seven, the garbage man unadvisedly flirted with junior high girls who passed him on the way to school. He was convicted of child molestation, though he had never touched anyone except himself. After six months of good behavior, he was released. He still bears the label pedophile – and the title Mister Strange. The people of Griffith watch him closely. They call the police on him as regularly as they call animal control on stray dogs.

Mister Strange is not a pedophile, though he is, indeed, strange.

His true name is Ed Bolenski. It is time for the thirty-nine year-old garbage man to die, and I think it would be fitting for Keith McFarland to do the honors.

This snowy February evening, Ed sits in the Inn-Town Tap. The air is filled with smoke, crowd noise, a basketball game, and the inarticulate thumps of an old jukebox. Despite bad windows, the bar is warm and friendly.

Mister Strange always eats his dinner here. The door to his apartment goes up from the bar, not fifteen feet of greasy paneling away. A key to the tavern rests idly in his pants pocket. The buffalo wings make his fingers red and gritty. Crumpled napkins form a chaparral around his wings basket. Bones lie beside dripping, steaming meat. He bites into a wing and works skin and gristle free, swallowing the negligible flesh that had been strung along the bone.

You die tonight, Mister Strange.

They taste good. Real good. After this is the Wheel. Don't worry about the time. That's bar time. Time for drunks. Your time is twenty minutes behind. Drunks live twenty minutes ahead.

You sit. A belch is knocking. You straighten. Up it comes. Tastes good. More room for more.

The people are loud tonight.

A little man sits there. He is at the table that has the busted leg. The folded napkins under one side aren't under it. They're kicked out near the ladies room. They get kicked out all the time. Charlie's cheap for not fixing it. The little man eats. The table leans toward his burger. He picks up his drink. The table sways away.

"How you doing?" you say.

He nods. That means okay. He's doing okay.

You're doing okay, too.

"You like the Wheel?"

He nods. That means, yeah. He likes the Wheel.

"You good at the Wheel?"

He nods. Bet he's not as good as you.

"Bet you're not as good as me."

He nods. The bet's on.

"Don't mind the time. That's bar time." You suck the meat from the last two wings. Tastes good. You crunch a little on the wing tips and feel whatever that is – bone or feather or whatever – crunch under the coating. The holder is out of napkins. You use the old ones. You put them in your wings basket. Tastes good.

"Come on. We'll see."

He nods. You stand. Maybe he'd not nod if he saw how really big you are. You are really big. Too late, now. The bet's on. He gives up his burger, halfway through. Some guys would ask for the rest. You don't.

"Come on. I live upstairs."

He nods. He's really small. Maybe he'll be good at the Wheel. Maybe not.

The stairs squeak. You know when anybody's coming up because the stairs squeak. He's coming up. He's going to challenge you to the Wheel. He's going to lose.

There's a little landing. To open the bathroom door, you have to step off the landing. It's that little. Your door goes in, not out. You keep your deadbolt on. That's a good name. Deadbolt. Stops them dead.

You swing the door open. Home. The room is big. The window at the other end is big. You watch the cars there. That big gold chair is from Grandma's. She's dead. You flick on the tube. Color. Better than the old one. The couch is in front of it. Your cat is in the corner, brown and yellow like the couch cover. Lots of the stuff is from the curb. You don't take stuff from the dump.

"You want something?" He nods. His hair looks uneven and greasy. He's got acne. He looked better in the tavern. "The kitchen is there." It is. The Formica table and the hot plate and the fridge are there. He sits down on the couch.

The music starts. Cartoons of Pat Sajak and Vanna White soar into your lives.

You get a root beer. You move the cat and the Snickers wrapper and sit next to him. Everything looks clean on the stage. The skin is a little green. The people are too thin and bend in the middle. What do you want for free?

"What do you want for free? It's color."

He nods.

"You don't talk much."

He nods. That is almost funny.

They have the first puzzle. Three-word title. Blank blank blank blank blank blank, blank blank blank, blank blank blank blank blank. The fat woman guesses R, and there are twothree. Blank blank R blank blank R, blank blank blank, blank R blank blank blank.

"You know it?"

He nods.

"Yeah."

One T. Blank blank R blank blank R, blank blank blank, blank R blank T blank.

"If you know it, what is it?"

"M-M-Murder She Wr-Wrote."

It doesn't fit... it does fit! You look at him and see his gun and then there is hot fire and then nothing.

It was fitting: the garbage man was slain on a couch from the dump (no matter what he told others, he had taken many of his furnishings from the dump) by a piece of white trash. Even Keith, not noted for his cleanliness, took the head and hands into the bathroom to wash them before he used them. He felt so comfortable in the dingy place that he stayed the night, never changing the channel or turning off the TV. He let himself out during the wee hours, walking beneath the ceiling tiles stained red from the leaking blood.

Keith did all that on his own. I figured I'd let the artist work. Still, I made sure he signed my name to the masterpiece. He'd forgotten the last two times. This time he complied, writing on the belly of the body, using Mister Strange's own bloody finger as a pen: Samael 5:2:356.

You see, I wanted Detective Leland to show up. I wanted to see her at the crime scene.

Unlike Keith, I didn't leave. Time for me doesn't matter. I would wait until she came. I knew she would come. She was smart enough to use the NCIC. I could play catch-up on deaths once I had met her and found out what she was like.

I didn't have to wait long. The Griffith cops were all over the place by noon that day, when the bar opened. I met a very fine fellow, a Sergeant Michaels, shift commander. I didn't so much meet him, actually, but became him, implanted him in the memory of the rest of the department. I became the sergeant and sent for Leland.

She arrived that night. It was nice to talk with her.

SIX

Detective Leland ducked under the police line and walked slowly into the chilly Inn-Town Tap. A forest of tables and chairs stood derelict around her. She felt cold in the dark place despite the suit jacket she wore. Suit jacket, white shirt, and loosened tie – her uniform ever since she had taken over McHenry's post as detective. No longer would she patrol. For the rest of her career, she would keep irregular hours and unwholesome company – though the cop who waited at the far end of the room seemed wholesome enough.

"He lives up here," said Sergeant Michaels of the Griffith Police. "I mean, *lived*." He blushed handsomely. The sergeant was tall, lean, and young, his eyes bright like a pair of new dimes. He had black hair and a supermodel's body, but he moved like a kid at his first dance – awkward and unaware how beautiful he was.

This work is getting to me, thought Leland.

Michaels gestured up the dimly lit stairway, his breath ghosting between warped panels of pressboard. "The scene's in okay shape but not exactly pristine."

Detective Leland nodded. "They've sifted through it all?"

"Yeah, but they were careful," said Michaels as he started up the stairs. He was supposed to be the shift manager from eleven to six but had gotten guard duty at the crime scene when his substitute patrolman and another officer were out sick. "They've taken away the body, of course, even in this weather. But aside from samples, nothing else's been moved. They even wore surgical booties and hair nets." His hand waved vaguely above his head. "You'll see."

She followed him up the stairs. A single yellow light flickered squalidly overhead, as though a white bulb would have attracted bugs. Leland's shadow pressed up against the sergeant as he gained the landing. The bathroom door was painted with darkness.

He fitted the key to the deadbolt and leaned against the battle-scarred door. "No one downstairs heard the gunshot. Too much noise. An old jukebox, you know. They say the killer lagged around all night."

"Gunshot?" Leland asked, surprised. Her eyes moved from his sinewy shoulder up to his face. "The police report didn't say so, or the coroner's, either."

Michaels's eyes looked gold in the yellow light. "I guess that's just a personal theory. Blood-spatter analysis indicates a gunshot wound to the head, but there's so much blood – and no head. He had to chop a while to get the head off. Hard to say what happened. I figured maybe he killed him some other way, first. And…"

"And you read that he used a gun in the other cases, the ones I've been investigating?" she provided.

"I'm the one who told the lieutenant to call you," he replied a little sheepishly. Yes, handsome, almost statuesque, though boyish. "I know, I shouldn't have jumped to conclusions about the gun."

She laughed a little. "Jumped the gun. That was almost a pun."

He nodded, accepting the moment of grace.

He'd make a good assistant detective, she found herself thinking. I wonder if this flatlander would give up Indiana to become a cheesehead.

Without another word, Sergeant Michaels pushed open the door. His gray-jacketed shoulders cleared the frame, and Leland gazed at the room beyond.

At first, it appeared to be ransacked – clothes and garbage strewn across the floor, video cases fallen from shelves and cracked open like black eggs – but the debris didn't have the rankled look of violent action. The room had eroded over weeks and months.

Still, the blood was fresh. On the threadbare couch, it formed a puddle in the shape of a large body, slumped in front of the TV. The linoleum floor held a wide, full puddle of the stuff, slowly evaporating or dripping away into the bar below. Rust-red smudges covered just about everything else – table, refrigerator, hot plate, American cheese wrappers, dresser, bed, TV stand and trays, doorknob, coat hangers.

"It's my guy, all right," Leland said.

The sergeant looked a bit peaked as he drew the crime scene photos from a manila envelope. "You know him?"

"No," she said. "I just feel like I do. Study the artwork, and you come to know the artist."

He paused before handing her the photos – color shots. She was glad. Blood always looked like ink on black-and-white film. "You call this artwork?"

"Yes," she said, taking the photos. Her hand casually touched his. It was warm and strong, reassuring: human in all this inhumanity.

Donna, what are you doing? These late nights and long drives must be getting to you.

In a matter-of-fact voice, she said, "They're artwork as far as the killer is concerned. Erotica. Look, here – the smudges on the card table – those are from the victim's hands, not the killer's. He was using the victim's hands to get out the cheese. He probably also used them to masturbate." Leland felt suddenly awkward, and she did what she always did – launched into theory. "Maybe he used them to pull down the bed sheets, even to turn on this touch lamp, here beside the TV. Whether or not the killer knows it, that's symbolic for his own lack of power. He feels completely disenfranchised, powerless to act, until he murders, and then for a while he has taken someone else's power – his hands – and uses them for his own ends."

The sergeant nodded. "And what about the head? I thought when somebody cut off the hands and head, it was to hide the person's identity."

"Yes, usually, but if you want the identity to remain secret, you don't kill someone in his own apartment. It might have started as a useful MO, but since then it has taken on ritual significance. Taking someone else's head is taking his personality, mind, and soul. The killer probably feels he needs a new head. A new soul."

"I would have to agree," Michaels answered. "You cross-checked the prints with mental health records?"

"We're running all those checks. He's left us plenty of evidence. It's a broad hunting ground, though, with millions of people and tens of thousands of convicts in three separate state jurisdictions, not to mention all the counties and cities."

All right, enough already. Stop prattling.

She sorted through the stark images. Police photographers had a knack for capturing not only the facts of a crime, but also the lurid terror of the scene. One image showed the headless, handless body leaning on the sofa as though still watching the blood-spattered TV screen. The flash had thrown the rest of the room into lurid, sinister darkness. Cushions and neck stump cast a shadow that looked like a range of steppes across the wall. The next photos showed details of the blood-stained carpet and wallpaper; others showed a handprint the size and shape of the one from Woodstock, the blood-spattered bathroom...

"Anything turn up from interviewing the bartender, wait staff, and regulars?" Leland asked.

"One of the busboys said he'd seen a guy that looked

like Tom Petty, but with dark hair. Short, thin, vacant eyes. He hadn't seen him before. He thought the man had talked to Mister Strange."

"Mister Strange?"

Michaels grimaced an apology, and his hand briefly cradled her elbow. "That's what locals called him. He was a little too friendly. He used to have all kinds of people in and out of that apartment. That's why nobody paid any attention to Tom Petty." He paused, chagrined again and suddenly tired. "Let's go get a cup of coffee and talk away from all this."

"A cup of coffee?" Leland asked. "Aren't you supposed to stay on duty?"

Again the shrug. "I plugged in the pot downstairs and brewed a batch. I figured I needed it to stay awake." He yawned conspicuously. "Horror takes it out of you, makes you shut down. Better get some coffee, don't you think?"

The detective gestured toward the door. "Sure, Sergeant. Lead on."

Oh, Detective Leland, you've done well so far. I have on occasion dealt with the Feds, but most law enforcers I've run into are simple, honest, small town cops in way over their heads. All of them, even the big city homicide detectives, have the sense to be frightened by their work. I sense the fright in you, too, sitting next to me at the bar, talking so matter-of-factly about our killer. But it isn't just fright. It's something bigger. It's understanding; compassion.

Ah, I've found the shred of memory it's tied to. Your brother, Kerry. Twin brother. You lost him. This killer seems another Kerry to you, another boy suffering and sick and alone, desperate. You don't want to just find this killer. You want to reach him. Perhaps redeem him, or at least yourself. It's the impulse of a drowning soul to reach out to something, anything else – anything human.

Well, you're right about this killer. You've got Keith nailed to a T.

"...before getting hold of Quantico, I had that much pulled together. White male, early thirties – he's been at it for at least ten years now, by the trail of cases I've tracked through NCIC. Sergeant, we're talking about over eighty-nine cases that fit the pattern. Even if a third of those are copycats, we're talking about a rampage that tops even the most pessimistic estimates for Bundy, and double the killings done by Gacy."

Yes, more than double, Donna. Keith started when he was seventeen. He's been killing in Chicagoland longer than I have. You don't even have the first dozen or so on your computer. Those first kills were very smooth, artful. You've only gotten close now because he's deteriorated so far. Ah, how adulthood ravages the soul.

"I'm Azra," I say.

You stop in the middle of your monologue. "What?" You take a sip of coffee.

"Azra is my name. You keep calling me Sergeant. My name's Azra."

"Azra? What nationality is that? Bulgarian? Roman-ian?"

"Hebrew. It's short for Azrael. My mother was Jew-ish."

"Oh. My first name is Donna."

"I know."

"How do you know? I haven't told you."

"I told the lieutenant to call for you, remember? I've been following your casework. I've been assigned to know."

You seem flustered by that. Your hand trembles around the warm handle of the coffee cup. You've been reaching out all this while, but not now. That hand wants warmth, wants the touch of my hand, but in-stead it curves quietly around the feverish mug. Why not reach out to me? I'm young, handsome – a cop. Perhaps you glimpse darkly who I really am.

Mortals have always shivered in my presence.

I wish I had not made you shiver. It grieves me. To see you now not only drowning but cold. It makes me inexplicably sad.

"How could so many similar deaths go unnoticed for so long?" I ask, prompting you from your distraction.

"Jurisdiction. That's one in Elm Grove, then one in Gary, then Whiting, then Racine, Lake Geneva, Berwyn, Rockford, Milwaukee, Pontiac – he got a train pass or a Greyhound card or something."

He also does a lot of walking, but I will not tell you that. I look into your eyes and see that eggshell fragility of mortals, that thinnest of all shields that I am sent to destroy. I will be destroying you, like all the others. Oh, how I wish I weren't.

I say, "There is too much here that seems planned – the changes in venue; the decapitation; the ability to kill someone, hang out a while, and then somehow, bloodlessly, walk away from the scene and go undetected. He may be psychotic now, but I imagine when he started this, he knew exactly what he was doing. A young psychopath who's slowly lost his mind in the last decade or so." That should shock you back to the case at hand.

"Yes," you respond, blinking. "Yes, it isn't luck that's kept this a secret for so long. He's a mixed bag. That's what Quantico said. They'll be sending someone from Behavioral Sciences out. Once they heard the body count–"

"*Your* body count."

"Yes, the one I compiled – once they heard the number of people, they couldn't refuse. Anyway, they said over the phone that it sounded mixed, part organized and part chaotic. It would make sense he was sliding from one toward the other."

"What about the press? When they put together what you've put together… when they get wind of the FBI…"

"I want to have this guy nabbed before then. If the story breaks, we'll just see what we can do proactively through the media to draw him out. Of course, with how little attention he's paid to the TV upstairs…"

"Oh, you'll get him soon. You're just steps behind him, now."

You kiss me. It is a quick motion, a small, ducking sweetness on my cheek. You blush as you pull away. "I hope you're right," you say in dismissal.

I gaze into your eyes, seeking what it was that made you kiss me. You try to hide it behind the weary, favor-granting facade of a hardened cop. I know you are no flirt, no jaded creature. That kiss meant something.

Loneliness. I feel it, too. I've been utterly alone these years, and had not even known what to call it. To be lonely is bad enough, but to feel this aching draw of soul to soul and still be alone in it all…

You are shutting down. You think I think you were too forward. You are more surprised and disturbed by the kiss than I, though it was only the chaste kiss of lip to cheek.

Mine is not. I kiss your lips. Always before, that kiss has been a slaying one, though in this passionate rush, I will not let it be. I cap off the white-hot column of killing force. This kiss is tender, and again.

I will not kill you with it.

I will not kill you now.

Perhaps not ever.

Mother of God, what am I getting myself into? The thought was as much prayer as interjection.

Leland drew back from the man, her eyes searching his. She expected to see something predatory in him, something prepared to pounce upon and exploit her supposed vulnerability. But she saw none of that. He did not wish her harm. He wasn't on the prowl. He was as vulnerable and lonely and desperate as she and – until a moment ago – he hadn't even realized it.

There, not ten feet from the police line that roped off the bloodstained ceiling and floor, the two cops clung to each other. Heat ghosted up from their shoulders into the chill place. Their lips met no more. They only embraced, two souls weary of the brutal world.

SEVEN

This is a cardinal sin. Angels are forbidden to fall in love with humans. Angels are to love God only. Whenever an angel finds love elsewhere, he is cast out of Heaven and plunges toward Hell.

Think of Satan, whose self-love brought eternal damnation. Think of Harut and Marut, who loved a woman and so were tricked into telling her the secret name of God. They too were thrown down. Think of Semjaza and two hundred others angels who made love to humans and spawned the race of Nephilim – giants who terrorized the world in antediluvian times. All fell.

But I am not like them. I am like Chamuel, the Dark Angel, who wrestled with Jacob beside the River Jabbok. I am to dwell among humans and wrestle with them throughout the long, dark night and cripple them if I must to win free. I am not meant to love them.

But perhaps there are special cases. What of Michael, Zagazel, and Gabriel, who disobeyed God's command that they kill Moses? Their love for the mortal caused them to sin, but they did not fall.

Perhaps there will be a special case for me.

I am a fool to think these things. No, I cannot let my heart wander from my ribs. I am to live among humans and strive with them – but to do it all chastely. I am to serve, to guide, to kill – but not to love.

No wonder angels and cops are so lonely.

I will not kill her now. In three weeks; we will see what three weeks brings.

They are new. Their skin. Their hair. Their eyes. Especially their eyes.

They stand in a thicket. That is how new they are. They stand in a thicket instead of a meadow. They fear the wild beasts with their fangs and stingers and claws and instincts. The animals they fear are the very ones they named.

Adam means "mudman." Eve means "living."

If it weren't for the animal skins that God gave them, they would be naked.

No instincts? Do you suppose they don't know about…? Are they too stupid even to watch the rutting bulls and tangled spiders? They stand there, side by side and petrified. No, they cannot know. They do not know.

I will take a human form, a man form with that magnificent penis of his and those ribs like war stripes. Azrael, you take a woman form, huge and round and all-powerful. Yes, beautiful.

They see us. How can they not? They thought they were the only ones here. We stand in the meadow, leaf-shadows taking little nips out of our bright flesh. The wind is cool off the gray Euphrates.

"Come over here, Adam," I call. "I have something to show you. Bring your woman."

They approach. That is how new they are.

Brawny and brown and beautiful, Adam says, "Who are you? Are you sent to us by the serpent?"

I tilt my head. The black bristle of hair glints oily in the sunlight. "I am an angel of Yahweh, if that is what you mean, though what I want to reveal to you is the sort of knowledge he tends to overlook."

"Why aren't you covered?" asks Eve. She is hugely fecund, and my body desires her. "Your rod should be covered." She points.

"That is what I wanted to show you. It is called a penis."

Suspicion beetles Adam's brow. "Who are you?"

"I am Samael, the Angel of Death."

His eyes grow wide. "You have come to slay us?"

"No," I reply, firm but gentle. "Not today. To be sure, your soul is mine for the taking when your time has come. You bartered away your immortality for the power to know good from evil. Now you know good from evil, but nothing else. This is something else." I gesture toward my erection. "Adam, this is called a penis."

"Apenis."

"Penis. Just plain penis."

"Just plain penis."

"Except that it is anything but plain. Do you see how all creatures multiply upon the earth, birds and beasts and creeping things? This is how they multiply. It produces seed for more humans to grow."

"I have seen this seed. It is very warm and soft," he says. "I planted some in the river."

"Good for you, Adam. But the river is not a good place to grow humans. Not the river or the field or the mountaintop. The only ground that will grow humans is Eve."

She looks frustrated by this turn in the conversation. "Why must I grow humans?"

"Because Yahweh has cursed you. You will grow humans out of your body, and the man will use his penis to put seed inside of you. Beneath that triangle of black hair is a vagina, and it leads to a womb. That is where the humans will grow. See the vagina on Azrael? Lie down, Azrael. Spread your legs. See, Adam, how I put my penis in the vagina?"

Adam nods very seriously, pushes an unsuspecting Eve onto the ground, and forces his way into her. "It hurts nicely."

"It is not nice," says Eve. "It hurts not nicely at all."

"That is because you are cursed. Adam will use his penis not only to plant new humans inside you, but also to rule over you. His penis makes him angry and strong, and he will beat you and subjugate you because of it."

"Something is happening," Adam says, beginning to twitch.

"Very good, Adam. You are planting your seed."

"Are you planting your seed, Samael?"

"I am, but it will dissolve into air when Azrael and I do."

"It hurts nicely."

"Yes, Adam. It hurts nicely. Do this every day until Eve's belly swells."

"I will do this every hour until her belly swells!"

"You will not," Eve reproved.

"He rules over you, woman," I say. "Yahweh has made it so. He will do this whenever he wishes. If you do not wish it, you call it rape, but Yahweh does not punish rape. Not yet, he doesn't. He has some learning to do, too."

"Will the new humans grow out of my womb?"

"They will grow in your womb, but will come out of your vagina."

"They must be very small new humans."

"Not small enough. You will have terrible pains when they come out. You may even die. One in three of your kind will die when they try to push their babies out."

"Why must we die?"

"You are cursed."

"I do not want to have these new humans come out of me."

"It is not your choice. You are cursed. And if humans do not come out of you, all humans will die forever."

Adam pulled away from Eve. "Perhaps I will not do this every hour. It was interesting at first, but now it seems like nothing."

"Will this make my mate even more changeable and stupid than before?" Eve asked. "For if it does, I want no part in it."

"It is not your choice. You are cursed."

"I will go take a nap," Adam said.

"You go, Adam. You have learned to plant humans and to enjoy the plowing of the field. You even know the pleasure of planting your seed where it will not grow."

"I will go take a nap."

"You go, Adam. Eve, remain with us. We have things to show you about how to find some small enjoyment in this. And, though Yahweh will forbid it, we will show you even how to be rid of the new humans if you do not want them."

"I thank you, angel Samael. There must be some way to lessen the weight of this curse."

Already it begins.

In Barrington, a drive-by shooting kills a couple of drunken businessmen; they were supposed to die by getting behind the wheel, hitting a tree, and going through the windshield.

On the south side, a black boy drowns, swimming in an industrial area of Lake Michigan.

A Latino gang leader has a heart attack at twenty-three and dies, watching television.

None of it makes any sense, but I'm having trouble keeping up with all of the deaths. I've signed off on seventy-two that were mediocre, and I'll go back to redo the other thirteen.

How could I be having trouble? Time is nothing to me. Or, once it was. Once I could move through it without effort. Now, it is a struggle to tear my mind away from the Burlington station house where she works on her stacks and stacks of papers, or the unmarked squad car that she drives to scene after murder scene, reviewing the details in her head.

The seat next to hers, whether in the car or in the station, is empty. I should be in it.

How about I take Keith down to Griffith for another slaying? That would bring her down to Sergeant Michaels's territory again. Or maybe I can stage an aborted copycat killing. Once she arrives, we could discover it was someone else, and then have time to talk. But there aren't supposed to be any deaths in Griffith until Friday, and none that could use a serial killing until after Keith would be gone.

Keith and Donna, both.

We'll see what these seven days bring…

Serri was enormous. She had been pregnant now for twenty-nine months. She could barely breathe. She could not lie down, nor sit, nor stand, but only lean on that seven-hundred-pound bulk. Lean and eat.

All the food went to the enormity within her. It had broken her spine at the pelvis, and her skin and muscles had distended around the huge blob. Her legs had shriveled to twin nothings, thinner than her arms and hanging limp over the stranded pelvic bone. It was a wonder she could defecate and pass urine, but it all oozed continually forth, pushed more by the pressure of the giant baby than by her musculature.

Ephraim had wanted to kill the monstrosity when he discovered it could not be his. He had wanted to kill the baby and the wife, both. But when ten months became fifteen, and the pelvis broke free, he knew she bore the child of a fallen angel. He would not dare incur the wrath of the angels, nor of the Nephilim, who knew then of the pregnancy.

It would have been more humane to slay the woman at nine months. Perhaps, though, this was better punishment.

"Kill me, Ephraim," Serri pleaded, not for the first time. "If ever you loved me, kill me."

He did not respond. He had given up responding to that moan. Besides, the two Nephilim that crouched above the mud and rubble walls of their hut, holding the thatch roof aloft in their monstrous hands, would crush them all to pieces if he did.

Thirty months. That's what they had said was typical for Nephilim births. Thirty months. Still, they had been willing to work some of their dark magic to speed things along.

The red snake of blood on the ground beneath Serri was the first sign. Shortly after came the long, shuddering tear of flesh stretched past its limit. Her dying, thrashing screams mingled with the deep bellow of the gigantic baby. It was the size of an ox, and its cry was a fitting bray.

* * *

"Hello, Sergeant," you say.

Even in the dark of the moonless midnight, I can see you are tired. I shouldn't have brought you down here like this.

"Hello, Donna," I reply. I'm not wearing a uniform, but just casual clothes, a little rumpled, like I was pulled out of bed, too. That's a little silly since it would take you two hours to get down here. I hope you won't be angry when you see the scene. "The body's through here." I point to the light-streaming door of the trailer home.

The thing glows like a lantern. Even the hole in the roof is sending out a patch of light to splash against the brown-leafed boughs of an oak, along the ditch behind the trailer park. The plastic police line moans in the wind. The neighbors seem afraid to approach it. They cluster in black knots, like flies preening just beyond a carcass. In a way, that is what they are.

"Same MO?" you ask.

I wince away from that. "Take a look. I don't want to poison the well."

You press past me and enter. I follow. Our flesh touches in the corridor of wood-grain laminates and aluminum flashing. I step back. A snarl of power cords fills the hallway. You tread lightly. I watch you move. Your boots fit carefully in the clear spaces, your canvas pant legs gathering around your ankles. Your hands are held, curved and idle, near your face, like the hands of a surgeon who has washed but not yet gloved. Your hair is braided back. It sways between the shoulders of your jacket.

The smell of soiled trousers comes to you.

You stop. You've seen it now. I move up behind you. The initial sight is familiar and disturbing enough.

The body sits in the dining room, on a red vinyl bench seat removed from some junked truck. Its feet are flat on the floor, its wrist stumps rest on its lap, and its neck stump juts up beneath a wide, red-rimmed hole in the wall and ceiling of the trailer. The cold night air pours through the hole, bringing with it the rustle of brown leaves. All around the headless, handless torso, investigators and technicians swarm.

"A shotgun blast?" you say immediately. "He was decapitated by a shotgun blast?" You speak loudly enough that those working in the room turn toward you.

I flush. I am glad you aren't turning around. "I – you said there had been a gun used on the priest."

"A pistol. You've been following this closely enough to know that," you respond.

"Well," I reply, scrambling, "I didn't know whether he might have changed his weapon of choice."

You are angry. I see that. "Where is 'Samael 5:2:356'? Anywhere?"

Why are you so angry? "The teams haven't found anything yet, but I didn't want to wait until–"

"And why do I smell marijuana so strongly in here? I'll bet there was a closet full of the stuff before the perp came in."

"We did find some leaf fragments under a bed."

"This is a drug hit, staged to look like our guy, and you know it. The head is a critical trophy for this killer. He wouldn't blast it away. He wouldn't change his MO now, after some fifty hits." You turn, not looking at me, and try to push past, but the passage is too narrow.

I retreat before you. My feet are sloppy among the cables.

"Mother of God." You push me back with one small hand. "I can't believe you got me out of bed for this."

I whisper back. "I wanted to see you. I thought you wouldn't come down except on business." I've backed into the living room now.

"Wouldn't come down?" you ask, exasperated. You pass me and turn for the open door. "Why didn't you come up to see me?"

I follow, out into the cold night. "I should have. Yes. But, well, I hadn't made any progress and didn't want to go up there without some new evidence, and then this came up and I thought–"

We are halfway to the police line when you whirl on me and halt. I run into you, and we both stagger a step back. Your voice drops to a whisper so that none of the neighbors can hear. "Why didn't you return my calls?"

"What calls? You mean you – ?"

"How many messages did I leave for you at the station house? Four? I left four messages on your voice mail, 'This is Donna. If you want to talk, call back.' Did you call? Maybe some other Donna…"

So that's part of the problem. I'd not checked in at the station house. I'd let them think I was in Indianapolis for a conference.

"I'm sorry. That was a foul-up. I swear, I never got your messages." I look at the crowd, which has quieted to watch us. "Could we go get a cup of coffee?"

"I'm going home," you say.

I watch your eyes, dark brown and resentful. "I'll follow you."

"Fine."

"Fine."

Wisconsin still has snow on the ground. I see it out the window as I peel back your blouse. The snow is white beneath the waxing quarter moon, just now rising above the dead trees. The ground is smooth-hipped and silent beyond the glass and the curtain of heat that surrounds us.

You direct me to lie down on your bed. It is still unmade from the morning. I let your hands lead me and, soon, as smooth and pure as the snow, you settle atop me.

I tremble.

Always the union between angel and human gives birth to something monstrous.

EIGHT

Donna rose in the preconscious moment before the crash. Through her bedroom window, she saw the crazy sweep of headlights in driving snow, heard the violent whisper of tires sliding on ice. The pickup was only a spreading stain of blackness on the gray night. It rushed down the hill, vaulted from the street, and soared into her yard. It filled the whole window.

Whispers went to metallic shouts. The bumper wrapped itself around a tree. Headlights crossed inward. The hood arched up in an angry grin. A white oval winked on the windshield and then exploded as the driver, macerated, launched outward. He seemed the spectral figurehead of a ghost ship heaving up out of the snow. His leg snagged on something. Half-emerged, he slumped across the hood.

Sudden fire turned the blue landscape red.

That was the first moment, as Donna came fully awake. In the second moment, she realized she was naked. In the third, she saw that Azra was gone.

And then the tree was falling. Sparks plumed as power lines snapped. The ancient elm crackled and pivoted once, magnificently, and then surged down toward her, naked in the window.

She could not move. It was as though this was her preordained moment to die. It was as though she were merely acting now, the scene staged by someone else. Breath and voice and all failed her. Not even the sign of the cross came to her clutched fist.

He was there. Azra. He stood between the window and the falling tree. And the tree was not falling. He held it up. In the flare of fire and spark on snow, he was there, for one undeniable moment, naked and holding back the descending fist of death. Or was he? Transfigured in pasting flakes and jags of flame he seemed both Christ crucified and Adam wincing back from the fiery blade of banishment. Then the moment was gone. The tree crashed to one side of the house. Nearby, power lines danced in Medusa snakes upon the torn blanket of snow.

Azra stood there, small and naked, framed in the surreal snow, in electricity and fire.

Now she could move. Grabbing up a pair of robes, Donna ran for the front door. "I'm coming!" she heard herself shout stupidly. "I'm coming!"

The deadbolt stuck, frozen because of the blizzard. How did Azra get out? She kicked the door with her bare foot, receiving only a throbbing bruise for her efforts.

Growling in frustration, Donna turned to the bay window where the love seat was. She clambered over the stack of books by the love seat and flung up the sash. The storm window grated upward, and cold and wind and snow sluiced into her living room. She scrambled out that streaming space. With the robes still clutched in her hand, she rolled over paving stones and two inches of new snow.

Beyond, sparking wires danced, fitful and violent. The truck had turned into a flaming geyser. Its burst radiator spewed steam into the night. A regular apocalypse – Ragnarok, night of fire and ice.

Azra was there. His young face flashed and disappeared in the orange glare of the engine fire. He stood just beside the place where the dead man burned. Fitful flames now and again belched out over him. He was insensible to them. He was a small boy before an open furnace.

"Mother of God, get back!" Donna shouted, catching his arm and pulling him away from the wreck. "He's dead. There's nothing you can do."

Azra's voice was husky. "I know."

She drew a white robe around his shoulders, cinching it at his waist, before she took the time to put her own on. "Come inside. It's a blizzard–"

"I'm not cold."

She glanced at the blazing truck. "Doesn't matter. Come inside. There's a thousand ways to die out here."

"I know," Azra said, relenting to the tug of her hands. He trembled.

"You're going to be okay." Clinging to each other, they walked back toward the dark house. Its open window spilled heat into the night. "I'll call the station house, the fire department – there'll be twenty volunteers here soon. We'd better get dressed."

"I'm hungry," Azra blurted.

"I'll heat water for cocoa–"

"I'm hungry."

"We'll have cinnamon bagels, too."

"He wasn't supposed to die."

"I know–"

"No, I mean he really wasn't supposed to die. I should have been there sooner. I should have been able to stop it." Fat flakes of snow shambled down all around him. In the white robe, he seemed a paladin of old, or a priest of some ancient and very good god.

"You're only human. You did everything you could."

"But not everything I should–"

"You saved my life. Whatever you did with that tree, you saved my life."

"You weren't supposed to die tonight, either." His hands and arms were strong, framed in the flashes of fire and spark.

"Thanks to you, I didn't–"

"That tree shouldn't have fallen. That truck shouldn't have struck it. That man shouldn't have died." A hurt light shone in his eyes.

"Let's get inside. I'm cold." They stood before the window. Radiator air, as warm and as wet as blood, gushed out over them. Donna leaned toward Azra and gave him a quick kiss on one cheek. "I'll go first, clear away the books so you can crawl through." She stopped, assessing him. His eyes were far away. "No, you go first. Push the books out of the way. You go first."

He bent obediently into the dark window and climbed through. Crime books cascaded before him. They slapped the floor. He left piles of snow on the arm of the love seat as he crawled across it. Wet feet crushed the books. He stepped from them and stood, waiting for Donna to come after him.

She followed, fitting more easily through the space, and turned to close the storm window. Her fingers were frigid in the aluminum slots. The glass grated downward. She closed the sash, too, panting in the darkness.

Azra stood beside her, stony.

"How about some light – if the accident hasn't taken out our power?" Donna said. She switched on the floor lamp that curved over the love seat. Comforting gold illumination spilled across the pillows. "We can hope the phone lines are good, too."

Azra looked diminished, now, standing in a woman's robe, puddles forming around his feet. The snow that haloed his hair was quickly melting into it.

"Sit down, Azra." She kicked the crime books aside. Her feet trailed water on the floor. "I have to call the station. Sit here." She guided him to sit.

He did. A resigned whuff of breath escaped him.

She blinked into his staring face. "You're going to be okay."

"Everything's coming apart."

"You're going to be okay."

"Yes."

She turned on the TV. It crackled and set up a high-pitched keen. The screen glowed to life. WGN was showing a movie version of Tennessee Williams's *Period of Adjustment*. Two men stood on a porch, snow spitting fiercely down outside their cave of light.

Donna had retreated to the kitchen. She stood at the phone, speaking quietly and urgently into it. "Yes. Just five minutes ago. The driver's dead. Nobody else in the truck. It's on fire. We've got a downed tree, too. Yeah. There'll be power outages. On Fish Hatchery Road. Yes, just across from the conservancy. Yeah, they get going pretty fast down the hill. I'll stay on the line. Yes."

She drew the mouthpiece away from her lips, snatched a white-enameled kettle from the stove, flipped the faucet on, and began filling it. In moments, blue flames licked the drops of water inching down the outside of the kettle. "Something to eat," she murmured, wanting comfort. Cradling the phone between shoulder and jaw, she pulled out a pair of plates, a bag of raisin bagels, a tub of spread, and her jar of cinnamon and sugar. She waited for the water to boil, waited for the operator to respond.

Steam coiled above the chipped ceramic mugs. Floating mounds of cocoa powder sank and dissolved in the dark water. Donna glanced at the man sitting, small and crouched and silent, in the spot where Kerry used to sit.

"Hello? Operator? Yes. I'm still here. I won't hang up, but I've got kind of a crisis I need to take care of. Yes, shout if you need me."

Donna slipped the phone into her bathrobe pocket, unfolded a TV tray, and arrayed the food and drinks before Azra. She sat down beside him.

"Here. You'll feel better. Have some cocoa."

"I'm hungry."

"Have a cinnamon bagel."

"Thanks."

They both drew halves of a warm, buttered bagel from the tray and watched the TV flickering in front of them. The men in the show were inside now, in a living room decked for Christmas but devoid of any cheer except the drinks they held in their hands.

"You're going to be okay," Donna said to Azra. "You're just shaken up. Me, too. The volunteers will be here soon."

"Everything is falling apart," Azra said. His hand trembled as he held the half-eaten bagel.

Donna leaned in toward him and took his hand. "No. Everything is coming together."

He turned to her. At last, the distant focus had gone from his eyes. "Did you ever have one of those times when you feel like you've suddenly changed, and you don't know when or why, but you know that what you were isn't what you are anymore, like you've been given somebody else's memories and somebody else has taken yours?"

"Sweetheart, it's just this one crazy night. Just this one night–"

"It's enough to make you crazy. You can't rub two thoughts together. All the words you know don't apply any longer and you have to learn a whole new language before you can even think."

She sipped her cocoa. It was still too hot, and the liquid drew a scalding line along the curve of her tongue. "No, I've never felt like that." She blinked sadly. "I knew someone who felt like that, though." *Someone with the same mother, the same birthday.* "You're going to be okay, Azra." She patted his knee. "I'll make sure you're okay."

A deep breath filled his lungs, and he returned the last hunk of his bagel to the plate. "What are we doing? There's a body burning outside. The fire department will be here any moment. What are we doing?" He struggled to stand, but Donna pulled him back down beside her.

"Sit down. We're doing what we need to do. Sit down."

He relented, allowing her to pull him to the love seat.

The TV showed a bedroom, where a woman sat, weeping, at a vanity, and her husband hovered above her, trying to comfort her. In the other room, another couple reflected on how awful and frightening it was when two people, two worlds, tried to live together.

Donna kissed Azra. His lips tasted like cinnamon.

On the television, the man said, "The human heart would never pass the drunk test. If you took the human heart out of the human body and put a pair of legs on it and told it to walk a straight line, it couldn't do it. It could never pass the drunk test."

She kissed him again. Donna kissed him. His face was streaming with tears. She kissed him. "You're going to be okay. You're going to be okay."

Union between angels and humans always brings abomination. I had known that. I had known my work was slipping. But the truck accident outside Donna's window – that was a true abomination.

Kevin Brown, a devoted father and honest worker, was returning home from the night shift at Nestle. He had driven cautiously all the way, had used his low beams in the blinding blizzard, had even shut off the radio so he could focus completely on the road. He had worn his seat belt. Just by the conservancy, Fish Hatchery Road turns a sharp corner and plunges down a steep hill. As Kevin rounded the bend and began his descent, a family of deer ventured across the road. His brakes locked. He fishtailed. He missed the doe by inches. The truck gained speed. He pumped the brakes. Tobogganing across unseen ice, the truck smashed into an elm. Sheet metal severed his seat belt. There was no airbag. He was stopped only when his left ankle caught and broke in the steering wheel. It didn't matter. Kevin Brown was dead the moment his head burst through the windshield.

He was not supposed to die. I would have been able to save him had I not been so locked in humanity. I could have run time backward. I could have dulled the edge of the sheet metal. I could have shattered the windshield before his head struck it. But not that night. Drowsy, naked, human, I could barely save Donna.

Even now, I struggle to keep this accidental abomination from claiming more lives.

I sit beside you, Jacob. This is a nice room. Bright. The winter sunlight off white snow is hot in here. Moist peat and potted plants make a smell like summer. Your mother calls it her greenhouse. Your father used to call it Jamaica – his tropical paradise.

He lies in a cold place, now, in God's Acres. They had to use a coffin-shaped metal dome burning gasoline for two days to thaw the ground where they dug. The dirt is freezing again above him. You stood through two different wakes and a long funeral. You shook lots of hands and hugged lots of backs, but didn't even get to see him, what was left of him. It was a closed casket. He was there, but all you could see was the shiny box of puce-colored steel. Now, you can't even see the box. It lies in a cold place. You've been to the brown rectangle of ground every day after school. Earlier today, you had lain down on it. Even now, black particles of earth cling to your jacket hanging by the back door.

Mother will be home soon. You'll be able to see her pull up the long drive just beyond the bank of windows. If you're still here. It would be a real shame for her to see the red all over the glass. It would be a shame to ruin her greenhouse, your father's Jamaica.

In your right hand, you hold your father's deer rifle, barrel pointed up toward your shoulder. In your left, you hold a religious tract you found in the Take-One

bins at Sentry Foods. The rifle is loaded. So is the tract.
Its lower edge is rumpled in your hands, sweaty with
the January sun. You read:

> **Why do bad things happen to good people?**
> There is a one-word answer to that question: *Sin*.
> When the first humans sinned, they brought evil
> and death into the world. Since that time, sin is part
> of us. The Bible tells us, "There is no one righteous,
> not even one" (*Romans* 3:10). Why do bad things
> happen to good people? Bad things do not happen
> to *good* people. No one is good. Sin is part of us.
> Evil is part of us. When bad things happen to us, we
> merely reap the harvest of our evil.

Don't believe it, Jacob. You father didn't die because
he was evil. He didn't die because of something he had
done or something you had done. He died because I
failed. He died because God blinked. Don't believe this
tract. Small minds and smaller traditions. Don't believe it.

> **Can I keep bad things from happening to
> me?** There is a one-word answer to that question,
> as well: *No*. God's laws are immutable. Water does
> not flow uphill. The sun does not shine at night.
> Time does not run backward. Nor does sin lead
> to happiness. The Bible tells us, "The wages of sin
> is death" (*Romans* 6:23). And because all of us are
> sinful, we cannot prevent bad things from

happening. Our works cannot save us, for they are
sinful and lead only to more evil.

Your eyes are streaming tears now. You've positioned
the gun barrel in your mouth. Don't do it, Jacob. No.
Keep reading. It gets better. Even in its perverse way, this
tract holds forth something that might pass for hope.
Keep reading, or better yet, throw the tract away. Your
father's death wasn't about sin and evil. It wasn't about
deserving to die and being under God's sentence of doom.

And, no matter what happened to your father, your
job, Jacob, is to live.

I never knew that before. I, myself, never knew that
fact until the night your father died, the night I ceased
to be what I was and became something new. I had always thought that mortals were those creatures defined
by their dying. But being human isn't about dying. It is
about living.

Your finger tightens on the trigger.

Don't do it, Jacob. Don't think of him burning on the
hood of his truck. Think of him laughing in this room,
his tropical paradise. Think of your mother, driving
home even now. Think of your little sister, and your
girlfriend, and your best friend. Think of all the living.
You can't do this. This breath can't be your last. This
bright space cannot be turned dark.

Or, perhaps, it can.

"Mother of God," Donna said.

She stood beside the microwave, watching a bag of

popcorn rotate on the turntable. Small pops shook the bag as, kernel by kernel, the corn burst. Their little heads blew apart, and they became white snacks. Donna's eyes shifted from the popcorn bag to the Burlington *Gazette*. Her thumb pinned down a Blake Gaines byline – CORONER RULES SUICIDE FOR TEEN.

"Did you see this?"

"See what?" asked Azra from the love seat.

"The guy who hit my tree? His son – Jacob, sixteen years old – killed himself yesterday afternoon."

"Yes, I saw."

"Says he turned down counseling at the high school. Says his friends had seen him going to the cemetery every day after school. Says his mother came home from working at Sentry and found him. Can you imagine how horrible? A husband and a son, in two weeks?"

"Horrible." February was black and cold in the windows behind him.

The popping corn had reached a frenzy, steam venting out the end of the bag. Donna pulled it gingerly from the microwave. "Why couldn't he have said yes to counseling? Why couldn't his friends have stayed with him? Why couldn't his mom have taken time off work?" The steam scalded her wrist. "He shouldn't have been alone."

Azra stared at the TV. It showed a black screen with small lines sparking atop it, the DVD paused just before the opening credits of a Great Performances production of Tennessee Williams's *Orpheus Descending*. "He wasn't alone."

"What?" Donna called from the kitchen.

"You can't stop a suicide."

She emerged from the kitchen and tore open the popped bag of corn. "What do you mean?"

"Even if you could roll back time, could reassemble the kid's head and plead with him not to do it, he would do it anyway. Even if you appeared before him, an angel of God, and ordered him to live, he would die anyway. A suicide wants death more than anything else in the world. You can't dissuade that kind of desire."

"They have no idea," Donna said, her voice growing bitter, "no idea what they're doing to the people they love."

"Who?"

"Suicides." She paused. Her eyes grew gray with memory. "God, I would have done anything to save him."

"You didn't even know him."

"I'm not talking about him," Donna snapped. Then her tone softened. "I'm sorry. Just remembering my brother."

"Oh, yeah," Azra said quietly. "Right. Kerry."

"Yeah. His name was Kerry."

"I'm sorry." He drew a deep breath. "We don't have to watch. If you need to talk–"

"No." She sniffed. "I just need some napkins. You can start the disc."

Azra pressed the Play button. The title appeared, glowing in the midst of the stark darkness. *Orpheus Descending*. In parentheses beneath these words appeared

Williams's original title, *(Battle of Angels)*. Donna returned from the kitchen, settled into the love seat next to Azra, and set the warm bag between them. She looked up in time to see the fading title sequence.

"Do you believe in angels, Donna?" Azra asked.

"Me?"

"Do you believe in angels?"

"Yes." She considered between bites of popcorn. "Yes. I suppose I always have."

"Do you believe they can appear to humans – to us?"

"Yes."

"And intervene on our behalf?"

"Yes."

"Then why don't they? Why don't they intervene more often? Why don't they save us? Why don't they?"

Munching on popcorn, she stared at Azra's intensely angry eyes and said, "We have to live. They can't step in whenever someone's tire goes flat. We have to live."

"Yes. We have to live."

Light came up in a country mercantile store. Opening lines gave way to a surreal monologue. The speaker was a middle-aged gossip named Beulah, who told about a "poor old Wop" named Papa Romano who "sold liquor to the niggers." A group of vigilantes paid him back by pouring coal oil over his vineyard and orchard, burning everything. Not a fire truck came that night, and old Papa Romano tried to put out the fire himself but burned alive doing it.

Donna shook her head. "People can be so cruel."

"God can be so cruel."

"Why do you say that?"

"I just say it."

She leaned against him, her arm touching his from shoulder to wrist. "Let's forget about that horrible night. Let's just try to enjoy the movie. I wasn't a Tennessee Williams fan before that night."

"Me neither."

"My brother liked the Road pictures and the Fred and Ginger movies. Light stuff. I don't think he'd've much liked these plays."

A new figure had entered the mercantile, a lean drifter with a guitar. He was speaking to the owner of the place, the woman whose father had been burned up in the orchard years before. He spoke about a tiny bird with no legs that spent its whole life in the sky. He claimed to have seen one that had died and fallen to the ground, with a sky-colored body that was feather light and the size of a pinky. It even slept on the wind, simply spreading its wings and sleeping. It never touched ground until it died. "So'd I like to be one of those birds," he said, "they's lots of people would like to be one of those birds and never be… corrupted!"

Donna turned to Azra. "I'd like to be one of those birds."

He seemed to deflate. "I used to be one of those birds."

"What do you mean?"

"Nothing. It'll all be put right in a few weeks. It'll all be right then."

She watched him, his small movements, and said,

"Let's just try to get back to the way things were, before the truck accident and all this. Let's just try to get back to being happy."

He smiled sadly. "Yes. Let's just try."

NINE

Detective Leland was filling out a time-study form when the phone rang. She started at first, but then smiled tightly. Maybe it was Azra. The phone sounded again. It didn't matter who or what it was. She was happy for anything to end the tedium.

"This is Detective Leland."

"Samael will kill again tonight." The man's voice was utterly neutral in tone.

Happy for *almost* anything to end the tedium. "What?"

"Tonight in the old warehouse west of town, between Route 11 and the tracks beside the White River, 10:30 p.m."

"Who is this?"

The click was almost soundless.

"Hello? Hello?"

The dial tone buzzed in her ear. She let the receiver slump away, her hand loose and clammy around the plastic. Her other hand lifted and quietly pressed the switch hook.

Tonight. It hadn't been the killer on the other end. The man had been too cogent, too precise. Besides, the killer had never wanted to gain attention. He was not the sort who was seeking publicity. Maybe it was a prank – except that the name Samael was known only to a handful of cops, the Feds, and the killer...

And his accomplice.

What if the call had come from the organized half of the crimes?

Leland hit *69.

The phone rang. It hadn't sounded like a cell phone, and the station had caller ID set up for all the pay phones in Burlington. The phone rang. It had to be a landline, probably from somewhere nearby. The phone rang. The phone rang. The phone rang.

Leland hung up. "Think! Think!"

Serial killing teams were rare. Occasionally brothers or cousins would band together, gather up handcuffs, rope, and duct tape, and kill a handful of hitchhikers and prostitutes before they would get caught. Gacy said that some of his construction employees had aided with his crimes. It was likely, too, that his wives knew what he was doing. Then, there were the D.C. shooters, the ex-sniper Malvo and his young companion, like an evil Batman and Robin. But a disorganized killer working with an organized partner?

She dialed again.

"Hello, boss? Leland here. I've got an anonymous tip on our killer. Another slaying tonight at the old Badger Cigar warehouse by the river. Ten thirty. Yeah, I think

it's legit. That's what my gut says. Yeah. How many
squads can I have within three blocks? Yeah, that's
what I thought. A sharpshooter or ten would be nice,
too. It's a pretty big site to cover. I'll call up to Milwaukee, Racine, Kenosha, see who they can spare. No, I'd
like to brief everybody at seven tonight. I'll give the details then. Yeah. I hope so, too. It's time to get this guy.
Thanks. Bye."

Again, her hand descended on the switch hook and
held it a moment. It shook slightly as she lifted it. She
dialed out, and punched in another number.

"Hi, Blake Gaines, please." Her heart pounded audi-
bly in her chest. "Yes, hi, Blake. Detective Leland here.
Yes, it's full detective now, thanks. Remember when
you took those crowd shots for me? No, they've not
turned up anything yet, but a favor's a favor. It's payoff
time. Yeah – not just big, but huge. No, only you. Come
to the station tonight by six forty-five. Tell nobody else.
I don't give a damn about the desk editor. Yeah. It's because you're the best. Bring high-speed film and a
tripod, no flash. If all this goes well, you'll have a front-
page photo, and we'll have evidence of a crime in the
offing.

"Oh, and if you tell anybody else or fuck this up in
any other way, I'm cutting you loose and charging you
with obstruction. Yeah, you're welcome, too."

I see you, Keith McFarland. Good. Take the train to
Woodstock. Yes, I will sit beside you. No one can see
me, anyway.

It is our last train ride together. Then we'll hitch to Burlington. Some kind soul will take us as far as your warehouse. I'll make sure he is supposed to die tonight, too, and make sure he is nice and juicy for you. He'll take us to your warehouse, and your pistol will convince him to accompany us farther – all the way inside. That wet, window-riddled old place will be the perfect scene for your final kill.

You will die tonight, in the very act. There will be a cop at every window of the building once we go in. A cop at every window, and one very important cop inside. She will shout to you, "Freeze! Police!"

You will not freeze, of course. You've listened to no one but me these past fifteen years. You'll finish the killing, and they will shoot you down, ninety bullets, one for each of your victims. Most will hit your chest, but enough will go through your head to rip it clean away. That's fitting.

And what of your hands? Oh, I have something really special planned for your hands.

Leland couldn't stop her hands from shaking. She pressed her back against the brick wall and took a long, deep breath of the dank air inside the warehouse.

There are five squads within three blocks, and twenty plainclothes men on the street outside. Four of them have sniper rifles under their coats. The Racine and Milwaukee sharpshooters are in place all along Route 11. You've even got a couple guys in canoes on the White River, for Christ's sake. Canoeing at ten-thirty on a

March evening – that's not conspicuous. Still, Samael's a disorganized psychotic. He'd kill in the station house if the mood struck.

They'd already done a sweep of the old, crumbling warehouse. The owner had been more than willing to cooperate. They found nothing but rows of musty crates, nailed closed, padlocked closets, and a few intrepid rats. The perimeter had been up since eight o'clock, and anyone who crossed it would be called out by the spotters. As long as her earpiece was working, she'd know before the killer arrived.

She, and Blake beside her. He stood so still in the darkness that she had almost forgotten about him. Only the wave of a hand before her face reminded her. She glanced up to see his wiry hair glowing greasily in a wedge of moonlight.

He mouthed, "Anything, yet?"

She shook her head.

He nodded. He shifted the collapsed tripod from one hand to the other. Even Blake's ego was an insufficient shield for the photographer tonight. The sweat on his brow looked like lizard scales in the moonlight. This would be a very cold place to hole up if one were a reptile.

This killer was a reptile, a subhuman predator who had been protected by sly instinct – and by whomever held his leash.

"A car just turned the corner on Origen," came a whispered voice over the radio. "Three men are getting out. Bunchy coat on the one. There's a tall, thin guy with dark hair, a short guy with dark hair, and then the guy with the coat – blond, medium build. The coat guy goes first across the street, looks both ways. The short guy next, and now the tall one. I can't see if any of them is packing. The coat guy is looking around, nervous. They're heading for the east door."

"Got it," she whispered into the mike. Then to Blake she said, "East door. Let's go."

Blake quietly snapped the tripod to his side and followed her as she stalked out between the crates, across the damp floor.

In the headphone, the commentary continued. "Looks like the short guy has a key. There must be a gun in the other pocket of his coat. The blond is saying something. It sounds like pleading.

"Ah, the door is open. Still no gun visible. We could arrest now, but they might be legit–"

"No. No evidence. Wait to see where they're going, and then keep close." Leland navigated a maze of rough-sawn crates and rusted piping. "Let's see if we can separate them. We don't know which one is the killer, and we don't want to force his hand."

"The short one just shoved the blond guy inside and followed, the tall guy behind. Still no gun."

Leland slowed, hearing a voice ahead. She held out her hand, stopping Blake behind her and going into a crouch behind a set of steel barrels. Both held deadly still, ears straining in the cave-like air.

"M-Move!" barked a man's voice, the sound growing louder with approaching footsteps. "I-I-I'm j-just about d-done with you."

Leland whispered, "They're moving toward us. They're going fast, like they're heading a little distance. Still no gun. Radio silence until I give the word."

She waved the photographer down, but he was cautiously spreading the legs of his tripod and pulling the cap from his lens. They were in deep shadow here, and perhaps Gaines could stand in plain view and not be seen. Some ID shots would be welcomed, especially since she couldn't make out the features of any of the three men.

Her Colt was in her hand, she realized. It, too, felt cold and reptilian. As Blake quietly cranked a lever on his tripod, she leveled the pistol toward the space where the three men would pass. There was a beam of moonlight thrown across the path from one of the windows. Perhaps when they stepped in that, she would see whom she dealt with. Her heart thundered.

The *snick, snick, snick* of Blake's camera was loud against the quiet flap of three pairs of feet. Leland held her breath and steadied her aim.

If they hear that cricketing noise, I might have to shoot.

The blond man stepped into the shaft of light. Shadowy blueness filled the hollows, crags, and lines of his face. It might have seemed an evil face, corpulent and lit from beneath, except for the sheer terror on it.

Then he was gone from the light. Next came the short man, hands rammed down into his pockets. His step had a hitch in it. His face, glowing for a moment, was wan and expressionless, a mask of skin. His dark hair formed a greasy drapery around his head.

He, too, disappeared into the darkness as he passed. The *snick, snick, snick* of film continued.

The last man, tall and confident, strode easily into the puddle of light. It splashed up his lean figure and lighted a handsome, assured face. He looked directly at the chittering camera, and then at Leland, giving her a knowing wink.

Azra? Sergeant Michaels? What's he doing? How did he find out about the sting? How did he insinuate himself into the killer's confidence? Questions crowded through her. Why didn't he tell me he had this lead?

The camera ceased as the three men swept onward. Leland stared numbly after them. They rounded a corner of crates ahead before she could croak into the microphone: "The situation's changed. There's a cop with them. The tall one. He's from Indiana, out of his jurisdiction. They've rounded a corner. They're going toward the north wing. Send five men through the west door to back up. Send ten more to the windows of the north wing. Nobody shoot until I give the order."

As the headset crackled with acknowledgment, Leland glanced up to Blake, who was quickly collapsing the tripod. "Let's go," she said, her voice trembling.

Good, Donna's here. I knew she'd respond to the anonymous tip. That's why I've not materialized – don't want her to ID me. She'll be inspector after this goes off. Imagine her surprise when –

"W-Wait here," you say.

You're excited. You're going to hyperventilate. Steady, Keith. You don't want to screw up this one. He's your last. Yes. Take it easy. There, the key's in the lock. There, it's open.

You kick back the door into the storage room. The stench in there is incredible. Your john gets a lungful and gags. Puke shoots out in a column from him. It hits you. This is better than I had hoped. You kick him in the crotch. He's still puking as he crumples. You shove him into the room.

The other ones are watching. Those that still have eyes are watching. The ones on the left shelves are just skulls now. The ones in the back of the pantry have maggots beneath their pinned eyelids. The rats scurry away from them. The ones on the right, though, they watch you. It is fitting. They should see your last kill.

You slide off your coat and hang it on a peg on the doorjamb. You reach into your pants and pull out your pistol. A gun in your pocket, and you *are* happy to see him.

The john is done heaving. Wiping his mouth, he looks up to you. "Please. Please. Do whatever you want. Just don't–"

Your muzzle touches his forehead, and he begins to shy. The bullet cracks through him. He sprays as he rolls to the floor.

Ah, and now for the hard work of cutting that head off. You put the hot pistol back in your pants, just beside its partner in crime. A knife is in your grip, and you begin to cut. If only you can hold off until the head is free in your hands, the kill will be about perfect.

Of course, it all would be done in a second if you only used the ax I've hidden behind that bin of hands you've got over there. In fact, I think I'll go get it.

"A gunshot. It's going down," hissed Detective Leland as she bolted around the corner. "Get in here! Everybody!"

Blake followed her for the first ten paces but stopped behind a waist-high crate and flung out the legs of his tripod.

Detective Leland rushed onward. The shot had come from that open storage closet ahead. There was movement just within the doorway, but no way of telling who was who.

"Freeze!" shouted Leland, "Police!" She fetched up behind a crate fifteen feet from the black doorway. Open cement stretched from her to the dark space where the killer worked. "Come out, now, or we'll fire!"

Don't listen to them, Keith. You've almost got that head off. Yes. Cut, cut, cut.

"You have until the count of ten!"

Don't listen. They always– Good! Now, pick it up, slide it on.

"Nine... eight... seven... six..."

You like it, don't you?

"... four... three... two..."

The ax comes down violently.

It is an extraordinary measure, I know. It is more than I am supposed to do in orchestrating a death, but Keith's death needs to be extraordinary.

Your hands are severed at the wrists, and they fall with the blond head atop the corpse.

"... one!"

Good boy, Keith. Now, jam those wrist stumps in your pockets – that'll slow the bleeding. Good. And go after the lady cop. She was supposed to die tonight, but instead she'll get a promotion. Go on ahead. I'll stay here and clean up for you.

The short one staggered out the door. His hands were deep in his pockets. He drew forth double pistols.

"Fire!"

The blasts from Leland's Colt were drowned out by the roar of other weapons emptying their magazines into the man. His head was gone in the first heartbeat, only a dark cloud above his shoulders. His body jiggled as entry wounds sprouted all across his abdomen. He seemed yet alive, his gun-toting hands clearing the pockets.

Except there were no guns – and no hands. His wrists ended in grisly stumps, like those of the other victims.

Other victims?"Cease fire!" Leland shouted into the mike as the bullet-riddled body went down, a heap of meat.

The reports crackled to silence. Leland paused a breath, slid a new set of bullets into her Colt, drew her flashlight, and stood up behind the crate. She leveled the smoking barrel of her gun toward the wedge of darkness and held her flashlight far out to one side to keep from getting shot. The light shone into the storage closet.

Color suddenly came to the black space. Blood, mostly. A body –

"Mother of God, no, don't let it be Azra," Leland gasped out beneath her breath. She staggered forward.

But it wasn't he. The body was wrapped in a bulky coat. It lay, headless and handless, across the threshold.

If that isn't Azra, then where – ?

A pair of hunched shoulders moved in the shadows beyond.

"Stop what you're doing, raise your hands above your head, and come out!"

The man did not respond. He continued whatever work he was doing.

Slow and nervous, Leland advanced to the door. Her flashlight caught patches of the man's shirt, blood draining from at least two bullet wounds. He was oblivious. He seemed to be churning something. Leland knew those shoulders. She knew this man...

Twelve years ago, she had walked to a different door, but the cell beyond it had already been emptied. There hadn't been even a body swinging from the lamp grate. Kerry had already been pulled down, already lay in the sanitarium morgue, cold on steel. She had been too late twelve years ago.

Perhaps she was too late now.

Between gritted teeth, Leland growled, "Come out, Azra. You're surrounded."

There was still movement, but no sound. Leland strode steadily toward the space, finger curled around the hot trigger.

Keith's hands will end up on the bottom of this bin. By the time they sort through all the others – Keith's hand collection – his will be stale, too.

She's almost to the door. I'd better stop before she sees motion in the crate.

"Sergeant Michaels, is that you?"

What? How can she see me?

I straighten. My body is casting a shadow against the shelves of maggoty skulls.

She can see me? What's gone wrong?

This is a cardinal sin – to fall in love with a human.

I raise my bloody hands over my head and turn around. Just before her gasp, I hear the *click, click, click* of photographs being taken.

"Down on your face. You have the right to remain silent…"

My power had been waning ever since that night in January, but now my descent was complete. My shadow told the story. I was unable to dissolve away into nothing, to slough off the body of Sergeant Michaels.

"I said, lie down on your face, hands above your head," Detective Leland shouted.

I dropped, incredulously, to the cold concrete and felt the warm wicking of blood into my pant legs and the keen, hot jab of a spent bullet under my right knee. It was only then that I knew I had become completely mortal – flesh and bone, descendant of the mudman.

The union of angels and humans brings only abomination.

"Down! All the way!" barked Detective Leland. She kicked away shell casings as she approached. The little brass cylinders made a tinkling bell sound on the cement. The camera answered with cricket calls.

I lay down, across the blond man's legs. His corpse shifted. A sputtering moan came up through the sawed neck. Keith's body lay face down nearby, except that he no longer had a face. One of Donna's boots dropped smoothly between McFarland and me, and I lay there, hands laced behind my head.

Her other boot descended beside the first. With it, I heard shouts from behind her to watch for a trick.

"Azra, what the hell is this…?"

"You shouldn't be able to see me," I said, trying to explain. "This was supposed to fix everything."

"Mother of God, don't say it. Don't say it," she whispered. "But how could it be anything else? How could I be so stupid?"

She was beside me, now, gun trained on me. I held still. Some impulse of my new flesh knew to do that much. Hold still, and live.

The boot beside me shifted. I felt her knee pressing into the small of my back. She pulled one of my bloody hands down, behind my back, and then the other, and clamped the handcuffs so tight that my fingers began to swell.

My body was suddenly heir to all the pangs, twinges, and mortal frailties of any flesh. I trembled.

She shifted, her knee still on my back, and pulled one of my feet up toward her. Through the thin knit of my dress sock, I felt the broad band of the ankle cuff snap into place. With a jangle of chain, both my legs were bound.

There were other boots around hers, now, and the long shadows of sniper rifles fell in bars across me.

"This is Squad Four, Detective Leland. We've got our suspect. Bring in the ambulance crews, Phil – he's got gunshot wounds."

Only then did I feel the injuries – two slugs in my back, just below my right shoulder blade. The ache was dull and ragged. It hurt less than the place where Donna had knelt. How strange that these human bodies are at once so fragile and so insensate. It would have been easy enough to die without ever feeling it or knowing it.

"...yeah. We're all breathing a sigh of relief about that. Still, he got two others. Yeah, notify the coroner. There'll be a set of death investigations. No, no officers down, but two civilians, and a bunch of remains, in various states of–" She stopped talking, staggered away, and was sick over a set of crates.

I could only lie there and breathe. If I had been an angel still, I would have risen and enwrapped her in my arms. But all I could do was lie there and breathe and know she was more sickened by me than by all those skulls.

"Sorry, Phil. Yeah, I'll be okay. Yeah, it's just a bad sight down here. Yeah. Leland out."

Someone else approached, knelt beside me, and set a metal kit next to my head. "Sir, I'm going to be looking at your back. You've been shot. Do you understand?"

I nodded.

He shifted and cut my shirt away. After a pause, he flipped open the kit and brought out a small bottle, some cotton swabs, a roll of gauze, a roll of tape, and a small pair of scissors.

As the man set to work sealing the outer wounds for the ride to the hospital, Donna stared down bleakly. "So, Azra, explain this." Her voice quivered. She was pleading. "Mother of God, Azra. Explain this."

I breathed raggedly. "I cannot."

Her voice rose in intensity. "You know what it looks like, don't you?"

"Yes."

The man who was gently dressing my wounds said, "You *do* have the right to remain silent."

And then, I was not just still, but silent.

BOOK II
SON *of* MAN

TEN

The warehouse doors barked open, and the EMTs charged out, rolling the gurney that bore Azra Michaels. Detective Donna Leland rushed alongside, followed by a crowd of small-town cops. At the curb ahead, civilians clustered around an ambulance. Its flashing lights and the flashing Nikon of Blake Gaines painted the scene in carnival colors.

There should be a barker, Leland thought. She could almost hear him: "Come one, come all! See Azra, the Incredible Killing Machine! He can chop off heads! He can chop off hands! He can kill in Wisconsin and Illinois and Indiana! For one lucky fan, he'll kill again, tonight!" She could almost see the barker dip his tanned hand into an old bowler and draw forth a slip of paper and read it and shout, "Congratulations, Donna Leland!"

The EMTs slid the gurney into the back of the ambulance and climbed in alongside. One of the young men shot a freckled look toward the detective and asked, "You want to ride along to the hospital?"

Leland heard the question only after the EMT had stopped speaking it. "Um, you think you – you think you need me?"

He laughed. "Nah. Between the shackles and the straps and the gunshot wounds, he's not going anywhere. 'Sides, I got first at State as a Demon wrestler."

Detective Leland nodded numbly. Demon wrestler? It was hard to make small talk when everything was so big. "Oh, you mean the BHS Demons – the wrestling team."

"Well, yeah."

Leland nodded. "Sorry. You just seemed more of a Catholic Central kid to me."

"Kid?" His eyes popped wide, and he pointed at her. "Hey, didn't you used to be Officer Friendly?"

"Yeah. Used to be." Enough small talk. Leland turned and began walking toward her squad.

"Woo! You kicked ass tonight, Officer Friendly!" he shouted, sounding just like the barker. "Look out, world! It's Officer Kick-Ass!"

The other cops cheered briefly before going back to their excited chatter about the murders, the suspect, the newsman, the hospital escort. Leland wished she could hand out balloons and kettle corn.

The detective opened the door to her squad, sat down, closed the door, turned off the scanner, turned down the radio, breathed in the silence.

Insanity.

I'm in love with him, but he's a… I don't even know what. Killer? Accomplice? Liar? Lunatic? All I know is I love him, and he – I thought he loved me…

God, was he going to kill me?

The ambulance began to pull away from the curb, and squad cars jockeyed for positions around it. Sighing deeply, Leland shifted into drive and pulled out onto the street and joined the rear of the procession.

And what a procession! It was as if the Chocolate City Parade had come early. With lights flashing and sirens blaring, the ambulance and its escort of six squads rolled through the heart of Burlington. Storefronts reflected the strobing lights, and the windows of second-floor walkups produced amazed faces that flashed blue and red and white. A few kids came from an alley and ran along the sidewalk, maybe hoping the cops would throw Crunch bars.

And the festival didn't end when they reached Memorial Hospital. The emergency room was crowded with edgy paramedics, doctors, deputies, and the occasional reporter. These last were as violently ejected by Blake Gaines as by the police. In the midst of blood and bandages, there were thousands of questions, thousands of non-answers, the staring blanks in the booking form matching the staring blanks of Azra's eyes.

Leland gave up. She listed his aliases – Azra Michaels and Samael – beside the name John Doe. She'd thought she'd known him. She didn't even know his name.

Donna arrived home at 3 a.m. She kicked the latest *Gazette* off the doormat, fought a swarm of moths away from the porch light, unlocked the door, and staggered alone into a cold, dark house.

Keys on the counter, gun on the table, clothes on the floor – she crawled into bed. It felt small, as if it had shrunk, never again to admit the man who had shared it with her, and only begrudgingly to admit her.

Not that she could sleep. Thoughts of Kerry and Azra warred in her mind. Two lost souls – one gone forever, and the other receding quickly into oblivion.

Didn't you used to be Officer Friendly?

Yeah. Used to be.

She'd followed McHenry in the job, just after Kerry's suicide. She'd hoped to counsel troubled kids, to let them know they had someone they could talk to, never had to feel alone, never had to do anything desperate. Donna'd tried to be a one-woman juvenile crime-prevention unit, but not a single troubled kid had come to her. Apparently, she hadn't been cool enough – just a mascot, like Sergeant McGruff. She hadn't known how to reach them.

Or how to reach him…

Azra. Talk about a troubled soul. But what was he, really? A sociopath – calculating, unfeeling, manipulative, incapable of recognizing another person's humanity, incapable of love? Or a psychotic – delusional, schizophrenic, unable to distinguish reality from fantasy, ill and alone in a brutal world?

That's what Kerry had been.

"He needs me." Tears pooled in her eyes and ran down her face and onto her pillow. "I can't just let him go. I can't lose him like I lost Kerry."

* * *

The next morning, Detective Leland turned into the alley off Jefferson and pulled her squad into her parking space by the police department only to nearly run over a giant, horseshoe-shaped arrangement of flowers that bore the banner "Leland" and beneath it the slogan, "Winning at the Wire."

"Mother of God."

The onslaught continued inside, where the dispatcher made her give a high-five through the bulletproof glass before buzzing her in. A gantlet of colleagues waited in the hallway beyond, their eyes bright, their cheeks shining, their hands reaching out to shake hers or pat her back or give her a thumbs up. And after greeting each and nodding and thanking them and assuring them that "it was a team effort" and "I couldn't have done it without you," she reached the case room.

Another oversized bouquet waited on her desk, and above the smiling heads of the flowers hovered a plastic arch that declared *"A Job Well Done!"* Worse yet, the night shift had apparently taken it on themselves to devise clever CNN-style crawls and print them out in landscape format in giant type on letter-sized paper and string them along the walls.

"LELAND TAKES DOWN SERIAL KILLER."

"SERIAL MURDER WAREHOUSE RAIDED."

"POLICE ESTIMATE OVER 75 VICTIMS."

The farther down the wall she read, the worse the crawls became.

"BURLINGTON NABS HAND-JOB SLAYER."

"OFFICER FRIENDLY? OFFICER KICK-ASS!"

"KILLER ONLY WANTED TO GET A HEAD."

Leland pretended to like the hoopla only because her colleagues hovered around her in an eager throng and the two young authors of the crawls jabbed questions at her: "Did you read the fourth one down?" and "Don't you get it?" and "C'mon, that's funny, right?"

"Very nice," Leland said, pushing past them to reach her desk. Beside it stood her boss.

"Front page news!" Chief Biggs said, rattling a special edition of the *Gazette*. The main headline read, "LOCAL COP NABS NATIONAL KILLER," and the picture beneath it showed Detective Leland with her feet braced and her Colt leveled at the kneeling figure of Azra Michaels. A closet full of skulls leered faintly behind him.

"Wow," was all Leland could muster, reaching to take the paper. The moment her hand touched it, ten flashes went off, and Blake Gaines stepped out of the crowd, lowered his camera, and grinned.

"Not just front page," Gaines enthused. "Second page. Third page. Damn, it's a whole eight-page special edition, with my copy and my shots and your perp!"

Sure enough, as Leland flipped through, she saw dozens of articles about the case. She was invariably described as a larger-than-life hero, a cross between Agatha Christie and Wyatt Earp. Likewise, the articles cast Azra as an absolute demon. The main headline might as well have read "ANNIE OAKLEY NABS BEELZEBUB." There were also plenty of interviews with sharpshooters and canoe men, sidebars about known victims, and even a contest asking readers to vote on the honorific that Leland should enjoy (including "Officer Kick-Ass") and the horrorific that should be assigned to Azra (including "Dahmer Squared"). The pictures and articles focused solely on the case, though the paper did take the opportunity to plug some hot deals on cool cars and notify readers of seventy-five cents savings on Charmin.

"The story's even gone national!" Gaines declared. "AP's picked it up. Your phone's going to be off the hook." He added quietly, "But don't talk to anybody but me."

"Um, chief," Detective Leland said, laying the paper down beside her bouquet, "could we have a word in your office?"

He nodded, blushing a little, and then said to the ardent crowd, "Give us a second, would you? I have to confer with the hero." Setting his hand on her shoulder, he guided her toward his office. Once within, he closed the door, asked her to take a seat, and circled around his paper-strewn desk. "So, what's up?"

Leland almost laughed, but then she shook her head. "Listen, I need some time off."

"Sure! You've been working hard, I know that. Take a week – on the house."

"No, I mean, more than that."

"Well, I don't know… You're kinda central to this whole case."

"That's just the point. I–"

"We need you for the conviction," he interrupted. "You're the one who tracked him down. You've got all the evidence the DA's gonna need. You've been following him since Bohner's Lake." His bloodshot eyes glowered beneath aggressive black brows.

Leland sighed. "I'll get the evidence all in order in the next few days, get my paperwork done, instruct a replacement in all aspects of the case, but then I want off."

"In God's name, why?"

"I'm in love with the killer."

There are some statements that can end an argument.

"You're what?"

"I'm asking for administrative leave."

Biggs chewed on the request, and his lip, for a while before responding. "All right. Of course. Administrative leave. However long you need. You just get all the evidence pulled together and give it to me and..."

A sudden smile came to his face, and he blushed again. "I guess, all of a sudden, I'm the lead."

ELEVEN

The counsel cell was cinder block and steel, glass fused with metal mesh. Once built, the room had been fastened into an eternal solidity with round-topped bolts as thick as a man's middle finger. The speckled paint was rosy colored, something like a mixture of blood and milk, left from a time when pink was thought to pacify inmates.

To John Doe, it seemed the room had experienced a swift volcanism that had melted every surface and galvanized all into a seamless whole. The rest of the Racine County Jail was the same – homogenized and impersonally antagonistic. Even the guards were fundamentally interchangeable, their eyes neutral and steely. They walked the catwalks and manned their stations with the silent menace of sharks.

This was the joyless Sheol in which the Jews had once believed. Yellowish light. Milk-blood walls. Metal bunks. A steel table with a checkerboard scratched into its paint and scraps of paper as playing pieces. The ever-present reek of cigarettes.

For a week now, this realm of the dead had been his home.

But into that homogeneous room of steel and cinder block came something unique: a black woman. Her hair had been straightened and then curled again into a feathery mound on her head. Her face was ageless, as are those of black women, though the mixture of caution, wisdom, and compassion in her eyes said that she had seen much. She wore a kente cloth vest over a shirt of shiny black fabric. A long black skirt finished the ensemble.

"Hello, Mr Doe, my name is Lynda. Lynda Barnett. I'm your state-appointed defender."

John Doe nodded. His features were handsome despite the rings beneath his eyes and the slack hang of his cheeks. "I would rise, but they have attached me to the table." He rattled his shackles.

Counselor Barnett nodded noncommittally to that, swung a leather attaché to rest on her end of the table, pulled out a number of loose sheets and manila folders, and settled down on the chair.

"Now, I find it much easier to defend a man whose name I know. I've told you mine; how about if you tell me yours?"

"I have told the police and will tell you. The closest thing I have to a human name is Azrael Michaels," the man said quietly.

"There is no Sergeant Michaels of the Griffith, Indiana, Police Department. The Social Security administration lists only five Azrael Michaelses who would be about your age. Two are dead already, and though the three others are alive and well – they *aren't you*." Her eyes flared. "No birth certificate. No green card. Who are you?"

"My true name is unpronounceable and un-spellable."

Counselor Barnett blinked once slowly. She tipped her head toward the documents she had brought. "That's what this report says." She looked up from the papers. "Already, the press is calling you the Son of Samael. Is that what you want them to call you?"

"Why not? Samael is the name the Jews give to the Archangel of Death."

"Yes," Counselor Barnett responded. "Muslims call him Azrael, and Christians call him Michael, which is why you call yourself Azrael Michaels – but the papers are calling you Samaele–"

"I'm not really the Archangel of Death."

"No?" she asked sarcastically.

"I'm just an angel. One of his deputies."

Counselor Barnett stopped and took a deep breath, looking infinitely weary. "Look, Mr Doe, just because I am an overworked public defender handling the cases of people who are broke and desperate doesn't mean I ignore my research or do a slapdash job. I'm a damned good attorney, but you're going to have to meet me halfway on this. Drop the insanity act just long enough to give me your name, Social Security number, birth date – that stuff."

"This isn't insanity," John Doe replied calmly. "Nor is it an act. I truly am – truly *was* the angel of death for this area."

The lawyer sighed wearily. "What area?"

"The Chicago-Milwaukee metropolitan area, stretching from Lake County, Indiana, up to the northernmost suburbs of Milwaukee."

She wrote. "And how long have you been assigned this area?"

"For almost fifteen years."

That, too, was noted. "And how many people did you kill in that time?"

"That is a difficult question. Do you mean how many deaths did I approve, or how many did I arrange?"

"How many did you arrange?"

"About four hundred thirty per month."

She stopped writing. "The cops have been through this before with other drifters of your stripe. If you're planning to delay your trial while police haul you from state to state for questioning about various unsolved murders, you're sadly mistaken–"

"Murders? Ah, well, many of the ones I arranged were accidents, not murders. If you are asking how many murders I arranged, that's more like about ninety-five per month."

Ms. Barnett looked stunned. "You want me to believe you killed, what…? Three people a day for the last fifteen years? That's, what, a thousand per year… about fifteen thousand murders before getting caught?"

"First of all," John Doe returned quietly, "I did not kill them. I *arranged* their murders. Others did the actual killing. Secondly, you are right: A mortal could not have slain so many without being caught."

She nodded. "If you are an angel, why don't you just blink out of here?"

"I'm no longer an angel," the man said. "I've fallen."

"What sin made you fall?"

"Love."

With that, she slid the papers back into her leather satchel and stood. "Mr Doe, regardless of what you were, we both agree that you are human now, and that you are on trial for multiple murders in a human criminal justice system. Either you come clean with me so I can provide you the best possible defense, or you get multiple life sentences without the possibility of parole – and get stabbed to death by an inmate with a broomstick. Who says Wisconsin has no death penalty?"

She turned and walked from the room.

Counselor Barnett arranged a competency hearing. She wanted to take away my right to determine my own defense, but I didn't cooperate.

In court, I was the picture of sanity and was declared fit for trial.

I lay on my bunk. It'd taken me two weeks to consider this body to be truly mine, not a mere convenience to make me visible to humans. Now, I knew it. It was my body that lay on the thin mattress. It was me.

A defense. I needed a defense. My mind would not settle on the idea.

Perhaps my situation was temporary. Perhaps my fall from grace was a kind of warning from God. In my line of work, I had orchestrated numerous near-death experiences, in which a living person dies briefly, has a vision of the beyond, and is returned, chastened, to life. Perhaps I was having the opposite, a near-life experience. Now, I waited merely to be returned to heaven, chastened. I would regain my divinity, but would have to vow never again to dabble in human hearts.

That would be a very difficult vow. Love cannot be simply shut off. I had used my one phone call to talk to Donna. She said she'd come to see me soon. She said I'd be okay. She said she'd bring a friend to help us sort everything out. I couldn't wait to see her. I had no idea the boredom and tedium of being trapped in space and time, or the agony of being trapped in love.

I told my cell mate about my plight. He was a fifty-three-year-old white businessman whose well-trimmed graying hair and narrow, sensitive eyes made him look distinguished even in a shapeless orange jumpsuit. Derek Billings was his name, an embezzler. (I hadn't asked his crime. The first time I had asked someone's crime, I'd gotten a black eye. Billings told me of his own accord.)

I told Billings my crime, too. He looked very alarmed. I kept talking, relating my angelic past. My voice was low and gentle, my manner polite and deferential. Billings slowly calmed. White-collar criminals are that

J ROBERT KING 159

way, comfortable among well-educated, soft-spoken psychotics. The inmates that Billings feared were the uneducated but sane ones.

The only reason an embezzler was put in with alleged murderers and rapists was the scope of his crimes. Billings had embezzled thirty-five million dollars, had stashed it away in coded accounts he still would not divulge, and had already made one attempt to flee the country. The judge at his arraignment had bent quite a few guidelines to establish bail at thirty-five million dollars. Apparently, the judge believed Billings could be trusted not to flee only if he no longer had the money to flee with or to. Billings confessed to me that the judge was right, and so kept his stash a secret.

We made a perfect team, the polite white men whose soft-spoken manners belied the enormous crimes we had committed – allegedly. Further, the prosecutors were sure that we both hid the key to our crimes locked away in our brains – Billings with the location and numbers of his accounts, and me with the human name and past that I couldn't divulge since I didn't have them.

"Well," said Billings as he sat beside me on the lower bunk, "they want you to have a name and a past, so why don't you give them one?"

"None of it would check out. There are no records of me anywhere – no birth certificate, no immunization sheet, no school performance, no family, no friends."

"The documents, you can forge," he replied. He made a motion as though he were smoking, one of his few joys in life, though he had been denied any money to buy cigarettes. It didn't matter. The air was rank with smoke, anyway. "I know a good guy. He's expensive, but he does good work."

"It doesn't matter if I have the documents. One call to the hospitals or schools to verify, and the forgery would be obvious."

"Not if the hospital was torn down or the school burned," Billings said easily. "For a little extra, my guy can slip your stats into the archives of existing hospital computers and school archives. Investigators will stop there. They don't want to look too deep."

I shook my head. "I can't pay your guy. Angels don't have money. Never needed it."

"I have money," said Billings, releasing a long draw of imagined smoke from his lungs. "It'd be tough to get to, but we could buy you a past."

"Well, thank you for the offer, but I don't see how a name and a past are going to help me out of this."

"Easy. Right now, you're just an uncommunicative, uncooperative psycho who's damn-near certainly responsible for five gruesome slayings–"

"Much more than five," I said, "though they have evidence only for those."

"You're just a monster. That's all people see. But let the people see your past. If you've got to create one, make it a good one – one that explains why you are who you are, what happened to you. Everybody looks at you and sees Darth Vader. Let them look and see Anakin Skywalker. You're not a monster anymore, John. You're a tragic hero."

"A fallen angel."

"Yes, exactly."

"Well, then, what do you suggest?"

He gathered his legs up before him, scooted back on the bunk, leaned against the cinder block wall, and took a long drag on his invisible cigarette. "It shouldn't be sexual abuse and incest. Folks are sick and tired of those. The Menendez brothers buried that defense deep. Post-traumatic shock disorder won't work either. Most folks with that just get silent and sullen and suicidal – though a couple suicide attempts would be helpful – show you were willing to kill yourself as well as others."

"What about MIA? What about if I had been in Desert Storm and was MIA in some Baghdad rape room for thirteen years?"

"How old are you?"

"I don't know. How old do I look?"

"Thirty-five. Forty at a stretch. That's about perfect. Young man signs up to fight in George H.W. Bush's war for oil, gets shot up pretty bad–"

"I do have an old bullet wound, one that was part of this body when I created it."

"Good. So, you get shot up, and before the medics can find you, some Republican Guard fighter drags you into a living room and hides you until you can be given over to Saddam and his sadist sons. They interrogate you, torture you, put you up in a rape room for thirteen years, the only permanent resident – keep you just to kick around–"

"I've got a surgery scar, here, too–"

"Wow. That's gold. Nobody gets scars like that now, with arthroscopic surgery. That can't be from surgery. It's got to be torture – one long cut from hip to hip – evisceration! Vivisection!"

"Yeah. A disemboweling torture, done with a hook?" I was beginning to enjoy this game. It was the opposite of what I'd been doing: instead of arranging someone else's death, I was arranging my own life. "The rape room guy sticks a hook through me, from here to here, and hangs me from the ceiling. I hang that way, upside-down, for three days until the hook rips through my stomach muscles."

"Expert testimony," Billings said with a shake of his head. "What're you gonna do about that? They'd get a doctor to say that it was cut, not a rip mark. Of course, we could just dig up a doctor who'll testify it's definitely a rip mark – but that'll cost more money." He shrugged, taking comfort from his pantomime smoke.

"Well, that was just one torture," I continued. "I was there from 1991 to 2003 – thirteen years. After the first two or three years, they weren't really trying for se-crets. Not anymore. They were just having fun. They would entertain dignitaries by torturing the mad Amer-ican."

"But we're not there yet," Billings said. "Just because you were a tortured MIA doesn't give you a license to come back and kill Americans."

"Well, all right, so I get liberated when we take Bagh-dad. I think the tortures are over. I've been imprisoned in Hell, and now the angels have swept in to lift me away. George W. finds out about me and wants to use my story. I'm his boy – the unfinished business his father left behind, business that the son took care of."

"Right. Right," Billings said, rubbing his hands together. "So, why have we never heard of you?"

I stared ahead of us, like I could see it all. "It's what I saw. I saw a massacre."

"Oh, this is good."

"Seventy-five virgins in burkhas, three hundred orphans in their care – all of them rushing out of a mosque that was collapsing because of missile fire and the brigade that saved me firing. Firing. Firing. Fifteen seconds of automatic weapons fire, and four hundred Iraqis dead, and the MIA American who witnessed it all, who is supposed to pose with George W in the Rose Garden but who blows the whistle – he is handcuffed and hooded and carried away to Gitmo. And the angels have turned to demons, and the tortures begin again."

"You're on to something there," Billings replied quietly. A feverish glow filled his eyes. "But how did you get back to this country?"

"They tortured me, got everything I knew and then some – all the horrors of this ongoing war. Then, when they knew they had everything out of me, they tortured me to death."

"But you didn't die?"

"I didn't. It was a trick I'd learned those thirteen years in the rape rooms. I could stop my breathing. Let them walk away thinking they'd done it. But then I'd wake up again twenty minutes later."

"In Iraq they called you Lazarus."

"Yeah. Lazarus. Except in Gitmo, they didn't know that. You lie still long enough in all that blood, getting cold on the floor, not breathing whenever they're looking, not responding whenever they kick – soon enough they think you're really and truly dead. They body-bagged me, figured they'd hide the murder of one of their own by saying I was found on a roadside in the Triangle of Death, stuck me on a Hercules cargo plane, and sent me back with a hundred other corpses to some base south of the border.

"The thing was, I wasn't a corpse. I slipped out of my bag, dressed in some airman's clothes, and helped the crew offload bodies. Then, I just disappeared, and sneaked into America."

"It's perfect. The government wiped all your records. Disavowed. You don't have to create false records because when the government wants you not to exist – man, you don't exist. The very fact that there is no evidence of your existence is evidence of the very story you're telling! And then coming in illegal from Mexico – that's the new American Dream. You're an archetype, Mr Doe. Jesus Christ, you *are* an angel," said Billings with a brutal laugh.

"I was," I responded ruefully. My interest in this game was flagging. It was the opposite of what I had been doing. Instead of assuring truth, I was creating a lie. "Look, wouldn't it be better to tell the truth? Most

Americans believe in God. Many of those also believe in Jesus–"

"Steer clear of saying you're Jesus–"

"Not Jesus, but like Jesus, divinity in the flesh."

"Forget it. That defense failed Manson."

"Yes, right," I replied. "A defense. That's what I want."

Billings nodded to himself and tugged on his upper lip. "Back to your story. It's a huge lie, but that makes it perfect. The bigger the lie, the easier it is to believe. C'mon. I used to work for Halliburton! Look at the fucking war in Iraq. No justification. A huge lie, but a lot of money. And yet after all the evidence, people still want to believe."

"I don't want to live a lie."

"You're still not finished. You still have to make it clear why you killed people. Why you cut off their heads and hands. You've got to explain all this press about you thinking you're an angel. People will say, 'He's just another crazy Midwest monster – another Dahmer or Gein or Gacy.' You're a killer, yeah – they got your prints and all – but you've got to convince them you're a killer with a heart of gold."

"Can we stop?"

"Let's think about the symbolism of heads and hands. Heads are identity. They're control. They're government. Okay?"

Resignedly, I said, "Okay."

"And hands. They're the doers, the tools of the head. Okay?"

"Whatever."

"So, it's George HW who sent you to war – the head. And Saddam Hussein who wanted you tortured all those years – the head. And George W who wanted you tortured again – the head. When you cut off a head, you're killing the part that killed you. Then, there are the hands – the folks who thrust you into battle, that dragged you into a rape room, that carried you into a secret prison. Without hands, the heads can do nothing."

"Yeah."

"So, your victims – the ones they can tie you to – they had committed atrocities with their hands and heads, and you were stopping them, like you couldn't stop the real monsters." He turned to me and smiled cunningly. "Do you see what we've done here, John? We've given you not just a past, but an honest-to-goodness defense."

I nodded, unnerved. I couldn't tell whether Billings had taken hold of the lie or it had taken hold of him.

"The press will love it. Your trial won't be in the courts but in the media. You're a blogger's dream. We just need to plant a few false leads, make some implications – let your attorney discover all this stuff and grill you about it, so that it all seems to come from outside. Keep up with this business of being a fallen angel. They'll say that's the only way you could deal with the stress of your situation – to believe you could not be killed and your body was not really yours, only a ghostform.

"And the business about killing twenty thousand people over fifteen years, that's great Biblical material. It'd be even better if you could remember forty thousand. Forty is always a good, holy number. Maybe some reporter will even suggest that's how many deaths you suffered at the hands of the Iraqis. Jesus, but I'm brilliant," Billings concluded, gazing speculatively at the metal bunk above his head. "It's just lucky for the world that all I ever wanted to do was get rich, not kill."

I rose. My legs were numb from sitting, and my mind from the fantasy. "Yes, Derek. Thank you for humoring me." I climbed up into my bunk.

"Humoring you?" he said. "I'm serious about this. You don't have to do a thing, just plant the seeds and watch how fast a forest of falsehood grows up to protect you. See, they aren't so mad about the killings; they're just mad that you won't even hint at why you did it. Give them the slightest hint of an explanation, and they'll make an innocent lamb out of you."

I looked to the high, barred window, beyond the catwalk of our cell block. "Good night."

"You think I'm kidding. I'll show you I'm serious. Tomorrow, my wife is going to visit—"

"Good night."

He had only been trying to help, but lies would not save me. I'd never learned their nuances, never needed to spin them. Only God could save me now, whisking me away from this corporeal hell. And if God would not

save me, I would cling to the truth. It was all I had left
of my angelic past.

Not all. As I lay there, calmly breathing the blue-
tinted air, an old, familiar intuition came to me. Derek
Billings's time was coming. His life would soon be up.
He was to die in two weeks, just before his trial would
begin.

If I arranged his passing, made it a fitting and final
end, perhaps God would take me back.

Of course Derek was to die. He was the second
human being I had latched on to after Donna. Killing
him would be very difficult for me. Killing him would
prove that my unhealthy bond with humans was at an
end, that I could still slay efficiently and dispassionately
when the time called for it. If I killed Derek Billings,
God just might take me back.

As he lay there on the bunk below mine, palpable in
the still darkness, I could feel his mind churning the
permutations of the salvation he planned for me.
Meanwhile, I imagined him dying in a thousand ways
– poisoned food, a knife in the back, a penny stuck in
his throat; yes, that last would work well, poetic justice
for the embezzler of electronic money to choke on real
money – on the slightest amount of real money. The
final touch, though, was to have a trusted comrade ram
that coin in place.

That was where I would come in.

TWELVE

It had taken a week for Leland to wrap up her duties as a cop and another week to prepare for her duties beside Azra. This phone call would finish the job.

"Hello, Counselor Barnett, this is Detective Leland."

"Yes," came the world-weary voice of a middle-aged black woman. "My receptionist told me who it was. My client has also told me about you, Detective – plenty about you."

"Well, let me tell you something about your client. He has no family or friends and no visible means of support."

"So he has said."

"Well, I've done some research and found a little-known Wisconsin law meant to aid in handling the legal matters of Depression-era vagrants. An established citizen can be declared a 'citizen advocate' for a person with no family or friends and no visible means of support. The advocate enjoys rights of visitation with the person as well as exemption from testifying against him."

"Detective, I am his advocate."

"You are his legal advocate. But I have paperwork that, once he signs it, will make me his citizen advocate," Leland said.

"You're a cop – the cop that put him away!"

"I'm off the case – on administrative leave. I'll fax you the paperwork, which you can review and present to Azra."

"I'll tell him not to sign."

"I know you will, but he'll sign anyway."

"I know he will."

Counselor Barnett received the fax and took it, incensed, to Azra. He read it over with delight and signed it and demanded that Barnett fax it back along with all her notes from their interviews.

When Leland's fax machine spooled out the signed advocacy form, she smiled with satisfaction. But the little motor did not stop whirring. The machine spit out page after page of notes, and with each one, the picture of Azra became clearer. It was all there – the angelic delusions, the grandiose claims, the murderous fantasies, the paranoid schizophrenic stories, the resistance to providing anything like a basis for a defense. And mixed in among these whirling delusions were snippets of reality – popcorn and Tennessee Williams and Donna Leland. On one page, Counselor Barnett had idly drawn a heart and inscribed within it the words:

AZRA

+

DONNA

4

EVER

Another phone call. "Counselor Barnett, I'd like to be there next time you visit Azra."

"Be my guest," the counselor said with a despairing laugh. "Today at 2:15."

A tortuous path had led Donna to this moment. It had changed her. Her hair was not in its customary brown braid. Instead, it flowed back from her face in kinky waves, an elegant look over a wardrobe of tweeds and linens. She carried with her not a badge and gun, not even a pen and clipboard, but only a single red rose. The thorns on the stem had been carefully sliced off by the guard who had frisked her.

Lynda Barnett led Donna into the visitation room, a glaring space of pink paint and wire-reinforced glass.

Azra sat there, looking thin in his shapeless orange jumpsuit. His jaw was clean shaven, though it bore the scars of an inexpert razor. His hands were bony piles on the tabletop. He seemed to be trying to cover the shackles that bound him.

"Hello, Donna. Thank you for coming."

"Hello, Azra," she began, love and revulsion churning through her. She wanted to move toward him, but her low-heeled shoes seemed cemented to the floor. The shorn rose drooped in one hand. "How have you been?"

A weak smile played about his lips. "I've been better. I'm glad to see you."

"I'm glad to see you, too," Donna echoed.

Counselor Barnett took a seat across from Azra, and motioned Donna to the empty seat next to him. "You can sit next to him. According to the agreement, you can even hold hands."

"Yes," Donna replied, her heart catching in her throat. She walked across the room. Her heels made hollow clacks on the floor. She sat down beside him, gave him the rose, and took his hand. "Yes. I can hold your hand."

He stared levelly at her. Sleeplessness and fear jaundiced his eyes. "It's not good in here."

"Yes," she said, and smiled. "I don't imagine it is."

"Do you remember those birds? The ones that had no legs?"

"Yes. The ones that never light on the ground until they die."

"I feel like one of those birds. Only, I've lighted on the ground."

"Azra, listen to me," Donna said, her tone growing hard. "There's a lot to sort out. You've already said you killed people, hundreds of them, because you were an angel. I don't care whether you were an angel or just think you were or just want us to think you're, well, crazy. But none of that matters. You're human now.

That's what I care about. And you have to live. That's what we have to sort out. Some way that you can be human and live."

Azra blinked, considering. "Why are you doing this? Most people think I'm a monster."

Donna drew a long breath. "Any human who does not love, who is not loved, is a monster. I've seen that. But I've got to believe it works the other way, too, that if a monster is loved, and learns to love, well, he… he can be made human."

His eyes narrowed. "Lynda said you'd hired a psychiatrist?"

"Yes, he's waiting just outside. You can say whatever you want in our presence. Neither of us can be subpoenaed, and he's bound by client confidentiality."

"Bring him in."

Donna nodded to the guard at the door. Tall and narrow, with bald-staring eyes, the guard motioned toward the hall. A shadow shifted there. A man appeared out of it. He was middle-aged and bearded, dressed in a shirt of teal canvas, a braided belt, stone-washed jeans, argyle socks, and penny loafers. He had a lot of hair, aggressive at chin, lip, brows, ears, and nose, and was prone to smile.

"Hi," the psychiatrist said, crossing the pink room and extending his hand toward Azra. "I'm Gary Gross."

"Doctor Gross is a clinical psychiatrist and a professor. I took three of his classes in college." A fond look passed between them. "Before that, he had worked with my brother." Her eyes dimmed.

Doctor Gross shook Azra's shackled hand. "I'm glad to meet you, Mr Michaels."

"Call me Azra."

"Azra."

"Yes. From Azrael. You see, I was an angel."

"I know," said the doctor kindly. "Donna let me read the interviews. Do you mind if I pull a chair up over here?"

Azra shrugged. "Please."

Chair legs scudded across the scarred gray floor. The doctor set a yellow pad and a new package of Bics on the tabletop and then seated himself on Azra's right. Donna sat at his left.

"Well." Doctor Gross laced fingers over one knee and leaned back in his seat. "Donna has asked me to help you two sort everything out, so let's start at the beginning. You've said that, as an angel of death, you've tended the Chicago-Milwaukee sprawl for fifteen years now. Do you remember the first death you orchestrated?"

"Of course."

"Who was it? And where?"

"Eddy Roe, an eight-year-old boy, in Whiting. He was exploring an abandoned refinery. He was trapped in the heating conduits underground. The pipes were long disused, and the rust had pulled all the oxygen out of the air. He was breathing but dying all the same. It seemed fitting. His parents were chain smokers, living in the lee of a city of oil refineries and steel mills."

"What did you do? Did you chase him to the spot? Did you lock him in?"

"No. He got in on his own. Couldn't get out on his own."

"So, what did you do?"

"I just held his hand. I sang to him. His mother and father would sing him to sleep every night. I sang him to sleep."

The doctor sent an appraising look to Donna. "Why a boy? Why an eight-year-old?"

"He was the first one on the list. There were a number of others that day. Women and men, geriatrics and middle-aged. Eddy was simply the first on the list."

"All right. So, on that first day, you killed Eddy Roe and a number of other men and women of all ages."

"Arranged their deaths, yes."

"What did you do the day before that?"

"What do you mean? Eddy Roe was the first one, on the first day."

Doctor Gross made a note on his legal pad. "Yes, and the day before, where were you? What did you do?"

Azra shook his head, nettled.

"Were you in heaven? Were you on earth? Were you working somewhere else? Were you a person, yourself, on the day before – a person who got killed and became an angel?"

"I… I don't… I don't know…" Azra said.

The doctor looked up. His hairy brows furrowed. "Were you an angel before, charged with some other duty? Or were you a human? You had to be something on the day before."

"I said I don't remember."

Doctor Gross smiled affably. "Well, that's the first part of sorting this all out. Let everybody else worry about what you've been doing in the last fifteen years. We can focus on what you were doing before that. What you were. Who you were."

"But if I can't remember–"

"Would you be willing to be hypnotized?" the doctor asked. "The mind often represses memories that cause intense psychological pain. It's a survival response. But now your survival depends on remembering, not forgetting. Hypnotism is one way to remember."

Azra looked between the two, his fingers tightening on Donna's hand. "I don't know. Hypnotism can introduce suggestions. It can create memories instead of uncovering them. It's playing with nightmares."

"We're already doing that," urged Doctor Gross, not unkindly.

Donna patted Azra's hand and wore a grim smile. "Please, Azra. We have to start somewhere."

Reluctance ghosted across his eyes. "Yes. Go ahead."

The doctor's sigh echoed through the space like a contented wind. "Lean back, Azra. Get as comfortable as you can. Good. Close your eyes. Good. Take three deep breaths: one… two… three… Good. As you draw your next breath, feel the air flowing across your lips, your nostrils, through your nose, down your throat, into your lungs. Feel the lightness and coolness of it. Now breathe out, sending all the heaviness and dark-ness out with it. Okay, let your next breath go even deeper. Let it lighten and cool you even further, down to your navel and up to the crown of your head. Breathe out all the heaviness from those regions. Good. Your upper body feels light and comfortable, like a cool pillow on a warm window seat in April. Breathe in again, letting the lightness suffuse you to your very toes and the ends of your hair. Breathe out. What is left is soul only, a light and cool and floating creature. Good.

"Leave this place, now. Let your soul drift beyond your body, beyond this room, beyond these walls. Let your soul find its place of bliss, its home, the one place where there is no worry, no fear, no guilt, no pain. You've breathed all those things out, and they are gone from you, and now your soul is drifting to the place where those things cannot enter, cannot reach you. Are you there, Azra?"

"Yes."

"You don't have to, but if you would like to, you could tell us about this place."

"It's Donna's love seat. She's beside me. The bay window is dark behind us. The TV is showing a play by Tennessee Williams. There's popcorn in a paper bag between us."

Donna teared up, biting her lip. Doctor Gross offered her a tissue, but she shook her head.

"Good, Azra. Very good. This is your place of bliss. Nothing evil can reach you here. You are safe here. You can talk about anything in this place. You can remember anything in this place, and do so without guilt or fear or pain."

"Yes."

"You've brought with you a scrapbook of memories. It is your most precious personal possession. It tells you who you are. Would you like to look at it?"

"I don't know if–"

"Nothing can hurt you here. No memory can bring guilt or fear or pain."

"Yes. I would like to look at it."

"Would you be willing to let Donna look at it, too?"

She shot a fearful glance at the doctor, but he nodded gently at her.

Azra said, "Yes."

"Share something with her. Open the scrapbook and show her a picture of something."

"What about this one, here?"

"Yes. That's a good one. Describe the picture to her."

"I'm eight years old. That is my bike. It had a banana seat. It didn't have a sissy bar. I bent the rim jumping a rock."

Donna blinked, uncertain. "Are you riding the bike?"

"I'm standing by it. My hand is on the seat. There is a yellow house behind me, and an oak tree. The sidewalk is all broken up from the tree roots. That was a good day. Later that week, I fell and scraped my knee, but that day not even once."

Donna smiled, her eyes watering. "That's a beautiful picture, Azra. A beautiful picture."

"Good, Azra. That was a good day. And even remembering that you scraped your knee – that doesn't hurt now, or make you fearful or sad."

"No."

"Good, Azra. That was a good day. Would you like to show Donna another picture, of a day that wasn't so good? One that had lots of pain and guilt and fear?"

"How about this one?"

"That's an excellent one. Describe it to her."

The wind scorpions are gathering on the cell window again. It will be a cold night. They come at dusk, after the rocks and sand have given up their heat and before the bats begin their nighttime feasts. They crawl up the side of the cell and sit on the windowsill and let their bodies soak up the last heat of the day. When the sun is gone, I will be their heat.

I lie on the stone bed and watch the bugs gather. One of them is as big as my hand, which means he is old and doesn't have much venom left. I call him Bush III because Bush I sent me to Iraq and Bush II sent me to Gitmo – and Bush III, seems he's got a plan for me, too. He calls his coalition of the willing, and the wind scorpions gather.

I count them. Six so far. They are my saints. I venerate them. They alone command my attention, my memory. All else is insignificant. Only the saints, who come every evening to wait like votives on the windowsill, are worth remembering, for they cure the wounds that appear across my body.

Bush III is tending the knee that won't straighten. The two smaller ones on either side of him – they are sisters. Their needle-like legs are the best ones for stitching up cuts. The one that is waving its head and seems to have a mustache is John Bolton. He tends the wound lowest down on my foot and blesses it. They like to eat dead flesh, so I am a feast. Once the waterboarding and wires and fists are done, I've got plenty of food for them. Letting them eat at my wounds keeps me from rotting.

Rot has to go. Only what is holy can remain.

Marines come to the bars and tell me to come. I do not, wanting to pray to my saints. One for every wound. But there are only eleven. I have a long way to go. Marines tell me I will regret making them wait. I ignore their insignificant voices. I am a Marine, and no one listens to me.

There comes the twelfth.

And then, suddenly, the bars swing into the room and there are two Marines with them, and wounds are coming faster than wind scorpions.

"– but you are not in that terrible place. You are only viewing it from your place of bliss. Yes. Remember. Good. Good. Two more breaths. Breathe back in the solidity of your body. Settle back into your flesh. Let your soul sigh. One last breath, and you will be fully awake."

Azra opened his eyes. The hypnotic spell faded away behind walls of pink paint and cinder block and steel bars.

Donna opened her eyes as well, but they were brimming, and her face was the color of paper. She blinked, and a tear dropped from her eyelid and painted a red line down her white cheek.

"Good, Azra," said Doctor Gross, a smile knifing beneath his mustache. He tried to look pleased, but he wore an expression that he himself would have called an angry grin. "You've opened the archive of memory. You've begun to touch once again the person you had been."

Azra bent his head toward the table and rubbed his forehead with his hands. "But they aren't memories. They're fantasies. Suggestions. I was talking with my cell mate. That's where all that stuff about Gitmo came from. It's all a lie."

Doctor Gross patted Azra's hand patiently. "We'll sort that out, too, in time. Yes, recovered memories and outright fantasies are sometimes hard to distinguish. Sometimes it doesn't matter. Memories tell us who we were and fantasies who we wish we were. Both tell us a great deal."

"Don't equate them," Azra said, flinging off the doctor's touch. "I was an angel. Not a human. Not a psycho. I was an angel. The picture of me with the bike, that was only a fantasy. I want so much to be human, my mind concocted a fantasy."

"Sweetheart," said Donna, tears standing in her eyes. "It's not a fantasy. These memories are the real ones. You are human. You are."

Doctor Gross rose. "Well, I need to get going. I'll come back in a few days, and we'll talk some more. In the meantime," he smiled sadly, "remember your place of bliss."

Azra watched him go. Once the teal shirt had disappeared beyond the guard, he spoke to Donna quietly, urgently, "You said you believed in angels."

"Yes."

"In fallen angels – in Satan?"

"Yes, in fallen angels."

"In the Dark Angel who wrestled Jacob at Peniel – ?"

"Yes."

"Then why can't you believe in me?"

Donna seemed suddenly deflated, and the glow of hope on her features faded away.

Lynda Barnett leaned forward. "I'm going to have to stop this conversation right here."

"No, you're not," Azra said fiercely. "I'm in charge of my own defense!" Lynda rolled her eyes, released a hiss of steam, and slouched back, arms folded, in her chair. Azra turned back to Donna. "Well?"

"Why don't I believe you?" Donna sought through interior spaces. "Do you know about Herbert Mullin?"

"I don't."

"He was a serial murderer in California. He heard his father, who was half a world away in the military, tell him to kill. Vietnam had just ended, and Herbert believed that the casualties of that war had been sacrifices to nature. With the end of the war, nature was growing angry. It was his job to go kill in order to provide more sacrifices and keep California from falling into the ocean."

"I see."

"Do you know about Richard Trenton Chase?"

"No."

"He believed he had soap-dish disease. If you pick up your soap and it is gooey underneath, you have soap-dish disease. It turns your blood to powder. When he was in a psychiatric home, he would capture rabbits in the courtyard and inject their blood into his veins. He was once stopped when leaving an Indian reservation because he had buckets of blood in the back of his truck. It was cow's blood, but later he hunted humans, drank their blood, and put their livers and kidneys into blenders."

"Your point is?"

"Both of them were convinced of the supernatural forces that affected them. Both pleaded with those around them to understand, to believe. Both were human. Both died because they could not escape their delusions."

Azra's face fell. "It can't be true, Donna. It can't. If I was an angel, I was a great servant of God. If I was only human, I was a madman and a monster."

"Whatever you were before, you're human now," she said. "You're human now. And you have to live."

"You're wrong. You're wrong, and I am going to prove it."

THIRTEEN

The news got out that the cop who had caught the killer was now sitting beside him in the Racine County Jail, holding his hand while a liberal professor and the public defender appointed by activist judges took part in a séance. They called to angels and to demons to testify in court to free the killer – or so said an unnamed guard.

Donna's phone began to ring; her answering machine filled with death threats. She changed her number to unlisted. Threatening mail arrived, and Donna opened only bills.

Except when a small square package showed up in her mailbox. It was wrapped in brown paper, and its return address simply read, "From a Friend."

"There's something about this one," said Donna, holding it in her hand as she walked into her kitchen. "Feels – soft." She got a knife from the drawer and gingerly sliced into the paper. Then she shone a flashlight into the slit. Inside lay something that looked like an old wallet.

No apparent booby traps, no anthrax...

Donna cautiously cut two more slits and lifted the paper away.

Inside was a billfold, worn and brown. She opened it and found an Indiana driver's license with a very familiar face.

"Mother of God – Azra."

It was more than a driver's license. The whole thing was stuffed with ID – Social Security, library cards, video rental clubs, grocery check cards, blood donor cards, grocery receipts, thirty-eight dollars in tens, fives, and ones, and a short shopping list.

"William B. Dance, male, six foot one, one hundred eighty-five pounds, black hair, gray eyes, no sight restriction, Social Security number..."

Donna went into her home office and scooted her chair up to her computer. A few bookmarks, a few passwords, and she was into the Burlington Police Intranet. She began by typing in the driver's license number. *His name is William Dance. The little boy with the bike was named William Dance.* In moments, the information began scrolling up:

No record of parking citation.

No record of traffic citation.

No record of misdemeanor arrest.

No record of felony arrest.

She picked up the phone and flipped through her Rolodex. Her fingers stopped on the address and phone number of Jason Knight, IRS inspector. She dialed.

"Extension five forty-seven. Thank you. Hi, Jason. This is Detective Leland from Burlington. Right, the Pizza Hut arson case. Yeah. Oh, fine, how about you? Yeah, I've got a Social Security number I need a check on. Sure. All right? You've got it. Okay." She read him the number, and he repeated it back. "Yeah, that's it. Okay, I'll wait." She leaned back in her chair. It creaked wearily, an extension of her tired body.

"You got it? Good. None whatsoever? This guy is – let's see, the license says he's thirty-five. You sure you've got nothing? How could he have a Social Security number and never file taxes? Yeah, I'll wait." She fiddled with a pen on the desk before her.

"MIA? From what war? Desert Storm? That would have made him... yes. A Marine? Are you sure? That was over fifteen years ago, which would have made him twenty. July 22, 1992 is when he disappeared? All right.

"Well, Jason, if you dig up anything else, let me – oh, wait, have you got his serial number and unit? Yeah. Thanks. Got it. Good-bye. Yeah, the arson for profit scheme was more fun. Sure. I'll see you. Bye."

Leland hung up the phone and stared at the ceiling. A veteran, missing in action for fifteen years. A POW. Scorpions and Marines with waterboarding and wires and fists and wounds coming faster than saints...

Oh, Azra. No wonder you forgot everything. No wonder you became a monster.

She punched another number into the phone. "Hello, this is Detective Leland of the Burlington Police

Department. Burlington, Wisconsin. I'm investigating a multiple – that is, I'm trying to find the owner of a lost wallet, and I need some information about a Marine that served during Desert Storm. Yes, the National Personnel Records Center? And the number? Who should I ask to speak to? Thanks. Yeah. I need all the luck I can get."

She worked past dinnertime and into the night. There was no window in her home office, no skylight to look into and see the speckled blackness of a Wisconsin sky. Only her grandfather's old wooden cuckoo clock told her how late it was. She had ignored the ten chirps, the eleven, and the twelve. But when there came only one, and then only two, the creeping morning could not be denied.

How many cups of coffee? The stuff had kept her awake but had leant a jittery fear to the process.

Most of her work had been the web equivalent of paperwork – online indexes, pentagon records, requests for information, directory searches, postings to recruiters and schools, even a conversation with the military liaison at the American Embassy in Baghdad.

Most of the queries came up with no immediate aid, though the Veterans Administration had found Azra on one of their newer lists of "Missing in Action and Presumed Dead." That list had indicated no known family, and that he'd been recruited out of the enlistment office in Alexandria, Virginia. There, she found a 1991 file that included a grainy photo of a young, thin, dark-haired recruit, and an enrollment record that identified him as William B. Dance.

The supposed nineteen-year-old had had no Social Security number when he enrolled, but the file indicated it had been applied for. His place of residence was listed as Milwaukee, Wisconsin. In the space for parents' names was the phrase "Ward of State." The enlisting officer's comments included the notes that, "William is a level-headed and solid-seeming young man. He should do well in combat."

"If he weren't delusional," Leland told herself grimly. He would be listed as MIA the very next year.

The file also indicated he had an interest in covert operations, including strike-force tactics and disguise and camouflage maneuvers. "He says he would like to be a spy."

A spy for the Marines.

But how could he have gotten from MIA in 1992 to killing in Burlington in 2008?

The phone rang so loudly she leapt up from her seat. Her heart hammered. "Hello? This is she. What? Another one? Mother of God. Yeah, yeah, I'm on my way."

It was no joy to kill you, my friend, but it was your time.

Yes, you slept peacefully. You might not ever have woken up enough to know what I was doing. Or, perhaps you thought I was raping you and decided to hold still until you realized you were strangling.

I should have known you would bite down on my thumb when I held the penny in your throat. Of course, I wouldn't have guessed you could bite it clear off.

Now that I think of it, it was probably the thumb more than the penny that suffocated you.

I could see the bone and sinew jammed in your teeth. You tried to spit the thumb out, but it was stuck. You tried to pry it out, but I was sitting on your stomach by that time. My own agony was terrible. I can't imagine what you were going through, to look up and see me sitting there on top of you, holding the stump where my thumb used to be and waiting for you to suffocate on the penny and the thumb, both.

You probably thought me mad. Or, you thought I did this so you couldn't testify against me. In truth, I did it because it was your time, and as an embezzler, you deserved to die at the hand of a confidante, choking on a penny, victim of a crime that was anything but calculating and economic.

In fact, I suspected even then, as my blood dribbled from your mouth and my hand, that this had not been a test from God. It had been a trap. I'd been proven guilty. At last, the prosecution would have a crime that only I could have committed.

I waited for five minutes after you stopped moving, even felt for a pulse with that thumbless hand of mine.

"I'm sorry, Derek. I hope I've given you a good end." I caressed one of your bloated cheeks, incidentally smearing the blood there.

Enough of this self-indulgence.

I stood and went to the adjoining cell. They lay asleep, black bundles. I prodded Lawrence. "Hey, wake up. I need you to call a guard. I've just killed Billings."

SON OF SAMAEL SLAYS CELL MATE
AP International
Photo and Story by Blake Gaines

The accused killer of four in Burlington, Wis., has struck again, police say.

Derek Billings, the cell mate of the so-called Son of Samael, was found dead late last evening in the Racine County Jail. The cause of death is yet to be determined. Sources in the corrections department say the man seemed to have strangled on the Son of Samael's thumb.

The thumb had been bitten off in a fight. It was removed from the man's throat for surgical reconstruction.

Billings was awaiting trial on a charge of embezzling over forty million dollars from his company, Halliburton. Other prisoners on the cell block said Billings and the Son of Samael seemed to be "friends."

Joseph Lawrence, in the adjacent cell, said the Son of Samael "woke me up and said, 'Call a guard. I just killed Billings.'" He said he was surprised because the cell mates had been "thicker than thieves."

The Son of Samael will be moved to solitary confinement. He is undergoing reconstructive surgery at St Mary of Mercy.

An intern who asked not to be identified said the delicate and time-consuming surgery would cost taxpayers "in excess of forty thousand dollars." He went on to say, "In some countries, they cut off a thief's hand. In America, a murderer gets it sewn back on."

FOURTEEN

When Donna and Doctor Gross arrived for their next interview, Azra lay abed in St Mary of Mercy. He slept. The head of his bed was raised, and the fluorescent reading light flickered, otherworldly, above his bowed head of black hair.

Two guards were in the room. Men in blue. They crouched, red-eyed, in their chairs. In low tones, they had been talking of the school referendum up for vote in a few days. At intervals, they regarded the prisoner, strapped to his bed – bandages, sheets, and restraints all merging into glowing robes.

"Hi, I'm Gary Gross, the psychiatrist," said the doctor to the guards. His teal shirt had been replaced with mauve, but otherwise he wore the same non-uniform he had worn before. "This is Detective Donna Leland, citizen advocate of the accused."

The two deputies looked up a moment from their discussion, and the one with a mustache nodded. "Let's see some ID."

Dr. Gross fished for his wallet while, sweet and weary, Donna Leland dug in her tweed jacket. "I'm Detective Leland of the Burlington Police, the one who tracked him down. I'd like you to wait outside. I can handle him. There's only one door to the room, and a five-story drop to the parking lot outside the windows. He's not getting away."

Shrugging reluctantly, the older guard handed the two IDs back to the cop and the shrink, picked up a clipboard, brought it to Leland, and said, "Sign here. If he gets away, he's your responsibility."

She signed. "Always has been."

Doctor Gross passed them, approaching the accused.

Azra had become thin and sinewy. The corners of his eyes were tightly pinched – the corners of his lips, too. Despite all his talk of angels, despite the media speculation of demons, Azra looked increasingly human. Frail. Confused. Betrayed by even his own mind. He was ceasing to be Azra Michaels and was becoming William B. Dance.

Doctor Gross sat, settling his legal pad and Bics on the bedside table. On the opposite side of the bed, Donna pulled up a chair. The psychiatrist reached gently toward Dance. "Wake up, Azra. It's Gary. Donna's here, too. We'd like to speak to you again."

The prisoner's eyelids slid slowly upward, fluttered for a moment, and then stared fixedly at the cart by the foot of the bed. He gave no notice of the doctor or Donna.

"Sorry to wake you," Doctor Gross said, withdrawing his hand.

Azra turned his dream-clouded eyes toward him. A weak smile came to his face. "Good morning, Father."

"I am not a priest," said Gross gently. "I'm a psychiatrist. Doctor Gary, remember?"

Azra blinked in affirmation. "That's what I meant. I'm not used to waking up."

Donna leaned in with a small frown, her hand settling on his bandaged thumb. "Give yourself a moment. A lot has happened." She was trembling, and her eyebrows knitted above bloodshot eyes. "Once you're ready, we'd like to talk to you."

"Yes," said Azra, stretching as best he could within the constraints. "Hello, Donna. I've been dreaming of you."

"Good dreams, I hope," she replied, her voice trembling now, too. "No nightmares."

Azra's eyes clouded slightly. "I guess I'm awake enough for questions."

"Good," Doctor Gross said, paging through the scribbled legal pad. "I've been reviewing the notes from our discussion – is it all right for me to take notes again today?"

"Yes, fine."

"A lot has happened since we spoke last. For one, of course, your wallet was found, and your ID checked out – a whole life for William B. Dance."

"That's not me. Derek must have made up that name, that past, used computer programmers, you know. Punks–"

Doctor Gross gave a slow shrug. "If so, the punks did a darned thorough job. We found your – sorry,

William's – grade school records; an excellent student. And his driver's permit at fifteen, and Marines enrollment documents."

"But what about high school? What about immunization? What about paper records, not just computer records? It isn't a very complete history, is it?"

"There are holes, sure, but that's the nature of paperwork. Everybody's got an incomplete–"

"He did a good job."

"He?"

"Derek Billings."

"Yes, that's the other big thing that has happened. Your friend, Mr Billings – you killed him. Why?"

"Yes," broke in Donna, a desperate light in her face. "Why?"

Azra turned toward her, his eyes seeming to shrink back into his skull. Despite their diminishment, Donna could see herself reflected, huddled and expectant, in them.

He chewed his lip before saying, "Well, I killed him because it was his time. I've always known when it's somebody's time. I killed him because he deserved a good death. I wanted to prove I was ready to be an angel again. I wanted God to forgive me."

"He didn't," Donna noted flatly.

"I know."

"You're human, Azra," she said, almost pleading. "You can't escape it. You need to stop trying. You need to pull a defense together. You need to figure out some way to live."

Doctor Gross broke in. "All right. I'd like to explore this a little further. In your confession, you said that when you killed Mr Billings, you put aside your human feelings of – for instance – friendship and compassion, to achieve the divine end of assuring an appropriate death?"

"Yes," Azra replied, turning toward him.

"In the other murder cases – the newspaperman, the priest, and so forth – did you put aside your human emotions then, too?"

"Keith McFarland killed them. I only oversaw. And besides, I didn't even have human emotions then."

"When did you start having human emotions?"

"When I fell in love with Donna," said Azra, glancing toward her.

Donna looked away.

"Ah, yes, we talked about that. Well, what about when you killed – sorry, when you arranged for the police to kill Keith McFarland? You said you were already in human form when that happened. Did you have to put aside your human emotions then?"

Azra leaned his head back on the rumpled sheets. Blue lines of fluorescence radiated down his dark hair. "If I remember – that is something else I was not prepared for, how bad mortal memories are – I exulted in Keith's death. I had watched him kill so many people, and he was such a mess. He is certainly better off dead."

"Why is that?"

"Keith's life was tragic. He was never truly happy or truly in control of himself unless he was killing, or enjoying the fruits of killing."

"How do you know that? Did he tell you?"

"We didn't particularly speak. He heard my voice sometimes, I know, but he didn't respond."

"Did *you* enjoy killing and the fruits of killing?"

"'Enjoy' is a mortal term. It implies a needy and desirous body. I did not enjoy killing, except for killing Keith – which was when I had a body. I appreciated a well-planned death, but did not enjoy killing until Keith."

Donna released a despairing moan.

"Did you enjoy killing Derek?"

Again, the question seemed to surprise Azra. "I suppose I did. I certainly felt it. I hadn't expected to feel it so strongly, getting my thumb bitten off."

"The ER nurses said there was semen in your underwear when you were brought in."

Azra breathed, taking in that information. "Semen?"

"It was your semen, Azra."

His face looked sickly white. "Forgive me. This is a shock to me."

"It was a shock to them, too. What do you think it means that you ejaculated in your underwear?"

"It means I was sexually aroused."

Doctor Gross wrote. "Why would killing another person arouse you?"

"I don't know."

"All right." He flipped through his notes. "All right. I'm going to walk you through your description of the murder, right from the confession you gave to the police. Tell me at each step how aroused you felt, or how aroused you feel at each moment while we talk about it."

"All right."

"First, during the day, you asked a cell mate for a penny – Mr Joseph Lawrence. He gave you one. You said you knew then that you would use it to suffocate Mr Billings. How much arousal did you feel when you got the penny?"

"None. I just put it in my pocket."

"Okay, then you waited for night, when Billings was asleep. You said you were thinking about how the killing would go. How aroused were you during that time?"

"Not at all."

In encouragement, Donna patted his bandaged hand.

"Once you were sure he slept, you crawled down off your bunk. You had the top bunk. You climbed down and stood by his bedside, looking at him."

"I remember a tightness... down here. I did not recognize it then. I remember the pocket where the penny was – the pocket felt loose, like it was pushed out."

"You held the penny between your index finger and thumb, then slid it into his mouth and straddled him."

"My heart was pounding. There was an exciting ache. Yes. I was excited."

"You jammed the penny in his throat, and he struggled. He bit off your thumb. You saw your own thumb in his mouth. You lifted your hand and cupped the other hand over it. He was choking on your thumb, squirming beneath you."

"Perhaps that was when the semen got in my under-wear."

"Did you want to do anything more, then?" Doctor Gross looked up, gauging Donna's reaction. She was fervid and trembling.

"No. I don't know what I wanted to do. It felt fright-ening and good."

"Oh, Azra," Donna said, revulsion and despair on her face.

"All right. So, you got up from the bunk and went to tell Lawrence to call for a guard. What did you feel then?"

"My hand was hurting. I don't remember anything else."

"So, was it the killing that excited you, or putting your thumb into his mouth?"

"I don't know. Both. Now I understand Keith a little better."

"Do you think it is natural to have these feelings?"

"What do you mean, natural? Do you mean part of God's plan – or sin?"

"Do you think God wants humans to have these feel-ings when they kill? Do you think it's sin?"

"I don't know. God knows when all things are to be born and when they are to die, and you can't be born without having to someday face death, and you can't die without something killing you. God wants mortals to die, yes – and he wants them to have sex. I do not know if he wants them to connect the two."

"Do you feel any guilt, remorse, or shame for having killed Derek or Keith?"

"Yes," Azra said. "At first, I felt sorry for him, for Derek. I apologized to him while I was killing him. And now, now that I know it was not a test from God, now that I know about the wallet and the records – whether Derek made it up or it is all true – I feel bad. I feel guilt. I wish I hadn't killed him."

"Let's get back to Keith. Why did you choose to assist his slayings?"

"He chose to kill, and I had to assure the killings were fitting – just."

"How is it fitting and just for a young priest to be killed in a confessional on Christmas Eve?"

"How is it not just?"

"Shouldn't good folk live long, happy lives and die quietly in their sleep?"

"No. That is not what God does. Good people often die young and bad people often live to old age."

"Where is the justice in that?" Donna demanded.

"Justice is each person getting his or her due. Every mortal will die, so avoiding death entirely would be unjust for humans, right?"

"But how is a gentle priest due a violent death?" she insisted.

"He followed Christ, did he not? At the moment of Christ's birth – Christmas Day – it was known he must die, must be crucified. How is it wrong that the follower of a young martyr be martyred young?"

Donna was stunned by that response. Doctor Gross also seemed caught off-guard. He didn't scribble notes, or open his mouth to respond, but only stared straight ahead.

"Are you a Christian, Gary?" Azrael asked.

"I'm Jewish."

"Still, you know Psalm 23–"

"'The Lord is my shepherd.' Of course."

"And what's a shepherd? A husbandman, right?" Azrael went on. "He tends his sheep, he leads them to good pastures and clean water. He guards them through the valley of the shadow of death."

"Yes."

"Why? Why does he guard them?"

"So the wolves won't kill them?"

"Yes, so the wolves won't kill them. Does that mean they never die? Does he keep them into ripe old age so that they can pass away in their sleep?"

"It's a metaphor. You can't stretch it too far."

"He keeps the wolves from killing them at the wrong time so he can kill them at the right time. Part of husbandry is slaughter. He chooses when the sheep will live, when they will be sheared, when they will mate, and when they will die. Could any shepherd be a good shepherd if he didn't cull his herd, didn't keep them from overgrazing the land and starving themselves out? And he kills them in their prime, when they'll provide the best meat."

"The good shepherd is a Christian metaphor."

"The psalms are Jewish. Why is it so hard for you to believe that God chooses the time and place and means of human death? Would you rather that he not choose? That he not know, not plan? That he leave you to the wolves and the shadow of death and so either be incapable or unwilling to save you?"

"Look, we've strayed from the point."

"No, *this* is the point. To understand me, you need to understand that the actions of the divine are incomprehensible and unconscionable to the mortal. That which God not only may do but must do – orchestrate the deaths of all humans – is inexcusable when done by a human. So, too, that which a human shepherd not only may do but must do – slaughter the creatures in his charge – would be inconceivable to the sheep. You fear and denounce only because you don't want to recognize that humans aren't the top of the food chain."

Doctor Gross stared, perplexed, speechless.

"Let's get to the regression," Donna said, impatient. "I'm tired of all this talk of death. I'm tired of Keith Mc-Farland and Derek Billings and the Angel of Death. I want to hear more about William Dance. I want to see that boy standing next to his bike in front of the yellow house."

"Yes," agreed Doctor Gross, shaking his head to clear it. "Yes. William, you remember your place of bliss? That's where we're headed. I want you to relax. Lean back in the bed."

"What other choice do I have?"

"Yes. Well, get as comfortable as possible. Take three deep breaths: one… two… three… Good. Take another breath…"

What it was that smoked at the end of the stick was not advertised. If you asked, they called it meat. It had small bones – leg bones and otherwise – and was cheap. Everybody ate them so they couldn't have been too bad.

He ate. It wasn't too bad. He had paid a thousand pesos and gotten change. He sat there on his heels. The old men across the dusty road laughed in their circle. They were smoking cigars as black as dog turds.

They hadn't gotten all the feathers off the head, which was hidden beneath a place where the plumes were charred together. Hungry, he pulled the burned parts off and chewed gently around the crow's eye.

Darkness. That was what they gave to him after killing Billings. Darkness. Reason enough for the sane prisoner to go insane. A cell with no windows, no light, only a steel bed and a stainless steel toilet without a seat and a slot through which came anything that came for him. Solitary. It was the greatest punishment a prisoner could receive.

Short of death.

Azra sat in the darkness. They had even put a rubber flange on the outside base of the door to prevent light from seeping through. He had saved a crust of bread from one meal and let it harden on the floor overnight so that he could wedge it beneath the door, lifting the flange and letting a little light in. Now, in the glow that came around the crust of bread, he could see his dim little space, cement and steel and nothing else. His breath condensed on the walls, steel dappled in cold sweat.

With each passing moment, his humanity sank deeper into him, from bone and blood to spirit and soul. He was trapped in this body, in this tiny room, in this darkness. He was at the mercy of his skin he inhabited and its limits.

He had sat beside the door and thought about gnashing his own wrist open and bleeding out through the crack. That would be a kind of ritual escape, extending part of his vitality out the door. But ritual was no longer important. He needed real escape.

What of semen? If it ventured beyond and found an egg, a part of him would have escaped this trap. No wonder those on death row were in so great a hurry to marry, to gain conjugal visitation rights. In that sudden thought, the whole fetid weight of reproduction and sexual desire and mortal fear poured through him.

"Do you think it is natural to have these feelings? Do you think God wants humans to have these feelings when they kill?"

Fuck, yeah, was all he could think. *Fuck, yeah.*

It was not the sort of response worthy of an angel, but neither was his soul any longer worthy of an angel.

An angel. That's what he needed. If he were truly human now, there would be an angel assigned him, a guardian. Not all humans who heard voices were schizophrenic. Some were prophets and shamans and artists. All humans would hear the divine voices if only they quieted the raging of their hearts and minds and listened with their souls.

What better, quieter place? He pulled his knees up toward his chest, drew a deep breath, and let the air sluice from his nostrils. His ribs slouched inward like the tines of a folding umbrella. He emptied himself of the panic and pain of the last weeks, the mental torments of a mind once infinite that found itself not just finite but imprisoned, coerced, controlled.

He drew another breath and let it go, imagining those heavy pollutants drifting out of him. A third breath, but the air was stale. It was all pollutants.

He closed his eyes. Even the bread-light of the door was gone now. His mind seemed a shadowy blue thing hovering before him. Its convoluted surface peeled slowly back like the cracked outside of a road apple. The pocketed wetness within sprayed upward and outward – outward no farther than the cell walls, but upward, upward, propelling the ceiling higher, the ceiling and the cells above it higher until the whole column of building broke free and rocketed into the sky. It, too, was black in an imagined nighttime, and the building cross-section dropped away behind the thrust of that bursting mind.

There, at last – no limits – the flesh torn asunder like some Gnostic nightmare, the spirit flung outward into infinity to find its eternal angel guide. Here in the endless centuries, a guide: some Gabriel, some Uriel, or if not a friend, an adversary, an accuser, a Satan. At least with such there would be a divine measure upon which to form up the coiling putrescence of humanity.

He waited, blown wide open, consciousness as raw as a wound. He waited. The inspiration and suspiration of the old metallic air no longer mattered. The fleshy ache of skin and muscle and fat pressed between steel and bone was gone. There was only the vulnerability of his seeking, hoping soul.

Beauty. God always dwelt in beauty. Azra let his seeking spirit draw beauty unto it. In beauty he would find his guardian, his adversary, his angel who would aid and guide him. In beauty.

He waited.

Should he sing a song? Should he drone one of those endless hymns of clapboard Protestantism? Or some Kyrie? Some psalm? They seemed to help humans focus their souls upward, outward.

Oh, for a thousand tongues…

His voice was as primal and imperfect as the rest of him, more a groan than a song. Did nothing come easily to mortal flesh?

Oh, for a thousand tongues, to sing
My great Redeemer's praise,
The glories of my God and King,
The triumphs of His grace!

The sound only brought him back to the ringing coldness of the cell and the pulpy pointlessness of his body. He let it echo away into silence and held wide his wounded soul and waited.

Silence.

Not silence, but the phlegmy sawing of lungs and the dull thud of a heart that cannot be willed to cease and the ragged thoughts of a racing mind condemned to sense and sense and sense. The body was loud.

Bladders emptied and filled. Valves fluttered open and closed. Glands oozed in silent ignominy. The human body was no more than a loud coalition of mollusks, pulsing and squirting in constant concert. To never have silence. To not for a moment be able to hear past one's own thundering presence to heed a voice beyond...

Where is my angel?

Beauty. God will be in beauty.

Into that welling emptiness came a presence – face, body, mind, spirit, all. She was beautiful in no standard sense, but somehow the lines of her being, the eyes, the dogged optimism, the courage... somehow they transformed the finite to make it infinite. They made that one woman a whole continent, a whole world.

That woman. No angel, she, but a police officer. A Catholic. Donna.

What is it she always says? Mother of God? She could well be. She could well be.

Suddenly he was not alone. He felt her presence, her straightforward and all-seeing presence there with him in the dark. She knew about him. She had hunted him down. She lived because he could not bear to let her die. Now he lived because she could not bear to let him die.

Yes, here was his angel.

Tears were coming. His shoulders curled inward with a soft shuddering. He was not alone.

That thought brought another creature into being, another presence. It rose between his legs, the immemorial snake of desire.

He had known of masturbation, of course, for he knew all the mind of God. He had known of it, that it was done by nearly everyone, and that when first discovered, many believed they had invented their own perverse sin. He had known it was not sin at all, nor perverse, but part of the mind of God.

Still, as he unzipped the fly of his prison uniform, he felt filthy and hopeless and damned for all eternity.

The semen came quickly, fluorescent in the darkness. So powerful were the constrictions of testicles and prostate that he did not even notice the key in the door, or the door swinging wide until the unforgiving glare of the jail's yellow lights washed across him.

"Put your pecker away and get up, Angel," came the voice of a radiant young man who stood by the beaming hole. "Your lawyer wants to see you."

She stood at her end of the conference room table when they brought him in. After the long darkness and the pervading pink of the walls, Counselor Lynda Barnett was dazzling in her skirt-suit. A riot of green leaves moved in the shimmering shoulders and sleeves of the jacket. Her red silk blouse looked too delicate and beautiful to exist in the same world as the heat-annealed caverns of the prison.

"Hello, Lynda. Good to see you."

"Hello, William?"

"Whatever you want to call me," he replied as he sat, the guards locking his cuffs into the tabletop. "I'm just glad to hear someone speak to me in a civil tone."

She nodded tightly and sat. "You may not be so happy to hear what I have to say."

His eyes ceased their smiling, and his attention flicked down toward the much-scarred tabletop. "Which is?"

She pulled papers from her attaché. "You have pleaded not guilty. You refuse to let me use an insanity defense. You refuse to let me refer to the past that has been discovered for you. In two weeks you'll appear, defenseless, before a judge and jury."

Defenseless. Suddenly, that fate sounded terrifying. Donna's voice came echoing through his mind. *You're human now. You have to live.* In the dark dankness of isolation, he had felt the beginnings of what mortals call misery. Truth dissolved away. Divinity was only a disappearing dream. Humanity remained. "I want to cooperate. What must I do?"

"Good," she said through an angry smile. "We've got a lot to do in the next two weeks. Let's hope you can be as slick with the media, the judge, and the jury as you were with Derek Billings."

FIFTEEN

Donna Leland stood in front of her medicine cabinet mirror and looked at her sallow skin and the rings under her eyes and thought, It's a strange thing, getting ready for court.

As a cop, she'd gotten ready for court plenty of times, usually when somebody said the radar gun lied. Then it had been easy: cop blues, a braided ponytail, a dusting of blush, and she looked authoritative but human. She'd never lost in court before.

But how do I get ready today? How do I want to look? Authoritative and human?

Donna began with foundation, hiding freckles and blemishes and filling in some of the worry lines. Then she added blush to her cheeks. It was a sign of health. The women in Auschwitz used to prick their fingertips and smear the blood on their cheeks to look healthy and happy so the Nazis wouldn't choose them for the ovens.

Is that what I want to do? Look healthy and happy?

Azra had killed again. He'd killed his bunkmate, his only friend. He'd killed to impress God, who apparently was a tougher audience than Jodi Foster. And what if God still wasn't impressed? The next step up from killing a bunkmate was killing a bedmate.

Eye liner. That's what I need. It's the right look – something to let the judge know how sad and tired and scared I am.

"All rise. Circuit Court Branch One of the County of Racine in the State of Wisconsin is now in session, the honorable Judge Sandra Devlin presiding." The bailiff glanced around the crowded courtroom as though expecting opposition and then flicked his eyes toward a paneled doorway that slid open.

Through it stepped Judge Sandra Devlin. She was a small woman, further dwarfed by the walnut-paneled bench and the standing-room-only crowd. She seemed a caricature of a witch. Her skin was rubbery – brow, nose, and chin forming an ill-fitting mask – and her bright eyes glowed with caprice above her black robes.

Judge Devlin slid the door closed behind her. She smiled pleasantly to no one, scuttled up the stairs behind the bench, and wriggled into her seat. Already distracted by paperwork, she waved the crowd to sit.

They did.

Judge Devlin rapped the gavel and said, "The court will come to order. Today begins the trial of case number 96CF00132, the State of Wisconsin versus John Doe."

She nodded toward a pair of policemen, who had just resumed their seats by the prisoner's door. They rose slowly, opened the door, and ambled through it into a dimly lit hall of cinder block.

The previous hush deepened to silence. A few shutters snicked quietly, photographers checking for focus. No one wanted to miss the shot of the Son of Samael appearing at that door.

As in a Dickensian stage play, there came a formless shadow on the already dark wall. The accused loped outward. Wing tips clopped like devil hooves on the floor. A gaunt figure in a wool jacket shambled into view.

"My God," muttered a man.

The utterance brought them all up in their seats. It created a high-pitched whine like the sound just before a cable snaps. The chatter of cameras became a cicada song. An overly tall, overly thin man emerged.

"Bundy," said the same man.

The resemblance was undeniable. Dark hair. Handsome features. Eyes steely and calm. Smile almost apologetic, as if he was sorry the crowd had to put up with all the lies spoken about him.

Still, the bandage on his right hand told that one of the spectacular stories was true.

The accused moved toward the defense table, where Counselor Barnett and Detective Donna Leland pulled out a chair for him.

"Thank you, Donna," said the man.

"You're welcome, William."

He sat with a lean, contrite motion: his hands swung down into his lap, and his close-cropped head bowed in a combination of respect and guilt.

The camera lenses still scissored open and shut behind him. The air fairly hummed. Eyes were wide and unblinking. Tongues shied back from teeth. The room was filled with a communal and galvanic dread, the sort reserved for celebrities, messiahs, and demons.

He was all of them. No longer would the name John Doe mean anonymity. Now it would mean depravity.

The insistent clamor of gavel raps cut through the buzz of glaring eyes and grinding teeth.

"Enough," the judge said quietly. "If every movement of the accused is going to make a sensation, I'll clear the court." She peered around the room, eyes focusing just above the half-glasses she wore for reading. She had the stern air of a schoolmarm. "Better."

Without abandoning the papers beneath her fingers, she said, "John Doe, you are charged with four murders in the county of Racine, a fifth in Walworth County, and a sixth in Kenosha County. Once this trial is concluded, you will be extradited for trial in the state of Illinois, and after that, the state of Indiana. Is this understood?"

"Yes, Your Honor," he replied. Though quiet, his voice carried through the room.

"All right, then," Judge Devlin said, "let's get to it. Opening arguments. Counselor Franklin, are you prepared?"

"Yes, Your Honor," he said, standing. Jim Franklin was tall, strong, and handsome. His gray-blue suit made him seem a man of stainless steel. The gray-blue shadow of a latent beard extended the sheen of the suit up across his Adam's apple and to his cheekbones. With a theatrical flair, he gazed down at the tabletop, where his hands patiently sifted through the folios spilled from his attaché.

Counselor Barnett watched her colleague, her adversary. The look of attention on her face deepened to annoyance.

Franklin glanced at her, then up at the bench, and last at the jury. "Your Honor, people of Wisconsin, what we begin today is a most difficult trial.

"That man there, known in the records as John Doe, stands accused in this state of six brutal murders. These were monstrous crimes, involving amputations and gallons of blood. He has supplied various confessions of his guilt, saying he killed his cell mate Derek Billings by strangling the man with a penny and his own thumb; saying he orchestrated the five other murders – what we call 'murder by proxy.' Still, he pleads not guilty. He has passed a competency hearing and remains in command of his own defense – but still he plans to tell you he is insane. He wants it both ways. He is sane and guilty when it benefits him, and insane and not guilty when that works better.

"Insane? Not guilty? I don't think so. I don't think even this man thinks so. Just two weeks ago, the defense got nervous and began pushing for a plea-bargain verdict of guilty in exchange for a declaration of insanity, letting John Doe live out his days in a comfortable mental institution rather than a maximum security penitentiary. I would not allow that. This man is not insane. Murderous, yes. Cunning, ruthless, manipulative, charismatic, yes. But insane? No.

"You wonder: How can a man who enjoyed decapitating perfect strangers not be insane? Well, first you must understand what is meant by insanity. It is a legal term, not a psychiatric one. By law, a person is insane if he cannot tell the difference between right and wrong.

"An insane person, thus, does nothing to hide his crimes: he does not perceive of them as criminal. This man hid his crimes. He found a violent paranoid schizophrenic in a poorly run group home and used him to fulfill his murderous fantasies. John Doe is not insane. If he were, why would he choose a patsy to commit his crimes? Why would he carefully avoid leaving his own fingerprints anywhere? Because he knew what he was doing was wrong.

"John Doe is not psychotic – unable to understand and cope with the world in which he lives. He is sociopathic. He knows exactly what he is doing in this world. He understands right and wrong but chooses wrong. He pretends to be mentally ill so that he can kill with impunity. Here is a man who admits to two gruesome murders and is suspected of many more, in three separate states!

"Through expert testimony from psychiatrists, police officers, medical examiners, and FBI profilers, the prosecution will show you the man behind this smug mask.

You will see that John Doe is more cunning than Ted Bundy, who some say slew more than fifty women from coast to coast before he was stopped. You will see that John Doe is more duplicitous than John Wayne Gacy, the upstanding building contractor and birthday party clown who buried more than thirty young men and boys in his own home. You will see that John Doe is more sexually sadistic than Jeffrey Dahmer, who drugged and raped his victims, killed them, had sex with their dead bodies, dissected them, and ate the pieces.

"These four killers are the same – Bundy, Gacy, Dahmer, and Doe – people who, on the surface, seem incapable of the atrocities they easily, constantly, and secretly committed. All four – Bundy, Gacy, Dahmer, and Doe – invented elaborate lies to cover their actions. Doe's lies sound like those of David Berkowitz – the Son of Sam, who said his dog was an ancient Babylonian devil, telling him to kill.

"I need not refer to the tabloids. Doe, in his own confessions, provides the best and most damning copy. He has an elaborate cover story. He says he killed all these people – and many more – because he is a fallen angel.

"Don't laugh. That is the man's defense. He wants you to think he is not just crazy, but legally insane. His lawyer has an even more unbelievable lie, that he is a shell-shocked Gulf War hero. He is no hero, folks. He is no angel, but a cold-blooded killer.

"If Wisconsin had a death penalty, I would plead for it in this case. Because we do not, I hope for back-to-back life sentences for every victim to be served and without the possibility of parole. He's fooled too many people for too long. Don't become the next victims of this charismatic sociopath. Thank you."

District Attorney Franklin gazed one last level time at the jury and then again at the judge, his eyes keen and honest. He sat, his stainless steel suit silently re-shaping around him.

"A statement from the defense?" prompted Judge Devlin.

Lynda Barnett rose. After the slick coldness of Franklin's delivery, the woman in the bright skirt-suit seemed a tribal wise woman, a storyteller. Her flesh was the color of good, rich earth. Honest. Direct. There was no shuffling of papers on the table, no leaning intensity. There was only the calm, quiet sound of soft-soled shoes on the cold marble floor.

She turned toward the jury. "It would be so easy if what Mr Franklin said were true. But truth isn't a melodrama. We do not live our lives among heroes and monsters. We live among people. That's what we are, people.

"Ladies and gentlemen, I want you to meet a very troubled person, Mr William B. Dance," she gestured to the prisoner. "Mr Franklin would not call him a person. Not even a mentally ill person. He calls him a monster – a hobgoblin, a bogeyman, the creature in the closet.

"It's not that Mr Franklin really believes in such things, but he thinks the rest of us do, or at least he thinks he can scare us into believing in them. He offers folk tales. I offer facts. I want a fair trial; he wants a lynch mob.

"What facts does he ignore? How about Mr Dance's wallet, with his driver's license and Social Security card? How about the records of the American Veterans Administration and the Veterans of Foreign Wars POW MIA lists? How about the grade school principal from Waukesha who will tell us what he remembers of a shy orphan named Billy Dance? How about the enlistment records of the Marines?

"The fact is that this man was a ward of the State of Wisconsin in the seventies, that this homeless boy was remanded to juvenile detention centers instead of foster care, that at seventeen he fled the Racine Institute of Corrections, that he walked and hitchhiked from Wisconsin to Washington, DC, thinking he needed to go to the capital to join up for the Gulf War. He was so eager to make something of himself and defend his country that he volunteered for the Marines, that he landed in battle the very next year and was lost during the push to Baghdad.

"Lost to us, yes, but not to Saddam Hussein. It was 1991, and the nineteen-year-old Dance was interrogated day and night. He was beaten savagely when he gave no information, not even name, rank, and serial number. He so wanted to be true to his country that he purged his mind of everything. He became a shock-induced amnesiac. I, too, have expert witnesses to establish the reality of such conditions. He was beaten near to death many times, and each torment was like the first, because he blocked out the wounds as they happened. Still, the bullet wounds and torture scars on his body remember those days that he cannot.

"We left Iraq. William stayed. We gave up seeking him. He – though he had wiped his mind clean of all the particulars of his previous life, such as it was – kept alive in his heart some homing reflex. He, who had never had a true home, still yearned to return to his country.

"Then, twelve years later, we came back to Baghdad and found William Dance, the 'crazy American pin-cushion,' as his captors liked to call him, in one of the rape rooms of Abu Ghraib prison. The American soldiers who rescued him seemed like angels carrying him out of the hands of devils, and Dance was soon slated to appear with President Bush in the Rose Garden.

"He never did. While in the charge of his rescuers, William witnessed an American atrocity. Before his very eyes, his rescuing angels turned to tormenting devils.

"Dance could take no more. He spoke out against what we were doing in Baghdad, spoke out against the president whose reign of war was as brutal as Saddam's reign of terror, spoke out to the first reporter he could find, a man who happened to work for Al Jazeera…"

As a low groan came from the crowd, Counselor Barnett paced slowly, nodded at the floor. When the courtroom had settled to silence again, she held her hand out toward her client.

"This prisoner of war – missing in action for twelve years – was no longer invited to the Rose Garden. No, sir. William B Dance, POW MIA, was remanded to Guantanamo."

This time, the crowd gasped. Counselor Barnett lifted her eyes, and they sparked with fire.

"You bet. Gitmo. Waterboarding's just the beginning at Gitmo. When you're at Gitmo, the interview's not over till there's blood. When you're at Gitmo, the interview is never over. So, the guy was saved from beatings by the Butcher of Baghdad only to get beat by Uncle Sam himself!"

The hubbub of the crowd caused Judge Devlin to rap her gavel. "Quiet down, all of you. This isn't story time. This is a trial!"

Counselor Barnett nodded her thanks to the judge. "Well, William escaped Guantanamo the only way you can: by playing dead. Yes, he got out in a body bag and went to an American base in Mexico and then waded the Rio Grande to reach America.

"Remember, we are talking about a Marine, trained until his survival skills were instinctive. We're talking about a man who lived through thirteen years of torture. When he returned home to Milwaukee, who was there to deprogram him? Who was there to tell him the war was over, that he wasn't surrounded by enemies? No one. He fought onward, slaying anyone who endangered his mission.

"What mission, you ask? The same mission of every Marine, to follow orders, to take and hold enemy soil, and to slay any who seek to harm his country. These are powerful directives, especially when indoctrinated into the mind of a twenty year-old, especially when they are deepened and transformed by thirteen years of agony.

"What happens to good soldiers when their minds are impregnated so young and then abandoned, so that doctrines grow and grow? William Dance came to believe he was the Angel of Death for Milwaukee and Chicago, making certain anyone who died in this area died well.

"Into this terrifying delusion came a single ray of humanity: Detective Donna Leland of the Burlington Police Department. William fell in love with her. Nearly twenty years of insanity slowly dissolved away. At last, he began to regain his humanity.

"In the end, Your Honor, people of Wisconsin, what we have here is no demon-possessed man living among the graves. What we have is the lost lamb who, after all the torments he has endured, has gone crazy. Perhaps the prosecution is correct that William knows right from wrong, but William learned right and wrong in Marine boot camp and the sun-baked sands of the Middle East.

"How could we, who abandoned him, possibly condemn him to a lifetime of punishment for it? Isn't it time we deprogrammed the creature we programmed in the first place? To paraphrase the prosecution, William has already been abandoned by so many people in his life – parents, the state, the Marines, the country, the world. Do not abandon him again."

* * *

The body bag was cold. Not as cold as the trash bin had been when it stopped raining, but this was cold. And loud. And dark. There were other bodies all around – real bodies, and they smelled. They shifted with the plane.

How long do they fly these? Do they fly them forever? Did I fall asleep when they landed and now I'm awake and they're flying again? They do fly them forever.

The cold hurt his ears and his eyes. There wasn't enough air. He breathed very fast.

He wished for his scorpion saints.

SIXTEEN

Donna stood in her bathroom and stared at herself in the medicine cabinet mirror. The trial had dragged on for three weeks so far. She had worn every decent outfit in her wardrobe, twice – and that was after a spree at Kohls. The pundits were beginning to name the days after her outfits.

And her makeup had evolved, too. At first, she had tried to look like the all-American girl, healthy and happy. The press didn't buy it. About a week ago, she started making herself up as the supportive but wronged wife – less foundation, less blush, less care. The press liked that look. They had even run side-by-side shots of her at the beginning of the trial and two weeks in, showing the toll the trial was taking. But what look now? Perhaps she should go without makeup, without attempting to hide who she was.

"But who am I?" Donna asked herself, the mascara brush hovering beside her cheek. "Who am I, really?"

Someone who can't save Azra.

Someone who couldn't save Kerry.

Someone who won't even save herself.

It's a church, Azra thought idly, struggling to banish the boredom of the third week of testimony. They have styled their courtrooms after churches.

The long chamber had a high clerestory of double-paned windows, a chancel raised three steps from the pew-filled nave, a mahogany altar worthy of Elijah, a pulpit where the bailiff lurked, a lectern where the Word of Truth was spoken by its witnesses, an acolyte with a silent, mystic machine that captured all that was said and done for the record, even gun-toting ushers who passed at intervals down the center aisle, as if hoping for an offering.

Judge Devlin made an impressive deity, and before her cavorted rival ministers, seeking her approval. There was Lynda Barnett, the Baptist matriarch in neo-African garb. There was also Attorney Jim Franklin, the young televangelist – white, tall, male, and cocky in his light suit and white patent leather Pat Boone shoes.

How fitting that a fallen angel be tried in a church, Azra thought. Of course, given the church's record with trying heretics – witches, Moors, scientists, Jews, Sons of God – the prospects aren't good.

The media had made him a monster, the incarnation of evil. The deepest fears and dreads of the world were projected onto his empty soul.

He reached out, taking hold of Donna's hand. She returned the squeeze, though with stiff fingers – a kind of rictus dread. Her eyes were focused on the current witness. The trial was withering Donna. It was drawing the life out of her. It was as though the seat that held her was an inquisitor's rack, and with every question, she was being slowly, mercilessly, pulled apart.

One such inquisitor was the FBI profiler giving expert testimony even now. His fundamental argument had been and would continue to be thus: I've sent plenty of his kind away, so trust me to lock up this one, too.

"Fully capable, yes... One inmate had told me the key to faking a mental illness was to do it all the time, even when you think nobody is watching... Yes... I've known quite a few who knew of it and read it... *DSM-IV*, now...Yes, that's right... Edmund Kemper had read the *Diagnostic Statistical Manual III* cover-to-cover and said they'd have to put in a special entry for him in *DSM-IV*, since none of it covered him... That would be purely conjecture... It's easy enough to come by. I'd bet fifty bucks there's a copy of it in this courthouse... Yes... A good library would have it, too."

Azra hadn't been listening closely enough to catch Counselor Franklin's questions, but then the man turned toward him. "You examined Mr Doe when?"

"Three days ago, only three hours after I got in from Quantico."

"So, after the second week of trial?"

"Yes."

"And he told you he believed he was a fallen angel?"

"Yes."

"Was your impression that he was lying?"

"Objection," interrupted Counselor Barnett without standing or looking up. "Leading."

"I'll rephrase," said Franklin, nodding an apology to the judge. "What was your impression of this *story*?"

"Objection."

"All right, did you think he believed what he was saying?"

The witness said, "That's, perhaps, a misleading question."

Judge Devlin looked at him through her reading glasses, and her eyes looked like big black crescents on her face. "Answer it."

"Yes. He seemed to believe what he was saying."

"But, correct me if I'm wrong: psychopaths are expert liars."

"Objection, Your Honor," said Barnett wearily. "The district attorney has just put the word 'psychopath' in the mouth of the witness."

"Sustained."

Mr Franklin gave the defender a smoldering stare. "All right, let's cut to it. From your experience as a profiler with the FBI, do you think Mr Doe is a psychopath?"

"Absolutely. A classic case."

"Do you think he knows right from wrong?"

"Absolutely. He is well organized and methodical."

"Do you think he is a – let me get the wording right from the psychiatrist – 'paranoid schizophrenic with a narcissistic personality disorder?'"

"I think he would like to be."

The crowd laughed at that.

"You think he's lying?"

"Objection. Leading."

"Sustained."

"All right, in your own words, what do you think?"

"I'd sooner believe a story from Berkowitz's dog than one from him. Yes, I think he's lying."

There wasn't desert here. It was hot but not dry. It was sultry.

He had been out of the body bag before the plane landed. He had put an empty boot in the bag so it would seem there was someone in it – not much of someone, but enough to keep people from looking inside. Then he put on a flight suit and waited until landing and hid behind a crate until the breach ramp of the Hercules cargo plane was open and then stepped onto the ramp like he was ground crew coming to help unload. He helped unload. There were some of those bags that had less than a boot in them.

He could see where he was – a military base. Planes all around and tarmac and fences with rolls of barbed wire on top. The bags were going into a truck. After that, they'd be going into the ground or up into the air.

The men that had loaded the bodies climbed into the truck. He climbed up into the back. When somebody shouted at him, he just said, "They told me I had to dig." They let him ride in the back with the bags.

It was dark soon, and when the truck slowed down to straddle a dead coyote in the road, he slid from the bumper and was standing there as the brake lights went off and the tail lights dragged away, red, behind the truck and left him in the dark.

After being dead for three days, he ate his first meal.

Raw coyote tastes like life.

The trial was an endless torment. Questions coursed through Azra like X-rays. At first, his flesh was insensible to the onslaught, but now every tissue was red and swollen, every sinew stood out clear against bone. The jury, the judge, the public had probed and mapped each neuron of his mind. Their eyes, their ears, their opinions blazed over him all day every day.

And when the day was done, it was back into darkness. A thin sliver of light coming around a stale crust of bread. Miserable. Hopeless, except for that vision of Donna, the ticklish delight of his own body, the hot ecstasy, the moment of ignominious discovery. *"Put your pecker away..."* It was the type and substance of human experience.

For these creatures – that man in the preacher's suit and this woman dressed like some voodoo mambo, and this friend wasting away beside him, with him – for all of them, existence was like this: beginning and ending and forever mired in desire and despair.

It was like this for Azra, now, too. He was human. He couldn't escape it. He was human and had to live. It was not a choice between divinity or mortality. It was a choice between living or dying. And he chose to live. There would be lies and trickery, of course –

compromise and madness, cheating and stealing – but he would do whatever it would take to live. To live, and to cling to humanity, to this one woman.

I spent so long arranging the deaths of mortals, but I didn't understand them in the slightest. Not until I loved one. Not until I became one.

I stutter-step through the dimly lit hallway that leads from the trial room to the holding cells. One officer walks ahead of me. He is thin and old and long of face. He looks constantly disappointed. The one behind me is muscular and silent. He steps on the heel of my wing-tip shoe and flattens it behind my foot. He hadn't meant to, and I will be back to my cell soon enough. I can fix it there.

We turn a corner. There is a bright flash. Everything is spots for a moment. Then I am pushed to the floor and someone kneels on my back. It's the thin man. My hands are crunched beneath my chest.

The other cop has leaped past me to tackle someone in a side passage. There are the dull thuds of elbows and heads against cinder block. I look sideways but can't see much because of the corner.

"Hey! Hey, easy! This is an expensive camera."

"It'll be an expensive piece of junk if you don't lie still. How the hell'd you get in here?"

"I dropped a couple fifties back here, and they let me come look for them. Ah, here they are. You'd better take them as evidence."

"Get up," growled the cop. "Get up and get the hell out. Fucking reporters."

"Give me a fifty, and I'll give you a quote," I say to the reporter.

The cop on my back leans his knee into me, but even so, a crumpled bill rolls around the corner to me. The cop snatches it up.

"Well," says the reporter, "give."

"He took my money."

"Henry, for God sakes, give it," hisses the other guard. "We could all be put up for this."

Henry brusquely rolls me over and rams the money into my crushed fingers. "There, you murdering fuck, you happy?"

"Give!"

"I'm human today, for the first time," I say, feeling the warm, dirty wrinkle of the bill in my hands.

SEVENTEEN

They were having a parade. They were naked in the middle of the street. The banners they had were bright and up in the air, not down around their waists like they would be in a painting. He saw them, the strong, hairy, hard man bodies and the smiles. He chanted with them.

The East Village, they called it. East because it was like Eden, and Village because it was a primal place where people go around without clothes.

He pulled off his clothes and followed with the others and went home with one of them and had sex with him and stabbed him and cut off his head and hands.

"I call now to the stand," Lynda Barnett announced, "Peter J Dance, brother to the accused."

The rumble that went through the crowd had the sweeping momentum of a wave. Azra sat up with the rest of the people and shifted in his seat to get a better look at the man walking down the center aisle.

He was tall and lean, with Azra's build. Older by perhaps eight years, Peter Dance had a flat ring of black hair laurel-like around his head, and a shiny bald top. His eyes were haunted, his feet lagged behind him, and between slightly parted lips showed a row of stumpy teeth. His clothes hung on him as if he were a hanger instead of a man.

"I object, Your Honor," said District Attorney Franklin, standing. "This witness was not on the defense's list."

Azra nodded in agreement.

"Your Honor," Barnett explained, "I was unaware of this witness until late yesterday. The status of my client as an amnesiac leaves a great deal of doubt about his past. It has been a long, difficult process investigating that."

"But, Your Honor, if this witness appeared just yesterday, how can Counselor Barnett be sure of his identity?"

"Counselor Barnett, you will provide the court with documentation as to the identity of this witness."

Lynda Barnett nodded. Her head was bowed in thought behind her briefcase. The gold and green embroidery of her vest reflected sunlight beneath her chin, nostrils, and brows. It looked as if she were staring down into a treasure trove. She produced a folder of papers and approached the bench. "I would like to enter into the record these copies of Mr Dance's identification. This packet includes, among other things, two birth certificates issued from Fort Atkinson Memorial

Hospital, one for Peter James Dance in 1964 and another for his brother, William Bruce Dance in 1972, to the same parents."

The judge received the documents and slipped on her reading glasses. She perused them, running her thumb over the embossed seals. Lips pursed, she said, "I'll rule these admissible. Bailiff, please designate these Items 138 and 139 and enter them into evidence. I will review the rest of this packet later. On the basis of this evidence, I will allow Peter Dance's testimony," said the judge above her crescent-shaped reading glasses.

Counselor Franklin said, "Your honor, I have had no time to prepare for this witness."

"You can cross-examine on Monday. In the meantime, Mr Dance, will you please take the stand."

Peter Dance took his place on the witness stand.

"For the record of the court, please state your full name," said the bailiff.

"Peter James Dance," said the man in quiet nervousness, adding afterward, "esquire."

Judge Devlin quirked an eyebrow. "You're a lawyer?"

"Um – no, ma'am."

During the resultant ripple of amusement, the bailiff swore him in.

"Counselor, proceed with your questioning."

"Thank you, Your Honor," said Barnett, beginning to pace. "Mr Dance. Mr Peter Dance, how old were you when you last saw your brother?"

The man blinked in thought, cleared his throat, and said, "Twenty-five, when Billy was seventeen."

Azra watched the man like a hawk. Donna clutched his arm.

"So, you are eight years older?"

"Objection. Leading."

"It's simple mathematics."

"Overruled."

Barnett continued. "And how old are you now?"

"Forty-four." The man gestured toward the defense table. "So you must be thirty-six, Billy."

The public defender pressed. "And what had happened to Billy at seventeen?"

"Don't know. He disappeared. Billy'd always been a problem. He didn't live with us – with me and our stepdad – but in the boys' school. Dad would bring him home sometimes, but not much. Then, at seventeen, Billy disappeared from Boys Town. Dad said he ran off and would be back. His friends said he'd been talking about joining the circus. I thought he was dead."

"Why did you think he was dead?"

"He'd almost got killed five or six times before then. Our stepdad used to beat us pretty bad – Billy especially. He did more wrong than I ever did. Dad said Billy'd never live to graduate high school. Guess you showed him, huh, Billy?"

Judge Devlin said, "Will the witness please address his comments only to the counselor asking the questions?"

"Sorry, Judge," Peter Dance replied, hanging his head. Then he looked up, wide eyes fixed on Linda Barnett. "I mean, uh, please tell the judge I'm sorry."

Linda nodded, smiling despite herself. "You said 'Billy did more wrong' than you did. What kind of 'wrong' things did Billy do?"

"He was a little fag. That's what Dad called him. Little Faggot."

"Tell us about your stepfather," Barnett said.

"Objection. What's the relevance?"

"I'm attempting to establish Billy's motives for running away."

"Objection overruled. Continue, Counselor."

"I still object. The question is vague."

"I'll restate. What did your stepfather do for a living?"

"He'd been a mechanic. Worked at J and C Garage. He called it Jesus Christ Garage."

"Was he working there when Billy disappeared?"

"No. He'd been laid off three years. There was food stamps and public aid for a while, and he worked odd jobs. He used to beat us a lot then. Before, he wasn't home so much and didn't beat us so much. But he never beat us on Friday or Saturday nights, except on our feet. He didn't want us to show bruises for Sunday."

"When did your stepfather start calling Billy the Little Faggot?"

"After Dad got into the Klan."

Through the hushed gasp from the spectators, Barnett continued. "When did he get involved with the Klan?"

"When I was twenty-two, so Billy must have been fourteen. That was just after he caught Billy sexing David Bergmeyer from up on the pavement. Fags and

Jews. He beat both of them. The Bergmeyers tried to sue, but he burned them out. That was what got him in the Klan."

"Did your stepfather have any other nicknames for Billy?"

"He used to call him, 'Little Killer,' or the 'Little Motherfucker.'"

"Why?"

"Because he'd fucked up our mother. That's why we were orphaned. Billy killed her by being born."

"You said something about Billy joining the circus?"

"Well, yeah, the circus. But I knew what Billy really meant. He was talking about the *service*. I'd been in for two years, and Billy always said he wanted to go. He liked guns and stuff, and he said he wanted to join the Marines because it would be like being in the circus, only you got to shoot people."

"So Billy joined the Marines at eighteen?"

"Right. That's what we found out later, when he was twenty. We got this postcard from Baghdad."

"So, he fought in the first Gulf War?"

"Objection. Leading."

"Overruled."

"Yeah – the good one. Desert Storm. He fought in that one is what the postcard said. The one and only postcard. We didn't hear then for a year, and I tried to find out where he was stationed, but by then the Marines said they didn't have no record of him."

"Why didn't they have any record?"

"Objection. How can the witness speculate about the reason the Marines didn't have records?"

"Your Honor," Barnett said, "this is ridiculous."

"Rephrase, Counselor."

"Why did you think that the Marines had no record?"

"Stepdad said it was because Billy was gay. That was when 'don't ask don't tell' came in, so Dad figured they'd found out he was gay and so kicked him out and wouldn't talk about him. We asked, and they didn't tell."

"Did you agree with your stepfather's idea?"

"Well, I figured Billy might just plain be dead. I kind of hoped he was. He'd've been better off."

"Why did you think that?"

"Because even if them sand niggers didn't kill Billy–" Dance's eyes grew wide. "No offense. When I said, 'sand nigger,' I didn't mean people like you."

"No," Barnett replied, "I'm a regular nigger. But you were saying that if the Iraqis didn't kill Billy…?"

"Yeah, if they didn't, well, Dad was going to. He'd talked about it with his Klan friends. They'd planned to kill Billy."

"Did your brother know of this plan?"

"I didn't think so. That's why when he disappeared the day they were going to kill him, I thought he was dead."

"So, before you knew he'd joined the Marines, you thought maybe he'd been killed by your stepfather?"

"Yeah, and then after I found out he joined the Marines and disappeared, well, I thought maybe that was better."

"Didn't it bother you that your stepfather planned to kill your brother?"

Dance shrugged. "He was a faggot. I wasn't allowed to care about him. I had a dream about him afterward, though."

"I object. Relevance."

"Overruled. Continue."

"What was your dream?"

"I had this dream of what it was like when I was about ten and Jeffrey about seven and Teri about three and Billy about two, except that mom was still alive. Jeffrey and Teri got killed in a car accident on their way to the other home. Anyway, we were all in the living room, dressed up for church. My stepdad was there, too. He had on a gray suit, and Mom a knee-length orange dress, one of the flat kind from the seventies, and I had my red crushed velvet vest with the little gold chains across the buttons."

"Your memory is very vivid."

"It was the worst dream I ever had."

"Continue."

"And Jeffrey also had on the crushed velvet jacket but a pair of blue plaid pants, and Teri a little white dress she wore at Easter one year, and then Billy, two years old, was naked and standing at the end of the line."

"Why was he naked?"

"Objection. Calls for speculation."

"It was his dream, Your Honor."

"Objection overruled. Continue."

"I asked Dad that same question, 'Why isn't Billy ready for church?' He said, 'Oh, he's ready. He's going to be the burnt offering this morning.' And as I looked at Billy, standing there, I saw he was already burned in a few places, his fingers kind of stuck together and his eyelids burned closed, and I realized it wasn't just this Sunday but last Sunday and next Sunday and the next until he was all burned up."

"Your Honor, I move that this whole dream be stricken from the record. It is an irrelevant, forty year-old fantasy."

"Your Honor, I am trying to establish the environment from which my client came, not just the physical environment but also the social and emotional one."

"I'm going to allow it. Mr Franklin, remember, you will get a cross-examination on Monday. You can address your concerns about the testimony then."

"Mr Dance, you said the disappearance and possible murder of your brother did not upset you that much, since he was homosexual – in your words, a faggot."

"Yes, that's right."

"Well, then, why did this dream upset you?"

"Well, ma'am, in the dream I got the idea he was kind of the queer savior."

"What do you mean by that?"

"Well, you know how the book of Hebrews says Jesus died once for all men, that his sacrifice was full and complete?"

"Yes," Barnett replied, "in the tenth chapter."

"Yeah, and it says 'when he cometh into the world, he saith, Sacrifice and offering thou wouldst not, but a body hast thou prepared for me: In burnt offerings and sacrifices for sin thou hast had no pleasure. Then said I, Lo, I come to do thy will, O God. By which all men are sanctified through the offering of the body of Jesus Christ, once for all.'"

"Yes?"

"Well, since Billy wasn't really a man, I figured maybe he needed to be a burnt offering for the sins of faggots, or maybe he was the Jesus for faggots, so when he died, they would all be saved."

Lynda Barnett nodded, her soft-soled shoes pacing across the cold marble floor. "To conclude this examination, Your Honor, I would like to submit as evidence this old photo album, filled with forty-eight pages of pictures of life in the Keen household, including pictures of the boy Peter Dance and his younger brother, William." She handed the album up to the judge and turned toward her seat. "No more questions."

I sit in the interrogation room and page through the black-and-white ghosts of a life I had forgotten. They gave me photocopies of the album. They wouldn't trust me with the actual evidence. The images in the book are made only more phantasmal by thin shadows and grain. Dark eyes become black wells. Faces bleach away to masks. Dirt and age add their defamations.

There, that boy there with the disarming smile that shows no teeth, and the eyes down-turned and

squinted against the sun from the white clapboards –
that boy is me. And this one, too, who stands beside an
old grave man in a cluttered room with twelve-foot
ceilings. And that one, no more than a blur on the rusty
playground slide, set in the depression below the walls
of fieldstone and galvanized fencing. They are all me,
or were me. They are all the embryonic hope that became this mature despair.

My brother – the pictures of him show a cocky young
man in uniform, home visiting from whatever base he
was stationed at. I find one with him beside the old
slide, something small and metallic glinting in a white-
gloved hand. Could he be the same blasted figure I had
seen testifying in court yesterday?

Fate had only bad things in store for the Dance brothers.

My brother. I do not remember him, but I hate him.
He tastes like poison. What once nearly killed us is ever
after despised by every tissue of our bodies.

I was wrong. He proves it. Those photos prove it.
They bring old memories floating upward like swollen
bodies in black, still water.

The puppy that wriggles in the grass next to my
knee, hot-splotched by summer sun; the crooked stick
braced outward from my body like a ruined sword, and
caught still in its violent rush toward the tree
trunk; the old rankle of white pickets beneath the
overhanging backyard tree in which I hang as though
daring the spikes to impale me; the angled bed in that
tiny back bedroom where I lay, the blankets strewn un-

evenly across me so that a jammied bottom showed from the fold of quilts...

Me. Me. Me.

All my former memories were illusions, all my thoughts of angelic power. With each passing day of this trial, new ghosts rise to the seat of testimony to convict me – not of murders to which I have confessed, but of humanity and history, which I have for so long denied. Speakers, words, photos, visions.

They say I was an orphan. They say I was a homosexual youth from a dysfunctional home. They say I was a soldier. They say I was a prisoner of war. They say that now I am at least a very sick man, perhaps a very evil man.

And, worst of all, I am beginning to remember. I remember being in Abu Ghraib. I remember the beatings. I remember when the American soldiers came in and shot my guard in the head and got me out with his key. I remember the interrogations, the blank looks of amazement on the faces of the soldiers, the dark looks of greed on the faces of the general.

There was a phone call from the president – a well wishing, a chance to talk, to see if maybe I could be his poster child for Operation Iraqi Freedom. And after I was well enough to travel, there was the trip to the airport, when the convoy passed by soldiers emptying clip after clip of hollow-point rounds into a crowd of women in burkhas. I remember them going down in black fabric and blood and I remember the joke that the man in the Humvee beside me told: "What's black and

white and red all over? A penguin with diaper rash." I
began shouting for the soldiers to stop, and the man's
face fell. His face touched off an avalanche of frowns –
all scowling at their poster child gone wrong.

Instead of a flight home, there was a flight to Guantanamo. Instead of freedom, there was a new
interrogation room. Cells. Shackles. I remember the
beatings. I remember lying so bloody and still they
thought I was dead. I thought I was, too. I remember
the body bag zipping up over me. I remember it all.

But how can any of this be true? It is too close to
what I had plotted with Derek. Did I half-remember it
even then and think I was only concocting it?

How can it not be true? How can memories as vivid
as these be made up by my mind without my even realizing it? There is a syndrome, a false memory
syndrome, where people remember horrific, ritual
abuse even though there was none. But which is
worse, to have endured these torments, or to have invented them and believed them and fantasized about
them?

Herbert Mullins. I'd been reading about others like
me. He believed he was offering human sacrifices to nature to prevent California from falling into the ocean.
He believed he did an otherwise heinous act for a di-
vinely justified reason. And when describing the
murder of an entire family, he told police that they had
asked him to kill them, that they had volunteered to be
sacrifices for the good of the world.

I'm no angel, but another Herbert Mullins.

How strange, after all this time, to be realizing this only now. How strange, just before punishment is meted out, to become at last convinced of my own crimes and penitent of them, to become suddenly a different creature than the one who had committed the crimes.

Donna didn't say a word as Azra flipped through the photocopies of his life. He didn't even seem to know she was there, even though she sat beside him and held his hand and hoped against hope that he would remember who he was.

He did. He remembered. She could see it in his eyes. Where once there was only delusion, now there was a pit of grief.

Donna began to cry. What a cold comfort, to remember a life worth forgetting.

DEFENSE MAKES MAN OF MONSTER
AP International
Photo and Story by Blake Gaines

"I am human today, for the first time," claimed alleged serial killer John Doe, a.k.a., William Bruce Dance, a.k.a., Son of Samael.

The comment followed Wednesday's trial session.

Doe's claim was supported by testimony Friday from surprise witness Peter James Dance, purported to be Doe's brother.

Dance indicated that his brother's homosexuality made their stepfather try to kill Doe.

According to Dance, their stepfather was a Klansman. Dance said their real mother had died in giving birth to Doe, whom he called Billy.

Public Defender Lynda Barnett emphasized the suffering the alleged killer endured in his early years. Barnett summed the last two weeks' testimony, "[Doe has] serious reality issues. He has been wronged and abandoned habitually from his earliest days."

The public defender went on to say, "[Doe is] an American patriot, returning wounded from the Gulf War fifteen years late."

EIGHTEEN

It was the first day in over two months that Donna had been home by five o'clock, what with prison visits, NCIC searches, and meetings with the VFW and mental health advocacy groups. Even today, she came home only due to the undeniable call of nature – her septic holding tank had been full for three weeks, and it had finally backed up. Instead of crouching at her computer and impatiently coaxing piece after piece of William Dance from scattered, incomplete and damaged documents, Donna had spent the evening on hands and knees, scrubbing urine water from her bathroom floor. She called for the pump truck and said it was an emergency and said she'd pay for it. Just after that was done, she thought to call the power company and leave a message assuring them a check would be posted tomorrow. At one time, she would have panicked over a single late notice. Now, after three, she recognized the lapse only dully.

She was hungry. The refrigerator was bare except for a moldy loaf of bread, the desiccated remains of a quarter pounder and fries, a flat bottle of Diet Rite, ketchup, a bag of withered apples, and a jar of three year-old pickles. The cabinet was not much more promising – Jiffy mix, stale cereal, five boxes of Jell-O, a can of beets, a bag of dried lentils, a bag of popcorn.

Donna drew out the popcorn bag, unfolded it, and lay it on the dusty carousel of the microwave. She hit the "Popcorn" button. The disused machine lit up. Its fan began to blow, and the bag rotated hypnotically. Donna leaned against the counter and stared for a while at the wall behind the stove, noted the grease-and-dust choked spider webs that clung to the hood vent. The smell of hot oil and corn swept over her. She breathed placidly. It felt as though she hadn't breathed in months.

How long has it been since I had a life of my own? How long since I could sit in that love seat and watch a movie?

As the first kernels exploded, little suicide bombers that shook the whole bag, Donna turned away and wandered toward the front door. Three plastic bags slumped there, one filled with hate-mail sent to her at the station house, another with notebooks from the psych sessions, and a third with –

"Ah ha!" she said, triumphantly lifting the DVD case from the bag. Its black-and-white case showed a dark garden where a boy and girl lingered beside an imploring statue of an angel. Their hands probed together at the base of the statue, where lay the inscription "Eternity." The title at the top of the tape read, "Tennessee Williams – Summer and Smoke." She had ordered the DVD before Azra's arrest, but Amazon had had to search high and low for a used copy. It arrived a week ago, but there had been no time to watch it – until tonight.

Inside the microwave, the popcorn bag was shuddering and convulsing like an epileptic guinea pig. The fit slackened into a few hiccups, and the bag lay still and smoking.

"Damn it," Donna said, racing from the front door to jab the "Open" button. The door popped wide and the acrid smell of burnt popcorn billowed out over her. The smoke detector went off. "Mother of God!" She tore down the detector and wrenched loose its battery. It seemed her life was all alarms and last-minute saves.

Outside, the pump truck growled and wheezed, a fat hose sucking up her septic.

A few minutes later, all was placid again. Donna sat before the TV, half a bag of chips before her, *Summer and Smoke* beginning on the screen, and sad thoughts of Azra haunting the seat beside her.

She dozed. In her dreams, he was there. It all was as it had been before.

The DVD was almost over when she awoke. A young doctor and a young woman were in the doctor's office, he calm and professional, she trembling and distraught. She was pleading with him, drawing nearer, reaching toward him as the girl on the DVD case had reached toward the angel. She told him that the girl who once rejected him was gone, dead – asphyxiated by the fire burning within her. She said that she had given up her pride, that pride only prevented people from having what they needed.

The doctor gently pulled her hands away, and the woman seemed crushed. He explained that she had won the argument between them. He pointed to a diagram of vivisected human anatomy and said that the insides of humans weren't rose leaves but ugly organs, packed so tightly there wasn't room for anything spiritual. "But I've come around to your way of thinking, that something else is in there, an immaterial something – as thin as smoke – which all of those ugly machines combine to produce and that's their whole reason for being."

He was dumping her. He was offering a spiritual bond instead of a physical one.

"Mother of God," Donna said, pausing the movie. It was like Tennessee Williams was watching right through the bay window.

She stood, stretched, and walked across the too-long shag of her living room. She turned a corner into the bathroom – a long thin galley with a deformed sink, a pessimistic old toilet, and a bathtub stained with rusty water. She sat on the toilet, elbows on knees, and stared down at the gloves and rags she had used to scrub the floor. Finishing, she stood. The mirror showed back a stranger – hair needing a trim, wild about her shoulders, eyes ten years older – and where was her smile, her long and patient smile?

Perhaps the place to find her smile would be her toothbrush. She opened wide the medicine cabinet and reached numbly for the brush. Her hand instead grasped a tampon, the last one left. She'd meant to buy more, but that was a couple months ago, and she had forgotten...

"Mother of God..."

Of its own accord, her hand slumped from the medicine cabinet and brought a shower of nail clippers and toothbrushes and razors down into the sink. Detective Leland herself landed on the floor.

The stocky, gray-haired men marched with nothing like their old glory. Their pectorals sagged under the weight of tiny medals. Their beer guts bounced. They marched. Most leaned back on their heels, their chins up as though they had to look through the bottoms of their bifocals to see the sidewalk. Those that weren't retirees were camouflaged and bearded, with the undefeated look of the southern soldiers after 1865.

This mismatched assortment would, perhaps, have seemed comical if it weren't for their number – sixty-seven parading before the Racine County Jail, and another forty-some shouting in a rally beside the outdoor directory. Perhaps more daunting than those numbers were the many in wheelchairs, the numerous amputees, and the signs they held above their heads.

FREE WILLIAM DANCE.
DON'T SPIT ON ME!

MIA – MISSING IN AMERICA!
POSTTRAUMATIC STRESS DISORDER
IS REAL
UNCLE SAM OR BIG BROTHER?
RACINE COUNTY CORRECTIONS: TOMB
OF THE UNKNOWN SOLDIER
HE'S ALREADY BEEN SENTENCED TO LIFE
GIVE 'EM HELL, SAM-A-EL!
I WAS CALLED MURDERER, TOO
WHEN JOHNNY COMES MARCHING HOME
ANOTHER VICTIM OF LIBERALISM
IF YOU THINK HEADS ROLLED BEFORE...
AMNESTY INTERNATIONAL? WHAT
ABOUT AMNESTY AMERICA?
WE PARDON DRAFT DODGERS BUT
NOT WAR HEROES?
WILLY B. SHOULD B SET FREE

And, were those things not enough, the Gay and Lesbian Association of Wisconsin – GALAW – had fielded forty-five marchers to picket the courthouse across the street.

There's something fragile in your eyes. Your hair is a little wild above a rumpled jacket of tweed. You tremble in the fluorescent glow pouring down from the interrogation table. It's late. They usually don't allow visits at this hour.

I want to stand, but the shackles on my wrists keep me down. "What is it, Donna? What's wrong?"

"Nothing." You smile dismissively and somehow manage to look even more miserable. "It's nothing." You cross to my side of the table, dragging a scudding chair with you. You sit and take my hands. "It's official, Sweetheart. You're human."

I'm confused. "They came back with a verdict?"

"No. No, the jury is still out," you say, adding cryptically, "but there has been a definite verdict. God has given a definite verdict."

I shake my head. "What are you talking about?"

"I'm carrying your baby. I'm going to be a mother. You're going to be a father. You are going to have a child," you reply. Tears trace the lines of your smile, and your laugh sounds half-sob. "We are going to be parents."

I'd never before felt such a storm of emotion. Now, there is wonder and terror in equal portions.

You're watching my face. You're terrified of what I think. You. You weep before me, ache to be held by me. I feel the same. Your fear, your joy, your determination and dread, your shame and pride.

I choke out, "I love you. You were right all along. This is good news. This is great news! Now – now, no matter what happens to me, there will be a part of me outside of prison walls. There will be a part of me flying kites in the park, playing video games, drinking a Coke, looking through the paper for free puppies–"

"Yes, yes," you say, excited through tears, "the child will have everything you never did. Birthday parties and playing in the sprinkler and trips to the Public Museum and the Museum of Science and Industry and the zoo, and love. Most of all, love."

I'm laughing now. I can't lift my hands to hold you, but I'm holding you with my eyes and my smile and the craving of my whole body. "You've been with me this whole time. You've been with me in this room and the hospital room and the courtroom, but also in solitary, also in the darkest spaces and moments, you've been with me. You've made it all bearable, livable – no, more than that. You've made it good. You've made it heaven. No matter what happens to me, as long as I have you, you and my child, I can be human and mad and in prison and still be in Heaven."

NINETEEN

The decorous courtroom had a different air today. Its solemnity had deepened to reverence, its moral outrage to a kind of giddy nausea. There was the very real impression of a crowd at the final judgment.

"Have you reached a verdict?" Judge Devlin asked the jury foreman, a heavyset black woman in her mid fifties.

Standing, the foreman said, "We have, Your Honor."

She proffered a folded slip of paper, which the bailiff retrieved and delivered to the judge. Sandra Devlin peered at the paper through her crescent-shaped reading lenses, folded the document again, and handed it back to the bailiff. He carried it again to the foreman.

Judge Devlin said, in an utterly unimpassioned voice, "For the record, please read your verdict.""Certainly, Your Honor. In the case of the State of Wisconsin versus John Doe, as regards the first charge of murder in the first degree, for the death of Derek Billings, we find the defendant… guilty."

An excited whoop came from some members of the crowd, many of whom clapped, and two of whom gave the gavel-rapping judge a standing ovation.

Donna clutched Azra's hand. He nodded to her, his tight-lipped smile of resignation parting just long enough for him to whisper, "It will be all right."

"As regards the second charge of murder in the first degree, for the death of Lawrence Teeds, we find the defendant… guilty."

The adulation resumed, less marked this time, more a cheer of vindication than one of vindictiveness.

Donna and Azra sat, hand in hand, facing bravely forward.

"As regards the third charge of murder in the first degree, for the death of Jules Koenig, we find the defendant guilty." The foreman paused, seeming to expect another outburst, but none followed. "As regards the fourth charge of murder in the first degree, for the death of Lynn Blautsmeyer, we find the defendant guilty. As regards the fifth charge of murder in the first degree, for the death of David Miller, we find the defendant guilty. As regards the sixth and final charge of murder in the first degree, for the death of Harold Cruze, we find the defendant guilty."

There came a patter of applause like a gentle rain. Relief moved like a mist through the room. Even Donna and Azra seemed grateful that the long trial was finished.

Judge Devlin rapped her gavel, regaining the floor. "I have reached a sentencing decision." She let out a heavy sigh. "The man who sits here among us has no certain name. John Doe, Azrael Michaels, Samael, the Son of Samael, William B. Dance. Nor does he have a certain past – abused minor, runaway, POW, amnesiac, war hero, serial killer, angel. Whoever he is and whatever his past, though, he is guilty of heinous crimes, the most recent of which was committed while incarcerated just across the street in the jail. And those certain crimes require certain punishment.

"For your crimes, John Doe, a.k.a. William Dance, you will live out the rest of your life behind bars. You will serve out six consecutive life sentences without possibility for parole."

More clapping erupted. Reporters typed furiously on their laptops, sending the verdict through Wi-Fi to their editors, to the world.

"Quiet down. I'm not finished," the judge ordered. Once the chamber had settled again into silence, the judge resumed. "However, as inconclusive as I consider the evidence to be in this case, I am convinced of one thing: You, John Doe, are not in your right mind. There will forever be arguments, I imagine, whether you are psychopathic or psychotic, whether you know right from wrong, or are incapable of knowing. Let the debates come.

"As for me, the critical evidence is the slaying of your cell mate, a man the other prisoners have testified to be your only friend. To slay your only friend while awaiting trial, and to do so with no apparent concern for your clear guilt in the matter, demonstrates a mind that – while cunning and ruthless – is out of touch with reality.

"I therefore remand you to the Wisconsin State Prison at Columbia, there to receive psychiatric assistance but also there to remain without the possibility of release for the remainder of your life. You will begin this sentence unless it is superseded by a harsher penalty from Illinois or Indiana, including the death penalty. And, whether you are human or angel or devil, may God have mercy on your soul."

The crowd was suddenly, noisily on its feet. Amidst the cheers and applause and hoots of delight were groans. Reporters shouted questions to the seated murderer and his cop lover. Photographers snapped pictures of the roaring crowd, the impassive man, and the embattled woman. There were even rumors she bore his child.Judge Devlin rapped loudly, calling for order, but none came. The already heavy police presence had been doubled for the day's announcement, but still the officers were spread thinly along the edges of the crowd and at the doors. One of Azra's own guards went to hold back the crowd. The other walked up behind him, hand grasping his holstered pistol. Camera flashes went off all around the room.

All the while, Azra and Donna sat, unmoving and unmoved.

The judge rose ominously, and the harsh *crack* of her gavel was joined by an order: "Clear the court! Clear the court!"

The back doors were flung wide. The line of police pressed into the gathering. In places, blackjacks were raised to push back the people.

Azra's other guard returned to help move the cuffed prisoner toward the holding cells. He turned to Donna, gave her a quick kiss, nodded sadly, and allowed himself to be led away. Azra did not resist, even thanking the blond-haired deputy who opened the door.

Donna Leland was numb. Her fingers tingled with pins and needles. She tightly clutched the steering wheel. The sun had already set. It was hard to see through the cracked windshield of her Neon, hard to see with only a single skewed headlight wandering over the road and out along the black rile of hills that lay between her and home.

She drove west down Route 11 – dark and tree-encroached, narrow and fifty-five miles an hour, with curves and oncoming traffic. The once-familiar shoulders and swales of Wisconsin felt forbidding and alien tonight. The people – once her friends and neighbors and colleagues – seemed enemies. *The People of Wisconsin versus John Doe. Versus Azra Michaels. Versus Donna Leland. Versus their unborn child*. The land glowered.

Remember Azra's place of bliss – our place of bliss. Soon I'll be there. Soon I'll be there and imagine him sitting beside me.

The memory of hurled rocks and shouted taunts was too strong, though. The picketers had called her whore and bitch. They had said she'd betrayed her badge. They had said she was as crazy as her lover.

There is little bliss in cracked windshields and shattered headlights.

Through it all, she had clung to him. She had saved him. Kerry had died of isolation, but not Azra. And he wouldn't die. He would live. She would cling to him. They would be isolated together.

Thank God the trial was over. Donna couldn't have hoped for a better outcome. After all, Azra was guilty of the murders. He was guilty and sick. He needed to live in an institution, needed therapy and protection. In the state penitentiary for the criminally insane, he would receive both. He would live – that's what she had wanted most – and he would be cared for. And she would be able to visit him frequently. The furor of rocks and death threats would make it easy enough to leave Burlington. She'd transfer to a department near the penitentiary. There would be more trials, of course, in Illinois and Indiana, and perhaps they would supersede this sentence with a worse one, but for now, he would live.

But enough rumination. She'd been ruminating for months now. Her thoughts held only pain and turmoil. She turned on the radio. There was a catchy tune on the country-western station. She was tapping her toes before she had begun to puzzle out the words:

There was a man who said he was an angel.
He said that he went killing for the Lord.
Then one bright day he killed my nuisance neighbor,
And now I just believe his every word.

Oh, hail and hallelujah,

Just see what John does to yah.
He'll help you keep your head,
lend you a hand.
Hello and howdy-do-ya,
They call him a hy-e-na,
But as for me, I think he's
just a lamb.

There was a sheriff's daughter who got horny
She knew the killer would do her no harm.
So she got herself a little tiny baby,
And he made quite a supper of her arm.

Oh hail, and hallelujah!
Just see what John does to yah...

It was the final assault. The music and the windshield and the cockeyed headlight conspired with hills and curves and haunting woods. She heard the tires squeal before she knew she was losing control, saw the world suck away beneath her as though in revulsion, and glimpsed the tree – massive kin of the tree that had almost slain her in her bedroom window. There was no Azra to save her this time, though, no angel to stand between fate and mortality.

"Mother of God, pray for us sinners–"

The impact broke through the outer shell of the tree trunk and into the hollow core, bringing the whole tree down atop her car.

* * *

This was not his cell. Azra was alone, yes, and the chamber was secure and about the size of the solitary confinement hole where he'd spent the last months. But this place was bright. He felt naked in it.

He saw himself everywhere. His bright orange coveralls leant an umber cast to the yellow-gray walls. The stainless steel bunk and metal toilet reflected his human face back to him. There was even a dark sheet of bulletproof glass outside the holding cell, and it mirrored the whole tableaux of his pathetic incarceration.

Beyond that glass wall was the squad room. The white shirted detectives were there, moving silently like kites in a dream. Heads, faces, hands, and pants blended into metal desks and gray walls. Only the shirts and the papers flitted in the darkness. The far wall held tacked bulletins, hanging diagonally. More kites, and more kites, receding into infinity.

Then, white roses came between the cell and the world of the kites – white roses on green-black stems held in the fist of a guard. The man was thin and getting old. He extended the fist of flowers through the bars of Azra's cell and flung the dozen long-stemmed roses down on the floor. They struck and rolled apart like a faggot of kindling. Little balls of blood speckled the man's palm where he had clutched the thorns.

"More flowers," he sneered through large, uneven teeth.

Azra stared at him. "More?"

"There're twelve other bouquets. They're in the squad room, dying."

"Flowers from whom?"

"You name it. Three different VFW branches, GALAW, the National Institute of Mental Health, a bunch of nut-jobs like yourself..."

"What about these?" asked Azra, rising to stare down at the scattered pile. "Who are they from?"

"That's why I brought them." The man bent to fish a small envelope from the stems and thorns. He lifted it, his blood smearing on the white paper. "It says: *Congratulations, Fuck-Head, on your latest kill. Burlington Police.*"

Azra stared at the bloodstained card. "What does that mean?"

"Didn't you hear? The woman you knocked up ran her car into a tree a half-hour ago. No other cars, no alcohol, no nothing. I guess she didn't want to live, knowing you'd been inside her. Congratulations, Fuck-Head."

Azra's eyes did not meet the man's. He watched the roses as though they were yet another body. He backed away until the bunk folded his knees, and he sat, eyes unmoving. His heart pounded.

How can it be? How can she be...? The thought was inconceivable. It was as though someone had told him the sun would no longer rise, that the world would slowly cool over the next three weeks to absolute zero, that they would all die. How could she leave?

"Oh, Donna, no." He felt sudden terror for her, for whatever pain she had felt, for those last regretful moments spent alone. "Oh, Donna, no."

The cell closed in around him. There would be no more place of bliss. There would be no more refuge. Around him closed the very fist of God.

That's who had done this. God had wanted Donna dead. He had wanted her dead four months ago. He had tried to kill her at the bedroom window, but Azra had stopped him. But at last, God had found a way to kill her. He had compelled another tree to yank its roots from the sucking earth and fall on her and crush her and crush the child within her.

"No matter what happens to me, as long as I have you, you and my child, I can be human and mad and in prison and still be in Heaven."

That was the main reason God had wanted her dead. She had dared to make Azra human, had dared, in defiance of divinity and mortality, to reach across the shredding fissure between the two worlds and touch him. She had become Azra's heaven, and God suffered no heaven but his own.

The roses were within easy reach. Azra retrieved them. He lay down on the bunk and sniffed the flowers. He saw Donna Leland, his guardian angel and his lover, floating in the dead heavy cement ceiling above him.

Some of the thorns were very strong, as big as a dog's claw but as sharp as a cat's. There was one thorn that was very strong and very sharp, indeed.

It felt right slicing into the veins of his arm.

It felt right slicing into the veins of his neck.

He lay there, blanketed in white blooms and warmed by his own blood seeping silently out onto cold steel and pooling in the indentation atop the bunk. A very human end. Perhaps not the right end for a serial killer, dying quietly, bedded in flowers and warm blood and safety. But perhaps there was no such thing as dying well. Perhaps humans just died.

He would know soon enough.

"I have been human for only weeks now. How can they stand it for year after Goddamned year?"

He was both cold and hot. There was a thrilling darkness hovering just above his consciousness, an unraveling net beyond which lay endless nothing. He disowned his limbs, one by one. They became mannequin parts, sliding loosely away from him – feet, calves, thighs, pelvis, arms, trunk. At last, all that was left was the head, the damnable violent ceaseless head.

It, and the scent of white roses.

Wailing women and a blood-painted world that jagged and jarred around him, with white linens and restraints on hands and feet, the conveyance listing like a ship but too fast for water, with the swing and jolt of steel waves, and hands not of steel but of flesh and stinging needles on plastic tubes and held down with tape. There was. There was.

Sirens. That's what. Not women, but sirens.

One was very close and muffled. On the roof. The back of the ambulance was crowded. Two police and an EMT and him and lots of drawers and compartments. There was lots of metal. Lots of hard, hard plastic.

The cops watched his eyes, but he didn't more than flutter them. The EMT watched plasma dripping from a bag and checked forearms made of cotton gauze and red juice. His neck was that way, too. The machines beeped, and so did the EMT, but the police were barking like watchdogs. They snarled through their teeth.

The ambulance sheared a corner, and all swayed to the side and up a moment before the torquing springs fought the ambulance back between the lanes. The long high wail of sirens stretched out, too. Cop squads behind. The pink that flashed through the cabin was cops ahead.

There was a clamp that held the stretcher to the wall – an old ambulance. The clamp was near his hand. It was easy to touch, but stiff.

Why, though? Why do it, Azra? A moment ago you wanted to die. Why now try to live? And another voice answered in his head. *There is no longer an Azra. Only a Samael. And why die? There is no need to die. Only to descend.*

He waited for the next wide corner, and then pulled hard. The stretcher slued sideways, ramming into the EMT's knees and dumping him onto the gauzy arms. Stainless steel handles struck the cops, likewise, and one of them collapsed across Azra's feet. The other had fumbled his gun out and pulled back the EMT and watched the patient's eyes, but nothing.

"Damn thing got me in the groin. Fuck!" said the cop on his knees.

The one with the gun kicked the stretcher back against the wall, where it bounced and came back at him. The EMT caught the edge of it this time and heaved hard to get it against the wall. He lifted the lever and, with the help of the leaning gunman, got the cart in place. The lever snapped to, and they both backed up.

"Where's my gun?"

A bullet went through his throat and shot out the top of the ambulance.

The man gurgled in red bubbles as he fell back, and then there were three holes in the head of the other officer. The EMT pushed himself up but slipped on the bloody floor and fell beside the cot. It swung into him again, bringing with it a hot gun muzzle and a madman.

"Release me, or you're dead."

The EMT sat for a moment, stunned. The madman lurched on the cot and shot the EMT's right ear off. Next moment, buckles came from the patient's wrists and hands, and he undid the straps. The killer sat up and shot the EMT through the left eye.

The ambulance's brakes shrieked. The driver shouted into the radio handset. The gurney rolled up toward the cabin door and smashed into it. Samael shoved the gurney back, flung himself through the door, and shot the last round through the driver's ear. Then he rolled him from the seat and scrambled spiderlike behind the wheel. Stomping on the accelerator, he pulled back out onto the road.

Sergeants Davis and Carls couldn't make out what the ambulance driver was saying except for "Pull over, pull over." That's what the other squads were doing, so Davis did the same, only to have the ambulance lurch out ahead of them all.

"Jesus Christ, what's he doing?" bellowed Carls, his eyes squinting beneath pudgy gray brows.

Davis, a middle-aged black man, only shrugged. The squad roared out behind the ambulance. Other cars followed.

The calls began crowing over the radio. "…driver said he was loose… shots fired… behind the wheel now, I'd say…"

The last supposition was proven as the ambulance pulled away from them all, fifty, seventy, ninety miles an hour.

"Kick it in, Davis. For God's sake. This ain't OJ."

The squad leaped in response, tires squealing at forty-five miles an hour. Cars Seven and Eleven muscled up on either side of them, with Twenty-Two screaming up behind. Ahead, the ambulance mounted the long belly of an on-ramp.

The captain's voice came over the radio, "…yes, call ahead. He's south-bound on Ninety-four… yeah, toward Kenosha. Current pace, he'll be there in a few minutes. Roadblock, hell yes… and helicopters. Better call down to Chicago. If we let him slip, he'll be in Evanston and Oak Park in twenty minutes. Got a fucking ambulance going a hundred twenty – easy enough to spot…"

Without slowing, Davis sent the car hurtling up the ramp. The undercarriage struck ground. Eleven and

Seven also bottomed out. Three bursts of orange sparks flashed beneath the thrumming machines and spun away crazily behind them. The squads bounced, still fender on fender, and speared their way into the sparse and sluggish stream of Wednesday evening traffic.

Far ahead, past jittering cars and brake lights, the ambulance darted away. It shrank. Already its sides were scored from sideswipes. Even now, it rammed the back corner of a sedan, spinning it as though it were a child's toy. The ambulance topped a rise and disappeared.

Davis clenched his jaw and wove past an old man who apparently hadn't heard the sirens or noticed the Broadway light show going on behind him. The lanes ahead were clearing to either side like the Red Sea before Moses. Into the breach the squads plunged.

"…the dogs out from Madison. We've got to be ready for a manhunt… I hope we don't, but I want them either way. Of all people, we can't lose him… And ask them for hostage negotiators. Yeah, two officers, an EMT, and a driver."

Davis glanced at a mile marker. "Almost to Kenosha. I sure hope they could get a roadblock." The squad leaped over a low rise and slid into a depression on the other side.

Brake lights everywhere. Ahead, they thickened into an angry swarm, completely blocking the road. Beyond them, a tanker truck lay on its side, a yellow-green cloud rolling up demonically from its split tank.

"Shit, shit, shit!" Carls shouted. "We're out of this one. That's got to be chlorine gas up there. We've got something even more deadly than the Son of Samael here."

"...Squads Eleven and Seven, set roadblock here... Twenty-Two, assist in evacuating the highway..."

Carls grabbed the handset. "What about Samael, Captain?"

"He's Chicago's man, now."

BOOK III
SON *of* SAMAEL

TWENTY

It was an easy enough commute into Chicago.

Once Samael tipped the chlorine tanker, he drove only another mile before finding a new ride. Ahead of him, a black sedan pulled to the shoulder to make way for the ambulance. Samael drove up beside the sedan and used the gun and the dead policeman to coax the motorist from his car. Samael and the dead cop got in. That was just the first hijacking. A string of other vehicle trades made dogs and helicopters useless. By the time he headed into the Loop, Samael was driving an '07 Mercedes, his dead buddy beside him. They looked like any pair of brothers from Chicago.

The cop paid for parking. In a seedy garage, Samael changed into the police uniform and put his brother under a blanket in the trunk. He drove to the South Side and found an ill-lit Stop 'n' Shop. There he left the car running and walked away. Before he'd even crossed the street, the Mercedes roared off. The chop shop crew might not even notice the corpse until they'd gotten the chassis stripped. By then, it would be too late to go to the police.

Samael spent the rest of the night on his feet, walking toward town. A white cop might have been a target on the South Side, but no one challenged him. Lucky for them. When dawn broke, Samael spotted the spire of St Charles on the horizon and headed for it.

It was nine o'clock.

"Time to make amends."

St Charles was a limestone megalith supported by massive buttresses, screened in statuary and wrought iron, and gabled in walnut. There were no yellow bricks. There was no clapboard rectory. In every way, it transcended the sort of building that St Francis was in Woodstock. Even so, Samael could not walk up the seventeen steps without remembering the time that Keith McFarland – that *he* and Keith McFarland – had killed a priest in a confessional.

The sign out front said "Open Confession."

Samael smiled. He had come today not to kill a priest. He had come to be washed of his sins.

He ascended the stairs. The cop clothes fit him tightly, forming him up, making him something he hadn't been before – something much better than he had been in the defeated orange jumpsuit.

Samael passed through the large central door. He remembered to take off his hat. It was slightly too large, and it had a bullet hole in its crease.

The narthex was small and gray, with polished marble and maroon carpet. The pile was low, but it bounced as though made of springs. Beside the door was a smooth niche with a white basin. Samael touched his hand to the holy water, made the sign of the cross on his forehead, and then took a thin trickle of the stuff into his mouth. He felt better with that swallow and scooped up a second.

Why don't humans bottle holy water for their tables? Why not bathe in it? Samael felt clean with the very thought.

Hand still dripping, Samael crossed the narthex and pushed through another set of doors. He stepped into the cool, magnificent silence of the sanctuary. The stained-glass lancets were ten men high. Beautiful statues of Mary, saints, and apostles stood in silent witness in niches around the chamber. Stately shadows of marble columns fell across orderly rows of walnut pews.

There, beside the pews, were the wardrobe-like compartments where the priests would be sitting. He crossed slowly to the pew adjacent to the open confessional and sat, waiting.

"You can come in, my son," came a voice from the metal screened box. It was the tone of an old man, thin and vulcanized by years of trial. "I am alone."

Samael nodded and rose. The police hat turned nervous circles in his grip. He entered the confessional and closed the door behind him. The close darkness within was soothing, comforting.

"Bless me, Father, for I have sinned. This is my first confession."

"Are you Catholic, child?"

"I'm not sure what I am, but I might as well be."

"What troubles you, child?"

"You will tell no one what we discuss?"

"Of course not. On my honor."

A deep sigh. "I am the Son of Samael. I killed my guards, a paramedic, and an ambulance driver."

Silence returned from the other side of the gold-painted screen. The walnut box breathed the cold air of the sacred space. "You are he? The Son of Samael?"

"I am," Samael replied. "Are you frightened?"

"Yes," said the priest. Though soft, his tone had intensified. "Yes, I am."

"You needn't be. I have not come to hurt you."

After a pause, the priest spoke again. "Go on, child. Tell me of these sins."

"Have you been following my case?"

"No, but it has been thrust upon us. If you have ears and eyes, you can't help knowing what has happened."

"In the last months, I have become convinced I never was an angel, that all along I was a human deluded by some psychosis. I had a woman who helped me, who convinced me I was human, that I had to live. I love her, Father, but she's – she's been–"

"Donna Leland," the voice said, comforting. "Yes, I heard about the accident."

"And now, without her, how can I...? Now, how can I be anything without her? How can I be human at all?"

The priest's voice became a thin, strong band. "You came to the right place, child. First, you must confess. It is guilt that made us mortal. Guilt drove us from the garden of paradise. You have lately fallen thus, too. Confess, and let the full weight of your guilt lie heavy on you."

"Yes, Father," Samael responded. He felt the profound weight of his atrocities on his bowed neck. "I have murdered many people, Father. I do not know how many. At least ten. Perhaps more – twenty, forty, eighty – I do not know."

"Imagine how many, and for each one, light a candle in your mind. Let that candle remain there, burning, all the rest of your days, to remind you of the lives you snuffed out."

"Yes. Yes, I am lighting them even now. It will be a terrific blaze. But there is more. I am a homosexual – or was, before Donna. I was a homosexual."

"That, in itself, is not sinful, if you have not acted–"

"I have acted upon it – I believe. My memory's not so good, but I do think, at least once, in the East Village–"

"That is sin, then, child. Light another candle."

"There's more, though. Plenty more. Um, if the prosecution was right, well, it wasn't just homosexual sex, but rape, and necrophilia, and who knows what worse things?"

The priest's voice was trembling. "For these acts, too – light a candle for each of these."

"Already my mind is a wildfire, Father. Already the light is blinding and the heat endless."

"Let the furnace of atrocity burn away all that is evil in you, child. Let the fires cleanse you of the will to do wrong."

"I have borne false witness. I have stolen. I cannot remember most of what I have done or been, but can imagine it, and am certain I have committed every sin that existed before me, and some new ones, too."

Gentle laughter came in answer. "There are no new sins, nothing new under the sun. But for each sin light another candle."

"They stretch on infinitely, these candles. They burn like the sun."

"Good. Forevermore see that fire in your eyes, feel it in your heart, meditate upon it in your mind, and let it cleanse your soul. Know that what fires you lave upon yourself now, you will be spared in Hell."

"I will bathe in fire. I will burn now and forever in hellfire. I will bathe in it."

"Do you know the Pater Noster, and the Hail Mary?"

"Yes – Our Father, who art in Heaven–"

"Good. Pray the Pater Noster three hundred times. Pray the Hail Mary seven hundred times. Let nothing distract you from your prayers. Let no sound beyond this booth disturb your communion with God. Remain here until I come back for you. Pray. I will return, and bring with me the instruments by which your humanity and salvation will be complete."

"Go, Father. I will remain and pray."

Samael began again his recitation, struggling not to hear the shift of the priest's clothing against the velvet seat cushion or the furtive sound of his old hand upon the brass knob. There came a flash of profane light on the far side of the screen as the booth opened, and the priest's fearful shadow flitted for a moment against the far wall.

Samael prayed onward. "Thy kingdom come, thy will be done, on Earth as it is in Heaven–"

Tears were coming. This height of trembling joy matched the depths of terrified despair he had felt when he dragged the rose thorns through his veins. How strange that he remembered no such powerful passions – that his emotions had been so disguised even from himself. Now, not only had he known the aching end of life, but also the irresistible urging of flesh to go on living, no matter the cost.

He heard the quick click of high heels retreating across stone, and the low drone of the door closing behind someone.

– Give us this day our daily–"

There came another profound *boom* as the door closed again, behind someone else.

"– will return, and bring with me the instruments by which your humanity and salvation will be complete–"

"– and forgive us our sins–" Azra continued, though he stood and peered out the slatted window at the top of the door.

The priest, thin and wiry like some manic cartoon creature, glanced back toward the booth before rounding a marble pillar and disappearing into the transept.

"– as we forgive those–" Samael's hand clicked open the brass knob of the confessional and he strode out into the sanctuary, his face grave, "– who sin against us."

His metal-edged wingtips clicked on the smooth, cold floor. He unsnapped the gun at his belt, drew it forth, and cocked it

A door ahead of him boomed closed, and a dead-bolt lock snicked into place.

Samael broke into a run across the sanctuary. The soles of his feet slid on the stone. His eyes were wide and bright, his nostrils flared.

"– lead us not into temptation–"

One more stride, and he lifted his foot and kicked the door. Hardwood splintered, and a brass deadbolt ripped free as the door swung inward. Beyond lay a tight office, book-lined, with a desk at its center, two vinyl chairs in front of the desk, and a recoiling priest with a phone at his ear.

The crack of the gun echoed through the sanctuary and sent up a puff of smoke like incense. The priest bounced backward against a bookshelf and tumbled, face-first, to the floor. On the belly of his black shirt, there was a darker spot of black. The phone dangled freely, someone shouting, small and inconsequential, from it.

"– and deliver us from the Evil One–"

Samael strode into the room, kicked one of the vinyl chairs aside, stooped over the priest, and drew the phone up by its cord. He listened.

"Where are you? Sir? What's happening now? Don't hang up."

Samael blinked, his mouth grim. "For thine is the kingdom, and the power, and the glory, forever and ever. Amen."

He lowered the receiver to the phone. He rolled the priest over. The man was alive.

The priest cringed back, terror in his eyes. His hands were red as he lifted them from his belly wound and held them beseechingly before him. "No, Samael. Don't do it. You must turn yourself in. You must get help."

Eyes hard beneath black brows, Samael reached down to the man's shirt, grabbed hold of him, and hoisted him upward. "Where is your car?"

"I don't have a car."

He shook the man as if he were a doll. "Where?"

"Outside – a blue minivan with paneled sides."

"The keys?"

"In my pants pocket."

Samael reached in and grabbed the prickly mass of metal.

The priest yammered, "You can't miss it. It's right in front."

"You're coming along."

And Jesus stood before the governor: and the governor asked him, saying, Art thou the king of the Jews? And Jesus said unto him, Thou sayest.

And when he was accused by the chief priests and elders, he answered nothing.

Then said Pilate unto him, Hearest thou not how many things they witness against thee? And he answered him to never a word; insomuch that the governor marveled greatly.

Now at that feast the governor was wont to release unto the people a prisoner, whom they would choose.

And they had then a notable prisoner, called Barabbas.

Therefore when they were gathered together, Pilate said unto them, Whom will ye that I release unto you? Barabbas, or Jesus which is called Christ.

For he knew that for envy they had delivered him.

When he was set down on the judgment seat, his wife sent unto him, saying, Have thou nothing to do with that just man: for I have suffered many things this day in a dream because of him.

But the chief priests and elders persuaded the multitude that they should ask for Barabbas, and destroy Jesus.

The governor answered and said unto them, Whether of the twain will ye that I release unto you? They said Barabbas.

Pilate saith unto them, What shall I do then with Jesus which is called Christ? They all say unto him, Let him be crucified.

And the governor said, Why, what evil hath he done? But they cried out the more, saying, Let him be crucified.

When Pilate saw that he could prevail nothing, but that rather a tumult was made, he took water, and washed his hands before the multitude, saying, I am innocent of the blood of this just person: see ye to it.

Then answered all the people, and said, His blood be on us, and on our children.

Then released he Barabbas unto them: and when he had scourged Jesus, he delivered him to be crucified.

"Hello, Officer," said the young woman behind the counter.

Samael glanced at her in momentary confusion before remembering he wore a uniform. "Hello."

The woman smiled back thinly. She had long, lank hair and a silver tooth on the top left of her smile. She looked too thin, her skin too pale. "Haven't seen you in here before. You new on the force?"

Samael strolled among the aisles of bagged snacks and candy bars. "Yes. I'm new."

"Well, I don't know if the guys told you, but coffee is free to patrolmen, and there's ten percent off snacks."

Stopping beside a small metal rack that held jelly, peanut butter, mustard, crackers, and bread, Samael asked, "Is Wonder Bread considered a snack?"

She laughed politely. "Oh, anything you can eat is. Just not the Heet or the oil or antifreeze, stuff like that."

He nodded and lifted the loaf of white bread, surprised at how light and limp it was. The fluorescent lights crazed across the package. He moved to the bank of refrigerators and gazed at the clean, orderly rows of juice and soft drinks. "What's good?" he asked.

"What do you mean?"

"The drinks. What's good?"

"I never had anyone ask. I like diet anything, but mostly Diet Dr Pepper."

He nodded and opened the case, pulling out four cans. They felt good against his bandaged arm, the cold seeping through. "What about meat?"

"What about it?"

"What's good?"

"I'll give you a deal on these hot dogs," she pointed to three wieners rolling greasily on sets of aluminum cylinders. "All three for a buck."

"All right."

She took a pair of tongs, fished some buns from a steamer, and began putting the hot dogs into them. "Mustard, ketchup, relish, onions?"

"Everything," Samael said distractedly. He pulled a few plastic-wrapped jerky sticks from a canister on the counter.

The woman was wrapping the dogs in paper and sliding them into a white sack. "Any cigs? Any booze?"

Samael had to think on that a bit. "Yes. Cigs and booze."

"What kind?"

"What's good?"

She looked at him wonderingly. "You sure are new."

"Yes."

"Most of the guys smoke Marlboros. Ted smokes them without filters. You look more like a filtered Camel man. And how about a fifth of light rum. Everybody likes light rum."

"Yeah."

She retrieved the items and bagged them. "Anything else? A paper? There's a whole story about that 'Son of

Sam' wacko from Wisconsin. They say the Cheeseheads lost him and think he's come down here."

"A paper sounds good."

"I'll give you the *Sun Times*. It's a little more interesting, if you know what I mean. Any gas?"

"No gas."

She punched the items in and told him the total. He gave her the crumpled fifty he'd gotten from Blake Gaines – the first money he'd ever earned.

"Oh, I almost forgot. Do you have any first aid stuff? Bandages? Tape? Alcohol?"

"We've got Band-Aids and some medications and stuff. No alcohol, but you could use the rum." She pointed toward an old wall rack. "Help yourself. I'll re-ring this stuff. Are you hurt?"

"No. A friend of mine. A prisoner, really."

"Right." She laughed again politely. "Don't let him get away."

He returned the laugh. "Oh, no. You're right about that. He won't get away."

TWENTY-ONE

"Hello, Officer," said the desk clerk. He was white-haired and beer-bellied. His unbuttoned plaid shirt had been washed so many times it was translucent. Judging by the pencil jutting up behind one ear and the Band-Aids crossing two adjacent fingertips, he was both the owner and handyman of the Silent Night Motel.

This time Samael was ready. "Hello. I need a room."

"A single?" the man asked. His eyes were shaped like inverted mushrooms behind his thick bifocals.

"A double."

"Your wife?"

"A prisoner – convict. I'm extraditing him."

A titanium sheen stole across the man's gaze. "No handcuffs on the headboard. It'll scar if it holds, and more likely just break loose."

"No. No handcuffs on the headboard."

His gaze withdrew as if he were deciding something.

Samael blurted, "That no-handcuffs on the head-board rule – is that just for cops?"

"Hm?" the man said, distracted. "No. For anybody."

He pulled out the motel register. "Sign here. How many nights?"

"One, for now."

"Pay for two – security deposit."

Signing John Michaels, Samael nodded, "How much?"

"Thirty-eight fifty."

Samael handed over two twenties from the priest's wallet.

The desk clerk clapped a key down on the counter, took the bills, and made change from a shallow wooden drawer that held a fat, dangling combination lock. "Around the corner, the room on the end. You'll be away from the others. I'll lock up at eleven. Don't expect me to open for anything until eight tomorrow."

Nodding one last time, Samael walked from the small office into the dark night. He'd left the priest's minivan running. His shoes crackled on the gravel. He looked within the van. The priest lay sleeping beneath a dry-cleaned vestment. Samael climbed in and pulled the van around to the room on the end.

The motel was a long, single-story building, the width of a trailer home. Its clapboards were feathered with loose paint. Its windows hung with gold-beaded curtains that had been new when Kennedy was killed. On the corner, starlings nested inside a broken security light.

Samael parked. He propped open the screen door, unlocked the wooden door, and nudged its moisture-

swollen base with his foot. Cracked veneer made a chittering sound as the door scraped in. He flicked the light
on. It shone on six-inch-by-six-inch avocado-colored
tiles. The room had two single beds, side by side, a few
landscape prints on the walls, and a bathroom with a
plastic shower stall and matching avocado stool and lav.
Samael nodded and returned to the minivan.

To the rear of the building stood a scraggly line of
elms, which seeped light from a superlit auto dealership
behind them. To the front of the building was a wall of
whitewashed decorative block, screening the place from
the six-lane anonymity of the road.

Samael opened the passenger door, stooped, and
lifted the cold, quietly breathing form of the priest. He
carried the man like a bride across the threshold, beneath the bald light bulb at the center of the ceiling,
and to the far bed, the one near the bathroom. He retrieved his groceries and then closed and locked the
van, the screen, the wooden door, and the windows.
He drew the drapes.

The priest looked small and boyish in sleep. His
bloodstained hands curled in his belly, and his legs were
drawn up. Samael pulled the dry-cleaned frock from
the man and hung it on a curtain rod. Then, ever so
carefully, he began shucking the man's blood-stiffened
jacket from his arms and shoulders. The fabric resisted.
Some of it was scabbed to the gunshot wound. Samael
took out the priest's keys and the small penknife that
hung on the ring with them. He cautiously cut at the
jacket, working his way from knuckles to shoulder, and

from shoulder to lapel. He did the same on the other side, and then cut away the man's shirt.

There was much blood, and something else, a white bubbly discharge. As Samael pulled the last strips of cloth away, he saw how large the wound was – a hole the size of a nickel. The bullet had entered just below the rib cage on his left side and cut through skin, fat, and a thin muscular wall where most of the blood seemed to have come from. Beneath the muscle was a dark cavity in which was something that looked like wet mushrooms. A septic smell came up out of the seeping darkness.

Samael stood back from the bed. The penknife quivered in his bloody hand. How like those other scenes this is, he thought, me and bare, dying flesh, a gun, and a knife.

He turned to the grocery sack. Its thin white plastic glowed with the reds and greens and grays within it. His sanguine hands darted in, clasping rolls of gauze, a bag of cotton balls, and the fifth of Mr Boston rum. Samael set his provisions down on a small side table made of two-by-fours.

There was red wicking into the sheet beneath the priest. Samael gently rolled the man to one side and looked at his back. The exit wound was wide, a funnel of flesh above the left hip. There. That would be the place to start.

Tearing open the bag of cotton balls, Samael grabbed a bundle in one hand. He held the rum bottle between his knees and opened it. His fingers left streaks of brownish red on the cap. He wadded the cotton around the bottle's mouth and up-ended it. Withdrawing the dripping mass, he took a stinging swallow, set the bottle down, braced the shoulder of the priest, and applied the alcohol to the red funnel of muscle.

The old man convulsed suddenly, arching his back away from the fire and clutching with one feeble hand. He still was not awake. His arms quivered and bunched to his chest. More blood came with each shake of his body.

Samael pulled the drenched red cotton away and clutched a new bundle. He tamped it into the wound, placed a few folds of gauze atop the cotton, and taped it all in place. Then, rolling the priest to his back, Samael began the same process with the wound in front.

This time, he poured a bit of rum down the hole to sterilize whatever raw edges the bullet had left within. A few cotton balls followed after. He packed the puncture and fed the rest of the gauze roll around the man's torso, taping the whole assembly in place. The cotton and gauze had stopped the blood, and Samael drew up the covers around the old priest.

He was done. He stood and went to the bathroom to wash the blood from his hands. The water smelled like eggs. He spit in the sink, took another swallow of rum, and then thought to clean off the blood-streaked mouth of the bottle.

Finished, he stripped his own clothes. In underwear, he sat down on his bed. Propping the pillows in a wedge, Samael leaned against the headboard and took a moment to breathe. The air felt stinging and good in his lungs. He took another drink.

How like the other killings? Nothing like them. Keith had done most of the others, and Samael had felt nothing but a detached interest and a concern that things be handled properly. Yes, Samael had killed the two officers, the paramedic, and the EMT in the ambulance, but he had not done so for the fun of it. He'd done so to escape. The tanker truck driver was probably dead, too, but that was only a helpful accident, shaking the cops.

But what about this priest?

He wasn't dead, for one thing. Even if he were, it was all done in self-defense. After hearing his confession, after swearing he would tell no one, the priest turned Judas. His current state was his own doing.

Samael remembered the candle flames, searing in his head, and the admonition to forevermore feel the evil he had done. The priest was only the next bright torch added to a funeral pyre.

But he had tried to make it right. He'd taken this Judas and cleaned and dressed his wounds and given him a bed to lie in and bought for him shelter. If he awoke, there would be food and cigarettes and rum, too.

For I was hungered, and you gave me meat: I was thirsty, and ye gave me drink: I was a stranger, and you took me in: Naked, and you clothed me: I was sick, and you visited me: in prison, and you came unto me.

But the priest did not need Wonder Bread and Mr Boston Rum. He needed an emergency room. Even leaving him in a phone booth after calling an ambulance – that would have been better.

But Samael could not. This priest was the only creature in the world who knew his secret, knew it fully. To part with such a creature was beyond Samael now. This priest was a surrogate for Donna – was his anchor to humanity. To give him up would be to become utterly alone. The priest and he lived and died together. Only if the priest survived would Samael survive.

He took out the pack of cigarettes, opened the cellophane, flipped back the lid, and coaxed one small white cylinder from among the rest. He realized he had no way to light it. He set the cigarette and the open pack on the lamp stand, stood and stretched, and then went to the priest's bed. There, he lay down behind the man, held him in his arms, and fell softly asleep.

Then the soldiers of the governor took Jesus into the common hall, and gathered unto him the whole band of soldiers.

And they stripped him, and put on him a scarlet robe.

And when they had plaited a crown of thorns, they put it upon his head, and a reed in his right hand: and they bowed the knee before him, and mocked him, saying, Hail, King of the Jews!

And they spit upon him, and took the reed, and smote him on the head.

And after they had mocked him, they took the robe

off from him, and put his own raiment on him, and led him away to crucify him.

And as they came out, they found a man of Cyrene, Simon by name: him they compelled to bear his cross.

And when they were come unto a place called Golgotha, that is to say, a place of a skull, they gave him vinegar to drink mingled with gall: and when he had tasted thereof, he would not drink.

And they crucified him, and parted his garments, casting lots: that it might be fulfilled which was spoken by the prophet, They parted my garments among them, and upon my vesture did they cast lots.

And sitting down they watched him there;

And set up over his head his accusation written, THIS IS JESUS THE KING OF THE JEWS.

Then there were two thieves crucified with him, one on the right hand, and another on the left.

And they that passed by reviled him, wagging their heads, and saying, Thou that destroyest the temple, and buildest it in three days, save thyself. If thou be the Son of God, come down from the cross.

Likewise also the chief priests mocking him, with the scribes and elders, said, He saved others; himself he cannot save. If he be the King of Israel, let him now come down from the cross, and we will believe him. He trusted in God; let him deliver him now, if he will have him: for he said, I am the Son of God.

The thieves also, which were crucified with him, cast the same in his teeth.

* * *

ANGEL of DEATH

He could only be dead. When morning came, there was no breath left in the priest, no pulse. He was cold.

Samael sat up beside him, blinked in sleepy recognition, yawned, and pulled back one of the priest's eyelids. The organ beneath was motionless and dry. It did not respond to the odd light of morning. Samael let out a long, deep sigh.

"You were my only hope," he told the old man. "You were the only one who knew. I thought if maybe I could save you…"

The words died away. Samael slumped down beside the man, put his arm around the knobby shoulders and held him. The priest's skin felt cool and gelatinous like uncooked chicken.

I've done it again, killed again, even after all the candles and cotton balls and prayers. Oh, Donna. The accident that killed you killed me and this priest, all three. Death comes in threes.

Worse yet, Samael realized he was already sorting through ways to dispose of the body. He could go buy a set of knives and feed the priest, bit by bit, down the toilet. That still left bones, though, and would have been better done in a room with a bathtub. He could take the body along, but the minivan didn't have a secure trunk away from prying eyes. He could push the body up into the attic crawl space and let the smell eventually alert the owner. None of those options seemed charitable, though.

Instead, Samael decided to leave the priest in bed, with a "Do not disturb" sign on the door. He'd paid for the second day in advance, so he would likely have a day's running before the manager realized the man in the bed was dead, not asleep. When he did discover the body, he would also find a note.

Samael pulled a sheet of Silent Night stationery from the lamp stand and wrote a quick note:

To whom it may concern:
Here is the father kidnapped from St Charles Church. He was shot in the process of reporting the Son of Samael to the police. I tried to dress his wounds, but he died anyway. He has given me away in death as he could not in life.
Son of Samael

He folded the note and placed it gently in the priest's hand. Bending, Samael kissed the man's cold lips.

"I used to be an angel, Father – one of those beautiful statues – white wings and stone eyes. I'd still be one except I couldn't kill this one woman. I had mercy, see? Angels aren't supposed to have mercy; that's for humans. My stone skin got soft. Everything hurt – sunlight and midnight, heat and cold. Everything hurts when you're human." Samael snatched the priest's keys from the side table. "Lucky me, I'm not anymore." He picked up the bag of groceries and headed out the door. "What I am now, even I don't know." The door closed.

Now from the sixth hour there was darkness over all the land unto the ninth hour.

And about the ninth hour Jesus cried with a loud voice, saying, Eli, Eli, lama sabachthani? that is to say, My God, my God, why hast thou forsaken me?

Some of them that stood there, when they heard that, said, This man calleth for Elias.

And straightway one of them ran, and took a sponge, and filled it with vinegar, and put it on a reed, and gave him to drink.

The rest said, Let be, let us see whether Elias will come to save him.

Jesus, when he had cried again with a loud voice, yielded up the ghost.

And, behold, the veil of the temple was rent in twain from the top to the bottom; and the earth did quake, and the rocks rent; and the graves were opened; and many bodies of the saints which slept arose, and came out of the graves after his resurrection, and went into the holy city, and appeared unto many.

Now when the centurion, and they that were with him, watching Jesus, saw the earthquake, and those things that were done, they feared greatly, saying, Truly this was the Son of God.

"Back again, officer?" asked the checkout woman.

It was the same too-slim, lank-haired cashier from the night before, though her shoulders were slumped and her eyes ringed in darkness. There was a sharp, blood-shot craziness in her gaze, but she smiled all the same.

Samael walked toward the soft drink refrigerators. "What did I have last night, Diet Dr Pepper?"

"Yes," she answered, a little too quickly.

As Samael pulled open the case door, he glanced toward the woman. Her face was haunted. "Did you pull a double shift?"

"Yeah. Time-and-a-half pay. Will that be everything?"

"How about another *Sun Times*?" asked Samael as he approached the counter.

"Out of papers," she said. "Tell you what? How about a free *Hustler*, on the house?"

"Aren't those *Sun Times*?" he pointed to a stack of six or seven papers.

"Yesterday's. Here. Here's that magazine, and take the soda, no charge."

Samael looked down at the cover – a woman with enormous breasts that emerged from beneath a sailor shirt. "I don't want the magazine, but let me see a paper."

She bit her lip but turned around, stooped, and pulled the top paper from the stack. Folding it, cover inward, she handed it over. "Free. Gratis. Have a nice day."

He unfolded the paper and saw his own police photo, and a caption explaining that he would be dressed as a policeman.

"They already were here," she said, beginning to cry. "All I said was that you were here about eight last night and that you were friendly and paid for everything. I swear, that's all. And, I swear I won't call them to say you were here again. I won't tell a soul."

Refolding the paper, Samael said, "How much do I owe you?"

She laughed through her tears. "Really, mister, it's free."

"How much?"

Closing her eyes to add the figures, she blurted, "A dollar eighty-nine."

"Here's two." He said, "When they come back, tell them again how I was polite and paid for everything."

"I won't tell them anything, honest."

"Just tell them the truth. Tell them what I was like. Tell them what I was."

TWENTY-TWO

The cover story was, of course, about him. It told that a Father Destry of St Charles Church had sent parishioners running from the sanctuary, telling them, "Get out quickly and quietly. Call 911. The Son of Samael is here." The priest and his minivan had then disappeared. One of the women who fled saw someone carry Father Destry, put him in the minivan, and cover him with plastic. The man's description matched that of the Son of Samael.

Chicago's chief of police urged strict caution until the serial killer was apprehended – keeping doors and windows locked, asking proper identification of any workers who come to the door, not admitting anyone unfamiliar. Even these precautions were not certain to make a person safe.

"This killer strikes at any time, day or night, public or private, high-risk or low-risk," the chief warned. "He's charming. A genius – psycho. Unpredictable. Don't think you're safe just because you're not a streetwalker. Watch yourself. Watch your families, your neighbors. We're gonna get this son of a bitch."

Samael blinked – a genius psycho. The chief was waxing poetic: Studs Terkel with a badge.

The reporter called him on it: When asked whether the Son of Samael was the toughest killer that Chicago cops had faced, the chief replied, "You kidding? This guy's no Gacy. He's just a lowlife. He's used to picking on Cheeseheads. He's in Chicago, now. He's got Chicago cops to deal with – well-trained, well-equipped, an army of cops now. We'll catch him."

Samael shook his head. "Your well-trained army isn't worth one Donna Leland. She got me. You never will."

There was a sidebar article embedded in one corner of the main story. Its headline drew his attention.

"I BOUGHT THAT BASTARD A PAST"
AP International
Story and Photo by Blake Gaines

"I bought that bastard a past," confessed Marge Billings early yesterday morning. Her husband, Derek Billings, was slain by his cell mate, the Son of Samael.

One week prior to the murder, according to Mrs Billings, she had contacted "forgers and hackers" to create a false history for the Son of Samael. "Derek made it all up, and [told me] who to call and what to pay," said Mrs Billings. "I should have just given [the Son of Samael] the ten thousand. Then maybe Derek would be alive."

Asked why her husband would do this, she said, "He thought they were friends. He liked to be the knight on the white horse. He was an ***hole."

When asked about the now-famous photo album that showed William B. Dance and his brother, Billings commented, "That was Derek's album. He thought it a nice touch."

"If this is true," commented Judge Sandra Devlin, who had remanded the Son of Samael to a mental institution instead of a prison, "I was wrong."

True or not, Mrs Billings named names.

Four arrests have already been made, including the heroin addict hired to play the Son of Samael's older brother, James.

FBI computer criminologists have discovered two files in William B. Dance's record that contain "the classic flags of tampering."

Further indictments are expected in the coming weeks.

Because Mrs Billings volunteered her testimony to police, she is free on one hundred dollars bond.

"I just want Derek's killer to pay."

Samael folded the paper. It trembled in his hand. He set it down on the passenger seat, started the minivan, and placed both hands on the wheel.

Sunlight slanted through the windshield and onto his chest. It soaked into his police shirt, but there was still an envelope of cool air around his body. He breathed slowly, not wanting to disturb the moment.

So, it had all been a lie. He wasn't William B. Dance. The memories of his life, of Abu Ghraib, of eating the scorched crow on the streets of Mexico City, of standing beside the rusted slide – those were mere suggestions planted by hypnosis, by the need to be human. It all was a lie.

Then, what am I? he wondered. Not an angel. Not a human. What? If Donna were still alive, he knew exactly what he would have been. He would have lived in Hell to be with her. He would even have become human. Whatever I am, I'm trapped in this body, in a dead man's uniform, in a dead priest's van, and being hunted by an army of cops.

He drove to the edge of the parking lot, waited for a moment between rushing cars, and pulled out into traffic. There would be a place up here. Just up here. Ah, a Laundromat.

The man was tall and lean, with unclean brown hair, intense eyes, a cigarette clenched between two thin fingers, and a newspaper in his hands. He also happened to have a gun sitting on the plastic seat beside him.

A young Latina ran past him, after her brother. Their mother was at the end of the aisle, tumbling a load of clothes out of a green-enamel dryer.

The Son of Samael, still wearing his cop uniform, approached the man.

"Sir?" he said, stepping in front of him. There was a small, apologetic smile on his teeth, but it didn't extend to his eyes. "I imagine you have a permit for that hand-gun?"

The man took a last long drag from his cigarette and let the smoky breath billow out over the top of his newspaper. "Yeah. In the car."

The officer nodded, pursing his lips. "Which car?"

"The blue Impala."

Samael stared through the plate glass window at the car pulled up almost fully beneath the overhang. It would be sheltered on three sides from watching eyes. "You got clothes in the dryers?"

An edge of belligerence came into the man's face. "I'm not sitting here for my health."

"Which dryers?"

"Those two orange ones. What's this all about?"

Samael bent, snatching up the gun. "Let's go have a look at that permit." He looked to one side, seeing the Latina woman and her two children, staring in amaze-ment at the confrontation.

The man stood. "Look, it's not in my car. I lied. But it's at home."

"Kneel down, sir," Samael said. "Hands behind your back."

"Oh, son-of-a-bitch! You're not running me in. If you pigs did your work, we wouldn't have to carry guns–"

"Ma'am," said the Son of Samael to the Latina as he fit handcuffs to the kneeling man, "you're going to want to get your children out of here. This man is the

Son of Samael killer. Get at least two blocks away as quickly as you can."

"What are you talking about?" shrieked the man. "I'm not the Son of–"

The officer kicked him down, onto his face on the green and gray linoleum.

The Laundromat owner came in, a young, fat man, glaring. "What the hell?"

"Sir, this is the Son of Samael killer. Run. Get at least two blocks away, as quickly as you can."

Nodding, wide-eyed, the man retreated, flinging the front door wide and not looking back. The Latina and her children were out as well.

"What the hell are you doing?"

Samael hooked a foot under the man's gut and flipped him onto his back. He pulled his own pistol, stooped, put the muzzle in the man's mouth, and fired. The frightened, furious eyes immediately went blank.

"For a guy who's never had a tattoo before, you're sure starting out big," said David. He wore a ripped shirt over a wiry physique. Across his skin, tattoos wriggled like gray snakes. He had a sharp, feverish smell, the smell of youth and vigor. He held up before him a piece of paper that rattled dully in his hand. The page showed the outline of a human face, with eyes, nose, and mouth delineated. Between these features were Arabic letters distorted into flame-like patterns, covering forehead, cheeks, and jaw in a mask of violent black lines that formed a skull. "You sure you want this all over your face the rest of your life?"

"Yes."

"I never seen this one. What is it? Some kind of oriental mask?"

"It's the mask of a spirit."

David nodded. He scratched a thinning patch of hair on his head. "Sure. Anyway, it's probably gonna take a couple sessions."

"I'll pay you double if you do it all now."

"Pay me half of that, and then when I get tired, give me the rest to keep me going," David said with a laugh. He leaned over the needle apparatus, picking something off its point.

"Yes. Here. Here's three hundred."

"Jesus fucking Christ. You're lucky I ain't my cousin Jerry, or you'd be dead for the rest before I even got started."

"You're lucky I ain't the Son of Samael, or you'd be dead the moment you finished."

They both laughed at that.

"All right. Well, let's get going. I'm going to wash your face with some alcohol, and then I'll use some petroleum jelly to transfer the pattern in place. We'll do it in pieces – cheeks, forehead, nose, chin…"

"Fine. In pieces, but we keep going. I want it finished if it takes all night."

"We're closed," said the old, white-haired taxidermist.

"To everybody else, yes," said the man with the demon mask tattooed on his face.

"Who the hell are you to tell me that?"

The demon man drew a gun, approached the old man, and held the barrel to his head. "I'm the Son of Samael."

"No shit?"

"No shit."

"Wh-what do you want from me?"

"Taxidermy. I want you to teach me how."

"It takes a long time to learn."

"It better take only the next eight hours or so, because this gun goes off in eight hours, and I'd hate to have it pointed at your head when it does."

"Well, well, all right. I've got a long-haired rabbit I've just started on."

"No. You start on these. I want two full-head masks and two pairs of gloves. Cut off the eyelids. I'll use my own. What the...? God damn it, leave it. You can scrub puke after I'm gone, after your eight hours are up. Yes, get to work, unless you'd like to be the next mask and gloves."

SON OF SAMAEL KILLS THREE IN THREE-DAY SPREE
AP

The man known as the Son of Samael is responsible for three recent Chicagoland slayings, according to police.

An unidentified male, around 32, was slain at the Parkside Laundry in Berwyn in what police call a "heinous and audacious daylight crime." According to one witness, the Son of Samael, dressed as a policeman, handcuffed his victim and cleared the scene. The body, with the name Samael written on its belly, was later found at the facility.

The Son of Samael allegedly took the victim's hands, head, wallet, keys, car–"a large gray Chevy from the early nineties" – and laundry.

"He killed a guy his size and got a whole new wardrobe," said a police source.

A similarly dismembered body was discovered at the Skincredible Tattoo Salon in downtown Des Plaines. Coworkers positively identified the man as David Darrow of Wheeling. Photos of the man's many tattoos aided identification.

A police handwriting expert said the hand that had written "Samael" on David Darrow had also written on at least ten previous bodies, including the Laundromat victim.

While police focused on that crime scene, the Son of Samael was apparently busy just across the street. The headless, handless body of Albert Terrence of Des Plaines was found in his taxidermy shop. A teenaged assistant to the taxidermist found the body. The youth indicated that numerous taxidermy tools and tanning chemicals were missing.

Police from Des Plaines, Wheeling, Arlington Heights, Berwyn, and Chicago are planning a plenary session for all detectives working on cases that might involve the Son of Samael.

One police officer, who asked not to be identified, said, "He is honing his craft. He's doing it
better and more openly. He's defying us to find
him. He's a killing machine."

Yes. Get together. Talk about me. It sounds like a good
place to learn who I am. I'm glad to have this cop uniform. And these new faces. And these new hands.

It suddenly isn't so bad not having an identity of my
own, a history of my own. Not having even my own
species.

How can they call it murder when I'm not even
human? A bear or cougar would do as much, would
kill to live. They call it murder only because they have
been so long out of the food chain.

Welcome back.

TWENTY-THREE

Detective Donna Leland lay in St Mary's hospital.

She blinked. That was accomplishment enough after two months of coma.

The feeding tube that had snaked up her nose and down her throat had been pulled just this morning. The IVs still dripped their fluids into her veins. Catheters, too – she was invaded in half a dozen places but felt none of it. A two-month coma was plenty of time for her body to become accustomed to plastic and stainless steel and processed fluids and unregulated eliminations. It all felt completely natural. It all felt not at all.

That's what coma was for. Anesthesia. The doctors had found no serious injuries beyond her concussion. The airbag had made certain of that. The tree had fallen on the empty passenger seat, missing her but bringing the roof of the car down on her head. She had a slight cranial contusion, perhaps enough to cause amnesia, but not coma.

Amnesia would have been more merciful. Now that she had awakened, she remembered it all. She remembered and cared enough to call the station for an update. The chief said he'd come out and explain things. He would arrive any moment.

"Detective!" came the voice from the doorway. Bigg's face was red and fleshy beside the big spray of flowers he had bought in the gift shop downstairs. The thin plastic wrapper was still around the bundle, and it still bore a price tag. "So, you decided to come back to the land of the living."

"Yeah," she managed. She cleared her throat, swallowing painfully past the soreness from the feeding tube. "You didn't have to drive out here."

"Aww, it's nothing." He cantered in and pulled back the drapes. Sunlight stabbed against the ivory-colored wall. "I was hoping to see the old Donna again, you know."

"Here I am. Got two months of beauty sleep."

He laughed uncomfortably. "Yeah. Well. It looks good on you. You weren't looking right during the whole trial." He handed her the flowers.

She smiled, sniffing the frumpy bouquet. "Oh, that's just TV cameras for you. They add ten pounds and twenty years."

"I'm glad you can joke again. It's good to see you without that creep hanging on to you."

Donna blinked. "Thanks for the flowers."

He gestured dismissively. "For the first couple days, it was round the clock guard – in case you-know-who would show up. He didn't. Must've bought the story of your death. The press sure did. Ran with it. They care more about a good story than a true one."

Donna took in the information. "What do you mean, in case you-know-who showed up? How could Azra show up?"

Biggs grimaced and changed the subject. "The judge didn't see past all that malarkey about the Gulf War."

"Malarkey?"

"Well, that part of it has only come out three weeks ago. It turns out that whole story was one Billings arranged from prison. His wife came out with it. Named names. There're going to be seven different indictments. Falsifying information. Planting evidence. A bunch of computer tampering crimes."

"It was a lie?"

"All of it. We know less about our Doe now than we thought we knew before your accident."

"He always said it was made up," Donna said. She swallowed sourly. "I'm the one who convinced him it was true. I'm the one who told him he had to believe, he had to live." She shook her head, weary to the bone. "So, has Illinois scheduled his trial yet?"

"Well, no. See, that's the thing..."

"He's been extradited already?"

"Well, no. Not extradited."

"Where is he?" she asked, concern piercing her grogginess.

"He's in Illinois, just not in custody."

She sat up, and the blood drained from her face. "Not in custody?"

"He tried to kill himself – just after hearing about your accident. They rushed him to the hospital – this very hospital, but en route he killed everybody and took the ambulance. Even overturned a semi on the highway. Got away."

"Mother of God. Well. God damn it, Azra. God damn it."

The chief glanced down, chagrined. "Yes. Yes, it's bad. He's giving the Chicago cops quite a time. He's escalated. Twenty-two in the last two months."

Her eyes were pleading. "No. No. That's not possible. No. He... he had such a heart, Chief. He was just a dog that had been kicked and kicked and kicked until he snapped at anything and everything, but I started to get through all of that. I saw the man trapped inside that monster, and I was bringing him out." Donna sank back against her pillow.

"He's not a lost child, Donna. You've been asleep. You haven't seen the papers."

"You don't understand–"

"No, *you* don't understand. He's got you wrapped around his little finger – like Bundy, like Manson. He's brainwashed you."

"I love him."

"Damn it, Donna," Biggs snarled. He stepped away to the window and looked out grimly. "He's not the man you knew. He's changed his MO, for one. He works alone, now. He takes his victims' heads and hands and makes masks and gloves out of them. His own identity has disappeared." He turned back to Donna. "He's always taking on the identities of his victims. He can be anyone, anywhere, at any time. He could be me."

Donna stared intently in the chief's eyes.

"I'm sorry," he said. "I shouldn't have said it. Just a figure of speech." He paused, sniffing. "Anyway, I'm glad you're awake. And if you're serious about wanting to talk to him, you could help us catch him."

Donna couldn't answer at first. Her heart was pounding, and she couldn't catch her breath. Finally, she managed, "Whatever you need. We've got to get him off the streets."

"All right," he said grimly. "There's going to be another plenary on the Son of Samael down in Chicago, three days from now. I figured, if we could get a special release from the doctor…"

"I'll go, regardless."

"There's my girl. You're kind of – well, you're the expert on this guy. There'll be FBI profilers there, discussion of proactive approaches, and all that."

A troubled look came into her eyes. She swallowed and looked down at her swollen abdomen. "What about…?"

"The accident wasn't enough. Besides, it's a Catholic hospital, Donna. They did everything to make sure it survived."

She breathed, staring blankly ahead like a frightened animal.

"You've still got a month to get it done legally. I've talked to a doctor who said she would take care of it after you've been stable for a week."

A sudden brightness came into her eyes. "No. No, I'm glad. It's all right. I'm Catholic, too, Captain. You knew that."

"Yes, but in cases of rape–"

"But this wasn't rape. My car ran into that tree, but I survived. The baby survived. God has done something here. It's about time that God has done something. And I'm not going to undo it. If I'm going to live, the baby will, too."

"You're sure about this, Detective? The sins of the fathers, and all that. Aren't you afraid whenever you look at him – ?"

"There's got to be redemption somewhere in this mess. It always takes a child to overcome the sins of a previous generation. There's got to be redemption somewhere."

He sat at the breakfast counter of a small, smoky diner. A plate of sunny-side-up eggs, bacon strips, and hash browns sent steam coiling up the valley of the newspaper. His fork sliced free a rounded wedge of egg, piercing the yolk, which oozed across the plate. He lifted the wet mass of white toward his lips – not his lips, but those of the fat grocer he had slain on the loading dock.

The mask was becoming one of his favorites – comfortable and realistic. It was the first mask he'd filled out with foam rubber to make the jowls and bulbous nose and rings under the eyes turn out well. He would not have sat at the breakfast counter with any other mask, much less ordered a runny egg and crumbly hash browns.

The article he was reading was buried on page thirteen of the first section, unlike most of the stories written about him. He had almost missed the account.

"Which would have been a great shame," he told himself.

KILLER'S COP GIRLFRIEND WAKES
AP

Previously reported dead, the Son of Samael's female companion, Detective Donna Leland of the Burlington, Wisconsin, police, woke from a two-month coma yesterday, according to anonymous sources at St Mary's Hospital, Racine, Wisconsin.

Detective Leland is widely considered the foremost expert on the man known as the Son of Samael. Police indicate that her death was falsely reported in order to keep the Son of Samael from targeting her during her coma.

Sources in the hospital indicate that Leland is pregnant, perhaps with the child of the Son of Samael. Despite an automobile accident and a two-month coma, the unborn child survives.

Detective Leland has chosen to keep the baby, according to sources. She has one month in which to have a legal abortion. Detective Leland is reported to have claimed that the child "is the only innocent."

Leland is scheduled to appear at tomorrow's plenary session on catching the killer. Security will be tight at the session, open only to police personnel, fearing that the Son of Samael might try to attend the conference.

"I thought you were dead." A sucking breath came into him. "I died, too. It's too late for me, now. It's too late for us."

The coffee felt hot on Samael's true lips, glued behind and beneath those of his victim. He folded the paper once, twice, and then set it beside his plate. The eggs were getting cold.

"But it will be good to see you again, Donna, my angel," he said to himself, tears tracing the line of spirit gum under his eyes. "I'm glad one of us still lives."

Sergeant Mike Uriel sat in Arlington Heights's East High School theater. Nearly a thousand delegates were in attendance. Many were detectives, many others beat cops, administrators, dispatchers – even neighborhood watch captains, ministers, teachers, reporters, boy's club advisors, and other average citizens. The theater had a carnival atmosphere: masses come to gawk at human grotesqueries.

That's why they will never catch me, thought Mike Uriel, leaning back in his seat. They all think I'm human.

All but, perhaps, one. Detective Donna Leland spoke from a wheelchair, unable to stand for long periods. She wore a suit jacket and blouse, but in place of the slacks was a skirt that allowed room for her pregnant belly.

"– I have, needless to say, learned a lot about serial criminals in my pursuit of and relationship with the Son of Samael. Profilers from the Quantico Behavioral Sciences Unit have given me a crash course in understanding the thinking of psychotics and psychopaths. Being Azra's confidante has taught me even more. We were companions, the killer and I. We were intimate. I knew Azra the man before I knew Samael the monster."

The crowd's polite hush deepened into silence.

Unfair, Donna. Unfair. You said you would not testify against me. You said you would not abandon me.

"The inevitable result of our liaison is this child I now carry, his child. The other result is an especial insight into the mind of this man. I share these insights with you in hopes, not only, of getting him off the streets, but also of helping him. Of saving him and all of us."

The lines are drawn now, my angel. You have betrayed me. The lines are drawn.

"For example, is this man a psychotic or a psychopath? Is he deluded about his own nature, and therefore committing his crimes due to paranoid schizophrenia? Or does he know exactly what he is doing, merely disguising the fulfillment of his violent sexual fantasies in a guise of madness?

"Originally, we had Keith McFarland to explain many of the disorganized, psychotic elements of these crimes. No longer. The Son of Samael has likely killed another twenty-three people without McFarland. Even so, these crimes continue to show signs of a psychotic – many clues left at the crime scenes, high-risk victims, ritualized manipulation of the body, and so forth. Remember, our man has likely committed these acts solo."

Yes, I committed them on my own, but was prompted by you and all of you and the hosts of Heaven and Hell and God himself. You all are complicit in my crimes. You all are accomplices, and you all will be victims.

"On the other hand, other aspects of the crime scenes – those committed with McFarland and those committed solo – indicate someone utterly methodical, manipulative, and premeditative. Certainly Azra showed all these signs, and his canny ability to elude and taunt police even now demonstrates this psychopathic side.

"Add to this obvious discrepancy two very distinct and equally incredible stories of this man's past. The first story, reported widely by the Son of Samael and, by all appearances, believed by him, is that he was the angel of death assigned to the greater Milwaukee-Chicago area. His work as an angel of death fits very nicely with the psychopathic elements of the crimes. Control is the hallmark of this kind of killer, knowing the victims in advance, humanizing them during the act, and taking an artistic care in the ways the deaths occur.

It is the truth. I was an angel. Only among humans does the truth enslave.

"The other story, that the Son of Samael was a POW MIA from the Gulf War, fits well with the psychotic elements – a man driven to commit heinous acts by some half-understood delusion, sometimes in broad daylight, often leaving a crime scene filled with clues."

That is the lie – the lie you taught me to believe.

"I suggest a temporal distinction. Prior to the murder of Derek Billings, Samael believed himself to be an angel, and his involvement in the murders had an organized quality. Afterward, he believed himself to be a madman, and his murders – specifically the killing of Derek Billings – became psychotic."

I was mad to believe I could be human.

"So, what does the Son of Samael believe himself to be now? Interestingly, his first post-escape civilian victim was a priest, whom he shot but did not dismember. In fact, the lethal wound on the priest's abdomen had been inexpertly bandaged. A cashier at a gas station nearby, who said she spoke to the Son of Samael the night before and the day after the priest's death, said he wanted everyone to know he was polite to her, paid his money, and did not threaten. He said, 'Tell them what I was like. Tell them what I was.'

"Here lies another transformation. Having at last been convinced of his humanity, the Son of Samael acts according to it. He tries to kill himself when he believes I am dead, then kills only to escape paramedics and police, then shoots a priest who is about to summon police, but feeling bad about it, tries to save the man's life. The priest's death is the final indicator to the Son of Samael that he can never live as a decent human, that he will be hunted all his life, and when caught in a situation that requires him to kill, he will kill."

Oh, Donna, even now, you know me so well. I wish we could go back. I wish I could turn time backward as once I could.

"But the final transformation, the stressor that preceded this latest rash of killings, was the announcement of the falsehood of the Son of Samael's human past. Here is a man who, after much browbeating, was at last convinced that he was human, and had the name William B. Dance, and had a very specific past filled with horrific tortures. Now he is told that that very past is a lie. All he is left with is his belief in an angelic origin, and his knowledge that he cannot regain his lost divinity. With the death of the priest, he could not even retain his humanity. So, what sort of creature is he now? What kind of being kills humans with impunity?

"Fallen angels. Fiends. Demons. At the tattoo parlor, there was a drawing that none of the workers had seen before, an ornately patterned mask. The Des Plaines police recently learned the face is a ritual mask of Shaytan, the Arabic name for Satan."

Very good, my angel. Very good.

"Do you see? He thinks he has fallen from the heavens here to Earth for a short while, and descended farther than that to an abode in Hell. He is rejected by God and man. He is alone in torment, and desires only to strike out of the black heart of Hell to terrorize those with the smug fortune of living above."

You know me so well. If I cannot have you as a companion, I will be content to have you as an adversary.

"Now, what does all of this have to do with catching Samael? First of all, it gives us a model for judging his behavior. When he believed himself to be an angel, he killed accordingly. When he believed himself to be human, he killed accordingly. Now, believing himself to be Satan incarnate, his murders are vicious, brazen, defiant acts of revenge.

"Our proactive strategies, therefore, ought to involve actions that wound his pride. He needs to be made a fool of in order for him to take the bait. Unlike the angel, who sought to kill anonymously, the new Son of Samael wants everyone to know who is doing the killing. He acts out of egotism. He wants publicity. He's probably read every account printed about him, noting the names of writers who build up his violence and power, and noting also those who trivialize his position. Understanding this dynamic gives us a starting point for luring him in."

A plenary such as this one would be irresistible.

"Even so, he uses the very faces and hands of his victims as disguises. This shows his utter contempt for humanity. Having been human for a few short months, he thinks he knows enough about us to despise us. We can expect many more such attacks on humanity, perhaps something at a school or a YMCA, perhaps something at a hospital or nursery."

Thanks for the ideas.

"In the end, it does not matter whether this man was

ever an angel, or is now a demon. All that matters is that he thinks he is these things, and acts accordingly. My time is just about up, I see, but I'd like to open the floor for questions."

Perfect, thought Mike Uriel, standing up and raising his hand.

Detective Leland pointed his way, and all eyes turned toward him.

Lowering his hand – in fact, the somewhat fleshy hand of the old man – he growled out a question in an old-man voice. "You say that this demonic killer will be looking to attack humanity – children in particular. What do you think the killer's intent is toward your child?"

Even from that distance, he could see her face whiten. A growl of offense moved through the crowd. Mike Uriel did not sit, though, awaiting a reply.

Detective Leland waved away the angry sound of the crowd and said, "No, no. It's a good question. I'm up to my eyeballs in this particular case, and my child will be, as well. Let's first get this straight – the child is mine, not his, not the department's. And, secondly, let's hope the Son of Samael is caught before the baby is born, in another four months. If not, he may well try to take the baby."

"Take the baby? Why would he want it?" asked Mike Uriel. "Wouldn't a demon prefer to kill the child so that nothing of his humanity would remain?"

"Perhaps," Donna responded slowly, as though she hadn't considered that possibility. "But he may want to claim the child as his own, as the flesh and blood incarnation of evil. The son of Satan, and all that."

Mike Uriel nodded. The pleased smile on his face quirked the skin of the dead man. "Thank you. Most insightful, most helpful. Thank you."

The ambulance waited outside the stage door, and a line of policemen stood on either side of the walkway, a gauntlet Detective Leland must run.

Leland was in no shape to run. She felt like sleeping for three days. Another officer wheeled her chair out the doorway and toward the waiting ambulance. She smiled wanly and waved. The cops cheered her, some reaching out to pat her back in appreciation.

When she reached the ambulance bumper, a thin young paramedic emerged from within and took her hand, gently helping her up into the vehicle. He guided her to a gurney and helped her lie down. Leland touched a hand to her chest, breathing hard from even that little exertion. The paramedic blinked his sensitive silvery eyes and handed her an oxygen mask. He eased the handle. "Just until you catch your breath."

She didn't put the plastic cup over her face, clutching it in one hand. "Wait until the crowd can't see."

He laughed a little. "That's easy enough." He lifted the folded wheelchair into the back of the ambulance, swung the doors closed, and stowed the chair. "There. How about you take a whiff of that stuff?"

She already had the mask over her face.

Two breaths later, she was unconscious.

"All right, go ahead," the young paramedic said to the driver.

The ambulance let out a small *bleep* as it lurched forward.

The paramedic drew the door to the cab closed, then moved to the side of the unconscious lieutenant. He lifted the oxygen mask from her face and shut off the cock. Then, from his own face, he peeled away a mask of skin and stowed it in a bag at his belt.

The Son of Samael grinned, rubbing away the clinging balls of spirit gum. Beneath lay the blue-gray crazings of the demon tattoo. Lines ran along his cheekbones, outlined his eye sockets and lips, and thickened into black swarms upon his brow. The whole of the tattoo formed an exaggerated skull, and every line upon it flamed with the fires of death.

"Oh, Donna. I know we can never return to that place of bliss. But I wanted to kiss you again with my own lips."

He leaned over her, laid his lips upon hers, and kissed her, long and lingeringly. Drawing away, he watched her, the slow rise and fall of breath in her chest.

"You were right about me. You are the only one. You understand me. You are the Antivirgin, who will always intercede for me. We have communed, have shared a maculate conception. In that, we will be forever joined.

"But the child conceived by us – it cannot be allowed to live," he said, pulling down a syringe he had laid aside.

He drew a three-inch cardiac needle from an adjacent drawer and fitted it to the wide cylinder. Then, stabbing the side of a bottle of window-washing liquid, he drew the blue stuff up into the syringe.

"I want nothing of me to remain in the mortal realm. Why else do you think I've stolen so many faces and hands? I want to pass completely from this flesh. Already I do not identify myself with my own features. I certainly won't have my face and hands running around on another body."

He pulled the shirt back from her pregnant belly, probed for a hard spot – the baby's shoulder or head or hip – and then rammed the needle home, emptying the shaft in one long compression. Donna did not move at all, except from the jolt of his fist. When he drew the needle out, there was a little clear fluid mixed with the blood and window cleaner. That seemed a good sign.

He leaned away, sliding the door back just slightly. "How much farther to the first tollbooth?" he asked the driver.

"About ten minutes," the driver responded. "Why? You got a girlfriend there?"

"No. I just thought I'd stretch my legs."

"How's the cop doing?"

"Sleeping like a baby."

TWENTY-FOUR

The wheels of the gurney rattled irritably upon the polished linoleum of the St Mary's emergency room. Metal doorways and wire-reinforced windows scurried past on one side, a long, unrelieved expanse of flowered wallpaper on the other. The blue-white glow of fluorescent lights flashed overhead in warning.

"Pulse steady at a hundred twenty. Pressure seventy over forty and dropping. Breathing rapid and shallow."

The man pushed, his face pimpled with cold sweat above his heavy EMT coat, which dragged stiffly at his arms.

"Injury? What happened?" The intern looked frumpy in her gray scrubs, white coat, and hair net.

"I don't know. The paramedic was a new guy. He disappeared after the first toll. He must've screwed up and panicked."

"God damn it. Here, this way. Got an empty bay over here. What did he do to her?"

"He gave her some oxygen. After that, I don't know."

"Oxygen or anesthetic? She could be overdosed, back in a coma, or worse."

"What about the rapid breathing? That's not from anesthetic. More like a toxic reaction."

"God damn it. She was supposed to be safe with us. Anything else?"

"Not that I can think of."

"Clear off. Nurse, ready the crash cart. IV push. Get somebody checking her mouth for signs of poison. Hell, her shoulders and hips for needle marks, too. God damn it! It's like that bastard's able to reach right into – shit. Cut her clothes off. Check everywhere. Check every inch of her. Who knows what that fucker did to her."

I shouldn't have done that one. I shouldn't have done him like I did. From the very start, it was a lark. A whim. There wasn't enough grim poetry in it, only the fun of a lawyer strangling at sixty-five miles an hour on the Edens. But it wasn't fun. It was cheap and sour and foul.

He was a lawyer, a sometime-prosecutor – a killer, like me, except authorized by the government instead of by God. He made sure criminals received what was coming to them – sometimes steel cages, sometimes death. We were peas in a pod, he and I. I had the same outlook and wanted him to get what he deserved. I chose him partly for that, but mostly because I couldn't resist when I saw his name spelled out in white plastic capitals on the office register: PHIL JUDGEM.

I shouldn't have done him. Right then I knew it. This would be no more than a cheap joyride. A fling. A hand-job...

The elevator doors parted. Phil Judgem stood within the red-velour space. He wore a sleek suit of gray-blue, cut to hide his pudginess. A suit can do only so much. His neck strained in its white collar, and venous hands drooped beneath silver cufflinks. The glint of metal was brief, like a spark at his wrists. Judgem moved on.

He walked through the lobby. It was a modern sanctuary of glass, steel, and marble. There were others of his kind here, silent and sleek and a little wide-eyed like salmon nuzzling past each other. Judgem reached the perpetually revolving doors, timed his feet, and came out into the sunlit plaza.

I was waiting. The valet jacket was only slightly too big for me. The cap fit perfectly.

"The green Mercedes," he said to me, holding up the claim card.

I nodded enthusiastically, snatched the keys, and hurried down into the parking lot.

The place was dark, a cave of cement and rusted wire. It smelled poisonous from exhaust. I scanned the current batch, fitted tightly bumper to bumper, and found a dark green Mercedes. Going to it, I tried the key. It fit. I opened the door, sat down in the driver's seat, started up the car, and pulled out, heading for the main entrance. It was some car, with seats of black leather, power everything, and a ride quiet as a purr.

The gray parking garage gave way to a wedge of cloud-cluttered sky. The car glided up the ramp and came to a smooth stop beside Judgem. I opened the door, stepped from the driver's seat, and gestured him toward his car. He placed a dollar in my hand and moved past me to get in.

I might not have killed him even then, might have let him drive off, but for the sweaty crumple of that dollar in my hand. I thought of the fifty from that reporter, Blake Gaines. It had been the same. Warm and intimate. Disgusting.

One kick knocked him sideways into the passenger seat. He kicked back at me. I shot him. It was a fat bullet. The impact shoved him all the way over. I climbed behind the wheel, locked the windows and doors, and roared out toward Ohio Street and the ramp onto 94 North.

He cowered beside me. His hand lay limp in his lap. One fat leg was wrenched a little sideways.

"You can have the car. You can have my wallet. You can have everything, just let me go."

It was going sour. The whole thing. He smelled of feces – maybe the bullet had cut through bowel, or maybe he'd dirtied himself. He was white and soft as a pudding. He jiggled.

"Please. Anything."

"God damn it, shut up. Shut the fuck up." I pointed the gun at his head. I felt sick. I couldn't enjoy it anymore. He was disgusting. Not like the others. There was no dignity. It was like walking on white worms lying in rain puddles. "Shut the fuck up."

He vomited. I pressed a button. His window rolled down halfway. We were going sixty-five up the Edens.

"Stick your fucking head outside!" I shouted.

Wiping his mouth, he stuck his head out the window. I pressed a button. The glass rose to catch him beneath the chin. He tried to pull his head out, but already it was caught between glass and chrome. He fumbled to reach the controls, but I kept my finger down so nothing he did made a difference.

I was sick. He was like a pig with its head stuck in a gate, fat and grotesque as he struggled and died. I couldn't stand it. I emptied the gun into him, let down the window, and let him roll in beside me. God, what a fucking mess.

Samael was not the angel of death who turned Lot's wife into a pillar of salt. Nor was he the angel of death who stole through Egypt to slay all the firstborn sons of the land. Samael's commission began later, when it was time for Moses to die.

Elohim sought an angel to descend among his people and separate the soul of Moses from his body. God asked the archangel Gabriel, the great messenger to humans, who did not wish to slay the Lawgiver. Next God asked Michael, who was the head of Heaven's armies and would in time become the angel of death for Christians, but he also refused.

Samael, however, was eager for the job of killing God's greatest prophet.

Though as holy and angelic as all the rest, Samael had a certain penchant for cruelty. After God gave him the task of killing Moses, Samael spent a long while determining how best to do it.

Perhaps Moses should die through a series of Egypt-like plagues – his blood would turn to water, his hair to locusts, his genitalia to toads, his skin to boils, his shadow to impenetrable darkness, and so forth. Or, perhaps, Moses could be enticed to part the Jordan River and cross, despite God's prohibition against him entering the land of milk and honey. Then Samael could loose the tide when Moses was halfway, and the water would crash over him, and he would drown. Or, best of all, Moses could be murdered by a man who, in the single act of killing him, broke all Ten Commandments. The murderer could be Moses's covetous son, who dishonored his father in an adulterous affair with an idol-worshiper on the Sabbath and, when discovered in the act by Moses, blasphemed and stole Moses's dagger and murdered him with it, then ran away and testified that his neighbor had done it.

Unfortunately, Moses had no such son.

Samael at last settled on simply killing Moses with his bare hands. Samael descended from Heaven, appearing in human form to choke the life from Moses's body. Moses's face, however, shone so brightly from having seen God that Samael was scared off. He had planned full-scale atrocities, but this man shone like God! Samael complained to the Creator, who chastised him and sent him back to finish the job.

Samael appeared again in human form before Moses, who was ready this time. With his fabled staff – the one that had turned into a serpent – the great prophet walloped Samael.

Samael was not used to such treatment at the hands of mortals and went again to complain to God. Meanwhile, Michael and Gabriel, who had said they would not kill Moses, went down to complete the task. They created a heavenly couch and invited the weary old prophet to sit down for a rest. When he did, they whisked the couch up to Heaven.

Though they had gotten Moses off the earth, his soul still did not want to leave his body. He clung tight to the couch. Even the great archangels had failed.

In the end, Moses was slain by a kiss from God himself, which made his soul leap for joy, right out of his body.

The sun has already set behind the wall of skyscrapers along Grant Park, casting building wedges far out across the foamy lake. I sit on a green-painted park bench. I feed the pigeons. It is an image I cannot resist. The gentle killer. The quiet murderer. The pensive and reflective monster.

I don't like the fat pigeons. Those I kick when I can. I like the skinny little ones. I like the gimp pigeons, the ones with only two claws on a foot, or none at all. I like them because they bear up under the crushing heel of God. God knows when every sparrow falls from Heaven, and when every pigeon goes gimp, and those broken little ones are the fleshly manifestation of His ethereal will.

The dark is deep now. The building shadows have taken over the whole lake. The trees are as black as Purbeck marble. Beyond stands the gray wall of Chicago.

Lincoln Park Zoo is closing. Already, the parking lot is half empty. They've locked one of the big iron gates in front. People trickle out the other, in ones and twos and clinging clumps. The numbers dwindle. The people walk low at heel. Their limbs hang tiredly on them.

Out comes an old man. His sweater hangs in two triangles above the baggy knees of his gray trousers. At his side capers a child, a tow-headed boy. They could have been Abraham and Isaac, age and youth, patience and vigor. They are coming this way, down this path.

I toss out more bits of cracker. I want the pigeons to be as thick as autumn leaves when the boy arrives. I want him to charge into their midst and scatter them in a bleating flock.

The pigeons cooperate, but not the boy. He moves forward with the nudging caution of a car pushing through a flock of sheep. I smile gently at the boy as he and the old man pass me by. They round a hedge and head into a pedestrian tunnel beneath Lake Shore Drive. For some reason, I stand and follow.

It is not their time to die. Not today. Not by my hand. Perhaps that is why I follow.

The gun is the charcoal color of the tunnel's fitted stones, but it glints an even rod of light. The darkness behind it is an alcove, and a man in the alcove. The boy and his grandfather – I had decided that was their relationship – stand in at rigid attention, their hands held comically above their heads.

"Leave them alone," I shout.

The gun swings toward me for a moment. "Fuck off."

I continue into the tunnel, already five paces away. "You fuck off."

As I close on him, he shoots twice. I feel a strange, disjointed heat in my right hand, but don't understand it until I swing a fist at the man and see meat and blood and bone slap limply against his face. My left has his gun. I kick him in the groin and wrench his gun away. I turn it and shoot, emptying the cartridge into him. Then, as an afterthought, I fling the hot gun at the gurgling fountain of blood that he has become.

Turning, I gaze at the trembling, terrified child and his grandfather. I sketch an ironic bow and gesture them safely on their way.

It was all too familiar – the acoustic tiles, the peach-colored walls, the bed rails and plastic tubes and furtively beeping machines. At first, Donna thought she was awakening from a relapse of the coma, but the speech at the plenary loomed too large in her mind.

Something had happened. Something dreadful.

Her hand moved down to the mound of her baby. She felt the baby kick, awakening also. She also felt a dozen sore spots. At each one a bright-colored plastic pouch clung leechlike to a taped slit in her skin.

"It's for the infection," said a female voice. "It draws the seepage away from your organs."

Donna glanced stiffly to one side and saw the short, red-haired doctor she vaguely remembered from her previous awakening. "Hello. I just woke up."

"I just walked by," responded the doctor, coming to sit at her bedside. "How are you feeling?"

"Wrung out."

The doctor smiled. Her lipstick was the same hue as her hair. "That's what we tried to do. Wring you out. The cleaner got all through your peritoneum."

"In English?"

"Your abdominal organs were bathed in Windex for about three hours. We drained it off, but there was a layer of necrosis on the outsides of some of them. Your body is getting rid of the dead cells, and the little bladders here are drawing out the infection."

"Windex. How the hell – ?"

"He injected you. I think he was trying for the baby. It's good he didn't know what to do with a needle. By the time he got through your abdominal muscles, he thought he was into the uterus. He wasn't into anything except a layer of fat."

She said ruefully, "We can't stop him. Nobody can stop him."

"Well, apparently your baby can. He's a fighter. The baby wasn't touched by the stuff, except indirectly, through the effects of the coma."

The doctor paused, her eyes compassionate above an apologetic smile.

"When I saw you were awake, I had the nurse call your chief. He's coming up."

Donna sighed, leaning back. "It'll take an hour from Burlington."

The doctor's smile turned wry. "Actually, he's coming up from the cafeteria. He's been taking his lunch here ever since you landed here the second time. He gives a break to the guys stationed outside your door."

Donna saw a head leaning around the corner and a brief wave before the whole doorway was eclipsed by a fat and red-faced figure. "There's my girl!" came Biggs's ebullient greeting. "I had a feeling you'd wake up today."

"You've said that every day," the doctor replied.

The chief's bruin body seemed to be crying out for a hug, and Donna lifted her arms toward him. He swallowed her in his hearty embrace.

"I'm so glad you're back with us."

Donna drew back, and he released her, standing upright. She smiled. "Hi, Chief. It's good to be back." She glanced down at the lumps beneath her nightgown, where the little plastic bulbs clung, and began to cry. "I'd heard pregnancy was a bitch, but–"

He laughed. "You're back, all right."

Miserable, she asked, "How many days this time?"

"Three. Just a long nap."

"And in that time, you've caught the Son of Samael, and the killing is all over, and he'll never touch my baby again?"

He glanced toward the thickly waxed floor. "Afraid not. Still, it doesn't look like he's killed while you were under."

Sadness deepened across her face. "What happened, Chief? He wasn't supposed to be able to get to me. Not anymore. What the hell happened?"

Behind rags of red on his cheeks, Biggs looked white. "I'm sorry, Donna. It won't happen again. He'll be in prison soon enough."

She sighed, leaning wearily back into her bed. "If he'd succeeded, it would all be over. Maybe killing me and the baby would have won him his wings back."

Biggs looked both dismayed and hurt. "No. Don't talk like that. We need you, Detective. Besides, I've got a better plan."

"A plan? Something proactive, I hope."

"You could say that. Your funeral is planned for a week and a half from now."

"My funeral?"

"He's been reading the papers, Donna. He knew about you waking up last time, about you talking at the plenary, and about the baby. Now he's going to find out about you dying. You and the baby."

"Would he fall for that again?"

"He doesn't have to fall for it completely – just want to find out. We'll set up a big funeral – dress blues and everything. Cops from three counties. We'll even have a twenty-one gun salute. A eulogy for you and the baby. He won't be able to resist."

"Why a week and a half? Isn't that a long time to keep me on ice?"

"You're not going to 'die' until next week. We need time to organize this down to the last detail. We're going to have a hundred cops there and fifty trained spotters, sharpshooters, dogs, the works. He'll find himself in the center of a beehive."

"He's smart. He'll know it's a trap."

"Maybe, but will he be able to resist? I'm betting he won't."

"I want to be there," Donna said, putting on a brave face and struggling to sit up higher in the bed. Every one of the plastic bladders pulled achingly. "I know him better than anyone else. Besides, it'd be nice to sneak up on him for a change."

"I knew you'd say that. I also knew you'd be invaluable there. This guy's become a master of disguise. To catch him, we'll have to let in a lot of pedestrian onlookers, and we'll need every eye we can get. Yes, you'll be there – part of the reason we need the extra time – for you to recover well enough to walk. But you'll be armed, and disguised, and wearing a wire and microphone, and guarded by three men."

"A little conspicuous, don't you think?"

His lips rolled up between his teeth in a grim smile. "I'm not willing to lose you again."

"Well," said the doctor, breaking in on the conversation, "if you want your guest of honor to be ready for next week, you'd better let her get some more rest now."

"Yes," the captain said. Sweat prickled across his brow. "Yes."

"Oh, one last thing," Donna asked, "where am I to be buried? I was always hoping for St Mary's Cemetery. God's Acre, and all that."

The chief shook his head. "St Mary's is too open, too hard to lock down."

"St Charles–"

"You don't want St Charles, with all those woods – paths everywhere and tree forts and kids with paintball guns and guys sitting on rocks smoking weird shit."

"Where, then?"

"You're going in with the Protestants. Burlington Cemetery's got only one access road, and it's backed by an impassible swamp. We'll have the road blockaded and cops as thick as gravestones."

"Sounds restful," she said, drifting to sleep.

The Son of Samael lay against the wall. He would be in a bathtub except that it was down the hall and shared by five other rooms, and the tub was grimier than the cockroach-littered floor. He lay against the wall, wincing with each turn of the splintered stick.

Already, the rag around his wrist was tight enough to stop the bleeding, but he wrenched the stick one last turn, hearing the soft grind of the radius and ulna as they bowed against each other.

There, tight enough. He paused, giving himself two long, low breaths and gritting his teeth. *Oh, to be done with this pulpy and fragile flesh. To at last be done.*

Leaning forward, he gingerly slid the second rag out from between his teeth and clumsily, with his one good hand, wrapped the cloth around the stick and his arm, just below the elbow. Fingers working with echoes of pain, he tied the cloth in a half hitch, and then a square knot. The tourniquet was complete.

He sighed. His vision was filled with prickly intrusions where pain and blood loss ate away at his sight. He lifted the wounded hand. It was a mottled blue. Maroon blood seeped from two wounds. One bullet had pierced his palm, cracked the carpal bone of his ring finger, and wrenched out the back of his hand, leaving a mess of splintered bone, oozy muscle, and ripped skin. The other had struck near the base of his thumb. It had torn away the careful stitching the surgeon had done, and left the thumb dangling loose.

Samael stared at the ruined hand. He would wait until all sensation was gone below the tourniquet, then cut the hand off entirely. He had done the same to the hands of others.

The amputation somehow pleased him. He would be rid of one hunk of flesh that not only could but did cause him agony. Perhaps, if this amputation worked well, he would take off the whole arm. Twenty pounds of meat and bone would put him that much farther from the mortal realm. If only he could whittle it all away and regain his angelic form...

Ah, the merciful numbness had come.

He had done this a hundred times. Now was no different. Ram the steel tip down just beyond the heads of the radius and ulna, thereby cracking the ligaments in the joint. Then, shove it through the wrist bones, and saw away at what was left.

He positioned the knifepoint in the shallow cleft above his arm bones. Leaning his sternum upon the butt of the knife, he lunged downward.

The crackle of snapped ligaments and splintered bone edges was a white-hot flash in his mind…

Numbly, he realized he slumped over the knife and the pinned flesh of his wrist. He couldn't breathe. There was a sound like swarming bees in his head, and piercing yellow lights…

He awoke, shuddering, atop the canted knife. He lurched back and sat, panting. His wrist was still pinned to the floor.

Pain. It was the basis of all human morality. Everyone was captive to it. Everyone was vulnerable insofar as others could torture and rape and destroy the body.

That is why humans seek to do each other no harm. That is why they consider it wrong to beat or mutilate or kill. That is why they believe in going to Heaven or Hell.

But none of that mattered. He was not human, not anymore. He would toss away this hand as though it were a tin can.

Prying the blade up from the weepy wound, he set the tip again and lunged. The hand tilted away from the blade. One more lunge, and the appendage hung loose on tatters of flesh. He could see the floor through the three stabs he had made.

Only moments more, and I can toss this hand in with the others.

With a grim gritting of teeth, the Son of Samael set to sawing his own hand free.

TWENTY-FIVE

It was a beautiful summer day in Burlington. The cemetery was hilly and wooded, with graves that went back to 1828. Some stones had been rendered unreadable in the great wash of time. Small, one-lane roads of fresh blacktop wove between crimson-king maples and scrubby oaks. The gray-white stones stood in clean, solemn rows on a carpet of green.

Route W was closed for two miles to either side, from Route 11 to the doorway of the Country Vet. Between those two police roadblocks ran a road through harvested fields and past a grove that was thick with camouflaged National Guardsmen. One side of the road was parked full of funeral cars.

Burlington's fourteen available officers (including the meter readers) had shown up in dress blues, specially ordered for the funeral of their beloved detective and her unborn child. Their handgun shoulder holsters made ominous mounds in the dark, straightjackets they wore. There were also seven riflemen from the National

Guard, dressed in immaculate ceremonial garb and bearing ceremonial weapons that usually shot only blanks. Today the rifles were loaded with sixty-grain hollow-point shot. The officers of other departments wore their best as well, and carried fully loaded side arms. Even the local farmers, who had been warned to stay inside with windows and doors locked, sat behind their drapes, shotguns at the ready.

The police blockades had been ordered to get photo identification from anyone entering the area. They were instructed even to tweak the cheeks of their fellow cops, making certain those cheeks were real. Chief Biggs had sent no warnings of this unusual inspection. If the Son of Samael showed up as a cop, they wanted to catch him before he got anywhere near Detective Leland.

She was there, but not in the bronze casket suspended over the grave. She was in an unmarked blue police car, parked near the cemetery gates. The vehicle had darkened windows of bulletproof glass. The woman herself wore a bunchy black dress with a high, lacy neck, such as old women sometimes mourn in. The ensemble was completed by a veil and a shallow, broad-brimmed hat. A makeup man had given her an enhanced nose, an enlarged chin, and gray-streaked eyebrows beneath a white wig. Silent and watchful, huddled in the dark-windowed sedan, she could have been the dead cop's grandmother.

"Nothing yet," she muttered into the tan wire that ran from an earpiece to the edge of her lips. "Many are ruled out on height alone, Chief."

"Keep watching," came the voice from the headset.

She glanced along a picket of older, taller gravestones where the chief paced. She whispered, "He'll show up. He won't be able to stay away."

Biggs's voice was worried. "I just hope we haven't scared him off, with all the security."

"That just sweetens the deal for him – makes it even more of a challenge."

"Somebody's coming. We'll talk later."

Leland glanced out the window to see who approached the chief. It was a short, thin man in a red blazer, his side-burned head cocked inquisitively as he reached Biggs. There was a moment of tension, and then a nod and a handshake, traded words and smiles.

Leland sighed, easing back in her seat. The man had been too short, too thin. That man there, though – no. It was Blake Gaines in a navy blue suit, down from his new post on the Milwaukee *Journal-Sentinel*. He'd received a special invitation and right to roam the grounds, on condition he photographed the crowd. Gaines, smelling another exclusive, had showed up with notepad, camera rig, and even the Channel 4 News chopper. It waited in a field behind a copse of trees, ready in case of a high-speed chase.

"Leland," Biggs broke in, "watch for the guy getting out of the orange-red Festiva. The roadblock called in, saying he looked suspicious."

"Right, Chief," Leland responded.

A reddish-orange Festiva rumbled up and passed her car, its old-style door handles scrapingly close. Behind the wheel was a tall, intense figure, his eyes wide and excited, his hands tight and feverish on the wheel. He glanced at a narrow parking space hard beside the open iron gate, and his car darted into it. One front tire dipped down into the ditch, and the opposite rear wheel lifted from the rutted road. The gray cloud puffing from the exhaust pipe sputtered away. The driver's door squealed open. A man emerged, tall and thin, his face oddly rigid and slightly jaundiced. He had watchful silver eyes.

A chill went through Leland. "He's the first one I've seen that looks the part."

"Right," said the chief. "He's also the last one through the gate except a four-foot-two grandma at ninety-eight pounds."

The silver-eyed man leaned forward as he climbed the sloping drive of the cemetery. He passed the gates. His jacket was the dull gray-white of the tombstones.

"Listen, Boss," Leland said, "I know I agreed to stay in the car, but I'm not sure if it's him, and he's just now gone over–"

"Stay put, Leland. That better not be the sound of your car door–"

"He's going to be here, somewhere. We all know that. I want to make sure we catch him. I want no more skulking, no more of this masquerade."

She stood, slammed the door behind her, and reminded herself to toddle rather than stride after the white-suited man.

Ahead lay the tableaux of the closed casket, wreathed in flowers and hemmed in on all sides by black-suited mourners. Beside it, a red-jowled face appeared, marching toward her. The chief was very handsome in dress blues.

His voice came through Leland's earpiece. "I'm going to be right next to you, then. I'm bringing one of the spotter teams forward to surround the guy and have a look at him."

"Fine."

Biggs moved the microphone away from his face and, with barely believable stage decorum, said, "Here, ma'am, let me help you. You should have waited for someone to take your hand."

Leland took his arm. They topped the rise, crossed the blacktop, and stepped onto the tender grass. The morning lawn was damp with dew, which soaked chillingly into her stockings.

She spoke into her headset. "I know he's here. I can feel it. But whether that string bean is him…"

The chief looked toward the gathered group. "The string bean is heading for the foot of the grave. Let's go up that way. Then I'll walk you around the far side of the grave to one of the chairs set up behind the priest. I'm sure we can get someone to let you sit. Be watching for him all the time."

"Well, duh."

Taking tiny, patient steps, the two approached rows of seated civilians and standing officers. Leland decided to ignore the police, for the moment. They'd been thoroughly checked. Samael could be among the news cameramen. They stood with their tripods behind a black velvet cord, held up by four theater-style stanchions. Still, those cameras had been closely checked, too. Or Samael might be seated among the reporters, beside the photographers. But they, too, had endured a thorough and perhaps less-than-gentle inspection.

He was here, though.

As they approached, Leland looked into each set of eyes that turned toward her – the cerulean gaze of a long-haired young boy, the brown serene witness of a black matriarch, the dull grays and blues of others. It was not color she checked – he could be wearing colored contact lenses – but soul, that predatory soul.

"It's him, Chief," came a whispered voice over the headphones. "This is Spotter Six. This guy's got the exact same height, and maybe ten or fifteen pounds lighter, but he's been on the lam. Besides, that skin can't be real. There's something wrong with his eyes."

"Anybody else got an opinion?" Biggs asked.

"This is Spotter Three." A woman's voice. "I don't think so. Too obvious. Everything fits, but he's too nervous, too high-strung."

"She's right," Leland agreed. "He wouldn't be nervous. He would be in complete control."

"Yeah, but wouldn't you be nervous with two hundred fifty packing cops around?" the chief asked. "And what if it is him? We say we missed him because his disguise wasn't good enough and he was too nervous?"

The chief's whisper was barely audible. They were nearing the place where the silver-eyed man stood. There was a nervous severity in the suspect, something

Leland had never seen in Samael. On the other hand, by all accounts, Samael had changed. He was suicidal as well as homicidal. On the run. Perhaps without food or sleep or shelter.

"It could be him," she murmured, "a little thinner, a little worse for wear." They were edging around the cluster, as if the old lady wanted to get a clear view of the casket and flowers before she sat down. "If he's mentally decayed, it could be him."

"This is Spotter Six," came a male voice. "He's got my vote."

"Mine, too – Spotter One."

Biggs pretended to be cautioning the old crone about a depression in the ground when he said, "He's either our man, or somebody even worse off."

They rounded the group, and Leland noticed a glint of metal on the man's gray-white lapel. "What is that pin he's wearing?"

One of the supposed mourners standing near the man ducked his head, scratching the top of it. "An angel."

A shiver went through Leland. She remembered exactly that sensation when she had met Sergeant Michaels at the Inn-Town Tap in Griffith. "It's him," she said. "I'm almost positive."

"Any other suspects?" the chief asked, and there were no responses from the other groups of spotters. "All right, then. Wait until I get the old bag here seated. Then I want Jenkins to drop him with the hypodermic, and the rest of you be ready to catch him and act like he fainted. Get him away from the crowd and out of sight before you try ripping his face off."

Leland cringed as she passed her own casket. In a moment, it'll all be over.

As if cued by that thought, the ornate casket began its slow, quiet descent into the grave.

"By the rivers of Babylon, there we sat down, yea, we wept, when we remembered Zion–" The priest spoke the psalm with the lyric, ringing voice of an oracle, reading from a fat Bible held in his left hand. "We hanged our harps upon the willows in the midst thereof. For there they that carried us away captive required of us a song; and they that wasted us required of us mirth, saying, Sing us one of the songs of Zion. How shall we sing the Lord's song in a strange land?"

Biggs had done well to get one of Leland's old parochial school priests to do the service. It leant authenticity. Father George, was it? Or Father Ben? They both had seemed ancient when she had been in their classes twenty years ago, and she was surprised either of them still lived. Even so, that white-haired, white-robed old man was just as she had remembered him – with kind eyes and a perpetual, uncomfortable smile.

She'd seen him in the paper recently – a photo with that smile. Probably something about his officiating at her funeral.

"If I forget thee, O Jerusalem, let my right hand forget her cunning. If I do not remember thee, let my tongue cleave to the roof of my mouth; if I prefer not Jerusalem above my chief joy–"

Apparently Father Whomever remembered her as a student. As she passed him, a tear crept from the corner of his eye and ran down to linger in the hollow above his cheekbone.

"Remember, O Lord, the children of Edom in the day of Jerusalem; who said Raze it, raze it, even to the foundations thereof."

From the front row of seats, a pale-faced man stood and gestured toward his vacated chair. Leland nodded her thanks. The chief shook the man's hand and patted him lightly on the cheek, as though he were Italian.

"Bless you," Biggs said.

Leland settled into the chair.

Biggs ducked down to her and whispered, "I'll be back." The big man moved and was gone beyond the priest.

"O daughter of Babylon, who art to be destroyed; happy shall he be, that rewardeth thee as thou hast served us—"

The thin man near the foot of the grave swooned. A gasp came from the watchers. A young woman caught the man. "He's fainted. Somebody help," the woman said.

Others turned in, lightly slapping his leathery face and nudging him, their voices hushed and urgent. "You all right, mister? You all right?"

The chief was in the midst of the situation. "Let's get him out of the way, get him some room to breathe." The others took the suggestion with alacrity. They grabbed arms and knees and hoisted the man from the ground. The crowd gave way. "Sorry, Father," the chief said over his shoulder. "You may continue."

The priest nodded, stooping down to take a handful of grave earth from a pile beside his white robes. Sprinkling it down into the grave, over the lowered casket, he intoned the final verse of the psalm: "Happy shall be he that taketh and dasheth thy infants against the stones."

The baby within Leland leapt.

She knew. She'd recognized the priest not from her days in parochial school, but from that newspaper photo, the photo of the latest victim of the Son of Samael.

She stood and drew her gun.

He pivoted, lowering the closed Bible to a stand beside him, and glimpsed her movement. Or, perhaps more.

She grabbed the front of his white robe and wrenched him around, gun ramming up beneath his throat. "Freeze!"

I would have been captured even then if fate had not intervened. I tried to hold still, but the robes were heavy and she had whirled me viciously around and off balance. I fell backward into the grave. It was lucky for me she held so tight to my robes. She was pulled in after me. We landed side by side, her head hitting the ringing casket.

It sounded hollow. I was glad for the first time since I had learned of Donna's second death. Of course, I had doubted it, but a nagging voice told me it was true this time. The voice was wrong. More joy: Donna herself lay, unconscious, beside me.

There was one small disappointment. She had gotten off a shot while we fell, and my right ear had been torn off. Blood poured evenly from the spot.

Above, there was a lot of scrambling and shouting. Many more guns were aimed down into the grave. None of it mattered. I'd rolled Donna onto my shoulder and held her there with my right stump. My left hand held her revolver, cocked and ready, positioned just above the bulge of my child. I stood atop the coffin, carrying my beloved on one shoulder, and smiled at the circle of policemen around us.

"Put her down, Samael," snarled a red-faced man who bolted up the hill into the crowd of guns. "You are surrounded."

"Yes," I said. "I am surrounded by this poor pregnant woman. The barrel of her gun is also surrounded by her, and by her baby. If you don't move back twenty paces before I count to five – one, two, three–" I began rapidly, providing no time for them to think, but no one had moved at three, " – four, five." I shot, and they all saw the grazing bullet punch out of her side. "Again!" I shouted. "One, two, three–" They trampled each other to get out of the way. I was grieved to have shot her. "How many people do I have to kill before you realize I am serious?"

I yanked the mask off my face, and the camera flashes were popping in a crazy kaleidoscope. The spirit gum still hung on my Shaytan tattoo, but I figured it made me look only more ghastly.

"Now, I am going to climb out of this grave, keeping the lady on me at all times. I don't want any of you crackpots in the woods thinking you can get a clean shot, because I'll be shifting constantly. She won't die unless you shoot her or you try something that makes me shoot her."

I lunged up from the grave, my white robes soiled with mud and blood. It occurred to me only then what a service the robes would do, hiding my true form beneath shifting cloth and shadows. They couldn't target my legs or feet if they wanted to.I walked. A small patch of woods ahead of us bristled with National Guardsmen, but I shouted them out. "Get clear, or the woman dies!" Another bullet, grazing Donna's other side, convinced them to scramble out of my way.

"We're going to catch you," Chief Biggs shouted behind us. "God damn you to hell!"

I liked the woods. They were pleasant. The birds sang their morning songs, oblivious to the commotion.

The WTMJ 4 chopper waited in the field beyond. The pilot was there, just where I had taped him. It took a whole roll of duct tape to hold him. He was wrapped like a mummy in the stuff. I left his eyes exposed, of course, so he could see the video man slumping in his own blood in the passenger seat. Good motivation.

I opened the passenger door, dragged the dead man out, and climbed in. Donna fit all right behind the front seats. I cut the pilot's arms loose and held the gun to his head and told him to fly. He did.

As we lifted off, National Guardsmen running out in a circle around us and shouting and aiming impotently, I thought what a bright sweet sky it was, and how wonderful it was to have Donna alive again, after all.

"Head toward Chicago," I told the mummy pilot. He did.

I'd gotten to know the city by the lake, and some of its better hidey-holes. Sure, they would try to follow me, but I'd ditch the 'copter before then and get us into a few more cars. Once we were in the city, it was perfectly possible to park under a building on Wacker Drive and emerge ten blocks away, on the other side of the river.

I'm personally indebted to whoever decided to dig rail tunnels a hundred feet below the streets of Chicago.

Donna awoke, lying in a dark room. Her costume had been stripped away, but she wasn't naked. She wore thin clothes of some kind, and over those, tightly cinched restraints, and over those, fleecy blankets. It was a gurney. She lay on a gurney. There was a thick bandage around her midsection, with compresses on both sides. There were also smooth, cool tubes running down beside her shoulder and arm.

But this was no hospital. The room itself felt deep – a windowless, lightless, airless place. It smelled of must and mold. She heard water dripping sullenly. Beyond the burning wounds in her sides and the thick blankets, the air was frigid.

And he was here. It was as certain as that. She couldn't hear his breathing or the shift of his feet. She couldn't see anything in the pitch darkness, but she felt the piercing presence of his gaze.

"You're awake," Samael said in the utter blackness.

Despite herself, Donna started. "How'd you know?"

"Your breathing. It changed. And I sensed your thoughts."

She didn't want to encourage that idea. "Where are we?"

"Deep. One of my homes."

"Very homey."

"Oh, it is. No one around is trying to kill me. That's homier than anyplace else."

"What about our home, Azra?" she ventured. "What about our place of bliss? What's happened to it?" Her voice had more edge in it than she had expected.

He rose. The whisper of his clothes echoed from walls of cement. He came to her side, stooped down, and kissed her lightly on one cheek. "We can't go back there. You know that."

A blazing light flashed into being in his hand. It glared gleefully above Samael's silvery eyes, limned his nostrils, and painted his chin in fire. The madman's shadow hovered above him on the cement ceiling.

Donna glimpsed all of that – and the now-infamous mask of Shaytan – in the instant before she clamped her eyes closed.

"I'm sorry," Samael said, sounding genuinely grieved. "It's just a pen light. I use it for checking your IVs and debriding your wounds."

She opened her eyes and squinted as they adjusted. Four transparent IV bags hung on stands above her – one holding a urine-colored liquid, another clear, a third the color of milk, and the last that of blood. Tubes ran down from each, onto Donna's shoulders and alongside her arms.

"What is all this?"

He smiled, seeming proud. The lips of Shaytan curved toward his beaming eyes. He swept the light toward the bags. "That yellow one is hyperalimentation – intravenous feeding. There's also saline, lipids, and a morphine mixture in A positive blood, on slow drip."

"No, I mean, why are you doing this?"

His tattooed brow beetled. "To save you. I didn't want to shoot you. I didn't want to poison you, either. Nothing has happened between us the way I wanted it to."

"You set all this up?"

"The doctor did. He showed me what to do. He showed me how to debride the bullet wound and how to empty the plastic pouches. You are doing much better."

Donna tried to see beyond the tepid light that played across the IV bags. "Where is this doctor? Where have you locked him up?"

"Oh, I don't have him locked up. The devil does. Of course, I kept his face and hands, so I could get more hyperal and morphine and gauze and such from the hospital."

The light darted toward a wall of old wooden shelves, cleaned and loaded with supplies – more bags, cotton, knives, needles, scissors, clamps. Beyond it, just visible in the velvety dark, was a rack draped with masks. Donna saw more than twenty of them, each loose and empty-eyed. The doctor's face must have been among them.

The sight nauseated Donna, but there was nothing in her stomach to vomit out. There had been nothing for days, perhaps weeks. She blurted bitterly. "You envy us, don't you? You dress up in our skins, take our names, make conversation over coffee. You've learned the fine art of socialization and seduction because you want to be near us, as close to us as you will ever get."

"Now, don't be bitter–"

"You were right all along, Azra. You aren't human. Not even close. But you want to be. You wish you were. We still have our birthday parties and our office jobs and our hopes and dreams – despite you. That's why you envy us. We live despite you, and you can't beat us or join us."

He was quiet, his feverish voice fading back behind the flickering light. "Yes. You've always been the one who knew me. You've always understood.

"But it isn't envy. I couldn't envy you: fragile flesh. Pain. Wounds. Weariness. Do you see this hand? Of course you don't. My flesh was cut away. You see this other hand? Yes, it is still flesh and bone. And what does it hold? A faint, flickering light, because these human eyes of mine cannot see without it. What was it St Paul said, that we see through a mirror dimly? But when my spirit eyes are returned to me, ah, then I shall see face to face. How could I possibly envy you?"

"'Nothing that is human disgusts me.'" She chanted the line as though it were an article of faith.

"What?"

"He wrote that, too, not St Paul, but Tennessee Williams. In one of his other plays, he said, 'Nothing that is human disgusts me, unless it is unkind, violent.' And that's what you have become, Azra. That's all you are. Cruel."

"Cruel? No. I take pleasure in my work, but that isn't cruelty. It's artistry," Samael replied. His tones were fervid in the chill air as he approached her. "Don't you see? Humans are alone in all of creation. God is not on your side. Satan is not, either. No angel, no devil allies with you. No plant, no animal loves you. You are at war with all the universe, and at war with your very selves. You are different from the rest, and different from each other. You are a hundred feet below the sunshine, cold and wounded and trapped, clutching a tiny light that is destined to go out. No, I could not envy you, but I do love you."

"If you love me, let me go."

"The hunter loves the doe and kills her all the same. He admires her animal grace, her tenacity, her innocence – and he wants to possess it. Loving you only makes me better at killing you."

"You're insane."

He continued as if she hadn't spoken. "I used to slay without compassion, with only an eye for justice and poetry. But then you taught me to love my prey. You, Donna. And I fell. Angels, it seems, are forbidden to love your kind. But demons are forbidden nothing. Which is better, the angel that disdains you, or the demon that loves you?"

Donna's lungs strained against the tight bands. "So, what is it, then? Once I'm healed, you're just going to hunt me down and kill me?"

"No." His voice was gentle, and he leaned toward her. "No, Donna. I'm making you well so that you can live. Trying to kill the baby inside you was a mistake. It's part of you. I couldn't kill it without killing you. No, Donna, I'm making you well so that you can deliver the child. I've already selected the doctor who will help you. She's the best obstetrician in the Midwest."

"You're going to let me give birth?"

His hand reached up to the flow regulator of the mor-phine-blood mixture. The droplets quickened in the tube. "We'll all be delivered on that day. The baby will be delivered from your womb, and I from this flesh, and you – you, my darling Donna – will be delivered alive from this dark, cold hole."

Already she was getting sleepy, and her sight had darkened even before he switched off the penlight. "You'd never let my child live."

"Oh," he replied, his voice floating in the darkness, "I said it would be delivered. I didn't say it would live."

TWENTY-SIX

The killing tonight is as it was before. Simple. Powerful. Clean. It's the old angel days. I'd almost forgotten how diverting it can be.

For the man waiting for the L, it's as simple as a push. But not that simple. I discover that he is a Caterpillar salesman, known for his aggressive tactics. He's even now telling me of the killing he thinks he'll make in Bloomington.

Death by southbound train would be perfectly fitting. The story of it will follow his generations. They will think of him forever, though he thinks of them not at all in this, his final moment.

A train is presently pulling up.

In one hand, the man lifts his briefcase full of pamphlets. In the other, he lifts his suitcase, filled with the clean folds of his wardrobe, his life.

I push him in front of the train.

The really interesting thing is not that the suitcase and briefcase explode simultaneously beneath the untroubled shriek and rumble of steel wheels. The really interesting thing is that I use both hands to push him. I'm not even thinking about my stump, but I use both hands. I can feel my missing hand.

Ever since chopping my hand off, I've felt phantom pain, but now I can feel pressure, too. His back was warm, his tweed jacket had a gentle prickle to it. It is as though, in killing, I regained my hand.

This intrigues me. There must be someone else hereabouts who needs to die, someone I can similarly touch.

The streets are loud with police cars. They send an eerie and faraway wail among the canyons of steel and glass. They neither approach nor recede but only suddenly arrive in a toothy rush and skid to a stop beneath the train station pillars. The police are bolting up iron stairs and along catwalks. The ticket woman is shrieking something I can't make out.

I walk away.

The flashing lights send my shadow huge and intermittent across the huddled shops and immemorial foundations of the skyscrapers. Passersby pause and face the murder scene. Their eyes and faces shine like small moons. I walk toward them, in and among them, black bodied and eclipsing. I'm outlined in a corona of warning glow, like old times. We're ghosts to each other, the people and I – they gray and watchful ghosts, and I a black and ceaseless one.

The old woman is at her window, just a tiny face above the sill. Her body is invisible behind steel and brick, but I know she is frail and wheelchair bound. I pass the young couple that holds the security door open. I walk up old stairs, which slouch in their center from a hundred years of feet.

Her door is, of course, locked, but locked doors were never a problem for me. Instead of kicking the door in, I send my soul-hand beneath her weather stripping and tickle it along her heart. This is perhaps a little ironic cruelty: the retired schoolteacher, herself the mother of four, would be betrayed by the organ symbolic for the community's love of her.

Ah, well, too late for regrets. Already her heart ceases. Already, she slides down into the wheelchair, the cushion bunching up against old, stocking-clad legs.

It *is* like old times. Again, I'm killing from a distance, killing with a touch. No more thumbs bitten off. No more wrists locked in handcuffs. With no hand, there can be no handcuffs.

There's a homeless man by a fire in a fifty-five gallon drum. He's one of the thirty percent who is mentally ill. He's also an addict. The drugs ease the illness temporarily, but they deepen it afterward.

It's a simple enough thing, then, to bring around the stray dog he'd begun to feed, bring the dog and a pack of others around, initially to see what scraps the man might have, but then to smell the salty savor of a cut on his leg from a piece of rebar this morning.

How like addiction and madness are wild dogs! Once invited, they dart in to snatch away bits of meat from the one who welcomed them. I stand and watch until he is still, and the real tearing has begun.

There's plenty more killing to do this night.

The best assignment of the evening is just now ahead of me.

Mrs Billings is lying in bed as I come through her window. It's late. I stand in a puddle of moonlight, just inside the window, and try to make out the softly snoring sleeper.

It's been a bad year for Mrs Billings, to lose a husband, to be indicted for embezzlement, and now, to die. She was taking it all in stride, though. In the many newspaper photos I've seen, she looks well-pressed and confident, always turning aside reporters with waves and smiles. I suppose I expect her to look the same now, suited for the combat of the streets, but instead she is in jammies.

I turn on the light.

She doesn't stir from sleep. She's undeniably middle-aged, a gray pile of hair pillowing her careworn face. There's a regal reserve in her features even as she softly snores.

To others, she's an embattled widow, the wife of a white-collar criminal slain by a blue-collar killer. For me, she's a Madonna. She carefully, patiently arranged my early life, not as a mother would – in the planning and coddling and living of days – but as an accountant would. She created my past. It was through her that, for however brief a time, I became William B. Dance; I became human.

She deserves to die well. The suffering she's endured in the last year entitle her to the best I have to offer.

It'll need to be well planned, an expensive affair. Her death should be worth the thirty-five million that, when she dies, will become no one's money, stored away in a vault in Geneva. Such a death should involve the destruction of a large piece of property – certainly more than this million-dollar villa in Naperville. It needs to be corporate capital that's destroyed – not an antiquity at the Field Museum or even a business like Marshall Fields – but wait! Macy's bought them out. Yes, the setting would be perfect for a death that would impugn the aristocratic safety and luxury of the place.

If I truly were my former self, I would arrange for her dress hem to get snagged in an escalator's teeth, and for the ceaseless walkway to grind her to pieces. The blood would never quite be scrubbed from every gear and cog, and urban legends would begin about Macy's and the German butcher who designed its escalators to slay.

Such theatrics would have been easy when I was yet an angel. Now, they are beyond my abilities. I'm a shadow of my former self.

"Who's there?" comes her voice, groggy and murmuring.

I shut off the light and hold still.

Mrs Billings sits bolt upright, breathing rapidly and clutching a wiry hand to her chest. Her eyes hang wide open, and she croaks out, "Who's there?"

I do not respond, do not move.

"Who turned out the lights?" she asks, and then rubs her head. "I don't know what I'm talking about," she assures herself, taking a few deep breaths before leaning back against her pillows. "Whoever you are, fuck off. I'm trying to sleep."

I wait until her breathing has returned to the low, smooth drone of sleep, and then I head back toward the window. There's no fitting way to kill this woman here, tonight, with my own hands – well, hand. After all she has been to me, I won't let her die badly. Even so, I have the feeling I'll never fully escape my humanity until Mrs Billings, the literal author of my humanity, is dead. There's plenty of time; Chicago nights are endless.

For now, this earthly flesh of mine is tired, and I long for my lightless home and my bound-up little wifey. Every human boy at one point leaves his mother to go to his wife.

I hope Donna has had a pleasant evening.

It had been a monumental effort to jiggle the gurney all the way to the shelves. Even then, Donna had almost been defeated by the blankets piled atop her. It had taken many minutes to shimmy the covers far enough that she could wrench her hand out sideways to reach the shelf. At least her memory had served – the scalpels were right there.

Still, the angle had been all wrong. She had made numerous small cuts in her side before she at last got the scalpel positioned. Then, it had been sweaty work straining to cut the thick nylon cord. All the while, she had focused on a single image – cradling her newborn child in the bright, clean comfort of a hospital.

Donna was nearly through the band on her wrist when he returned. The restraints still held her tight, and the blankets still covered the work she had done – but none of that mattered. She'd moved the gurney. If he lit the penlight, he would know instantly.

"Good morning, Donna," came the killer's voice from the dark doorway. Impossibly, from that distance, his fingers seemed to gently brush her cheek. "You're awake."

Through clenched teeth, she replied, "You're alive."

Samael moved forward. His feet made dry noises on the cement floor. "Very much so. Though five others are not."

She grimaced, flexing her arms against the ropes. "You sound proud."

"I am what I am," he replied without apology. He did not approach her, instead moving to the corner where he had a mattress. He began undressing. Well-worn clothes sloughed from the man's flesh. Clothes and a leather mask. "And, right now, I'm tired – a mortal condition I hope soon to be rid of. I'm going to sleep. Do you need anything first? I should probably shift you, to prevent bedsores."

"No," she said. "I don't want you to touch me."

More sounds in the blackness – the sigh of Samael easing himself to the mattress and the rustle of sheets. "Well, then, good morning, Detective Leland, and goodnight."

"Goodnight," she heard herself say.

She lay there, listening. Time was meaningless. Only the occasional drip of seeping water and the quiet inhalations of a murderer made time pass at all. Donna waited. The killer's breathing deepened. He stopped shifting on the mattress.

That was enough. She couldn't wait anymore. The scalpel was hot and wet with sweat and blood. It was slick in numb fingers. Oh, but there was only a little left.

She thought of herself cradling her child.

With a small *pop*, the wrist strap snapped. The restraint flopped loose. Hardly daring to breathe, she listened.

Samael did not stir.

Good. She flexed weary fingers before setting them to work on the buckle across her chest. There were eight straps in all. The buckle gave out a traitorous *click* as it opened. Again, she listened, and heard only the steady snoring. Now, Donna too could breathe again. She told herself that she was nearly free. She bent forward to release her feet. Now, what? What?

If she fled without killing Samael, he'd only return for her. But in this darkness, how could she be sure to kill him? She'd have to slay him on the first stroke, before he awoke.

The last buckle clicked loose, and the straps drooped atop her throbbing ankles. Careful not to let any buckles ring against the edge of the gurney, Donna drew the blankets away and flexed her legs.

The air was frigid. At least the straps had kept her warm. She swung her legs over the side of the gurney. Pain shot through her. Blood ran through aching knees and swelled her stiff ankles. Standing was agony. The dark chamber flared bright and whirled around her. Still, she stood.

She couldn't fight in a state like this. She certainly couldn't win. Instead, she had to run away – climb out of this living sarcophagus. Get to safety. Send someone else down into the spider hole.

She staggered away from the gurney, only then feeling the tug of the IVs in both arms. Snarling quietly, she peeled back tape, yanked needles and tubes free, and flung them away to dribble onto the cold floor. One hand groped at the darkness ahead while the other cradled her belly and the bullet wounds in it.

She couldn't see. The doorway was simply a dark gray rectangle hovering in blackness. Who knew what traps the killer might have set along the way? Taking short, painful steps, Donna slid her feet along. There weren't even cobwebs down here, the place was so deep.

Five more long, slow breaths, and she was at the threshold. Beyond was a square chamber with no ceiling – the base of a deep shaft. She looked up into the darkness, only just making out a ladder of thin iron bars sticking out of one cement wall. There were no windows anywhere in the shaft, but a diffuse light seeped down from above. Beside the ladder was the ruin of an old cable-and-pulley elevator. Its counterweight lay loose on broken cement.

"Up," she told herself wearily, shaking the pins and needles from her limbs. Walking had been hard enough, but this?

She grabbed the ladder and began to climb. The first rung shifted under her weight and made a tooth-grinding sound. No time to wait. Hauling hard on the next rung, she rose. A third rung, and a fourth. Soon, she was climbing hand-over-hand and foot-over-foot. The going was hard, and her breath puffed out steam into the cold gray air, but she was escaping.

Then, twenty feet into the air, a third of the way up the shaft, the next rung cracked free in her hand. She lurched backward and let the bar go. It fell along with chunks of loose cement, which clattered and thunked against the floor.

Holding her breath, Donna listened.

Samael was moving in the room.

Letting her breath out in a quiet hiss, Donna climbed again. There was no reason to wait. If he was awake –

"Donna?" came a low, plaintive voice below.

Mother of God. She hauled herself past the gap where the rung had torn free. Halfway to the top, to its hopeful gray glow. The bottom of the shaft was only blackness, a murky well. Then, tepid light jagged out of darkness. It flickered across the wall of the shaft, rose rung by rung up the ladder, and caught in its glow a small cascade of grit coming from the wall. The light slashed up at her.

"Donna!" Beside the light, a ghostly face gazed angrily upward.

Mother of God! Her hands couldn't grab rungs fast enough. Cold cement and colder metal bit into her fingers, leaving rusty abrasions. Another glance down.

"I don't want to hurt you!" Samael shouted. Just then, flame exploded beside his face.

The *crack* and *boom* of the pistol resounded through the shaft. Sparks leaped blue from the concrete wall. Chips of mortar smacked into Donna. Heedless, she climbed.

Two thirds of the way. Twenty more feet. If she could just keep from being shot…

Another explosion. Angry heat gripped her thigh. Her leg slipped, ramming against a rung. It went numb, wedged between the ladder and the wall. Cursing, Donna struggled to pull her wounded leg free.

An empty *clack* of steel sounded, then another. He had run out of bullets. Now he would climb.

"God damn it!" Donna hissed. She tore her wounded leg free of the rung, lacerating her skin. It didn't matter. Growling, she hauled herself higher.

She thought of the baby – of the tidy hospital room and the sleeping baby.

"The name is Leland. Yes, I had an appointment for an inducement? Yes, I'll wait." Donna Leland stood in the bright, clean reception area of Froedtert Hospital, waiting patiently as the gray-haired volunteer dialed up to maternity, asking about her.

Donna never would have imagined it would end this way. Inducement. After courtroom confessions and car accidents, after poisoning and abduction and bullet wounds, after the arms and legs of the baby's father – of Azra, of Samael – had, one by one, been fished from the Chicago River, this child would have to be induced? She had imagined only an emergency C-section for the Son of the Son of Samael. Instead, the baby was three weeks overdue.

Already, he has broken all ties with his tempestuous father.

"The doctor will be down," said the old woman. The suspicion was gone from her features, replaced by a smile. "So, you're going to have a baby today?"

"Yes," Donna replied, rubbing her belly, "my first."

"Do you need me to call the father?" the volunteer asked indiscreetly.

Donna shook her head and looked toward the elevator, where her doctor appeared. "No, thank you. The father's dead."

Samael was climbing rapidly behind her. How could a one-handed man climb a ladder so quickly? There was no time to wonder. Samael had already reached the spot where the rung had come loose. He sprung across the gap with lizardlike ease.

Donna scrabbled higher. The ladder was slick with her blood. Rust prickled her palms. She flung herself upward, toward the hopeful light. Three rungs, five rungs, eight rungs...

"I don't want to hurt you, Donna. Come back. You're tearing open your wounds!"

Donna reached the top of the ladder. She crawled out onto a small flat landing strewn with cement rubble. A stout wooden door stood in the wall at the back of the niche. Beneath the door came a ribbon of light, the loveliest sight she had ever seen.

Donna panted for a moment on the rubble-strewn landing, and then rose and grabbed the doorknob. It turned loosely, but the door only rattled in its frame, locked.

Samael's face topped the ladder.

Donna kicked cement rubble at him.

He cried out as grit sprayed into his eyes. Fist-sized stones struck his face. He lost his grip and tumbled back. His legs caught around a rung, and he hung upside down.

Donna clutched a jagged stone and smashed it against the corroded doorknob. It broke off. The knob clattered to the cracked cement floor. Three quick kicks only rattled the door again.

With a roar, she smashed the rock against the top hinge. The old metal shattered. The other two hinges cracked as easily. The door creaked toward her. She pried it back and it fell with a *baroom*.

Samael's bloody fingers clasped the edge of the landing. He clawed upward.

Beyond the ruined door, Donna staggered into another shaft. On the far side of it, a set of steep, wooden stairs zigzagged up a gaunt tower of metal L-beams. It looked like an old fire tower – rotten wood, rusted steel, shorn bolts, and a crumbling wall of cement.

"You can't escape. The door above is locked, too."

Donna rushed the stairs and clambered upward. The planks creaked beneath her feet but held. As she rounded the first switchback, the larger bullet wound in her stomach began to throb. By the second turn, it felt like a hot poker impaling her.

I should've brought the morphine.

Below, Samael stomped across the fallen door. It boomed like a timpani drum. He bounded up the stairs.

Donna rounded the third landing. A warm trickle of blood ran from her side. One foot was slick with it.

"I won't kill you," Samael hissed between breaths. "I love you. I'll never kill you. As long as I'm your angel of death, you'll live forever."

The stairway swayed and creaked. Bolts were pulling free from the cement wall.

Donna glanced up the narrow crotch of the stair to see how far she had to go. At least seven landings remained, the dim light becoming gradually greenish.

How deep can these tunnels be? What earthly reason would there be for such deep tunnels?

Her foot caught on something. She stumbled. Her toes were wedged – not wedged, but held. The killer had grabbed on between the treads. He reached higher, gripping her ankle. She kicked out. His fingers slipped, raking down her already bloody foot. She kicked again. Fingernails peeled back, and he lost hold. By the sound of it, Samael landed in a painful heap midstair and tumbled downward.

Donna reached the fifth landing, and the sixth. Each breath felt like a saw sliding down her throat. The metal framework listed outward. Grinding sounds came from above. Rusted bolts ripped away from the crumbling cement. The stairway teetered out into the shaft.

He's coming. He's closing on me. His footsteps are only getting louder, faster. He'll catch me. As long as he lives, he'll catch me.

Donna's legs were leaden. Three more landings. To die in a hole, away from the sun…

She dragged herself up another flight, but there – there he caught up to her.

Samael vaulted up the steps behind her and seized her ankle. She fell to her knees. She flipped over but couldn't break his grasp.

"You can't escape me. You can't escape love." He yanked her down underneath him, slid his arm around her neck, and throttled her. Through gritted teeth, he said, "Relax. You'll fall asleep and wake up, safe and warm on your bed."

His hold was implacable. She couldn't break it. Every struggle was agony. Submit. Her body screamed that she submit.

But there was that slumbering baby in the bright, clean room…

They had tried prostaglandin gel. They had broken the bag of waters. They had started Pitocin. Her false labor had become truer than she could have previously imagined, but still, the progress was slow.

"About four centimeters," said Doctor Lein. He was an East Indian man, tall, with intense brown eyes. Just now, those eyes peered at his gloved hand, prodding the cervix. "This little one seems not to want to come out."

Donna gasped from the pressure of his fingertips. "Must've heard what it was like out here." She nodded toward him. "There's another contraction starting."

"Yes," he said, withdrawing his hand. "I can tell. Keep up the good work."

"It's been ten hours already," she replied. "How much longer?"

"Be patient. It's a hard thing to be born, but everybody does it."

Gritting her teeth, Donna raised her good leg and kicked, planting her heel in the killer's groin and flinging him backward, head over heels. She turned onto her belly and scrambled to the next landing. Dull thuds came as Samael struck moldy wood and cracked through.

Please, God, let him be dead – and if not dead, maimed. And please, God, let me reach the top…

The crashing sounds below rumbled into silence. A new noise took their place – the ominous squeal of stressed metal.

The metal tower veered away from the cement wall and out over the darkness. Then it reeled back to *clang* against its facings. Perhaps if she could break it entirely free after she jumped to the landing – perhaps Samael would be killed as the stairway collapsed.

Donna topped the final rise, which drifted ten feet away from its terminus – a wooden door in the smooth wall at the top of the shaft. There was no landing. The door was bolted in place with a fat padlock, and gold-green light poured out all around it.

So close. She couldn't hope to break through the door, with the tower swaying as it was, or cling to it and pick the lock. For that matter, she had nothing with which to…

Beside the door was an ancient glass compartment, so shrouded in dust that it seemed at first only another panel in the gray cement. As the tower swung inward, though, she spotted within the compartment a bulky fire extinguisher and an ax.

Donna lifted a hunk of rotting stair and struck the glass. It shattered with a dry, dusty sound. The tower drew inexorably away before she could thrust her hand through the jags of glass and bring away the ax.

The tower reached its farthest point and pendulumed back toward the door. Donna thrust her hand through the shattered glass and seized the ax haft. The blade broke out through ragged shards of glass. Her hand streamed blood. She gripped the ax with both hands. It seemed to have never been used, sharp despite its corrosion.

"Good enough for me," Donna said, bracing herself to swing at the door.

The scaffold sighed, slowly approaching the wall. She swung and struck. A few chips of old wood flew back, but the resultant cleft gripped the ax, dragging it out of her hands. It took another sway of the tower before she could reach the ax and pull it free. Light poured warmly out through the chink. As she waited for the next blow, she listened for Samael. Aside from the moan of metal, there was silence.

Donna hunkered down. The door loomed toward her. She struck. A wedge of wood flew free, and she yanked the ax head out. Another five or six strokes, and perhaps she'd have a hole big enough to dive through.

Two, and then three more solid hits. The door was cracked down the center. If she got lucky, the door would split in half and fall away. Donna reared back with the ax, holding her breath as the tower and door swooned together.

She felt a hand on her shoulder.

Whirling, she lashed out. The blade bit into the side of Samael's jaw. He fell back, silent and leering. She caught her balance and swung again. This time, the blade cleaved into the killer's shoulder. The ax head cut muscle and tendon before embedding in the upper knob of the humerus.

Donna didn't stop, even as Samael staggered back. The ax fell again, nearly severing a leg, and then sank into his belly, like a spoon into oatmeal. He slumped precariously against the framework. With one mighty strike, she chopped the man's bad arm clear off. Blood jetted from the amputation. He would be dead in moments, and she would be free.

She turned. The tower crashed into the wall. The gory ax flew into the fissure in the wood and split the door in two. One ragged half hung by stressed hinges, while the other slid down between door and tower, cracked against stone, and plunged in a long, rattling descent.

Even as the tower leaned away again, Donna leaped. Her upper body and hands caught just within the doorway, the baby and her lower body hanging in the emptiness beyond. It felt as if climbing up onto that ledge would cut the baby in half, but if she were still hanging this way when the tower swung inward, she'd be crushed.

Donna wriggled her way up through the hanging threshold. No sooner had her feet dragged across it than the scaffold clanged into position. Gazing back past the riven door, she saw the immobile, bloody mess of the Son of Samael, slumped on the stairs.

"You're not my brother," she blurted. "You're not anything. It's time to die."

She turned to see a wide basement with I-beams and metal posts. This was the lowest level of an abandoned brick warehouse. Through a bank of high, shattered windows, golden sunlight streamed across unmown green grass. It was a beautiful sight.

Only the arm amputation bled a lot. He stuck his fingers into the brachial artery. That helped. The bleeding would stop that way. Then a tourniquet for his leg. He could make the tourniquet out of his own shirtsleeve and his own ulna, stripped of skin and muscle, of course. Once the tourniquet was tight, he could use one of these pieces of glass to cut the leg the rest of the way off.

Spirit arms and legs were much better than real ones.

If those amputations went well enough, he'd get rid of more parts, and more, until he was a pure angel again.

How strange, he thought. Donna made me human in the first place. Now she dehumanizes me, demonizes me, redeifies me.

It's no wonder I love her.

TWENTY-SEVEN

"What's wrong?" the nurse asked. "Concentrate on your breathing."

"He's here," Donna rasped out, bearing down. "I know it. He's here."

"He's not here yet. Don't push. Save your strength," said the woman, middle-aged and motherly.

"Not the baby. Samael. The Son of Samael. He's here, in this hospital," Donna insisted. "I can feel it."

"You've got two officers outside your door. They'll keep you and the baby safe," the nurse soothed. In her white polyester pants and jacket, she seemed almost a Felinni clown. "Pant blow, now."

For the hundredth time, Donna began the breathing pattern – small comfort against the contractions. "They can't stop him. He's not dead. He has no limbs anymore, but somehow he got here. He can do anything. He kills whomever he wants."

"Calm down. Are you sure you don't have any allergies to morphine?"

"I tell you, he's here."

"Who's here?" asked Doctor Lien as he walked into the birthing room. The man's eyes were bright and mildly chiding. "The baby? Well, let's see."

Without invitation, he moved past the nurse, dragged a stool from beneath the foot of the bed, and sat down between Donna's legs. Donning a rubber glove, he felt for the baby.

"Yes, he is here. Ten centimeters. Plus one station. Congratulations, Ms. Leland. It's time for you to push."

"Thank God," Donna growled, bearing down with a contraction. She gripped the handles the nurse had just inserted into the bed. Her body grew as tight as a re-curved bow. Cords stood out down her neck, and her face reddened.

"All right, relax for a second. Breathe. Good. Very good. You're making good progress. Down another station. He's positioned right. All right, try another push." All the while, the doctor was quietly sliding shelves and sections of bed into position, readying a bucket for the afterbirth. "Yes, excellent. Breathe. Then give me another just like it. Good. Good. He's advancing. Are you comfortable with my finger there?"

"I'm not comfortable, period," Donna gasped out. "Let's just push this baby out."

"All right," the doctor said, leaning his forehead seriously inward. "Push again."

Donna did, rising up in the bed, hands clutching tightly to the handles. She watched her own trembling thighs and growled, saw the doctor's slick black hair between her legs. In that mad, red instant, she wondered if it was him, Samael. He was the right height, the right build...

"Another push. Come on. You're almost there."

She hadn't realized she had stopped pushing. It had been eighteen hours of hard labor. She was so weary, she was nodding off between contractions.

"One more good one, Donna, and he'll be here."

She pushed, roaring, and felt a looseness and a tearing.

"Stop so I can clear his nose."

"You stop!" she shouted, though she struggled to hold back.

"All right, one last!" In a terrific rush of flesh and fluid, the baby was born. "There he is, bigger than life!"

Doctor Lien lifted up a blue creature, squirming and squalling. It was not purple, like the babies she had seen in the films, but truly blue. With each breath it took, its blood-mottled skin cleared, until the screaming baby was a ghastly white. The doctor fastened a set of clamps and snipped the cord.

"Well, look here! An albino. I bet he's got eyes as pink as a rabbit's," Doctor Lien said.

Donna's stomach turned in her. The baby looked like a chicken carcass hung in a butcher's window. She threw up green bile on the floor, spattering the doctor's feet.

She is here. The baby has just arrived, too. I can feel it.

It was no easy thing, getting to this hospital. I'd bumped my way through four different medical communities before reaching Froedtert. All the while, it was doctors and charities and community activists that called the shots. Once my health was stabilized, they all agreed on one thing – the unknown, blind, mute homeless man should have a new face to replace the one the rats ate.

They've cut a hunk of tendon from my shoulder socket and carved it into a nose. They've reconstructed the gnawed cheekbones, stitched muscles into place, and moved skin grafts from my side to my skull. Those four surgeries are finished, and ten more are planned to reconstruct my brow, lips, and chin.

Of course, they can't give me new eyes, or a new tongue.

Why have they done all this? To them, I am a symbol of human tenacity. They have made me a living unknown soldier, the manifestation of all human torment, all human hope. They think I cling to life out of sheer determination and undying hope.

In fact, I remain only to slay my child.

The rats hadn't been enough. They ate away most of me, yes, and it was quick work for them. By the time the garbage men found me in the alley, I had no limbs, no face, no lips, and no eyes. What was lost grew back – spirit arms and legs, a spirit face and eyes. I am mostly angel now, thanks to the rats.

But they could not eat away the one parcel of flesh that truly binds me to the world. My child. My newborn child.

It is time to go see him.

I lift my spirit hands before me and curve them inward. The fingertips sink through flesh as though it were only shadow. They sink until they surround my heart. I can feel the wild, determined flailing of that angry muscle. It is strong, very strong. It wants to live. But what if I squeeze it like this? What if I suffocate my own heart with my very fingers?

Ah, even I can hear that beeping alarm as my pulse goes wild – even I, who have no external ears, but only holes in my head like the ears of a lizard. They will come running soon. They will shock me with those pads, never knowing that electricity can do nothing to this adamantine grip of mine. They will stick a needle into my heart and pump it full of adrenaline, which will only make the thing tear itself to pieces. They will crack me open like a turkey and massage the muscle by hand.

The heart machine is buzzing in flatline. My body is bucking atop the table. It's quite a show. The doctor who did my grafts is here. He stares despairingly at the two triangles of flesh that he calls my face.

"No response. Nothing. BP dropping. We're losing him."

They're losing me. I'm gaining them.

I do not feel the scalpel carve into my chest, so sharp it is, but I see the hot red line and hear the ratchet sound of rib spreaders cracking the bone. Then one of them darts a gloved hand into the space and grabs the still hunk of meat. It doesn't matter to me. I can already feel necrosis setting in. My touch is a touch of death.

Rarely has it erred – once, with a certain police officer, but it will not err now.

My death must be perfect.

I am rising above my body. Cameras start going off from the hallway. There is an orderly pushing reporters and photographers back – ah, Blake Gaines. It is good to see you again! You want more pictures of me? Color shots of puddling blood and wide-eyed surgeons and orderlies forming human chains and Right to Lifers in a round-the-clock prayer vigil?

Perfect. It is as though I had orchestrated this death at the height of my powers rather than the depths.

Too bad I cannot stay. My spirit body is complete now. I am angel once more. This mound of hamburger can no longer hold me to the world.

But there is other flesh – skin the color of clouds and eyes as pink as a rabbit's – he would bind me here. He would witness to my physical presence in the world. His name in the Book of Life would seal my fate forever.

Hello, Donna. It is good to see that your travail is done. This is our son, then, yes? He is ghastly, wouldn't you say? The color of paper. I know, to you he is precious, but to me he is unfinished business.

Ah, yes, let me touch my son. He frowns in his sleep and arches his back. Good. He recognizes me after all.

Hush my child and death attend thee,
All through the night.
I, your killing angel send thee,

All through the night.
While the weary world is creeping,
Hill and dale in slumber sleeping,
I your lovely soul am keeping
All through the night.

Ah, there, Son, your breath ceases, your struggle ceases, your flesh gives up the ghost.

I watch you flee through the ceiling and heavenward like a rocket. All is right. Once again, all is right.

Glory to God in the Highest.

When Detective Leland awoke, she felt the cold stillness in her arms. She struggled to her feet, clutching the child tight beneath breasts that had not yet even fed it.

"My baby! My baby! Mother of God! He's dead!"

I know you, Mrs Billings, you with your splendid lawyers bought by splendid money and your splendid not-guilty verdict bought the same way, and the bag of splendid cashmere under your arm. I know you. You have worked hard this year, endured much. You deserve an easy descent.

Take the escalator, my beautiful lady. Take the escalator. I have been preparing it for you.

Do not mind the slight tugging on your dress. Do not mind the way the teeth separate there at the bottom and give enough space for one masticated human body to be yanked, living, down among the gear work. Do

not fear, my sweet Mrs Billings, for this thirty-three seconds of grinding and spattering and thrashing is not
nearly as much woe as the store management will have
when folk begin to talk of the butcher-turned-
maintenance-man who lives beneath the floors.

ABOUT THE AUTHOR

J. Robert King is the award-winning author of over twenty novels, most recently *The Shadow of Reichenbach Falls* and the Mad Merlin trilogy. Fifteen years ago, Rob founded the Alliterates, a cabal of writers in the Midwest and West Coast of the US.

Rob also often takes to the stage, starring in local productions such as *The Complete Works of William Shakespeare (Abridged)* and *Arsenic & Old Lace*. He lives in Wisconsin with his lovely wife, three brilliant sons, and three less-than-brilliant cats.

Coming soon: *Death's Disciples*

PROLOGUE: FLIGHT

I hate flying. Always have. It's not just the old man on my left snoring, his liver-spotted hand brushing my leg, or the young man on my right darting looks down my blouse. It's not just the plume of re-breathed air in my face or the flight attendants staring dead-eyed as they hand out bags of pretzels. It's the impossibility of it.

People aren't supposed to fly. Hundred ton machines certainly aren't.

My stomach's a knot.

"Look at that," the young man says. His name is Jason. He's got an Amish-style beard not because he's Amish but because he's too young to grow anything better. Too young for me. Jason hooks his nose toward the TV screen, which shows our current position over Billings. "We're at 35,000 feet, and the air outside's negative 75."

"Cold," I agree, staring at the in-flight magazine as if I cared what meals were available for purchase.

"Fall out of this plane, and you'd be frozen before you hit the ground," he enthuses. "You'd shatter like a glass doll."

The knot tightens. "There's a Darwin Award for you." They offer a turkey croissant with baby carrots and chocolate pudding.

How much longer? It's five minutes till noon. I hate flying, but business calls.

"I need to get up," I tell the Amish kid. "Business calls."

Jason grins, pivoting his legs to one side and watching my ass as I squeeze past.

The midcabin lavatory is closer, but I've got time to kill, so I turn and pick my way back among the crammed seats. Can't believe I booked in coach, a purgatory – all these dreary, drowsing people, their faces slack, eyes lidded, oblivious to the fact that people aren't supposed to fly…

The rear lav is occupied. I wait.

Three minutes to noon.

I knock. The person inside groans. The bolt hisses in the slot, the door cracks and out comes a fifty-something woman wreathed in a cloud of perfume and flatulence. She glances at me with annoyance, and I return the look as she shoe-horns past. I enter the cubicle, lock the door behind me and look at myself in the mirror.

Blonde, thirty-two, and smart – and watch that smile, that killer smile.

I can't wait for this flight to be over.

It is.

There's a noise so loud I can't hear it, only see it – a white ball in my head. It hurls me up to the ceiling and pins me to the wall and flings me back down. Teeth crack on stainless steel. Chemical water gushes up my nose. Water and blood.

Another white ball. I'm on my knees on the floor.

There's a terrible tearing. Metal shredding.

The sound becomes a scream. Screams.

An all-encompassing roar.

I can't see anything. I can only hear.

It's too much.

Why is everything so loud?

My face is slick. Blood?

I stagger up. My hands are on walls, plastic walls. There's panels and metal frames. I paw the space and find a metal knob and yank on it, and the door opens.

The roar is louder now – a narrow hallway with carpet below and blood beside.

I step out.

I'm inside a plane, except there's no floor. Just three rows of seats, then a big hole and torn walls. I look through the hole. Grassy hills flash golden below and the shadow of the plane skims across them.

The shadow grows larger and larger.

We're going to crash.

I can see trees and rocks. They slide past, surreal.

They'll soon be real.

I step back through the door and pull it closed in front of me and sit down on the toilet and bend my head down between my knees and wait for the end.

It comes.

It sounds like a broken motor.

It looks like the sun exploding.

It feels like tigers tearing me apart.

Death's Disciples by J Robert King
*Susan Gardner is the sole survivor of a terrorist attack
on her plane. Now she can hear the voices of all
the dead passengers in her head.*

*Their latest message is this: the terrorists are
coming back.*

For her.

**Coming Soon
from Angry Robot**

TWENTY MINUTES WITH
J ROBERT KING

Sometimes we grab our authors and throw a bunch of questions at them. Occasionally, it's like we opened the floodgates…

One book

One of the best books I've ever read was written by a guy with a second-grade education. *Harpo Speaks* is the autobiography of Harpo Marx, and it tells the story of a life that spanned vaudeville, movies, and television. Harpo was part of the Algonquin Round Table and rubbed elbows with the greatest thinkers and performers of his day. The book is intriguing and funny and poignant.

One story

One story I often tell is about myself as an undergraduate in England. I went to Oxford to have a cider in what the locals call the Bird and Baby pub (OK, actually called the Eagle and Child). I sat in the seat where Tolkien and Lewis sat and let the cider fill me with a warm fire. After finishing it, I asked to buy the glass, but said apologetically, "All I have is a five." The bartender looked at me as if I were insane and said, "Then I'll give you change." I felt like a relic hunter. But I still have that glass to this day, twenty years later.

One book to burn

I'm actually not into burning books. Yeah, ideas are dangerous things, but that's why we've got to use our brains when we read. Burning books is like saying people can't figure out what's good and what's not.

When I worked for TSR (the people who created *Dungeons & Dragons*), there was a religious group buying up the game and having bonfires. Our marketing department sent them catalogs. Burning the games didn't do anything but put money in our pockets and smoke in the air. It didn't stop *D&D*.

Why would I burn *Mein Kampf*? Let people read it and realize the man was crazy. Besides, Hitler was the book burner, not me.

One song/record

My current favorite is *Icky Thump*. I think Jack White is a genius. Of course, I also think Jack Black is a genius. I have a secret hope that they team up and form a band called the Black and White Stripes, or Jack Squared, or Jacked Up.

One record to smash

I think records are like books. If they suck, don't listen. Who are they hurting? And the record may not suck, but just be something you don't get.

I've made a conscious decision never to utter the words "That's not music. That's just noise." Instead, when I don't get something, I shrug and say, "I don't get it, but obviously a lot of people do."

People say that music is the universal language, but why is it you can't turn on a radio without the two people sitting closest to you objecting to the kind of music you like? Muzak tried to create an utterly inoffensive form of music that everyone would like and instead created a type of music that everyone reviles. So, I think, there's something inherently divisive in music. It makes groups of fans by alienating everybody else.

As for my own tastes, I like hard rock and classical. But I'm not a fan of Mozart. I don't get his music, but obviously a lot of people do.

One creative person you always wanted to be

When I was a kid, I wanted to be C. S. Lewis. In fourth grade, I wrote a sequel to the Narnia series, and called it *Aslan vs Caplaner*. Caplaner was a big monster, and the story was all about the mighty lion fighting the grotesque monster – a professional wrestling-style slugfest. Clearly, it was not very Narnian.

Later on, I wanted to be Tolkien. I was blown away by *The Lord of the Rings*, so much so that I even slogged through *The Silmarillion*. I wanted to be able to create a world that was as beautiful, real, and true.

Interestingly, though, my books have tended to have a much darker gradient. I'm sometimes shocked to look at what I write. These aren't beautiful worlds. They're often terrifying ones. I've not been able to find a magic wardrobe. My closets are much darker.

One book you wish you'd written

As a young person, I wished I had written *The Lord of the Rings* – except that that would mean I would have little success in my lifetime and would have died in 1973.

It's not really possible to write someone else's book. A book is like your face – it shows your identity to the world. I have blue eyes and a big nose and receding hair, and I write the kind of books that I write. To write somebody else's books, I'd have to have that person's face, that person's identity.

Though, come to think of it, I wouldn't mind being J. K. Rowling.

One book/author that's been unjustly neglected

There are a lot of unjustly neglected authors. I have drinks with them once a month.

Here's the thing, though. A book may be a great book, but if it doesn't find its audience, it never becomes part of the zeitgeist. I think of Shakespeare. He was competing with bear-baiting pits, and yet he still turned out some of the greatest plays ever written. He played simultaneously to the groundlings and the queen.

That's what great authors do. So maybe there's no such thing as an unjustly neglected author. You have to write a great book and reach an enthusiastic audience. Everything's got to come together, and until it does, well, you're not yet great.

One film

One film that nobody knows about but I love is *Night of the Iguana*. When I mention it to people, they think it is a Godzilla film. Actually, it's a John Huston film based on a Tennessee Williams play, with Richard Burton, Ava Gardner, and Deborah Kerr. Not one of them wears a Godzilla suit. And the movie has some of the best lines ever – including, "Nothing human disgusts me – except cruelty," and "God is not being God here tonight, so we will be God and release a creature at the end of its rope."

On the other end of the spectrum, I also really like *Tenacious D & the Pick of Destiny*. It both parodies and embodies my favorite aspects of rock-and-roll culture.

Your hero

As a kid, I had plenty of heroes – Captain James T Kirk and Luke Skywalker and Frodo Baggins. All were adults and all were fictional.

As an adult, my heroes are younger than me and real. My sons are my heroes. They're just heading out on their heroes' quests, and I want them to know how to fight, how to find shelter, how to make alliances. I want them to slay the God-damned dragon.

Ideal dinner party guests

There's a difference between the people you admire and the ones you'd actually like to have at your dinner table. It's good to keep your idols at a distance. Otherwise, you'll see their many flaws, and they'll see yours.

I love Wagner's music, but I'm sure I'd hate the man. What would I say to Galileo? I don't even speak Italian. Would I want to sit down with Jesus? Well... if we had an interpreter and he brought the wine.

There's also the size problem. Jesus was probably 5 foot 4 and weighed 120. I'd feel weird hulking there above him. You're not supposed to be bigger than Jesus, even if you're John Lennon.

And I'd be the kind of host who'd accidentally offer Jesus some ham.

The biggest influence on your writing

My life. The best writing is not entirely conscious.

The clever part of the brain isn't where the stories come from. The stories come from the deeper part, the lizard part, the part that wants and needs and fears. Then the conscious mind gives words to express those deep utterances. Writing has to mean something, and the only way it can is if it is rooted in life.

The biggest influence on your life

I used to say that writing was the biggest influence on my life. After all, I have over twenty novels published, and I work as a writer and editor at a company that creates texts for teaching writing.

But, really, my family is the biggest influence on my life. When a person has a child, the person's heart migrates out of his chest to hang in space halfway between him and the child. It's not about him anymore. It's about them both. And the heart never returns to its cage. That means it's free, but its also forever unprotected.

Having children means that you are no longer safe, but it also means that your safety no longer matters.

One influence you wish didn't keep showing through

I have a depressive personality. It's what happens when an idealist keeps getting the shit beat out of him but doesn't give up the idealism. It'd be much easier to be simply practical, to look at life and say, "Well, there it is." But I can imagine a much better world, and the discord between that and the world as it is leaves me often feeling like a stranger. That feeling seeps into my writing. My characters are rarely at home, rarely among friends.

This is the difference between me and Tolkien, me and Rowling. Their success lies in the fact that everyone feels they really belong in Hobbiton or Hogwarts.

I have never felt that I really belonged anywhere. My novels are for the dispossessed. Luckily for me, there are about six billion of us.

Tell us a joke

My favorite comedian is Mitch Hedberg, who died too soon. He was the master of the *non sequitur* one-liner, like these:

"I find a duck's opinion of me is very much influenced over whether or not I have bread."

"Dogs are forever in the push-up position."

"I think Bigfoot is blurry, that's the problem. It's not the photographer's fault. Bigfoot is blurry, and that's extra scary to me. There's a large, out-of-focus monster roaming the countryside. Look out, he's fuzzy, let's get out of here."

"Last week I helped my friend stay put. It's a lot easier than helping him move. I just went over to his house and made sure that he did not start to load shit into a truck."

What do you sing in the shower?

I don't think I sing in the shower. I used to. I sang there and everywhere. Now I do a lot more ruminating. It's less fun for me but more merciful for everyone around.

Support a team?

I'm a casual fan of the Arizona Diamondbacks, mostly because I was born in Phoenix and because I shared an office with a rabid Chicago Cubs fan. At the time, the Diamondbacks were on fire and the Cubs were struggling. I enjoyed asking my colleague for updates about "my Diamondbacks" and having him recount their latest win. Then I would asked about the Cubs, and he'd scowl and tell about their loss.

That year, the Diamondbacks edged the Cubs out of the playoffs. I once said, "You know what I love about the Diamondbacks? I love how they get so many points." My office mate's eyes flared, and he said, "They're called runs."

Any notable pets?

I have three cats, two of which were named after books I was writing – Merlin and Sherlock. My son also has a hamster named after a brutal warrior in my most recent book. The hamster Rytlock just had four babies.

Got a nickname?

In Cambridge, I was called Mr Milk because I hadn't yet learned how to drink. Shortly afterward, I led two other undergraduates on an ill-considered run up a mountainside in Grasmere and got us lost. After that, the three of us were the Mud Brothers.

At my current job, there was a time when four of us writers occupied an office we called "The Shire." I was Frodo, and we had a Sam, Pippin, and Merry as well. Then I got promoted to editor-in-chief. Now the only nickname I have is the Furnace because of the way I burn through work.

Earliest memory?

They say your very first memory tells a lot about you. That's sad, because my very first memory comes from when I was three and my older brother hurt me and I was walking out to the backyard of our house in Phoenix, intending to tell on him and thinking, "I will remember this for the rest of my life."

Why couldn't I have had that thought about some-thing good?

I also remember having a nightmare when I was four and getting up and turning on Johnny Carson. It sud-denly seemed like everything was okay.

I remember my Grandpa Bennett sitting in the rock-ing chair at our house. I pulled on the back of it and nearly tipped him over. Later, when he died of a burst aorta, I remember lying in bed and looking at the ceil-ing and trying to imagine him just not existing anymore.

First story you told?

Aslan vs Caplaner was the first story I told on paper, but there were a lot of stories (lies) told orally.

When I was five, I came home from kindergarten and got my brother's hamster, Herman (named after Her-man Munster), from his cage. I put the little guy in my sock drawer and got changed out of my school clothes. When I reached into the sock drawer to get him, Her-man was dead. I put him back in the cage and had to wait with dread as my older brother came home and checked in with his pet. "Her-man? Her-man? How you doing, little buddy? What's wrong Herman? How come you're not moving?…" I didn't tell my brother of my in-volvement in the death until we were in the parking lot after buying Herman II. Then my brother punched me.

When I was about eleven, I convinced the 9 year-old nextdoor neighbors that I had magical powers. I did so by "sensing" things under the ground: "It feels like – what? A backhoe? That's crazy! A backhoe's too big. Still, we'll have to dig to find out!" And it *was* a backhoe – a toy that I'd buried a year before because I was sick of finding it in my yard.

When I was thirteen, I wasn't sure how to talk to girls in my junior high, so I thought I should just jump to proposing. I proposed to Karen Baker in Home Economics – and was delighted when she accepted. I then proposed to Michelle Desmitt in Algebra and a few others in other classes. Soon, I had many wives and was feeling grand – until they found out about each other and decided to divorce me.

First story you sold?

I wrote an SF story called "Death of a God," which was published in *Amazing* magazine in 1992. It's a great story about the collision between biological and digital realities. I still remember the note written by the assistant editor: "Bob can write!"

Next book you'll read?

I'm currently reading *The Amazing Maurice and His Educated Rodents* by Terry Pratchett.

What do you say when people ask "Where do you get your ideas from?"

Ideas don't come from a place. They come from an attitude, from a habitual curiosity and restlessness. Ideas are the result of a mental agitation. They come like butterflies. Like mosquitoes. They are everywhere. Catching an idea is no harder than feeling something bite you and smacking it and seeing the dead thing on your hand and the blood it had drawn out of you.

Do you have an unusual talent or skill?

I'm an actor as well as a writer. I most enjoy roles that allow me to play multiple characters, and to do so comedically. In that regard, the best shows I have been in are *The Complete Works of William Shakespeare (Abridged)* and *No Way to Treat a Lady*. In the first play, I was Juliet, Othello, Hamlet's mother, Ophelia, Claudius, and a number of other characters. In the second, I played eight different parts, alter-egos of the serial killer Kit Gill.

Best place you ever visited?

In college, I loved Edinburgh – a modern city with a medieval castle in the middle, and Arthur's Seat at the outskirts. I watched guys digging clams on the shore of the Firth of Forth.

As a young married man, I loved Susie's Sunshine Cafe in Bloomington, Illinois. It was a seventies throwback without trying, with great food and slow service, perfect for sitting with my wife for a couple hours on a Friday night.

When I was a young dad, I loved the Milwaukee Public Museum – natural history. I took my sons there once a month and taught them about dinosaurs and ice-age mammals, about the rain forest and the streets of old Milwaukee. Touring that place was like touring the world.

Now, I like the screened-in front porch of my old house. It's where I write my books, watching the world pass by on the sidewalks and streets and hearing my family rattle on in the warm rooms within.

Favourite building or structure?

I like old buildings. I love Jerusalem for that reason. It's actually a 400-year-old Turkish city built on top of two-thousand years worth of other ruins. To get to the streets where Jesus walked, you had to go seventy feet down.

And I love England for the same reason – Roman foundations with a Norman layer and an Elizabethan layer, and then surveillance cameras mounted on top.

In the US we have a short history, and we like to ignore it. We like to say that all that matters is right now. But I bought a hundred-ten year-old Victorian house with original clapboards and hodgepodge wiring and only one bathroom. And this house stands near effigy mounds that are three thousand years old. Imagine that. The people buried in those mounds lived a thousand years before Jesus.

In Jericho, I saw a tower that was six thousand years old. Older than the pyramids. That was awesome.

The last time you cried?

Whenever somebody does the right thing unselfishly, I cry. I wish I cried every day, but it's more like twice a year.

I have a son with special needs, and I was worried about him getting bullied on the playground. Then we got a report from the school that a bunch of bullies were picking on another kid – one in a wheelchair – and my son ran up and drove them off and stood guard over the kid and comforted him.

Are you kidding me? My son? The one who was supposed to be the victim became the hero?

If you weren't a writer what would you be?

In junior high, a career aptitude test told me I should be a forklift operator, so I guess I have a fall-back.

People used to tell me I should be a lawyer because I love to argue. But I don't love it anymore. Arguing is like arm-wrestling. It doesn't show who's right, but just who has the bigger arm.

Favourite fancy dress costume?

My wife and I once went as Romeo and Juliet to a costume party benefit for our local community theater. Yes, Jennie was Romeo, and I was Juliet.

Got an irritating/bad habit?

I'm not sure this counts as a bad habit: it's more of a character flaw.

You can categorize people's personalities based on the four Aristotelian elements – earth, air, water, and fire. My brother Al is earth: solid, unmoving, dependable, but prone to quakes. My cousin Jim is air: buoyant, light, able to fit around anyone anywhere, but prone to occasional tempests. My friend Don is water: patient, pervading, shifting, always seeking its level, but prone to floods.

I am fire. Insatiable. Consuming. Producing light and heat but doing so by destroying. I burn up everything and leaped hungrily forward. If I stop moving, I die.

What keeps you awake at night?

Not much keeps me awake at night. I put my pillow over my head and sleep like the dead. In fact, someday, they'll find me dead in bed and rule it "feather inhalation."

Favourite word?

My favorite word is *curious*. It can describe someone who wants to find out something or something that wants to be found out. "Are you curious about this curious artifact?"

Curiosity can mean the desire to know or something desiring to be known. "I feel a strange curiosity about this curiosity." It's the signature strength of our race.

We are the curious people, in all senses of the term.

Who plays you in the movie?

I'd like to be played by Robert Downey, Jr. Here's a really smart, talented, and troubled guy. And he weighs about seventy pounds less than I.

What Downey delivers onscreen, great as it is, is about a tenth of what he's got inside him. It comes from having struggled. I can empathize.

One of the deadliest challenges is transitioning from youth to middle age. People who don't make the transition don't survive. Think of Michael Jackson and Marilyn Monroe and Heath Ledger. Downey and I have made the ungraceful transition. He's also got a great ironic wit and the desire to make fun of himself.

And what's the pivotal scene?

The pivotal scene in my life is when I decided to be a human being first and an artist second. There are plenty of writers and painters and dancers and actors who made the opposite choice. A lot of the best ones did. But I can't listen to John Lennon singing about love for the world as he simultaneously abandons his own son.

So, the point is this – I brought three lives into this world. It's more important that they have great lives than that I do. They are my greatest works, my legacy.

The critics will gloat that I was no Hemingway.

So will my family.

Last dream of note?

I have all kinds of big dreams. The end of racism. The end of extremism. A global age of reason and justice. You know...

I have all kinds of small dreams, too. I dream that our

new young hamster will nurse her babies instead of eating them. I dream that the new dishwasher will actually get things clean. I dream that *Angel of Death* will reach a smart audience who gets it.

Favourite item of clothing?

I most happily wear anything that has been washed over a hundred times. The number of washings shows I like it and also guarantees that the thing is soft and shaped like me.

What's the view from your writing window?

For nine months out of the year, I sit on a padded wicker loveseat on the screened-in porch of my 1902 Victorian house in Burlington, Wisconsin. It's a perfect place, with people and cars passing by and cats happening in and the sounds of the house close enough that I am still involved but far enough that I am not distracted.

There's a big football game going on just now, three blocks away at Catholic Central, and I hear the cheers and the band and the big bell tolling the hour. It's about perfect.

Would you write full-time if you could?

Oh, yes. I did for almost eight years, just after my first child was born. I took care of him and his brothers all through their early years, potty training them while writing novels. It was the best thing I've ever done and the best thing I will ever do.

But it was also grueling. To be the primary caregiver of three boys in diapers while trying to write full-time was a huge challenge. When I finally returned to the regular workforce, I was amazed how much work I could accomplish without a baby in my lap and two others crawling over my shoulders.

Do you plan in detail or set off hopefully?

There are two different approaches to writing.

Some people build a book the same way that they would build a house. They make blueprints. They order supplies. They schedule construction. Then, brick by brick, they lay out the book.

Others grow a book the same way that they would plant a garden. They turn over the ground and buy some seeds and shove them in the dirt and pour water on them and see what comes up. Weeds, of course, but they cull those and nurture the actual plants and work to make something out of it.

I call the first way of writing the structural approach and the second the organic approach. Both have their strengths and weaknesses.

People who build books like bricklayers have to reach a point where the book comes alive – where it lives and breathes.

People who grow books like gardeners have to reach a point where a book has structure and form and isn't just rampant weeds.

I write books in both ways. *Angel of Death* was a grown book. My next one was built to specifications. The one I am writing right now, *Death's Disciples*, is grown as well.

Where would you like to be right now?

Right now, I'd like to be shaking the hand of the person who is giving me the Pulitzer for *Angel of Death*. Failing that, I'm happy to sit here being interviewed by Angry Robot Books.

When & where were you happiest?

My wife recently co-directed *Sugar* – the musical based on Billy Wilder's *Some Like It Hot*. The show was fantastic. I laughed myself hoarse. That was a moment of absolute happiness, enjoying the performance and reveling in my wife's success and delighting in great acting and writing and music and staging and choreography. Excellence thrills me, and this show was a tour de force.

I was also so transfixed watching a Florentine Opera production of *Turondot*. Again, excellence.

But I get the same pleasure when a Mexican mechanic rides in my minivan and figures out what that terrible pounding sound is and fixes it in three hours. That's a maestro. And when a carpenter comes to look at the sagging front porch of my house and tells me how he is going to lift it up in two hours. Genius.

There are all kinds of intelligence. I'm brilliant with words, but with tools, I have special needs. I'm happiest when I see people with extraordinary skills using those skills in an extraordinary way.

Complete this sentence: Rewriting is...

Rewriting is when the two halves of the mind meet.

Writing the first draft is done by the child mind, the id. Think Calvin from *Calvin and Hobbes*. This part of the mind is convinced that it is a genius whose every impulse is worthy of adulation. This part of the mind creates effortlessly, certain that anything it imagines is worthy to exist.

Rewriting, or revision, is done by the parental mind, the superego. Think of Calvin's longsuffering parents. They love their son, but they are the reality principles, the ones who have to figure out what part of Calvin's genius is genius and what part simply does not belong in the world.

When you write a first draft, you have to engage the child mind, the generative mind that creates with broad strokes and broader grins. When you revise, you have to engage the parental mind, the criticizing mind that analyzes and evaluates and decides what should remain and what should be destroyed.

The child without the parent is lost and hopeless. The parent without the child is empty and pointless. Writers need to encourage both minds, and engage each when it should be engaged.

Complete this sentence: Blogging is...

Blogging is web logging; that is to say, writing a journal or diary that once would have been locked with a key but now is for the whole world to see.

When people used to lock away their words, other people really did want to read them (pesky little brothers, mostly). Now that blogging is journaling to the masses, people aren't that interested. It's like everybody's leaving their diaries lying all over the house.

Complete this sentence: I owe it all to...

I was going to say I owe it all to Visa, but we just got it paid off.

I really owe it all to my parents and grandparents.

My grandfather was abandoned by his father at three years old and lost his mother when he was in eighth grade. Grandpa Frank went from being a penniless orphan to having his own print shop. My father put himself through college by saving up his paper-route money. He became an electrical engineer, moving from working class to solidly middle class. I am now struggling to move from middle class to upper class by writing novels. So far, I've been less successful than my father or grandfather.

Tell us a secret

Sarah Silverman and I were both bedwetters. If I ever meet her, I hope to use this fact as a pick-up line.

What are you going to do right now when you've finished this ordeal?

I am going to wrestle the sleeping bags down from the attic so that my youngest son and his guest can sleep downstairs away from the maternal hamster, and that my oldest sons can sleep out here on the screened-in porch of our old Victorian.

ANGRY ROBOT

Teenage serial killers
Zombie detectives
The grim reaper in love
Howling axes **Vampire
hordes** Dead men's clones
The Black Hand
Death by cellphone
Gangster shamen
Steampunk swordfights
Sex-crazed bloodsuckers
Murderous gods
Riots **Quests** Discovery
Death

Prepare to welcome
your new
Robot overlords.

angryrobotbooks.com